I0661808

A NEW RECRUIT FOR THE RESISTANCE GIRLS

ALICE G. MAY

Boldwood

First published in Great Britain in 2025 by Boldwood Books Ltd.

Copyright © Alice G. May, 2025

Cover Design by Colin Thomas

Cover Images: Colin Thomas, iStock, Dave Dunford, Daniel Klein and Bob's Bits

The moral right of Alice G. May to be identified as the author of this work has been asserted in accordance with the Copyright, Designs and Patents Act 1988.

All rights reserved. No part of this book may be reproduced in any form or by any electronic or mechanical means, including information storage and retrieval systems, without written permission from the author, except for the use of brief quotations in a book review. This book is a work of fiction and, except in the case of historical fact, any resemblance to actual persons, living or dead, is purely coincidental.

Every effort has been made to obtain the necessary permissions with reference to copyright material, both illustrative and quoted. We apologise for any omissions in this respect and will be pleased to make the appropriate acknowledgements in any future edition.

A CIP catalogue record for this book is available from the British Library.

Paperback ISBN 978-1-83703-513-7

Large Print ISBN 978-1-83703-512-0

Hardback ISBN 978-1-83703-511-3

Trade Paperback ISBN 978-1-80656-028-8

Ebook ISBN 978-1-83703-514-4

Kindle ISBN 978-1-83703-515-1

Audio CD ISBN 978-1-83703-506-9

MP3 CD ISBN 978-1-83703-507-6

Digital audio download ISBN 978-1-83703-508-3

This book is printed on certified sustainable paper. Boldwood Books is dedicated to putting sustainability at the heart of our business. For more information please visit https://www.boldwoodbooks.com/about-us/sustainability/

Boldwood Books Ltd, 23 Bowerdean Street, London, SW6 3TN

www.boldwoodbooks.com

*For all the brave scientists
and support staff who worked tirelessly
to help turn the tide of war.
Also
for
R.S.W.
and
Nigel and Gill
(a.k.a. Mum and Dad)*

1

APRIL 1942

I didn't know what to say to break the silence. I'd never seen Connie so furious. She seemed fine when we left our shared billet in the Nissen huts. With each step since, she'd become progressively quieter and more withdrawn. Normally an even-tempered soul, Connie's anger surged between us like a tempestuous sea. Anger directed at me. I should have expected it.

Dressed in an understated outfit similar to mine – grey-green corduroy trousers and a thick, olive-green woollen jumper over a soft grey woollen shirt, she wore her hair tied back with a brown silk scarf. Our clothes had been supplied by the army. Yet, they were not a uniform. Instead, they were designed to be unremarkable, easily dismissed. To an observer, we could be friends out to share a woodland walk together in the glorious afternoon sunshine, if it weren't for the kitbags slung across our shoulders and the gas mask box straps swinging from our hands. The fact that Connie marched ahead of me through the trees, refusing to acknowledge my existence, was another giveaway that something was afoot.

'Connie, please,' I said, breaking into a little half-jog to catch up.

The increased pace of her boots, scrunching leaf litter underfoot with each outraged step, was the only reply. As we approached the vast lawns at the rear of Hannington Hall, the ornate construction of the stunning stately home came into view; a huge contrast to the huts, bell tents and other temporary military accommodation units tucked out of sight in the woodland behind us.

A circle of female recruits for the resistance, all wearing loose, practical army-issue clothing, were gathered on the grass ahead watching a demonstration of hand-to-hand combat.

Now was my last chance to clear the air. With the war as fraught as it was, and the missions we might be sent on so dangerous, it was entirely possible that I might never see Connie again. The thought of my sweet friend leaving and, heaven forbid, possibly dying, still hating me, was unbearable.

I grabbed her arm, forcing her to stop. 'Will you look at me?'

She glared and shook me off, a muscle twitching in her jaw. 'What am I looking at, Fliss?' She crossed her arms. 'We've been together for nearly four weeks, now. You, me, Wren, Lexi, Jo and Louisa. Strangers training alongside each other. Living in the same barracks. We all thought you were one of us. Another brand-new recruit for this secret women's army Major Stapleton is building.'

'That's exactly what I am.'

She sighed. 'I'm not stupid. *We've* been training to protect the country from Nazi invasion but it turns out we needed protecting from you.'

I couldn't have been more shocked if she'd slapped me. 'Connie! How can you say that?'

'You just admitted that you've worked with Major Stapleton for nearly two years.'

It did sound bad and a wave of sadness made my throat tight. 'I'm still me, Connie,' I whispered.

'That's my point, Fliss.' She shook her head. 'I don't know who you are. I don't even know your real name.'

'To be fair, I don't know your real name either.' One of the rules of this place was that we shouldn't share personal details with the others training alongside us. It was safer for everyone that way. What we didn't know couldn't be divulged under torture.

Her eyes swam with unshed tears. 'I thought we were friends but you've been spying on us.'

'I haven't.'

'Yes, you have. The more I think about it, the more obvious it is. You've been listening in and reporting back. For all I know, you're the reason I'm about to be told I have to leave. What did you tell them? "Oh! Connie's too soft. She hasn't got what it takes."'

'No!' Her words were like a knife to my heart. 'I'd never say that. And anyway, it isn't true. You doubt yourself. You shouldn't. We all think you're amazing.'

She huffed in disbelief and looked away.

'Honestly, Connie, I know it looks bad. Please believe me, it's not like that.'

'What else can I think? We're training our hardest and learning all these new skills. And *you're* pretending to do the same, when really you're under-cover, keeping an eye on *us*.' She moved to march on.

I dashed around in front of her, cutting off her escape. 'I was asked to assess the training scheme. Not to assess you.'

'Pull the other one. It's got a clatter trap on it.'

If her expression hadn't been so deadly, her reference to yesterday's lesson on how to set trip alarms to stop enemy agents creeping up on you in the field would have made me laugh.

'I'm telling the truth,' I said. 'It took ages for the top brass to allow Major Stapleton to set up a training scheme for women. They only agreed because Britain is losing this damned war. If America hadn't joined us last December, most likely we'd already be under Nazi rule.' I shuddered at the thought.

She watched me intently, making no move to speak.

I checked over my shoulder and dropped my voice. 'Look. There's a limit to what I can say because of the whole *Official Secrets* thing. You know that, so don't repeat this. Special ops have built hidden bunkers and caches of weapons and supplies all over the south and east of England, in the past eighteen months. They've been training teams of men to go undercover and sabotage an invading force. Very brave men, ready to form a resistance here in Britain.'

'And?' she said.

'Things had to get really bad before the higher-ups would consider training women.'

Connie gave a low growl of frustration. 'Well, that's just typical. They're a bunch of dinosaurs who want us all cowering at home rather than actually doing something useful.'

'Not all men are like that,' I said, loath to contradict her, but also not wanting to ignore the fact that I'd had the privilege of working with some very forward-thinking men in the last few years. One in particular sprang to mind, but I pushed all thoughts of him away. He was too distracting. 'You're right though. Most men underestimate our abilities. However, while this war is truly awful, it's *forcing* attitudes to women to change.'

'About time, too,' she said. 'Women can go undercover just as easily as men, easier in some cases.'

'Yes, they can. The major and I have spent the last year proving that.'

'How?'

I shook my head. 'I can't say. It's confidential. But, now that we have, women trained here will form the backbone of the British Resistance. It's far easier for us to take visible positions in occupied territory. We can keep an eye on the enemy and report back, connecting individual, self-contained cells of resistance operatives to each other via secret radio comms. And if things really deteriorate, we can go underground too.'

'And make life hell for the invaders.' Connie's words were steeped in steely determination.

'Exactly. But it's dangerous.'

'I don't care.'

'You should care,' I said. '*We* are only the second cohort of women recruits to come through the Hannington Hall training scheme. The major needs to know that the program is fit for purpose. That it genuinely teaches you skills that will help. Who better to test it out than me? I've already had experience of working undercover.' I put a hand over my heart. 'I wasn't deceiving you for the hell of it, Connie. It had to be real to be of value.'

She grunted and scraped a toe against the ground. 'What's it like working undercover?'

The question threw me. There were things I couldn't share. Part of Connie's anger was due to a fear of the unknown, rather than my actions. Scaring her unnecessarily before she started wouldn't help. I chose my next words with care. 'It's tough. The only way to survive is to keep your head and follow your training. That's why Major Stapleton is so keen to get this right. She feels responsible for all of us.'

'You say *us* like you haven't been reporting back.'

'I haven't,' I said. 'I genuinely didn't expect our little group to bond in the way we have, Connie. You are all talented and extremely brave. It's a privilege to have shared a hut with you, these last few weeks. And I'll always have your back. You can trust me.' I needed her to believe me. Thus far, my experience of undercover work had been as a lone wolf. Operating in plain sight, watching for enemy agents, whilst reporting back to the major in secret. It was isolating and bruising in many ways. In contrast, the camaraderie of the last few weeks had been wonderful. I felt connected to Connie, Wren, Jo, Lexi and Louisa in a way I hadn't anticipated. 'Working with you all has been wonderful. I've learned so much from you.'

'Like what?'

'That it doesn't matter that we don't know much about each other. We know the important stuff. We care what happens to one another and that even though we're about to be separated and sent off on different missions, we'll support each other no matter what. Because we will. Admit it, Connie. We're friends. Aren't we?'

Several beats passed before she sighed. 'Fine. All right, yes, we're friends.'

Pent-up air exploded from my lungs as I pulled her into a hug. 'I meant it when I said I've got your back.'

We clung to each other briefly before she disengaged. Levelling a glare of steel at me that told me there was far more to Connie than I had ever appreciated, she said, 'But, if you let me down again, Fliss, I'll never forgive you.'

'I won't.' I shook my head, relief making my eyes suspiciously wet. 'I promise.'

I fell into step beside her and we emerged from the trees that skirted the lawns and climbed the stone steps onto the patio at the back of the hall. As we reached a set of French windows, the glass criss-crossed with brown anti-blast tape, she asked, 'Do you know why Major Stapleton is pulling me out of training early?'

'I don't. Sorry. I'm sure she has a good reason.'

'Like what?'

'Either she thinks you won't need the information in the last two weeks of the program, or, she needs you somewhere now. For an operation that can't wait. Something that requires someone with your particular skill set.' I opened the door and waved for her to go ahead of me. 'She's really good at pairing the right person with the right operation.'

We crossed a large room furnished with serviceable chairs and benches. Ornate cornicing overhead watched our progress. Bare floorboards echoed our footsteps back at us. The whole building smelt of beeswax polish laid down over hundreds of years, and the memory of ancient fires in now empty grates.

We hurried down a corridor, passing several other trainees en route to their next class, and negotiated a narrow set of steps down to the basement.

As we reached the room that led to Major Stapleton's office, Connie gave a heavy sigh. 'I'd have liked to finish the whole training scheme.'

I gave her shoulder a quick squeeze before opening the door.

Sergeant Miller sat at a desk inside. A short, angular woman, she gave every appearance of having been ironed into her ATS uniform whilst wearing it. She looked up as we approached and smiled. 'You've arrived. Jolly good. The major is keen to see you, Connie. I'll take you in.' She got to her feet in one fluid motion. 'Meanwhile, Fliss, she asks if you wouldn't mind familiarising yourself with these reports.' She tapped a pile of documents set out before her. 'You can use my desk if you like. I have a few errands to run.'

'Thank you, Sergeant,' I replied. I flashed Connie a grin full of encouragement.

Sergeant Miller herded Connie over to Major Stapleton's door, knocked and ushered her in, before turning back to me. 'Perhaps you could answer the telephone if it rings and take a message?'

'Of course,' I said. Slipping back into the role of secretary would be no hardship. The last few years had taught me to adapt to whatever situation I found myself in as quickly as possible. I pulled the first document towards me as she left.

Alone in the room, my recent conversation with Connie still ringing in my ears, it was hard to concentrate. Instead, my mind raced back two years to when this whole adventure started; to the old me. Someone who didn't know how to sabotage engines, cut telephone lines and blow up electrical substations. A woman who wouldn't dream of killing someone with her bare hands.

That version of me didn't watch for danger around every corner. She didn't suspect everyone of having the worst possible motives and she didn't live in fear of an enemy invasion destroying everything she loves. That Felicity Makepeace – Fliss to my friends – didn't exist any more. I was stronger now. I knew who I was and what I could do. And I'd be damned if I let anyone push me around ever again.

Would I do it all again if I got the chance?

Yes. I absolutely would. It had been hard, but I wouldn't miss being the me I was now for anything.

2

TWO YEARS EARLIER, 1940

'Right, Felicity,' said Da, coming into the office from the workshop as I was putting the cover on my typewriter. He pulled an oily rag from the pocket of his overalls and wiped his hands. 'That's the Harrisons' van serviced. Can you drop it back to them tomorrow?'

I made a note on the pad on my desk. 'I'll do it first thing in the morning,' I said, unable to suppress a grin. The best part of my day was sailing through the streets of Bristol behind the wheel of a decent vehicle. The Harrisons' van was a 998c Morris 10 with barely a hundred miles on the odometer. It was a beautiful deep green with shiny brass headlamps. Gorgeous.

'Grand. And, while you are out, one of the delivery trucks at the bakery on Market Street is making a strange knocking noise,' he said. 'Are you able to pick that up for us?'

I forced my grin to stay on my face despite the sinking feeling his words triggered. Deliveries were fun. But pick-ups? Not so much. The trucks weren't a problem; it was the owners. Men hate handing the keys of their vehicles to a woman. It's a fact. You'd think with Germany marching into Poland nearly six months back, war being declared, and men going off to fight in droves, they would have other things to worry about. If I had tuppence for every time a grouchy fella fixed sceptical eyes on me and demanded, 'Are you sure you can drive?' I'd be a rich woman.

I always replied, 'Yes, sir,' keeping my eyes lowered and my tone respectful.

No point triggering a row. Women drivers were becoming more common and not just on farms out in the countryside. I wasn't doing anything wrong, but it didn't stop the narrow-eyed glares. Even producing my licence, with my name, Felicity Makepeace, stamped across it didn't always allay suspicion.

Da started Makepeace Motors twenty years ago, the year I was born. I'd grown up living and breathing engines. I could drive them, all of them, no matter how big. I could fix them too, although that was a step too far for most and best not mentioned. Manoeuvring vehicles around on the car lot, and in and out of the workshop, had become my job the minute my legs were long enough to reach the pedals. Driving was second nature to me.

I made a mental note to scrape my unruly brown curls back under a cap the next day, and rather than my usual smart divided skirt and blouse, I'd wear loose-fitting overalls, to hide my figure. Thanks to my five-foot-eight-inch height and slim build, if I kept my head down and said as little as possible, I would probably get away without challenge.

Da raised his voice. 'Did you hear me, Fliss?'

'Yes, Da. I'll do it on my way back.'

'Grand.' He opened the door to the small changing area and disappeared inside, reappearing a few minutes later having swapped his overalls for grey trousers and a smart brown jumper. 'Tell your ma I'm calling in at the Whistling Ferret on my way home. Can you close up for me?' He disappeared into the early evening gloom on the street outside.

The door banged shut behind him. A sense of calm settled over the room. I tidied away the documents on my desk and made sure there was blank paper left in my notepad and that my pencils were sharp for the next day. The instructor at the secretarial evening course I'd attended often said the key to being an efficient secretary was having freshly sharpened pencils and a pad of paper on hand at all times. I switched off the desk lamp and retrieved my favourite bright-green woollen coat from the hook on the wall beside the grey metal filing cabinet. After slipping my arms into the sleeves, I fastened the belt around my waist. My eyes wandered over to the workshop door. I rarely set foot through it these days, not since... well, anyway.

I grimaced. Dad had asked me to lock up. He didn't usually do that. By rights, I should check everything was straight in there before I left.

Stepping into the cavernous space, I closed my eyes and took a deep breath. The heady mix of engine oil and petrol brought such happy memories, like handing Da wrenches and sprockets when I was six or seven. Holding bowls for oil changes when I was ten. Replacing spark plugs on my twelfth birthday. Life had been perfect, then. Getting covered in oil alongside him, listening to him describe the new engines coming on the market, it was all I ever wanted to do. I had foolishly assumed we'd spend forever working on engines together.

I ignored the sad resignation tugging at my heart. When I'd left school at fourteen, Ma put her foot down and overnight, the workshop door had closed to me because it wasn't fitting for a grown woman to work with engines. If I hadn't proved useful with shorthand and typing, I'd not be at Makepeace Motors at all. Now, instead of tuning engines, I shuffled paper all day and the most challenging mechanical repair that cropped up was changing the ribbon on my typewriter. Da had taken on a couple of junior mechanics, one after another, neither of whom knew as much as I did, but they had one advantage I didn't. They were men.

I pushed the memory aside and scanned the workshop for anything out of place. A beautiful 1937 Opel Kadett Drophead, all polished burgundy panels and gleaming chrome trim had just received a new set of tyres. It was a stunning motor; practical, with clean rounded lines. Next to it was a Ford Model B Roadster in need of a service. Having two private vehicles in the workshop was rare, regardless of the war and fuel rationing. We usually serviced essential supply trucks and delivery vans.

A few tools had been left scattered over one of the workbenches. I tutted and hurried over to tidy up, relishing the weight of them in my hands.

That was when I heard it: the soft roll of inspection trolley wheels on concrete, the scrape of boot heels and the clang of a spanner dropped on stone. I mentally kicked myself. Jake Derwent, the only junior mechanic we had left, now that all able-bodied men were in the armed forces, and the one I made a point of avoiding. If only he hadn't failed his medical. He was usually gone by four and I should have checked before coming in. Every muscle in my body tensed as his bulky form appeared from behind the Kadett and I shuddered. I had tried to like him, I really had. Tall and fair, he was relatively good-looking, but something about him made my skin crawl. There was a predatory watchfulness to him. I couldn't explain why it bothered me.

'Well, well, well,' he said. 'We don't often see you in here, Felicity. Do we?'

I swallowed, striving for a normal tone. 'Da asked me to lock up. He didn't say you were still here.' *Why didn't he say?* It made no sense. If Jake was here, and Da knew that, there was no need for me to lock up.

Jake waved a hand at the car he'd been working on. 'I'm just finishing up.' He paced towards me, his eyes never leaving my face.

I forced my lips to smile and backed away. 'I didn't mean to disturb you. I'll go.'

'No, don't,' he said, his voice smooth as silk. He flicked his fringe back from his forehead. 'I thought you and me could step out together on Friday. We could go to the pictures.'

'Oh!' My mind went blank. 'I uh... I don't... uh—'

In an instant, he was by my side. 'Don't say no.' He grabbed my right wrist in one meaty paw.

'I'm sorry,' I said. 'I really don't think Da would—'

'Your da won't mind,' he said. 'I already asked his permission.' A menacing edge crept into his tone. The look in his eye brought to mind a cat toying with a mouse. He squeezed, hard enough to force a small whimper from me.

'You're hurting me.' I gasped.

'I am. Aren't I?' An evil light sparked in his eyes and his grip tightened. He was enjoying seeing my pain.

I clamped down on a moan, refusing to give him the satisfaction of knowing how scared I was. 'Let me go,' I said, through gritted teeth.

He leaned closer, a blast of foul breath washing over me. 'You haven't answered my question.'

'Technically, you didn't ask a question.'

'I told you, your da said it's a good idea.'

He squeezed again, this time with a twist, making me squeal. I bent sideways to try and ease the agony, my breath coming in short, sharp gasps. Da and Ma brought Jake up in conversation all the time these days. Was this why Da had asked me to lock up?

Jake eased the pressure, allowing me to straighten, and reached for my other hand, lifting it up between us, rubbing at my bare ring finger. 'If it's a question you want—'

'Please don't,' I whispered, trying not to gag on rising horror and the smell of stale sweat and nicotine coiling around us. This couldn't be happening.

'You're a pretty girl, Fliss. We'd be good together.'

'No!' I said, tugging my fingers free, unable to hide the mounting panic in my voice.

The iron clamp on my wrist tightened again, the bones grinding against each other. Any minute now something would snap. A swishy pounding started in my ears. The teasing light in his eyes vanished and a deep furrow appeared across his brow. He loomed closer, crowding me against the workbench. 'Your da wants you married. He said as much. And there aren't many menfolk around, what with the war. You better start treating me right.'

Da wouldn't want this, though. However, arguing with Jake wasn't an option. I needed to do whatever was necessary to get him to let me go before he broke my arm.

'You're right.' The words exploded on a wave of pain. I forced a smile and a nervous giggle. 'I don't mean no, as in *no*.' I placed my palm on his vast chest and poured a lightness I didn't feel into my words. 'Of course, I don't. I mean... well, it's just... Jake, this is all very sudden.'

The pain in my wrist eased a fraction.

I fluttered my eyelashes in what I hoped approximated maidenly modesty rather than pure terror. 'You have to give a girl time to think.'

His eyes narrowed. 'What's there to think about?'

'Well...' I cast around for something innocuous to say, something he might believe. 'Well, what to wear, for starters. I've not walked out with anyone, before. Not properly.' That wasn't exactly true. I'd been to dances with friends, but there had been no one serious. Apart from Carl Edwards, that is. The older brother of one of my friends from school; tall, dark and handsome, he was the image of Errol Flynn. He'd turned up at Makepeace Motors at the end of the day, about eight months ago, and asked if he could escort me home. It was nice; he made me laugh and he came every day for two whole weeks. I'd begun to think that maybe... well... never mind. The long and short of it is he stopped coming. And the next time I bumped into his sister, Suzie, she refused to talk to me. I still don't know what I did wrong. I shook the memory away and focused on my immediate problem. 'You want me to look nice for you, don't you?'

'Fair play,' Jake grunted and stepped back, releasing me. 'You get yourself gussied up nice. I'll call for you at six on Friday.'

I fixed my eyes on the floor, nodded and edged away. As soon as there was enough room, I turned and dashed back into the office, crammed my red beret on my head, grabbed my handbag, gloves and gas mask from my desk, scurried out into the street, and broke into a run.

3

I was two blocks away, by the time the iron band of terror that was welded around my torso eased. I slowed to a walk and took my first full breath of air in what seemed like hours. Damn it all to hell. What the devil was I going to do? The mere thought of spending time with Jake made me feel as if ten thousand cockroaches were crawling all over me. How come I could see that there was something sinister about him, when no one else could? I had tried to tell Ma he made me feel uncomfortable, but she'd laughed and said I was being silly. And Da often joked that Jake was so good at his job it was a shame he wasn't part of the family. I stopped short in horror, as the most awful penny dropped. They really did want me to marry him.

Granite-like resolve settled over me. I wasn't in any hurry to get married. If I did decide to shackle myself to a man, I'd have more taste than to choose a monster like Jake. Not on your Nellie. I'd make that crystal clear to Ma, the minute I got home.

I glanced at my watch. Damn it, I was going to miss my bus. The kick pleats of my skirt flapped against my shins as I ran, and the heels of my court shoes clopped on the pavement like the hooves of a cantering horse. With my bag and gas mask box clutched to my chest, I rounded a corner to see the bus already at the stop, the conductor stood on the rear platform ready to ring the bell.

I waved a frantic arm. 'Please wait.' Adding a final burst of speed, I leapt on, grabbing the shiny pole to steady myself.

The conductor, an older gentleman in a dark blue uniform and thick glasses, peered down at me from under his peaked hat and then glanced back along the road in the direction I had come. 'You running from someone, love?'

I shook my head and held out two pennies for a ticket. 'Just keen to get home.'

He punched a hole in the slip of blue card and handed it over. I tried to stop my hands shaking as I accepted it and tucked it into my pocket.

'Take a seat,' he urged, pressing the bell twice to tell the driver to move on.

The engine thrummed beneath my feet. I shuffled to the nearest empty seat, sank down and tried to calm myself as the bus resumed its route.

A couple of stops later, three girls got on. Wrapped warmly in belted coats with bright scarves and hats, they chattered merrily as they looked for space to settle. Two took the double bench behind me and the third perched in the free seat by my side. She swivelled away from me and peered over the back of the seat in order to continue her conversation with her friends, saying, 'I told her. I said, "Ma, as soon as I'm old enough, I'm joining the ATS."'

The girl, seated immediately behind me, said, 'You don't want to be doing that, Vi.'

'Why not?' demanded Vi. 'Our Vera did it. She says she's having great fun.'

'Your Vera is as daft as a brush,' replied the one behind me, her words dripping with sarcasm.

'You take that back, Trish!' demanded Vi.

'What's the ATS?' came a timid question from the third girl, sat diagonally behind me.

Vi tutted. 'Don't you know anything, Sal? It's the Auxiliary Territorial Service. The women's branch of the army.'

'Oh!' There was a pause, then Sal asked, 'Isn't joining the army, or the air force, dangerous?'

'Nah,' said Vi. 'Women don't go into battle. They do safe jobs.'

'They can get jolly close to the action, mind,' said Trish, her tone dry. 'My grandma worked at the front during the last war. She volunteered as a nurse.'

'She didn't fight though, did she?' countered Vi. 'Anyway, it's got to be more exciting than sticking around here.'

'Where did they send your Vera, then?' asked Sal.

'This big army base near London. She did basic training first and was then assigned a post. She says there are lots of handsome officers too. That's what I want. A good-looking fella and a bit of excitement.'

There were interested murmurs from the other two girls. Given my recent encounter with Jake, a good-looking fella and a bit of excitement were not high on my wish list. Nevertheless, the idea of leaving Bristol lodged in my brain. It wasn't something that had ever crossed my mind before.

The bus slowed for the next stop. All three girls got to their feet and shuffled towards the rear platform.

As they stepped out, Trish asked, 'Where did your Vera go to sign up for this ATS, then?'

I turned my head to catch Vi's reply as, one by one, they hopped out onto the pavement.

'There's a recruiter in the library on Market Street,' came the faint response.

The library. I hadn't realised it was a recruitment station, despite the fact that I went there all the time and I'd seen posters about the ATS. Interesting.

The double ding sounded again and the bus rumbled on, leaving the trio behind. My mind went into a freefall of possibilities. Friday night was four days away. Jake had been clear that no wasn't an acceptable answer. What if I followed Vera's example, joined the ATS and got posted far away, somewhere Jake would never find me? Even as the idea arrived, I dismissed it. I was being silly. There was no need to leave. I would simply sit my parents down and explain that Jake wasn't the man for me. All would be well.

4

Back at the house, one of the newer semi-detached properties near St Paul's, the savoury scent of Lord Woolton pie welcomed me as I stepped inside. I hung my outer things and my gas mask on the pegs behind the front door and pushed the draught excluder into place with my foot. Pulling aside the blackout curtain, which hung across the hallway about three feet behind the door, I stepped around the regulation sand and water buckets onto the black and white diamond-tiled floor before sweeping the curtain back into place behind me. Fingers of warmth reached towards me from the parlour where my younger brothers were playing before a meagre fire. The few months when they'd been evacuated at the start of the war had been very peaceful. However, Ma had been beside herself without them. The threat of bombing predicted in the papers hadn't materialised, so she had brought them home at Christmas and not sent them back.

'Neeeeaawww!' shrieked George, waving a toy plane in the air. 'I'm coming to get you.'

'You can't catch me,' William yelled back. 'Mine's a Hurricane.'

I stepped back as both charged past. They chased each other up the stairs, making aeroplane engine and explosion noises. In the six years since George's arrival and the four since William's, I'd learned that with babies, boys in particular, noise and chaos went hand in hand. I loved them, even though their arrival had meant I became invisible overnight. With sons to inherit the business, at last, Da listened to Ma's grumbles that it wasn't fitting for a girl to work as a mechanic. Hence my shift sideways into the office to send out bills, order engine parts and organise the servicing schedules. It wasn't the same but at least it gave me something more challenging to get my teeth into than staying at home rocking babies for Ma.

I wandered down the hall, past the dining room to the kitchen. The unexpected sight of Ma pulling the steaming pie from the oven herself brought me up short.

'Where's Edith?' I asked, glancing around for the daily who usually helped Ma around the house. Other than Nana – who was sat in her rocking chair in the corner, wrapped in a shawl, humming to herself and completely oblivious to the world, the cat fast asleep on her lap – the kitchen was empty.

Ma placed the pie down on the sideboard with a thump. 'She's given her notice.'

'Did she say why?'

She wiped her brow with the back of her hand. 'She's moving back to her village to look after her parents.'

'Goodness. That's a blow.'

'It's to be expected given the war. And being in the country will be safer for her than Bristol.' She gave me a quick kiss on the cheek. 'Anyway, how did work go, today, love?'

I dredged up a smile. 'Good, thanks.' I didn't mean to tell her straight away. I'd planned to wait until Da was back too. But I couldn't keep the pretence up. The thought of seeing Jake the next day made me want to heave. 'Uh... No! Actually, Ma, it wasn't good at all.'

Her brow creased in concern. 'Whatever's the matter?'

I ducked my head. 'It's Jake. He... uh...' Why was it so difficult to say the words?

'Oh!' She clasped her hands together. 'Did he ask to step out with you, at last? That's wonderful news. He's such a charming young man. Gladys.' She turned to Nana. 'Gladys? Did you hear that? Our Fliss has a sweetheart.'

Nana ignored her and kept on rocking and humming, locked in her own little world.

'You mean, you knew he was going to ask me?' My voice was barely above a whisper.

She bobbed up and down, like a child at Christmas. 'I suspected as much.'

'Why didn't you warn me?'

'It wasn't my place. Your father said he was sweet on you and that he'd asked for permission to court you. Which is exactly what he should do. He's a nice young man.'

'No, Ma—'

'It's so romantic. Isn't it, Gladys?'

Nana kept humming.

I shook my head. 'It's not romantic. And he's not nice, Ma. He really isn't.'

She laughed. 'Don't be daft. He likes you. You're just shy.'

'He hurt me, look.' I showed her my wrist. Clear prints from Jake's fingers darkened my skin.

Her brow crinkled. 'I'm sure he didn't mean it, Fliss. He's a big strapping lad. He probably doesn't know his own strength, love. You'll have to tell him to be gentle.'

'He enjoyed hurting me.'

'You're overreacting.' She tutted and turned back to the stove, muttering, 'These potatoes will be done in a minute. Can you set the table, please, love?'

'I don't want anything to do with him.'

'Now, listen here.' She whirled to face me. 'You're twenty. It's time you started thinking about your future. Jake will be a good provider. He'll always have steady work at Makepeace Motors.'

'I can't—'

'Your da agrees with me. You're lucky to have Jake, what with lads joining up left, right and centre. It's a blessing he failed his medical and won't have to go and fight.'

I closed my eyes, counting to ten. Arguing with Ma when she was in this sort of mood never ended well.

'Your da says skilled labour is going to be a real issue if this war isn't over soon. And you and Jake getting wed would—'

'Wed?' The word came out as a squeak. I'd seen women married to violent men: their unexplained bruises, their stoic, bowed shoulders. That was never going to be me. No matter what Ma said. 'Ma! I'm not going to marry him.'

'Why ever not?' She threw the pot holder on the table and turned to me with her hands on her hips. 'I wasn't going to tell you like this, only Edith leaving me in the lurch, gives me no choice. I'm taking the boys and Nana to live with your Aunty Mo in Raglan.'

Startled by the change in subject, I sensed a possible escape route. 'That's a good idea, Ma. It'll be safer there. The war is going to get worse before it gets better. I reckon Bristol will be a target for bombs soon enough, what with the dockyards and everything.'

'The problem is Mo hasn't room for you, too.' She sniffed. 'And you can't stay here without me if you're not married. People will talk. Marrying Jake solves that. He can move in here and you can look after both him and your da while I'm gone.' She had clearly made her mind up.

The bottom dropped away from my stomach as if I had fallen off a cliff and was plummeting towards the rocks below with no way of saving myself. 'He's dangerous, Ma,' I muttered, rising horror threatening to choke me.

'You haven't given him a chance.' She waved a pointy finger under my nose. 'You'll accept his offer to walk out on Friday, my girl. You'll have a lovely time, you'll see. Then, come Sunday, he can visit us here for his tea. We'll welcome him into the family, properly.' A huge crash sounded from overhead. Ma's hands flew to her cheeks. 'Oh Lord! What are those boys up to?' She spun on her heels and headed for the stairs, calling back over her shoulder, 'Don't be difficult, Fliss. For once, just do as you're told.'

I stared after her, a growing sense of helplessness festering in my belly. My wrist throbbed and icy cold fingers of fear slithered around my heart. I stumbled over to the stool near Nana and sat down, forcing myself to take slow deep breaths.

'I can't marry him,' I muttered to myself. 'I won't.' The creak of the rocking chair stilled. The tuneless humming stopped. I looked into her careworn, rheumy eyes. 'What do I do, Nana?'

She met my gaze and, for the first time in a long time, it seemed as if the old Nana was looking back.

'What do I do, Nana?' I whispered, again. 'Do I stay, and risk being forced to marry a man who will hurt me, or do I run?'

'Run,' she said, as if it was the easiest thing in the world. She resumed her rocking and humming, the fleeting moment of lucidity gone. Had she merely been repeating the last word I said, or did she mean it? It was hard to believe that I was even considering it. Yet the more I thought about leaving, the more it made sense. While running away was a scary prospect, the idea of being trapped into marriage with Jake terrified me. Pulling a vanishing act might be the only way to save my life. What on earth was I going to do?

* * *

After a night spent tossing and turning, my wrist aching and my conversation with Ma going around and around my head, I concluded that I didn't have a choice. Ma's mind was made up, and there was no point appealing to Da – he always agreed with her. I had to leave to save myself, and the ATS sounded like a sensible way to do it. The fact that I needed to be on Market Street in the morning anyway – exactly where Vi said Vera had signed up – seemed like a sign. I could deliver the Harrisons' van, and go straight to the library to see what the enlistment process involved. Then maybe, if it felt like the right thing to do, I could... well, I could decide when I was there. Afterwards, I'd pick up the bakery truck and get back to work with no one the wiser.

As a plan, it made sense. I was hit with a confusing mix of elation at having an escape route, marred by a crushing sense of doom. If I left Bristol, Ma and Da might never forgive me. Yet, if I stayed, I might never be able to forgive myself.

5

The public lending library on Market Street was a two-storey Georgian building set back from the road. Carved stone steps led up to a red-brick-fronted structure with a pale stone trim and large sash windows. The air inside carried the essence of books and old wood, the most comforting smell in the world, in my opinion. I hurried to the main desk, keeping my footsteps light so as not to disturb the hushed atmosphere.

'Good morning, Miss Makepeace,' said the librarian, a young woman with ruddy cheeks and a bright smile. She didn't bat an eyelid at my scruffy overcoat and cap. 'We don't usually see you until Saturday.'

'Hi, Miss Turner,' I murmured. 'I'm not looking for books today. I heard there was an ATS recruiter here.'

'Are you joining up?' Her eyes sparkled with excitement. 'Good for you.'

'I'm not sure yet, so if you see Ma, please don't tell her.'

'Not a word, I promise.' She drew a small criss-cross motion with one finger over her heart. 'You'll need to go up to the manager's office.' She pointed across the hallway. 'Through that door, up two flights of stairs and along the corridor to the end. Knock on the last door and then take a seat outside. She'll call you in when she's ready.'

I nodded my thanks and followed her instructions. Stood outside the door, I took a moment to straighten my appearance, pulling the cap from my head and smoothing back a few stray strands of hair. That I was in loose-fitting trousers and a tunic was unfortunate, but couldn't be helped. They were clean and had no obvious holes. Even so, I decided to keep my coat on to hide my unusual ensemble and knocked on the door.

Before I could take a seat, a voice called out, 'Come in.'

Inside, a petite woman with neat brown hair wearing a sage green ATS uniform with shiny brass buttons sat behind a desk. Shrewd eyes ran over me from head to toe.

'Good morning,' she said. 'I'm Major Stapleton. And you are?'

I stiffened my spine and moved to stand before her. 'Felicity Makepeace, ma'am.'

She indicated a chair in front of the desk. 'Take a seat, Miss Makepeace. Do I take it you are here to join the ATS?'

'Yes, ma'am.'

She rummaged in a desk drawer. 'Bear with me. I just need to find the right form. Staff Sergeant Bennet, who usually runs this recruiting office, is sadly ill. I'm filling in for a few days. Ah! Here we are.' She withdrew a piece of paper, pausing to gift me with an intense stare. 'Please understand, we consider the ATS to be part of the army. Technically, we don't have full military status yet. We're working towards it and, as a result, even though current recruits are essentially volunteers, you are expected to take your ATS role seriously. Do you understand? Commitment is essential.'

'Of course,' I said.

She let out a heavy sigh. 'Senior figures – and by that, I mean the men in charge – believe that women have no place in the military. It's an outdated notion of chivalry, that we women need to be kept at home, safe and sound, while the menfolk defend our country. Things have changed since the last war.'

'Thank heaven,' I said with feeling. 'We have the vote, for a start. And better education. And the right to have jobs. Although, if you ask me, things could do with changing more.'

She blinked, as if she hadn't expected me to speak.

I silently cursed myself for letting my tongue run away. 'Sorry for interrupting you, ma'am.'

She shook her head. 'You have strong opinions. That's nothing to be ashamed of. Tell me.' She waved one hand in the air. 'And this is nothing to do with the interview process. I am merely intrigued. Do *you* have a job?'

'Yes, ma'am.' I told her about Makepeace Motors.

'I see. And you can drive too. Jolly well done you.' She leaned forward. 'What made you decide to join up? Don't worry, there's no right or wrong answer. I'm interested in your motivation. We're on a bit of a recruitment drive to increase numbers.'

My mind raced. Should I be completely candid with her? While I'd be damned if I revealed my awful situation with Jake, it was refreshing to be asked my opinion on something. 'I think women should have exactly the same rights as men, and that includes the right to defend our country if we want to.'

Her lips stretched into a broad smile, the sort that crinkles the sides of your eyes. 'Well said. Well said indeed. You clearly have a good head on your shoulders. We could do with a few more of you in the ATS. This isn't some little jolly for girls who want a bit of excitement or to meet a few handsome officers. War is a serious business.'

'I agree,' I said. *Poor Vi might be in for a shock when she signed up.*

The major held out the paper towards me. 'Excellent. In which case, I suggest you take this form away with you. Have a think over the next few days and have a chat with your family. When you are sure that this is what you want, complete it and bring it back. The next intake for basic training for our local units is in three weeks.'

My heart sank like a ship's anchor thrown overboard with no tether. It hadn't occurred to me that I might have to wait. I didn't have a week, let alone three. I reached to take the form from her. To my surprise, she didn't let go of it. Instead, her eyes travelled to my wrist. My cuff had slipped back revealing livid bruises. Abandoning the paper, I tugged my sleeve down and cradled my wrist on my lap. My cheeks burned. So much for the impression I'd given of being a strong independent woman.

There was a beat or two of silence, before the major asked, her voice brisk, 'How quickly were you hoping to join us?'

'As soon as possible,' I muttered.

She ran her finger down a list on her desk. 'There are no spaces in the local units, at all. However, there is one possibility.' Her lips compressed into a straight line. 'I'll make a telephone call and see what I can do. You'll have to go further afield than we would usually send girls from Bristol.'

'I don't mind.' I edged forward in my seat, relief that I might actually manage to escape from Jake caused hot tears to crowd the backs of my eyes. I blinked them away. 'I'm happy to go anywhere.'

She lifted the handset from the black Bakelite telephone on her desk and then paused, sighed, and replaced it back on the cradle. 'I keep forgetting. This isn't working and the engineer can't come to fix it until tomorrow. I'm so sorry, I can't leave the office unattended to go and use the public one.'

To have a possible escape route within my grasp only for it to be whipped away was almost too much to bear. I found myself on my feet without realising I was going to move at all. 'Do you mind if I take a look at it, ma'am?'

She raised one curious eyebrow. 'Be my guest.'

It was one of the newer designs with a rotary dial. I lifted the handset and listened. Nothing. I pushed the zero around the dial and watched it spin back. No operator offered to direct my call. 'It's probably a loose wire,' I muttered, following the flex from the base of the telephone to the socket in the wall and disconnecting it. 'I'll put this back in a minute. No point risking an electric shock while I take a look inside.' I returned to the handset and unscrewed the cover from the mouthpiece.

'Do you know much about telephones?' asked the major.

More confident now that I had something mechanical to fidget with, I shot her a quick smile. 'Not really. Although, I took the one at Makepeace Motors apart when it was first installed.' Da's furious reaction when he found his brand-new investment in pieces on my desk wasn't something I'd forget in a hurry.

'Why?' She sounded genuinely interested.

I shrugged. 'Curiosity, more than anything. I like to know how things work and it was a slow day.'

'What did you learn?'

'That there's a thin plate in the mouthpiece here.' I pointed it out so that she could see what I meant. 'That vibrates when you speak and that converts the sound into an electrical pulse. Only, there's nothing wrong with this one. Maybe the problem is in the earpiece.' I screwed the cap back on and turned my attention to dismantling the other end of the handset. 'Anyway, those pulses travel along the wire to the telephone you are calling. Once there, a receiver converts the signal back into sound in the earpiece. Aha! I can see the problem. There is a loose wire. Can you see?' I turned it to show her.

She glanced from the nest of wires to me, a calculating expression on her face. 'Can you fix it?'

'I could if I had the right tools. I'll have to improvise. Do you have a paperclip?'

She rummaged in a drawer and produced one.

I unravelled it and bent the end into a small hook. 'Do you mind holding the handset steady for me?'

Major Stapleton complied and watched with interest as I slid the paperclip into the earpiece, to snag the offending wire. I plucked a bobby pin from my hair and used the two to manoeuvre the wire back into place. 'There. Hopefully, that should do it.' I screwed the cover back on and placed the handset on the cradle before reconnecting the main flex to the socket on the wall. 'Have a try.'

Major Stapleton held the receiver to her ear. 'I have a dialling tone!' The surprise in her voice matched the expression on her face. 'Goodness. You did it.'

'It's temporary. Your engineer can sort it out properly, tomorrow.'

'Thank you.' Her eyes flicked to my wrist and then to my face. 'Why don't you pop along to the building next door for a basic medical, while I make those calls I mentioned. There's a recruitment drive for the main army there this week and they have a medical team on standby. If the doctor confirms that you're fit to join up, and your vaccinations are up to date, come straight back and I should have an answer for you about whether or not I can place you somewhere.'

* * *

Twenty minutes later, having submitted to being prodded and poked, asked a range of basic health questions and given a tetanus shot, I was back with a completed medical form to hand her.

'Excellent.' She scanned it. 'Good news. I've managed to secure you a place. Will tomorrow be soon enough for you to be ready to leave?'

'Tomorrow is perfect,' I said, unable to keep the tidal wave of relief that swamped me from showing in my voice. A second later, that relief was followed by a surge of panic. What would Ma and Da say? How would I tell them? The memory of Jake's sneering face elbowed its way to the forefront of my mind and I knew I had no choice. I was doing this, no matter what. 'Do my family need to know where I'm going?'

'That is up to you. I would advise informing them that you're joining up. Whether that is done via letter or face to face is your choice. We don't want them reporting you missing. The police have enough to do. Bear in mind that you don't have to reveal exactly where you're going. I can make a note on your file to keep details of your posting confidential in any relevant communication moving forward.'

'Thank you. Do you have any idea what I might be doing?'

She steepled her fingers. 'The ATS is still in its infancy, Miss Makepeace. We are barely more than eighteen months old and some of our systems are not yet fully established. You will have to bear with us.'

'I can do that.'

'Everyone hopes that this war will be done and dusted in a jiffy. With each month that passes, that is looking less and less likely. I hope to be proved wrong, of course. Nevertheless, an extended period of conflict will mean more and more opportunities for women as things develop.' She returned her glasses to her nose. 'Which is my long-winded way of saying, unfortunately the ATS is only able to offer relatively menial appointments to recruits at the moment; supportive roles in cleaning, catering and basic office work.'

'That's fine.' I just wanted to get away. Staying here and looking after Da and Jake would involve cleaning, catering and office work. At least with the ATS, I wouldn't be shackled to Jake for life.

'I've found you a place in a new unit in Dorset. The facility is small and still under construction so you will have to be adaptable. If you keep your head down and do your duty, you never know where the ATS will take you.'

'It sounds perfect.'

She beamed. 'In which case, I'll let them know to expect you. Any other questions?'

'What should I take with me?'

'As little as possible. Minimal personal possessions are advised. You will be issued with a uniform. Bring your identity card, ration book, gas mask, basic toiletries and undergarments. Travel in practical clothing and a pair of sturdy shoes if you have them. Bedding and a towel are provided. I'd advise long johns for under your pyjamas, although they are not strictly in accordance with regulation. All the recruits tell me the nights are cold.' A twinkle appeared in her eye. 'The army doesn't issue bed socks, you know.'

The ghost of a smile tugged at my lips. The cold didn't scare me. I could survive anything if it meant I didn't have to spend the rest of my days living in fear of Jake. Having escape tantalisingly close made me almost giddy with excitement.

The major sat back. 'A word to the wise. Uniform sizing can be erratic. Bring a needle, thread and safety pins if you have them. We don't allow permanent alteration of your uniform because it remains the property of the army. Having said that, the odd stitch here and there that can be undone and any other temporary adjustments are acceptable.'

'I see. And where should I report?'

She rubbed her chin. 'Can you get to Bristol Temple Meads Station before nine?'

My mind whirled. It would be tight, but it was possible. 'Yes.'

'Then report to the station master when you arrive. I'll make sure he has a ticket ready for you and information about where you are headed.' She frowned. 'It is my job, when I'm not filling in for sick colleagues, to promote the interests of the ATS. To make sure that we are developing into an effective force and offering as much as we can. As such I will be paying regular visits to each of the companies deployed in the south and east of England, to make sure that all is running smoothly. Wherever you end up posted, you can expect to see me, from time to time. I am also on the lookout for any privates who show particular initiative.'

That sounded interesting. If there was an opportunity to advance, maybe I could get promoted to more challenging duties. 'What sort of initiative?'

'I'm not sure yet,' said Major Stapleton, tipping her head to one side. 'It's just an idea I'm working on. I believe that women have much to offer given the right circumstances.' She picked up a pen from her desk and unscrewed the cap. 'We had better get this form filled in then, hadn't we? May I see your identity papers?' Within ten minutes, the paperwork was complete. She got to her feet. 'From this moment forward, you are a member of the ATS serving your king and country. Congratulations and good luck.'

'Thank you, ma'am.' I stood and shook the hand she offered, and left the building with a spring in my step. Now that I had made the decision to go, I couldn't wait to get started. This time tomorrow, I would be on my way. Jake would be a distant memory. I hardened my heart to the ripple of regret that the thought of leaving my family and everything I had ever known triggered. This was the only option I had. It was time to look forward, not back.

6

The bus to Bristol Temple Meads was the same one I always caught in the mornings. The route went right past Makepeace Motors at a quarter past the hour, and would arrive at the station at eight minutes to nine, which should give me just enough time to get my ticket. I dare not take an earlier bus; Ma might get suspicious. The only way for this plan to succeed was to act completely normally, right up until the moment I didn't get off the bus for work.

I dressed exactly as I would any other day: a long, dove-grey divided skirt, which was both smart and practical, a cream blouse with a fitted grey waistcoat and a flowered silk scarf tied around my neck. I added thick woollen tights and sturdy boots rather than my court shoes, which given the cold weather wasn't particularly suspicious. I'd snuck into the pantry the night before, when Ma was distracted putting the boys to bed, and plucked my ration book from the old biscuit tin on the top shelf. I packed it, with my identity papers and the other meagre possessions I was taking, into a small leather satchel hidden under my bed. After a breakfast of dry toast, I said goodbye and left Ma and the boys in the dining room eating, just as I always did, pausing in the hall to look back and take a mental picture of them that I could carry in my heart. The realisation that I might never see them again almost made me change my mind.

Ma looked up, a frown on her face. 'What on earth are you dilly-dallying for?'

I shook my head, flashed her a sad smile, muttered goodbye again before dashing upstairs, to grab my satchel. Back downstairs, I shrugged into my coat and hat and left.

The front door closed behind me with a satisfying clunk. I stared at it for a few seconds wondering if I would ever return, then a thrum of excitement germinated in my belly. I was really doing this. I walked to the bus stop at the end of the road, trying to act normally. Inside, I was all a tremble, convinced that at any second Ma would find the letter I'd left on my pillow and come charging out to stop me.

Writing that letter had been one of the hardest things I'd ever had to do. Hot, salty tears had trickled down my cheeks as I searched for the right words.

> *Dear Ma and Da,*
>
> *By the time you find this, I will have left Bristol.*
>
> *Ma's decision to take Nana and the boys to Aunty Mo's is sensible. They'll be safe there and the countryside will be good for them.*
>
> *I know Aunty Mo doesn't have room for me and that Ma is worried about me staying in Bristol without her. So I've joined up instead.*
>
> *I'll be safe, I promise. I'll be billeted with lots of other women and we'll all work hard to help win this awful war.*
>
> *I can't say where I am being posted, yet, but please don't worry about me.*
>
> *With all my love,*
>
> *Fliss*
>
> *x*

I could only hope that I had struck the right tone. As well as not mentioning where I was going, I had avoided all reference to which service I had joined, to make tracking me down much harder.

It was a relief to see the bus turn into the road and glide to a halt. As soon as I'd paid my fare and we were underway, I began to breathe more easily.

I checked my watch countless times as we crawled along the streets of Bristol. My usual stop came, but I didn't get off. The bus lurched on, approaching Makepeace Motors. I stared out of the window, hoping for a last glimpse of the yard as we passed. To my horror, a familiar bulky figure stood on the street outside. Having just arrived for work, Jake looked up as the bus drew level.

Before I could duck out of sight, our eyes locked. His brow knit. An ominous scowl twisted his lips.

I shrank back from the window in terror, telling myself that it would be fine; he didn't know what I was planning. I could barely stay in my seat, the urge to run was so strong. I forced myself to focus on the road ahead. Every second that passed the bus was taking me further away from him, closer to safety.

Bristol Temple Meads station, with its four-turreted clocktower and red-brick frontage, finally loomed into view and I hurried to be the first to disembark the instant the bus stopped. The slope up to the main station entrance was alive with hustle and bustle, with deliveries being made and troops gathering for deployment. I edged past a group of uniformed officers and skirted around a pile of packing cases piled high on the pavement.

A shout rang out from behind.

I turned. Dear Lord. No!

Jake, a few hundred feet away and bearing down on me at speed, had a face like thunder. Behind him, the Ford Roadster from the workshop sat abandoned at the side of the road, two wheels up on the kerb. It made sense that he'd have worked out where I was heading. He knew the bus routes, the same as I did, and in the sports car, he'd have easily been able to get here before me.

I ran, my heart in my mouth. There was only one thought in my head. Escape.

Inside the station, the vast concourse was packed. Steam hissed, whistles shrieked and the scent of hot metal and smoke filled the air. I dashed into the crowd and kept moving, ignoring the sharp pain of a stitch under my ribs. Sweat trickled between my shoulder blades. In my mind's eye, Jake was mere feet behind and about to grab me. I slipped past a queue of people waiting to buy newspapers and threw myself into an alcove out of sight. Leaning against the wall with my eyes closed, I battled to stop my limbs trembling and prayed that he hadn't seen me.

A quick check of my wristwatch told me it was four minutes to nine. I had to get to the station master. Peering out from my hidey-hole, I saw Jake march up and down just inside the station entrance, glowering in all directions, then he threw his hands in the air and stormed off towards platform one. I could only assume that he intended to search the whole station until he found me.

I ducked my head and walked purposefully in the opposite direction, towards the ticket office, sending up a small prayer to heaven that there was no queue. The uniformed man behind the counter nodded as I approached. 'How can I help you, miss?'

'I was told to report to the station master. My name is Felicity Makepeace.'

He tugged out his pocket watch and frowned at it. 'You're late. It's nearly nine.'

'I know, I am sorry.' One leg twitched as I silently urged the man to hurry.

'Your train is already at platform seven. You have six minutes, so look sharp. Here.' He thrust an envelope at me.

'Thanks.' I tore it open. There was a letter and joining papers inside. I scanned the letter.

Private Makepeace,

I have arranged for you to complete your basic ATS training at Foxhalt Hall, which is on the Dorset/Hampshire border near Fordingbridge.

Take the 0905 hours train to Salisbury, then the 1030 hours bus on to Fordingbridge.

You will be met outside Fordingbridge post office for your journey on to Foxhalt.

I wish you every luck with your endeavours and urge you to serve your country well.

Yours sincerely,

Major Belinda Stapleton

Foxhalt Hall. I'd never heard of it. Chances were that Jake had never heard of it either. I could feel safe in the knowledge that he would never find me there. There was a ticket still inside the envelope.

Aware that time was short, I hurried towards platform seven, the paperwork from the major and the envelope with the ticket clutched in my fist like a lifeline. Glancing back, I saw to my horror that Jake wasn't far away. Fortunately, thanks to the sheer number of troops between us, he hadn't spotted me. I ducked behind a stall laden with flowers where a soldier was buying a rose for a pretty woman clutching his arm.

The flower seller, an older woman dressed in a long dark skirt and a thick woollen cardigan the colour of a clear blue summer sky, pocketed his money before peering curiously at me. 'Is everything all right, love?' she asked. 'You look like the hounds of hell are on your tail.'

A short gasp of horrified laughter was out before I could stop it. 'That's one way to describe him.' I slapped a hand over my mouth pushing down a whimper of fear.

She frowned. 'Some fella bothering you?'

I gave a jerky nod.

'You can hide right under the stall if it'll help,' she said. 'There's quite a big gap under the table. I can drape the cloth to cover you.'

I shook my head. 'Thank you, but my train leaves in a few minutes. If I can get to it, I can escape him for good.'

She stood so that her body shielded me from view and crossed her arms staring out over the concourse. 'Is it that great lump over there.' She nodded towards Jake.

'How could you tell?'

'I've met his type before.'

A thought occurred to me. 'I don't suppose you'd...? No. Sorry, I shouldn't ask. It's too dangerous.'

'Ask the question,' she said. '*I'll* decide if it's too dangerous.'

I ran a hand down the arm of my coat. 'Would you put on my coat and hat? They're bright and quite noticeable. Perhaps you could lead him away? It might give me enough time to get to platform seven.'

She sucked her teeth, her eyes narrowed. 'How will you get your coat back?'

'I won't.'

She grinned and stuck out her hand. 'Go on. Hand them over. A nice coat and hat are always worth taking a risk for.' She called over to a boy shining shoes a few yards away. 'Billy, watch the flowers for me. I'll be back in a sec.' She shrugged out of her cardigan and held it out to me. 'Here, love. You take my cardie. Fair exchange is no robbery, right?'

I passed her my coat and hat and watched her saunter through the crowds in Jake's direction, keeping her head down so that the brim of the hat covered her face. Without waiting to see if he took the bait, I dashed off in the opposite direction.

The sharp chill air seared in and out of my lungs as I ran. My satchel and gas mask bounced against my back, and my boots pounded the flagstones. Pushing all thought of Jake from my mind, I focused on setting one foot in front of the other in a steady, maintainable rhythm. I dodged around people in my way, my eyes darting in all directions, searching for signs to platform seven. There. I took the steps two at a time, every muscle in my body protesting.

A sharp double toot from the guard's whistle cut through the air and a booming voice called, 'All aboard.' The ominous clunking sound of train doors slamming reached my ears. My one chance at escape was about to pull out of the station without me. Spurred on by desperation, I scampered across the platform towards the train.

The sharp grate of metal on metal sounded as the couplings took the strain. The thrum of the immense engine was so loud I felt it reverberate through my bones. The carriages began to move, slowly at first, then gaining in speed. I cantered alongside the last door of the rear carriage, my heart galloping in time with my feet, like a herd of stampeding horses. I eyed the distance from the platform to the train, hoping against hope that I could, somehow, manage to get aboard. Just as I was about to give up, the door flew open and a hand extended.

'Well, hurry up and jump, if you're coming,' said a voice.

Without allowing myself to think, I grasped the hand and jumped.

7

I sailed through the air, landing inside the carriage in an undignified heap with my belongings all around me. The door shut with a satisfying kerchunk, reducing the clatter and rattle of the train's rolling stock to muted growls and rhythmic tremors beneath me. Ignoring my smarting kneecaps, I glanced up to thank the owner of the hand for his assistance. My gaze locked with a pair of stunning blue eyes that made me gasp. A tall, slim man in a three-piece brown worsted suit leaned over me. The shadow he cast conjured up the ghost of Jake's looming presence in the workshop and I couldn't stop myself from cringing away.

He straightened, a hint of concern crowding his eyes. 'Forgive me,' he said, stepping back. 'We haven't been properly introduced.' He raised his trilby hat along with his eyebrows. 'I'm Daniel. Pleased to meet you. May I help you up?' He slowly put out a hand as if to a nervous child.

My gaze ping-ponged from his hand to his face and back again and the strangest sensation came over me, as if I suddenly recognised him as someone I had always been searching for. Which was utterly ridiculous. Nevertheless, I couldn't spend my life on the floor of a train carriage, so I accepted his assistance. A disconcerting jolt of electricity ran up my arm the second my fingers touched his. As soon as I had regained my feet, I jerked my hand free and shuffled back against the wall of the carriage to create as much distance between us as possible. With my palm to my chest to help slow my breathing, I searched in vain for something to say.

He smiled, as if there were nothing unusual about our encounter. 'Did you know, most people arrive early for public transport? The guards prefer passengers to not risk life and limb when boarding.' There was a distinct teasing note in his voice.

Apart from those mesmerising eyes, there was nothing particularly striking about him. He was an inch or two taller than me, with strong features: a slightly too big nose, a fractionally too wide mouth. He wasn't unattractive, yet not classically good-looking either. I was at a loss to explain his magnetic attraction.

'Hmm,' he said, when I didn't reply. 'A woman of mystery. Perhaps you're on the run from the police.' He laughed. 'Have I aided and abetted a fugitive?'

I ducked my head, my cheeks burning. 'Don't be silly.'

'You can speak. Wonderful. I was beginning to think you'd left your voice behind on the platform. Do you have a name?'

'Fliss.' Noting the disparity between his immaculate appearance, and mine, I set about straightening my clothes.

'Come on, Fliss,' he said, picking up a kitbag that lurked at his feet. He jerked his head to indicate that I should follow.

The sensible part of my brain reminded me that he was a complete stranger and an unknown quantity. Yet, the pull to go with him was strong. This wasn't the same as being alone in the workshop with Jake. A train was a public space; I should be safe enough. 'Where are we going?'

'I suggest we find a compartment to hide in, before the guard comes to tell you off.' His lips twitched. 'I don't know about you, but I can do without being ejected at the next station.'

I cursed under my breath. He was right. A run-in with the guard was the last thing I needed. I scurried behind him, tucking a stray lock of hair behind my ear, my satchel bashing against my legs. He loped along the corridor, glancing into each compartment he passed. The train was relatively full, rather than rammed with troops in the way the news reels often implied. It wasn't long before he found a compartment he thought suitable. I hesitated to enter until I saw two other occupants within: an elderly woman peering through half-moon glasses at the pages of a book, and a portly gentleman with a red face who was fast asleep. Daniel slid the glass door open and gestured for me to precede him.

Inside, the scent of ancient pipe smoke and worn leather lingered in the air, hinting at countless past passengers.

Daniel stowed our baggage in the overhead netting before running his eyes over me thoughtfully. 'The guard probably got a good look at you. And that rather... uh... relaxed hairstyle of yours is quite memorable.'

My hand shot to my head. I tugged a compact from a little pocket in my waistcoat and flipped open the mirror. 'Oh dear.' The neat chignon I had arranged that morning was gone. Most of the bobby pins were a distant memory too. Wild curls tumbled in all directions.

'I don't mean to imply that you're not perfect as you are, of course.' He tipped his head on one side. 'It's a shame you can't change your appearance enough that he won't recognise you.'

Maybe it was a rush of adrenaline triggered by successfully escaping Jake; for some reason Daniel's words sounded like a challenge. One I couldn't resist.

'I bet you I can,' I said.

Surprised amusement lit up his face. 'Go on then.'

'Fine. Watch this.'

I tugged my silk scarf free of my neck, shook it out and folded it into a triangle. Brushing my curls back from my face with my fingers, I laid the scarf over the top, gathered the ends together and twisted it all into a long rope that I arranged around my head and then tucked the ends in. The result was a pretty headwrap hiding every strand of hair.

He gave a low whistle. 'Impressive.'

'I'm not finished.' I shrugged off the cardigan and unbuttoned my waistcoat before pulling my blouse free from my skirt. Bundling up both waistcoat and cardigan into a ball, I stuffed them under my top and sat down in a seat next to the window. With my arms arranged on either side of the fake 'bump' to hold it in place, I rested my head against the glass and stared out at the outskirts of Bristol rushing by, and said, 'Who would dream of disturbing an exhausted, expectant mother?'

Daniel snorted. 'That might actually work. Let's hope he doesn't ask you to stand up.'

A commotion sounded outside in the corridor. 'Where is she?' came an irate voice followed by the sound of a door sliding roughly aside and muttered conversation.

'It sounds like we're on.' The spicy scent of his aftershave floated over me as he took the seat next to mine. He picked up a newspaper, abandoned on a seat nearby, and flicked it open.

My eyes drifted to those of the woman sat opposite and I nearly groaned out loud. We'd been carrying on as if she wasn't present. There was no time to explain. To beg for her help. She'd give me away for certain. My stomach lurched. I could be thrown off the train at the next station. It would be a disaster. I'd never make it to Foxhalt by myself. What on earth would happen then? I couldn't go home. I closed my eyes to hold back tears of frustration. There was nothing I could do, other than commit to this course of action and hope for the best.

The door swished open. I threw the woman opposite an imploring look before feigning sleep, keeping my lashes parted a fraction so that I could see what was going on. 'Everyone on your feet,' demanded the guard. He shook the man near the door. 'Stand up, sir. Let me look at you.'

The man spluttered awake and grumbled to his feet. 'What on earth is going on?'

'I'm looking for a girl.'

'Do I look like a girl?' growled the man. He shuffled in a circle before sitting back down and closing his eyes again.

I felt rather than saw Daniel rising from the seat beside me. The newspaper rustled. He spoke with hushed urgency. 'Please don't disturb my wife, sir. She finds travel exhausting in her condition.'

I could almost hear the cogs of the guard's brain turning as he ran narrowed eyes over me. He scratched his head and glanced across the compartment with a frown at the woman opposite. 'A girl jumped on board this train when it was already underway.'

'It's a long time since I was a girl,' she said, an arch look spilling over the top of her glasses. 'And if you think a heavily pregnant woman is capable of leaping onto a moving train, you're dafter than you look.'

The guard cast me one final intense look and turned away. 'She looks nothing like her, anyway.' Seconds later he was gone.

'I'd stay like that for a few more minutes if I were you,' said the old lady, returning her attention to her book. 'In case he doubles back.'

I leaned forward. 'Thank you. I didn't expect you to cover for me, but I am so grateful that you did.'

Mischief rippled across her face. 'I never said that *you* were heavily pregnant. He jumped to his own conclusions.' She turned to Daniel. 'However, I do think your friend just won her bet, young man.'

Daniel grinned. 'I think she did too.'

A piercing whistle sounded. The rhythmic rocking of the train changed as it began to slow. 'This will be my stop,' said the woman, gathering her things. 'Good luck to you both. And thank you for adding a bit of excitement to an otherwise boring journey.' She slipped into the corridor. The man in the corner shook himself awake, heaved a huge case down from the luggage rack and ambled off too.

Daniel lowered himself back onto the seat beside me. 'I take it you have a ticket,' he said.

'Of course I have a ticket,' I said, rummaging in the front pocket of my satchel for the envelope and producing it. 'Here it is. Oh!'

'Have you lost something?'

I checked inside the envelope again. 'There was a letter too, and...' I slipped my hand back into my pocket. Nothing. At some point since switching coats with the flower seller and getting on the train, I had lost Major Stapleton's letter *and* my joining papers. 'They've gone.'

'Were they important?'

'Very.' I sighed. 'They were my joining instructions for the ATS, and had all my travel details too.'

'Can you remember what they said?'

I dropped my head into my hands with a groan and tried to visualise the letter. 'I was to get off in Salisbury and then catch a bus to... Fordingbridge, I think. Then...' I bit my lip. 'Someone was meeting me to take me to a place called Foxhalt. I remember that because of the fox bit in the name.'

'Do you have enough money for the bus fare?' he asked.

'Yes. I do.'

'Then I shouldn't worry, if I were you. You can check at the bus station when you buy your ticket. The conductors know everywhere on their routes. If you say you're heading for this Foxhalt, they'll be able to advise you.'

He was right. However, losing the major's papers rattled me. Somewhere lying on a platform in Bristol Temple Meads Station were documents with not only my name but where I was going on them. And there was nothing I could do about it other than hope some janitor swept them up and threw them away.

What if they didn't? What if Jake found them and...? No. I couldn't go there.

'Is there a problem?' He was examining me as if I were a curious specimen of plant that he had no idea how to categorise.

I shook my head. 'It doesn't matter.' Thinking of Jake reminded me that you couldn't be too careful with men. And Daniel and I were now alone in the carriage. Not that he had done anything to make me think he was dangerous. Even so, it would be sensible to remember that I barely knew him and should be careful what I said and did. It was time to change the subject. Keep things light. Divert the subject onto him. 'Where are you heading?'

'Southampton.' He said the word as if it tasted bad.

'You don't sound very happy about that.'

He waved a dismissive hand. 'It's a long story.'

'How long?' I waved my ticket and shot him a mischievous look, the urge to tease a smile from him overcoming my reticence. 'I have until Salisbury, remember? And it looks like we've been delayed anyway.' I nodded out of the window. Having moved out of the station, the train had stopped completely with no indication of why. 'We could be here ages. Plenty of time for a long story.' I'd much rather talk about him than me.

'If you insist,' he said. 'Don't blame me if you're bored to tears.'

'Deal.'

'I've been trying to join up ever since war broke out.' He lifted a shoulder and let it drop. 'I thought, rather than wait to be called, why not just do it. I'm young, fit and single.'

For some reason, that last bit of information lifted my spirits.

'It seems only fair for me to fight in place of someone who maybe can't, or perhaps someone who has dependents,' he continued. 'Army, navy, air force, I don't mind which.'

'That's very brave of you.' And yet, he wasn't in uniform.

'Not brave at all, as it turned out.' He grimaced. 'I failed the medical.'

'Oh!'

'I tried all three services in London. And then, I travelled to Cardiff to visit my uncle and I thought I'd try again there. I was hoping another recruiting office might come to a different decision.'

'They didn't?'

'No.' His shoulders sank, giving him a haunted air. He was either a very good actor or genuinely disappointed not to serve. Whereas Jake had been cock-a-hoop not to be called up. 'It's ridiculous,' he insisted. 'There's nothing wrong with me.'

'Nothing?' I raised an eyebrow and fixed him with the sort of stare I usually reserved for my brothers when they were being flexible with the truth.

He scowled. 'Nothing apart from a slightly duff elbow.'

'Duff how?'

He looked down at the back of his hands. 'I broke it falling out of a tree, years ago. I was eight. It set badly. I mean, it works well enough; I just don't have the full range of movement that other people have. See?' He held both arms in front of him, one straightened fully and the other didn't, stopping halfway. 'It's not a serious problem. I manage just fine.' He moved his forearms, rotating them so that his hands twisted from being palm down to palm up and back. The motion of the left arm was noticeably more limited and jerkier than the right. He huffed in disgust. 'They wouldn't listen. And I've been warned not to waste the time of any other recruitment offices.'

'So, why are you going to Southampton?'

He dropped his arms into his lap with a grunt. 'Apparently, there's some government office there that will tell me what I *am* allowed to do.'

'That's good,' I said. 'Did they give you any idea what that might be?'

'No. Not a clue. They could send me anywhere in the country to do, pretty much anything.' He wrinkled his nose in disgust. 'At least it's something, I suppose. Anyway. That's enough about me.'

The train jerked as we started moving once again. 'Oh, thank goodness,' I said, checking the time. 'If we are too late into Salisbury, I might miss my lift at Fordingbridge.'

Daniel was easy company. He was happy to chat about diverse subjects from the latest news broadcasts about the progress of the war to the effects of rationing and even music. We discovered a mutual love for Glenn Miller and Ella Fitzgerald. Against my better judgement, I felt a strange pang of loss when we finally drew into Salisbury station.

'Would you mind if I wrote to you?' said Daniel, as he lifted my bag down. 'Once I'm settled somewhere, I mean. Perhaps you can let me know that you arrived safely.'

'I... uh... I don't know.' This was meant to be my fresh new start. It wasn't just about escaping Jake. This was a chance to build a life I had some control over. Did I need a man complicating things? I'd enjoyed talking to him and he seemed perfectly lovely, but I didn't *know* him. What if I was jumping from one awful man situation into another?

'I tell you what,' he said. 'Let's leave it to chance. I'll write to "Fliss" at the ATS in "Foxhalt", which is all I really know about you. I'll include my contact details. If it reaches you, you can decide if you want to write back. How's that?'

That seemed fair. I nodded my agreement.

There was genuine kindness in his eyes. 'It was nice meeting you.'

'And you. Good luck and safe journey, Daniel.' I pressed a quick kiss to his cheek, surprised when that same spark of electricity I'd experienced before when we touched shot between us again. I lifted one hand to my lips to cover my confusion, turned away and melted into the crowd. The platform was packed with troops trying to board the train. I threaded my way between them towards the station exit. What on earth had possessed me to kiss him? I hugged the sensation of that sizzling contact to myself. He was nothing like Jake; that was for sure. Perhaps I should have agreed to write to him. No. I shook my head. I didn't need any ties. I'd escaped everything. For the first time in my life, I was free.

I shrugged myself deeper into the flower seller's cardigan to ward off the chill and went in search of the bus station. With every step I took, my spirits lifted as I looked forward to whatever this new life of mine would bring.

8

The bus wound its way through country lanes bound by hedgerows that sprouted a profusion of early spring growth. I drank in the bold patchwork of countryside colours, from the blue sky and green verges to bright yellow daffodils and purple crocuses. A slow-moving tractor brought a frustrating delay, followed by a herd of cows that drifted across the road, ignoring the young lad desperately trying to encourage them back into a field. I was eventually deposited outside the post office in the small market town of Fordingbridge, nearly an hour later than I was supposed to have arrived. Other passengers disembarked and bustled past me as I stood on the pavement wondering if whoever was meeting me was still there.

A vehicle door slammed off to my left. A tall woman with an hourglass figure, dressed in a sergeant's uniform, stood next to a small military truck. I shouldered my gas mask and satchel and approached her.

Pausing in the act of pulling on leather gloves, she looked up, her lips pursed. 'If you're Felicity Makepeace, you're late.'

'I'm sorry, ma'am.'

'Where are your joining papers?'

Nausea puddled in my stomach. 'I'm sorry, ma'am. I've lost them.'

'Do you have your identity card?'

'Yes.' Fortunately, that had been securely packed in my bag. I handed it over. She glared at the cramped print and then at my face. 'Makepeace,' she muttered. 'I'll just have to hope that you are who you say you are. This is most irregular. It's bad enough that you're joining us midway through a training program, you could at least be organised. *And* on time. You're in the army now.'

The admonishment was a little tough given every government broadcast urged patience with the inevitable delays of wartime travel. I bit back a sharp retort. 'Yes, ma'am.'

She gave a brisk nod. 'I'm Sergeant Beaconsfield. Stow your gear in the back and let's get going.'

I hurried to comply, taking a moment to examine the truck. Da had spoken about the War Office's use of Morris CS8 trucks with approval. We'd recently had a couple in the yard to work on but I'd not driven one. Two-wheel drive with an eight-foot wheelbase, it had a six-cylinder engine. This was an early model with an open cab that had small glass sections in front of both driver and passenger to deflect the wind. A folding canvas canopy overhead provided shelter from the rain, and the rear compartment was large enough to seat eight on sideways wooden benches.

'Do stop dawdling,' she said.

I scrambled into the passenger seat.

'Like trucks, do you?' she asked.

I nodded, fighting to find my voice. She couldn't have been more than a few years older than me, but in her smart uniform, with red lipstick and neat auburn curls that stopped just above her collar, she oozed a confidence and glamour that I could never aspire to.

'By rights, we should be in the pony and trap, what with petrol rationing, but—' she waved towards the post office '—there was an urgent telegram that needed to be sent so Commander Carter said to drive.' The engine roared into life. She gave the gearstick a determined wiggle before ramming it into first, and the truck leapt forwards like a startled rabbit darting from the undergrowth.

'Commander Carter?' I asked, clutching at my seat and trying not to wince at the sound of grating gears.

She raised her voice above the noise. 'Commander Carter is in charge of the Foxhalt training base. She's only allowed you to join us as a special favour for Major Stapleton. I hope you're going to be worth all the trouble you're causing.'

I concentrated on staying in my seat as she weaved an erratic path down the road. 'I hope so too.'

We drove in silence for several minutes. I was glad when we left Fordingbridge behind and spilled back onto the narrow country lanes. Hurtling along at breakneck speed was less stressful when there were no pedestrians nearby. We approached a crossroads. She stamped on the brakes briefly, slowing our pace, making my teeth rattle. Jiggling the gearstick again, she muttered, 'There must be a gear here somewhere.' I saw the muscles in her jaw clench as she forced the lever forward. The truck groaned and jerked as if it were planning to leap off the road entirely. 'Blast it!' she cursed, under her breath, steering us around a corner.

I couldn't help myself. She was going to wreck the transmission if she wasn't careful. 'Have you tried double declutching?'

She swerved into a lay-by and brought us to a screeching halt that almost had me headbutting the dash. Fixing me with a cool stare, she said, 'Are you telling me how to drive, Makepeace?'

I cleared my throat. 'I wouldn't dream of it, ma'am. I'm sure you already know that the unsynchronised transmissions in trucks can make gear changes tricky.'

Her reply was crisp. 'Everyone knows that.'

'Fortunately, doing it in two stages, by depressing the clutch and going out of gear and into neutral first, before releasing the clutch and then re-depressing it before slipping into the new gear, does produce surprisingly good results.'

'That goes without saying,' she huffed, and pulled away again, this time at a more reasonable speed. A few moments later, she demanded, 'Have you passed your driving test?'

'Yes, ma'am. I took it the minute I was old enough.'

'Then you must be older than you look,' she said. 'Seeing as tests have been suspended since the war started.'

'Thank you, ma'am. I'm twenty.'

She sniffed. 'I'm used to a sports car. My father taught me to drive in a Bentley. A little thing. Two-seater. Moved like the wind.'

That explained her penchant for speed. 'Lucky you. They're beautiful cars.'

'I find this... monstrosity... unnecessarily cumbersome.'

It explained why she was riding the accelerator so hard. 'Trucks are particularly heavy,' I agreed.

The next time she changed gear, I could see her attempting to follow my suggestion. The resultant transition was less traumatic for both the vehicle and me. Unfortunately, that was the moment a deer chose to jump over the hedge straight into our path.

We both screamed.

Sergeant Beaconsfield stamped on the brakes and swerved, missing the animal's rump by mere inches. The truck skidded several feet. The rear swung out ready to fishtail. Her arms braced against the steering wheel, she lifted her foot off the brakes and stamped down again, fighting to regain control. I could see her battling to turn into the skid. Releasing my death grip on the dash, I grabbed the wheel to help.

Together, we began to win.

The back end of the truck steadied. Our momentum slowed.

There was a loud bang. We lurched forward one last time and juddered to a halt.

'That was close,' I said, peering out of the cab and back up the road to the deer, glad to see it jumping into a field on the other side, completely oblivious to the carnage it had just caused.

Sergeant Beaconsfield didn't move. She sat staring at the wheel, her face pale, that muscle in her jaw twitching again.

'I've never had a deer jump in front of me,' I said. 'It's not the sort of thing that happens in the city. You did well to miss it. Shall I see what that bang was?' I hopped down from the cab and scurried around to the bonnet, glad to feel solid ground beneath my feet. The damage was clear.

'Oh! Lawks. We've got a flat,' I said, staring at the useless strips of rubber that hung from the front passenger wheel. 'We must have hit something sharp.' I scanned the road. 'It was probably that pothole. What bad luck. Shall I check the spare?'

She didn't respond.

Convinced the best thing to do was keep talking, I hurried around to the rear of the truck and peered underneath. 'Nothing here.' I examined the rest of the vehicle until I found the spare nestled in a covered box between the cab and the rear section. 'Ah! There it is, behind your seat. Forgive me, ma'am. I'm going to have to ask you to step out.'

'Umm... yes. Of course.' Her voice seemed to come from a million miles away and her movements were sluggish. I released the spare wheel from the storage housing and we lifted it down together.

Sergeant Beaconsfield stood a few feet away and watched as I placed the jack under the main chassis and cranked the front corner of the vehicle high enough to enable me to release the wheel nuts on the wheel with the damaged tyre. She pulled a pack of Camel cigarettes from the pocket of her uniform and offered me one. I shook my head. Smoking had never appealed and naked flames near fuel and oils in the workshop were a daft idea. She shrugged and lit one for herself, inhaled deeply and blew out a stream of smoke that caught on the gentle breeze and floated away like a trail of dandelion seeds.

'How come you know so much about trucks?' she said.

I pulled the damaged wheel from the axle, hopping back as it thumped down onto the road. 'My father owns a repair shop.'

She took another long drag on her cigarette.

I heaved the damaged wheel onto its side and dragged it out of the way, before busying myself setting the spare in place and tightening the nuts.

'Who exactly are you?' she asked.

I looked up, bewildered. 'I'm sorry?'

'Clearly something about you merits special treatment. Or you wouldn't be allowed to join a training period midway through.' She stared up the road. 'Are you related to someone important somehow? Is that why they're letting you break the rules?'

'No,' I said, unable to keep astonishment from my voice. Was that why she was so prickly? She thought I had pulled strings 'Nothing like that.'

'It must be something. Come on. You can tell me.'

I'd never felt less like confiding in someone in my life. 'Honestly. There's nothing to tell.'

'What is your connection to Major Stapleton?'

'I met her two days ago.'

Her lips compressed in dissatisfaction. 'Don't lie to me.'

'Why do you think I'm lying?'

'Don't you know who Major Stapleton is?'

I shook my head.

'She's connected,' she said. 'She knows everyone. I've heard she has fingers in all sorts of pies, all the way up to government level. Do you expect me to believe that a recruit suddenly arriving mid-program, with no proper papers, following a telephone endorsement from the major, isn't strange?'

She seemed to be almost talking to herself, and there was little point repeating myself. She was right, though. It was odd. Major Stapleton had clearly moved heaven and earth to get me into Foxhalt. Why would she do that for someone she didn't know? Was it simply that she'd seen my bruises, put two and two together, and wanted to help me get away? On reflection, probably not. Somehow, I didn't think kindness was the major's main motivating factor. She'd seemed a very determined woman. I wondered what that might mean and realised I had better keep my wits about me moving forward, just in case.

With the new wheel securely attached, I gathered up the tools and replaced both them and the damaged tyre in the appropriate compartment, before wiping my hands on a rag. 'We're good to go, ma'am.'

She took a final drag of her cigarette and stamped the butt out on the ground. 'Whoever you are, and whatever your secret is, don't expect me to go easy on you. I'll be watching to make sure you catch up on all the training you've missed.'

'I'll do my best, ma'am.' I meant it. Life at Foxhalt was going to be tougher than I'd bargained for with Sergeant Beaconsfield on my back. Regardless, I was determined to make a success of it.

'Right.' She held out the key. 'You drive. I'll direct.'

9

Foxhalt Hall turned out to be a three-storey, pale stone mansion set in manicured grounds. I tried not to stare at the large sash windows and ornate columns as I steered the truck along the swooping gravel drive, past the main house and on through an area of broadleaf woodland to a small lake. Beyond the lake, Sergeant Beaconsfield directed me to park in a courtyard. A wooden stable block stood to the left, a large barn to the right, and straight ahead was a pretty red-brick building smothered in ivy. She hopped down from the truck and headed towards the latter.

'Come along, Makepeace.'

I grabbed my gear from the back and hurried after her as she strode through the front entrance, marched along a wood-panelled hallway and through an open doorway at the far end. The room we arrived in was a generously proportioned dining room with décor that hinted at prosperous times gone by. The smell of fresh bread and vegetable soup made my mouth water. Several groups of women in ATS uniforms sat around tables eating a meal.

Indistinct chatter stilled the minute the sergeant's presence was registered.

Everyone stood to attention.

'At ease,' said Sergeant Beaconsfield. The recruits resumed their seats. 'This is Private Makepeace. She is joining us for the remainder of the training period.'

All eyes turned to me, the atmosphere heavy with unspoken questions. My stomach chose that moment to announce that it hadn't been fed since breakfast. The loud, unladylike grumble made everyone laugh. My cheeks burned.

Sergeant Beaconsfield called out, 'Private Moore?'

A chair scraped the floor on the far side of the room and a dainty brunette with smiling eyes and dimples stood up. 'Yes, Sergeant.'

'You are in charge of getting Private Makepeace settled. You had better make sure she eats something.'

'Yes, Sergeant.'

'Show her where she is to sleep, get her into uniform and bring her back to me. I'll be outside Commander Carter's office at fourteen hundred hours.'

'Yes, ma'am.'

'Don't be late.' She gave a brisk nod, turned and left.

Silence filled the room before general chatter resumed as the women went back to their meals. Private Moore beckoned me over and dragged out a spare chair. 'Here, sit. I'll get you some food.'

I glanced around, wondering where to put my things. Seeing a sideboard under the window, I placed my gas mask and satchel on top and steeled myself to join Private Moore and her companions. I'd concentrated so much on getting away, I hadn't really thought about what it might be like when I arrived. What if they didn't like me? I'd had friends at school, but I'd always been considered a bit of an oddity because of my obsession with engines and, since leaving school, all the girls I knew had married and had babies, moving into a world I wasn't a part of. I squared my shoulders and turned to slip into my seat, ready to smile at my new companions.

Further down the table, a heavy-set woman with mousy hair and a strong jaw leaned forward, asking, 'What did you do to Beaky to put her in such a foul mood?'

'Beaky?' I asked.

She tipped her head towards the door. 'Sergeant Beaconsfield. She's usually all right, only, today, she looks like someone has slapped her round the face with a dead fish.'

Telling them all the reasons why I'd upset the sergeant wouldn't achieve anything so I just shook my head. 'I have no idea.'

'Well, whatever it was, don't do it again,' said the woman.

'Give her a break, Carole,' said Private Moore, placing a bowl of steaming soup in front of me. 'I'm Kitty, by the way,' she said.

'Hi, Kitty,' I said. 'I'm Felicity. My friends call me Fliss.'

The woman the other side of me filled a glass of water and passed it over. 'I'm Rosie,' she said, tipping her head towards the other two. 'That's Jane, and that's Pam. We all bunk together.' Each woman nodded in turn.

'It's nice to meet you.' I smiled around the table, before taking a mouthful of soup. 'Wow!' I glanced down into my bowl in surprise. 'That might be the best soup I've ever had.'

Carole snorted. 'You can say what you like about this place—'

'And you usually do,' teased Pam, leaning back in her chair, tucking a stray lock of blonde hair behind one ear with long graceful fingers.

Carole ignored the interruption. '—but the food is excellent.'

There were general murmurs of agreement.

Kitty giggled. 'Don't mind Carole. She's always like that. Pass the bread down, girls.'

'How come you're late?' asked Pam, handing over a plate of sliced national loaf.

'It's a long story,' I said, not wanting to get into it. 'What have I missed?'

Rosie snorted again. 'Not much.'

Kitty tutted. 'Don't be like that, Rosie.'

'Why not?' Rosie scraped at her soup bowl. 'Apart from the right way to make beds, peel potatoes, cook and clean, we've been learning how to march. It's not difficult.'

'Marching is not that easy,' grumbled Carole.

'That's because you don't know your left from your right,' said Rosie.

Marching did sound rather dull. Major Stapleton had warned me that life in the ATS would be mundane. I realised a small part of me had been hoping for a bit of excitement. 'Why are we marching?' I asked.

'My brother said it's important when you're in the army to be able to move troops around in an organised fashion,' explained Kitty.

'That doesn't stop it being boring,' said Rosie.

'Stop being such a grump, Rosie. Whatever will Fliss think?' Pam grinned. 'Mind you, you're right about the beds and potatoes and stuff. It is all a bit basic.'

'Which is why it's called basic training,' said Carole. 'I'm happy cooking. I was worried we'd be doing technical things. Cooking I can handle.'

Kitty scraped her empty soup bowl for the last mouthful before setting her spoon down. 'The other ATS centres are attached to actual army bases. Foxhalt is new and we're only the third set of recruits to come through here. They're still working stuff out.'

I searched for something diplomatic to say. 'This house is nice, isn't it?'

'It's the old dower house to the main manor,' said Kitty. 'Apparently, the current Lady Winton's mother-in-law used to live here.'

'Winton?' I asked.

'The family that owns this whole estate,' said Rosie.

'Rumour has it that Beaky's related to them,' said Pam. 'On the wrong side of the blanket, if you know what I mean.'

'Where did you hear that?' said Kitty.

Pam shrugged. 'I can't remember. I bet that's how she got her posting here.'

Carole sniffed. 'If she was proper gentry, they'd have bought her an officer's commission rather than letting her join the rank and file with us. That lot look after their own. They buy themselves nice cushy positions rather than work their way up.'

I filed that interesting snippet of information away for later consideration. Perhaps being illegitimate had something to do with why Beaky was so defensive. It might explain why she seemed to think I'd pulled strings for special treatment. Working out how to get her on my side could be the key to making sure my time at Foxhalt was a success.

A bell sounded somewhere in the house. The girls at one of the other tables started collecting up bowls and plates. I stood up with mine, intent on following suit.

'Leave them, Fliss,' said Kitty. 'We're not on clear-up duty today. Grab your kit; I'll show you around. We'd better start with getting you some uniform.'

* * *

Twenty minutes later, my arms laden with government-issue clothing, I followed her up a beautifully carved wooden staircase. Pale sections in the middle of each step showed where a carpet runner used to be. Our footsteps echoed as we crossed the first floor, to the rear of the building. Kitty opened a door that revealed another staircase. Cramped and twisted, it took us up to a long empty corridor with doors on either side.

'These are the old servants' quarters,' said Kitty. 'There are proper barracks being built out the back. Nissen huts. They'll be ready soon. For the time being we're bunked up here. It's a bit of a crush. Look.' She flung open a door to reveal a room with two sets of bunk beds. Four trunks were stacked along the far wall under a small window. She closed the door and moved on to a door right at the end of the corridor. 'The problem is we weren't expecting you, and there's no space to put another bed in any of these rooms, so you're in here.' Her face flushed a deep red as she turned the handle. 'I'm really sorry. We cleared out all the junk and tried to make it nice.'

The door hinged outwards into the corridor rather than inwards like all the others. I could see why straight away. It was a cupboard. The space inside was just big enough to take a small metal bedframe, leaving a minuscule section of floorspace free. The ceiling sloped down at a sharp angle on two sides, making it impossible to stand up straight if you were anywhere other than right by the door.

'At least I won't have to worry about blackout blinds,' I joked, noting the absence of a window.

Kitty's laugh held a note of relief. 'And you won't have to listen to Rosie snoring either. Only, don't tell her I said that.'

I grinned. 'I won't. And I'll be fine in here.'

She pointed at the bed. 'Pay attention to how the bed and your blankets are arranged.'

I glanced at the bare bed with all the blankets folded neatly on top of the pillow.

'That's how we are expected to leave our rooms in the morning before we go down for breakfast,' she said. 'We had a whole teaching session on it. I'll show you how to do it this evening, especially how to fold everything. There's a trick to it.'

'Thank you.'

'And see the mattress, how it's made up of those three square-shaped sections laid next to each other? They're called biscuits. When you make the bed up, there's a way of putting the bottom sheet on that holds them all together. Mind you, the biscuits are quite thin and can shift around if you wriggle too much in the night. My advice is, if you find a comfy spot, don't move unless you have to.' She shrugged. 'You get used to it, and they're not too bad really.'

'Thanks for the heads-up,' I said, laying the heavy pile of clothes down in the centre of the bed. There was so much information to take in that my head was beginning to throb. I couldn't help but wonder what I had got myself into, but I only had to remember Jake to remind myself why I was here. It would be fine. If I worked hard, I'd settle in, in no time.

She glanced at her watch. 'We'd better get a wriggle on. You should change into your main uniform. Leave the overalls and boots for tomorrow's work session. I'll wait out here.'

Alone in the cupboard with the door shut, I was engulfed in complete darkness. I stuck my head back out into the corridor. 'I'm going to have to leave the door open, Kitty, or I won't be able to see anything.'

She giggled. 'I didn't think of that. We've an electric light in our room, but of course a cupboard wouldn't have one. We'll have to get you a candle or something for later.'

'I'm surprised there's electricity out here at all. I thought most rural places weren't connected to the national grid yet,' I said, as I ducked back in to get changed.

'We've got a temporary generator until they can connect us properly,' said Kitty. 'It's mainly so the telephone works, and they've run lights off it, too. They're a bit dim, mind. Not to worry though, we have a ready supply of candles.'

'That's good.' I stripped out of my things, trying not to knock my elbows against the walls or bang my head on the ceiling, and tried on the uniform. The fabric of the jacket and skirt was the usual unexciting green/brown colour and was hardwearing, and scratchy. Fortunately, the flannel blouse was soft against the skin and wouldn't drive me mad, and I had brought a petticoat that would shield my legs from the skirt. Once I had selected the best-fitting pieces, I folded all the others up and stepped out into the corridor. 'What do you think? I've had to pin the waistband of the skirt. I hope it doesn't show.'

It felt strange to be in uniform for the first time. I'd seen more and more women dressed like this in recent weeks and thought they looked very smart, especially with the shiny buttons and neat belt buckle. Now, here I was, dressed like them. It was surprising how good that felt. I'd never been part of a big organisation before. It had always just been me. I brushed a hand down my jacket, smoothing out the fabric, a sense of pride I didn't expect making me stand tall and straighten my shoulders. This whole thing had started out as a way to escape. That wasn't the case any more. I'd never particularly hankered to

join the army, yet something about this felt right. In a funny way, maybe Jake
had done me a favour. Maybe this was exactly where I was supposed to be.

Kitty ran assessing eyes all over me. 'Turn around.' She tugged at my jacket.
'Now turn back.' She straightened my tie. 'You look good. It suits you. Come on,
let's get you down to Beaky so you can meet Commander Carter.'

10

Commander Carter's office was a large airy room at the front of the house. Light streamed in from a stunning bay window. The walls were a delicate apricot shade and the lingering scent of woodsmoke told of years of roaring fires in the carved marble hearth. It must have been beautiful when the Dowager Lady Winton had lived there. Sadly, wartime deprivations were starting to bite and any form of fire in the grate, whether roaring or not, was a thing of the past. I shivered as I stood before the commander's desk, though whether that was from nerves or the cold I couldn't decide.

She was a trim woman with the excellent posture of a former dancer and stood several inches taller than me. Her silvered hair was pulled back into a tight bun, and the brass buttons on her uniform glittered like stars.

'So, you're the special recruit Major Stapleton has sent me,' she said in a soft voice. 'The one she said demonstrated extraordinary initiative in her interview.'

Beaky cleared her throat to get my attention. She made a point of standing more upright and straightening her shoulders, then jerked her head towards the commander. 'Answer the commander, Makepeace.'

I tried to copy the way Beaky was standing. 'I don't know about special, ma'am, but Major Stapleton did send me, yes.'

'And what made you want to join the ATS in such a hurry?' asked the commander.

I could almost hear Beaky's ears pricking up. She was waiting for an answer, but I was damned if I was going to give it to her. My reasons for joining were my own. 'I want to do my duty, ma'am.'

'So much that you couldn't wait for the usual procedures to be followed?' The commander's tone was mild with a hint of steel underneath.

'Yes, ma'am.'

'I understand there was an incident on your way here.'

'Ma'am?' My stomach tightened. How could she possibly know about Jake chasing me onto the train?

'With the truck,' she prompted.

'I've already filed a report, ma'am,' said Beaky. 'There was a pothole.'

'I am aware of that, Sergeant,' said the commander. She didn't take her eyes from me, yet she was clearly speaking to Beaky. 'I am also aware that you have applied for a promotion. Isn't that so?'

'Yes, ma'am,' said Beaky.

'You have been warned about driving too fast on several occasions. If you have been speeding again, you will have to be reprimanded rather than promoted. There is a war on; replacing vehicle parts is expensive.'

A barely audible hiss came from my side. I didn't dare look at Beaky. Cold sweat trickled down my spine. The last thing I needed was to make her hate me even more.

I felt as if the commander could see right into my soul. 'Tell the truth, Private. Did the sergeant's speed cause the damage to the vehicle?'

Relief washed through me. Thank goodness she had phrased it like that. I shook my head. 'No, ma'am. A deer jumped in front of us with no warning. The sergeant handled the situation with skill and efficiency. She avoided the obstacle and although we skidded, she brought the truck back under control as soon as possible. Shredding the tyre on the pothole was unavoidable.'

Commander Carter gave a brisk nod. 'In which case, I commend you for assisting as she changed the tyre. Welcome to Foxhalt.'

Assisting? I blinked. 'Thank you, ma'am.'

She turned to Beaky. 'Am I right in thinking there is a session on first aid with Sergeant Matthews this afternoon.'

'Yes, ma'am, at fourteen thirty hours.'

Commander Carter checked her wristwatch. 'In which case, you had better both head off, or you will be late. That will be all.'

Beaky saluted and turned smartly on her heel. I did my best to copy and left the room, closing the door behind me. I hurried to keep up with Beaky, my mind spiralling. Would the fact that I covered for her make her less antagonistic, or might it just make her worse? She wasn't to know that I'd never tell on her. She might think I'd use the information about her driving and the flat tyre to blackmail her. She already thought I'd pulled strings to get here, so she might think me capable of all sorts of things. Oh, why did things have to be so difficult?

11

'Come along, Makepeace. Don't dawdle.' Beaky marched off down the corridor to another room that held the same air of faded grandeur as the office we had just left. A decorative ceiling rose and carved panelling on the walls contrasted with rows of simple ladder-back chairs facing a serviceable wooden table laden with first aid supplies near the window. A faint scent of carbolic soap hung in the air. The rest of the recruits from the dining room were gathered, waiting for the session to begin. I hurried to join Kitty, who was sat right at the back. Beaky went to stand by the window.

Sergeant Matthews strode into the room, her movements brisk and efficient. When she reached the table, the hum of conversation stopped and everyone stood to attention. She looked up and smiled. 'Good afternoon. Please be seated.' The rustle and scuff of chair legs against the floor followed before attentive silence settled over the room.

Over the next half an hour, the sergeant outlined basic first aid, from where we might find first aid kits at any of the bases we might be posted, to the contents of those kits and how we should use them. Everything she said made sense and I paid careful attention. Eventually, Sergeant Matthews clapped her hands and said, 'Now we come to the part of the class when you get to put some of this theory into practice. Please pair up with the partners you had last time and we'll do some bandaging.'

Kitty shot me an apologetic look. 'I was with Carole, last time. Sorry.'

'That's fine,' I replied stretching my back as I rose from my chair. 'Don't worry. I'll be fine.'

Sergeant Matthews approached. 'Is there a problem here?'

'Private Makepeace is new,' said Kitty. 'She doesn't have a partner.'

'Not to worry,' said the sergeant, flashing me a bright smile. She turned and beckoned Beaky over. 'We have an odd number here, Sergeant. Please allow our new arrival to run through the bandaging techniques on you.'

The tight lines that appeared around Beaky's mouth made it clear she'd prefer to swallow wasps. She gestured me over to a corner of the room and handed me a couple of bandages and a sling. 'Let's see how much of that you absorbed.'

With her eyes watching my every move, my usual dexterity abandoned me. With fat fumbling fingers, I made a complete hash of bandaging her wrist.

She wrenched her hand away from me with a loud tut. 'What are you trying to do? Cut off my circulation?'

'I'm sorry, I—'

'Put out your hand.'

Without thinking, I tugged up my sleeve as I complied.

Beaky gasped.

Damn. My bruises were a livid purple. I snatched my arm back and pulled my cuff down. Ducking my head, I held out my other hand.

Beaky didn't speak for several long seconds, then she cleared her throat. 'Yes... well... as Sergeant Matthews said, the wrist is one of the more awkward parts of the body to bandage effectively. However, with a few simple tricks, you can stabilise a damaged joint effectively. You can also use this system to apply pressure to a wound on that same joint.' With brisk, efficient movements she demonstrated.

I watched her systematically wrap my wrist and hand with the bandage. 'You make it look easy.'

She shot me a searching look, as if checking to see if I was being sarcastic.

'I mean it,' I said.

She shrugged. 'It gets easier with practice.' She pressed my fingertips gently and watched as the skin paled and then returned to a healthy pink. 'You don't want the bandage to be too tight, or you can do more damage than good. Now. You try it.'

I unwrapped my wrist, rolled the bandage back up and then slowly repeated the exercise on Beaky's wrist. This time, with more success. Beaky gave a grunt of approval. That small reaction from her meant the world. Maybe, if I was really careful how I handled her, she would stop being so wary around me.

A bell sounded in the distance. Sergeant Matthews raised her voice so that all could hear. 'That's the end of the session. Thank you for your attention. Please clear up before you move on to your next assignment.'

I muttered my thanks to Beaky for partnering me and joined Kitty by the table to rewind bandages and put them away. 'What do we do now, Kitty?'

She wrinkled her nose. 'We have basic chores. There's a rota. You're probably not on it yet. I'll show you where it is. The life of an ATS girl isn't exactly glamorous. They're the types of everyday tasks that might be useful at any of the bases we could be sent to. Then, we have supper and some downtime before bed at eight.'

As we made our way towards the door, Beaky intercepted us. 'Makepeace. I'd like a word.'

Kitty threw me a wide-eyed look. I watched her and the rest of my classmates disappear, and wished I could go with them.

Beaky closed the door. 'What happened to your arm?'

I slid my wrist behind my back. 'Nothing, ma'am.'

A moment of silence followed, broken only by the rhythmic tick from a baby grandfather clock stood to attention in the corner of the room.

'Look. I'm not being nosy,' she said. 'I just need to know if I ought to report it.'

The last thing I wanted was what happened with Jake to follow me here. He was in the past and this was my future, something shiny and new that he had no business affecting. If I told Beaky she would tell the commander and it would just get messy.

'Please leave it, ma'am? I'm fine.' There was only one way to stop her forcing the issue. 'You owe me a favour,' I muttered.

Her eyebrows shot up. 'How do you figure that?'

'I covered for you. You were speeding and you know you were. *And* I let the commander think you changed that tyre.' How I kept my tone steady when I was shaking inside, I don't know.

'I didn't say it was me. She assumed it was.'

'And you didn't correct her.'

We stared at each other for several seconds in a tense stand-off before Beaky sighed and shook her head. 'Fine. I won't report it, if you tell me why Major Stapleton vouched for you. What did you do in your interview with her that showed such extraordinary initiative?'

Is that all she wanted to know? It seemed a small price to pay. 'I fixed her telephone.'

Beaky looked stunned. 'How?'

I raised one shoulder and let it drop. 'I can fix most things given a chance. It's just what I do.'

Beaky huffed. 'I'm not sure whether to believe you. Initiative or not, Make-peace, from now on if you set one toe out of line, I'll come down on you like a lorry load of bricks.' She turned on her heel and stalked from the room.

I stood listening to the clock in the corner tick steadily on, aware that I had just made the situation with Beaky a thousand times worse.

12

That evening, after a hot meal of vegetable stew with a delicious serving of bread pudding afterwards, I helped wash dishes and then climbed the stairs to bed. An icy draught snatched at my ankles as I reached the top floor, the warmth of the kitchen a distant memory already. A candle and box of matches sat just inside the door to my cupboard bedroom. I lit the candle and set about making the bed and changing into my pyjamas before folding my uniform carefully for the next morning. Pulling back the two scratchy woollen blankets, I stared down at the thin straw mattress and limp pillow. A brief flash of homesickness made my knees wobble. *Don't be silly. Home isn't an option.* I'd made a choice. I was on my own and it was for the best, despite that prickle of hot tears lurking behind my eyes.

A scuffling sound came from the corridor. Intrigued, I opened the door a crack to see Kitty outside brandishing a cloth-wrapped package.

'I thought you might like to borrow my hot water bottle,' she said. 'The first night somewhere new is always rough. At least, if you're warm, you should be able to sleep.'

It would be rude to refuse such kindness, and I didn't relish the thought of quivering with cold all night. 'Are you sure?' I said, taking the warm bundle from her, my tears of despair turning to ones of gratitude. 'What about you, though?'

She grinned. 'I got used to how chilly it is a long time ago. Go on, shove it under your blankets and then come and have some cocoa in our room. Carole was last to finish in the kitchen. She brought up a flask for us.'

I did as she suggested, slipped the blue cardigan on over my pyjamas and followed her next door. Blackout blinds were in place at the windows. Rosie, Pam and Carole sat on the floor looking at cards with pictures on them.

'Carole doesn't sleep in here,' explained Kitty. 'She's from next door.'

'We let her in, because she bribes us,' said Jane with a grin. She was sat on one of the lower bunks rubbing cold cream on her face. 'I'll do anything for cocoa.'

'How did your first day go, Fliss?' asked Carole, handing me a mug.

'It was certainly eventful,' I said with a chuckle. Tendrils of steam wafted up from the surface of the liquid; the warm, rich, chocolatey smell offering comfort on so many levels. 'Thank you for including me.'

'Don't get used to it,' said Carole, her tone abrupt.

'Honestly, Carole,' Pam gave her a nudge. 'You could start a war all by yourself with the way you talk sometimes.' She rolled her eyes at me. 'Ignore her, Fliss. She doesn't mean it.'

'I can't help it if people are oversensitive,' muttered Carole.

Kitty giggled. 'What she means is, don't get used to the cocoa, Fliss. Not, don't get used to being included.'

I gave a tentative smile. The way they teased each other spoke of genuine affection. Perhaps, in time, I'd become part of this happy little group too.

'Cocoa is a rare treat,' said Rosie, tying a silk scarf around her head to secure the sponge rollers in her hair. 'So, Fliss, tell us what you did before joining up.'

'Oh, I worked for my father as a secretary,' I said, hoping to leave it at that. 'What are you looking at?' I asked, sinking down to sit cross-legged on the floor beside Pam.

She passed over a couple of cards. 'We're supposed to be able to identify aircraft in flight, so we know which are enemy planes as opposed to friendly ones. See.' She handed me one. It showed a detailed picture on one side of the card and a silhouette of the plane as it would appear from underneath against the sky on the other.

'Gosh,' I said. 'That's interesting. I suppose we're going to learn all sorts of things to help fight the war.'

Rosie lay back on her bunk with a dramatic sigh. 'I'd rather learn something that will help me get a job afterwards.'

'What sort of job?' I asked.

She sat up, a sparkle in her eye. 'I'd like to be a secretary, like you. I'd work in an office and have a typewriter and... hey, can you teach me to type, Fliss?'

Startled, I nearly choked on my cocoa.

'How is she supposed to do that without a typewriter, you dozy mare?' said Carole.

Rosie's face fell.

'You're right, Carole, it would be difficult,' I said. 'Mind you, there are lots of other things I can show you, Rosie.'

The sparkle was back. 'Like what?'

'Shorthand, filing, how to lay out professional letters.' I raised a hand palm up. 'It's all important. The shorthand is the key, I think. If you can master that, you'll get a job easily. As for typing, I can draw out what all the keys on the typewriter look like on a piece of paper. You can get used to where they are and what they do. And then, if we ever do get near a typewriter... well, then it's just a case of practising.'

Rosie grinned. 'Perfect. Yes, please.' She scrambled off her bunk and dug in one of the trunks to produce paper and a pencil, and passed them over.

Kitty sat forward. 'Would you draw one for me, too, Fliss?'

I shrugged. 'Of course. I'd be happy to.' It only took me a few minutes to complete it, by which time, Jane had decided she wanted one too. Then, I showed them the most common symbols used in shorthand. It felt good to be able to share what I knew and I began to hope that this was something solid I could offer in exchange for the chance to build proper friendships with them.

* * *

Twenty minutes later, a bell sounded from the depths of the house. The girls all drained their mugs as one.

'That's five minutes to lights out,' said Kitty. 'We've just enough time to visit the lav and do our teeth. You and Carole had better scoot before Beaky comes around to check we're all in bed. Sleep well, Fliss.'

I said goodnight and, after a quick scrub of my teeth, scurried back to my cupboard and dived under the covers. It wasn't long before I was fast asleep.

* * *

The subsequent days were filled with a variety of repetitive tasks. Some were physically demanding, leaving us exhausted and covered in dirt, others not so much. We wore overalls for really mucky jobs like clearing woodland to site bell tents and digging foundations for Nissen huts. It was tough going; nevertheless, working together as a team proved rewarding. The weather was crisp and dry and spending time out of doors in the fresh air and the early spring sunshine was no great hardship.

Once the foundations were set, we moved on to build the upper sections of the Nissen huts. The next cohort of trainees would be twice the size of ours and more accommodation was essential. Erecting the curved, prefabricated corrugated metal sheeting took longer than I expected. Then, as each hut was completed, we hauled in furniture and put together bed frames.

Towards the end of the week, as Kitty and I sat together outside one of the huts stuffing mattress biscuits with straw, the strange sensation of being watched crept over me. I cast furtive glances all around, trying to work out why.

'Are you all right?' asked Kitty.

I shook myself. 'It feels like someone is watching me, but I can't see anyone.'

'It's probably Beaky,' she said. 'She always seems to be on at you about something, which is strange because she's usually all right. A bit bossy but fine.'

It was true. No one else rubbed Beaky up the wrong way like I did. We'd got off on the wrong foot and I couldn't think how to set things right.

'Watch out,' hissed Kitty. 'Here she is.' She turned away and busied herself with the next mattress.

Beaky's shadow loomed over us. 'Makepeace,' she barked. 'Why are you never where I need you to be?'

Responding in the same sharp tone would get me nowhere. I pushed the biscuit I was working on aside and stood up. 'Forgive me, ma'am. Where do you need me to be?'

'There's a problem with the generator and the trooper who usually looks after it is on leave. If you're as good at fixing things as you claim, then you should be able to get it going.' There was a distinct challenge to her words.

'I'll do my best, ma'am.' I dusted off my hands, unable to believe my luck. Being actively asked to work on a piece of mechanical equipment was like a dream come true. Usually, people demanded I stay away from them. Maybe, if I did a good job, Beaky would start to appreciate that I wasn't trying to cause trouble.

She waved a dismissive hand. 'Off you go. I'll be along soon to see how you're getting on. If you can't fix it, we'll know you've been less than honest about your abilities, won't we?'

'Yes, ma'am.' So that was it. A direct challenge. I'd never worked on a generator before. I had to hope that I was up to it. I gave a smart salute and hurried off to get started.

* * *

Half an hour later, in a lean-to shed built against the side of the dower house, I was up to my elbows in sump oil. The generator was a standard army-issue Alco, robust and efficient, powered by a Villiers engine. Fortunately for me, there was a manual available for both and a set of tools. My delight at working on machinery again was tempered by concern. I had to get this right. Taking a steady, step-by-step approach, I worked my way around the series of green metal compartments that comprised the whole unit, until I tracked down the problem. Satisfied that it would now work, I was giving the whole machine a quick service, when Beaky appeared.

'How are you getting on?' she demanded.

I finished screwing the cap back on the sump oil and grabbed a rag to wipe my hands. 'Fine, thank you, ma'am.'

'What's wrong with it?'

'The choke was jammed. That's this bit.' I pointed to a small section over the fuel tank on the main engine. 'It controls the flow of air into the carburettor and helps to get the right mix of air and fuel to start the engine. If you limit the air, when the engine is cold, it's easier to get it going. Once it's warmed up, you can allow more air in and it won't stall.'

'Can you fix it?'

'Already done, ma'am,' I said, taking care not to sound triumphant. 'I was just about to try firing it up.'

She crossed her arms. 'Go on, then. Let's see.'

I wound the starting rope around the pulley. With Beaky watching my every move, my hands started to shake. This was the moment of truth. If the engine started, I was vindicated. If it didn't... well, it didn't bear thinking what her reaction might be. I gripped the handle and pulled.

Nothing happened.

'Aha!' she crowed.

'Just a minute, ma'am, please,' I said, fighting to stop panic from wholly consuming me. My fingers had all the dexterity of fat sausages as I adjusted the choke again and rewound the pull cord. I gave a swift, sharp jerk on the rope and, to my relief, the engine jumped into life. 'There we go,' I said. 'It was just feeling a bit shy.' I listened to the sound of the motor and adjusted the choke in gradual increments until it was fully out. The engine sounded smooth and steady. 'Power should be fully restored inside the house, now, ma'am.'

She pursed her lips before giving me a brisk nod. 'Well done, Makepeace. I'll go and tell the commander. Clear up here and get back to the others.'

I watched her march away, ridiculously pleased with those three words. *Well done, Makepeace.* Perhaps she and I could turn a corner now.

13

The rest of basic training passed without incident. We studied emergency protocol drills, how to build makeshift stretchers and carry casualties using a human cradle seat made from our forearms. Then came basic food prep, hygiene and canteen operations, organising supplies and stocktaking. Evenings were filled with our allocated duties on the cleaning and catering rotas, with a little downtime to unwind before bed. Kitty, Jane and Rosie often used this time to practise their shorthand and ask me for other secretarial tips.

Eventually, we gathered in the classroom on the last day to find out where we were to be posted.

'I wonder where they are sending us?' said Jane.

'Do you think we'll be together?' asked Kitty, her eyes round.

'I hope so,' I said and meant it. Cheerful and upbeat, Kitty was a joy to be around. 'We work well together. It makes no sense to train us as a team and then break us up.'

'You're assuming there's coherent thinking going on,' said Carole with a wry smile.

'Hush!' said Rosie. 'They're here.'

Silence fell as Commander Carter marched to the front of the room. Sergeant Matthews followed with Beaky hard on her heels. The air was thick with tension.

Commander Carter cleared her throat. 'Congratulations on reaching the final day of basic training. You have worked hard and are ready to become full members of the ATS. It is my duty now, to reveal your first postings. Remember, these are placements where you are needed. You will be doing your bit to help your country establish solid defences against the enemy. You will not be going alone. Sergeant Matthews will be going with one group and the newly appointed Staff Sergeant Beaconsfield will be going with the other. I am sure you will want to join me in congratulating Staff Sergeant Beaconsfield on her promotion.'

Applause rippled around the room.

Commander Carter continued, 'The following names are those going with Sergeant Matthews. Please gather in the dining room where she will brief you on the specifics of your posting. Everyone else, remain here for Staff Sergeant Beaconsfield to do the same.'

I crossed my fingers that we would be called to go downstairs. Life with Sergeant Matthews would be easier. As each name was called out it became clear that my prayers were not going to be answered.

Kitty turned to me, her eyes full. 'We're staying together. Isn't that great?'

'Yes. It's wonderful.' I flashed an extra enthusiastic smile at her to cover how torn I was. It was a surprise to see Pam leave with Sergeant Matthews' group. She gave us a little wave and a shrug as she joined several of her other friends as they filed out. While a small part of me wanted to go with her, I was happy to be staying with Kitty and the others. Beaky, however, was still an unknown quantity. Would promotion make her easier to work with, or more difficult? Only time would tell.

As soon as everyone who needed to had left the room, Beaky moved to the front. 'Does anyone here know what radio detection finding, or RDF, is?' she asked.

'It's something to do with spotting enemy planes, isn't it?' said Julie, a short woman with an eager-to-please manner, sat on the far side of the room.

'Indeed, it is.' Approval flitted across Beaky's face. 'With the war escalating, the government are putting certain resources into place to make sure that we are in the best position to fight. Part of that includes the Chain Home system.'

'I read about that in the paper,' said Rosie.

I had too. There had been several articles that mentioned Chain Home. 'It's a series of radio masts, isn't it?' I said.

'There's a Chain Home station near my grandparents' house,' said a woman at the back of the room.

'I wonder how they work,' came another voice.

'Settle down, please,' said Beaky. 'And yes, Chain Home is a series of sites with telecommunication aerials that have been established all along the south and east coast of England facing outwards over the English Channel. It's a relatively new technology, developed since the last war, to detect incoming enemy aircraft.'

Kitty shuffled closer to me, whispering, 'It's scary how close the fighting is getting.'

I patted her arm.

Beaky continued. 'We're being sent to the Chain Home site at Renscombe Down on the cliffs near a village called Worth Matravers in Dorset. The site is being expanded to house a research facility.'

'Researching what?' asked Rosie.

'I don't have specifics,' said Beaky. 'The details are confidential. However, the overall aim is to advance telecommunication technology vital for our country's security – work that could make all the difference in the outcome of the war.'

There was a murmur of interest and one woman held her hand up. 'Will we be doing the research?'

I held my breath, hope battling common sense. The chance to be directly involved in something that would help to defend the country against attack would be incredible.

Beaky's next words were like a bucket of cold water in the face. 'Of course not. The scientists will handle that. Our orders are to support the operational team charged with developing the site to accommodate a huge influx of personnel. After that, we will be responsible for general housekeeping and will also assist the catering crew.'

Carole rolled her eyes and muttered, 'Basically, we'll be the cleaners, and if we're really lucky, they'll let us wash dirty dishes too.'

Beaky ignored the interruption. 'We will be billeted in the nearby town of Swanage and take a bus out to the site each day. We will make ourselves useful in whatever way we can. Our orders are simply to get the job done. Is that understood?'

There was a chorus of 'Yes, ma'am.'

'We will leave tomorrow morning at oh-nine-hundred hours. I suggest you spend this evening packing. Make sure that you are downstairs in the courtyard ready to leave on time. Dismissed.'

As we filed from the room, a buzz of speculation hung in the air as everyone chattered about where we were going. It was impossible not to join in with the general excitement. This was my first real adventure with the ATS. I may have joined up on impulse to avoid being forced to marry Jake, but I had found something else here, something more than escape. I had found friends and a purpose. I didn't care how mundane the work was. We would build something together and help our country to win the war. I couldn't wait to get stuck in.

As I passed Beaky, she barked, 'Makepeace. We're travelling in the Morris tomorrow. You're driving.'

I snapped the crispest salute I could manage, to hide the fact that my heart was sinking faster than a dropped anvil at the thought of the two of us stuck in the cab together for hours. 'Yes, ma'am. And congratulations on your promotion, ma'am.'

'Thank you.'

The satisfied wiggle she gave of her shoulders, like a bantam hen fluffing out feathers before strutting off, gave me plenty to think about that night as I packed my things. What if the best way to handle her was complete deference? Rather than trying to convince her *I* was the perfect soldier, perhaps I should act as though *she* was the perfect superior officer. There was no way of knowing if it would work. Either way, it was worth a try.

14

That creeping sensation of being watched returned as I helped pack the truck early the next morning. Again, there was no sign of anyone, no matter how hard I looked. I dismissed it and concentrated on the job in hand.

The troop were in good spirits as they all clambered aboard. Just as I was about to slip into the driver's seat, Commander Carter's secretary came out with a small hessian sack in her hands.

'Hold on, please,' she called. 'The post came late yesterday and there are a few personal letters.' The envelopes she passed to the girls in the back were greeted with squeals of delight. 'That's all. Unless... well... I've had this one here for nearly a week, but I have no idea who it's for. It just says Fliss, Foxhalt, Dorset.'

'Oh!' I said, my hand springing to cover my mouth. 'That's me.' It must be from Daniel. Like he promised. He'd said he would address it like that. A deliciously warm feeling spread across my chest. And here it was.

The secretary pushed her glasses up her nose and blinked like a confused owl. 'I thought your name was Felicity.'

'It is, but my friends call me Fliss.'

'In which case, this is definitely for you.'

'Thank you.' I took the envelope and tore it open. Daniel's sloped handwriting was neat and attractive without being fussy.

Dear Fliss,

I hope this reaches you and that Foxhalt has proven to be all you were hoping for. I also hope that you weren't forced to jump on any more moving vehicles in order to get there.

I arrived in Southampton safely and have been allocated to a training centre where my skills can be developed to support the war effort. It feels good to know that I am doing something useful at last.

I include my current address above. If there is any chance you might wish to stay in contact, I would be glad to know how you are.

Either way, I send you my best wishes,

Daniel (Evans)

A whistle came from the back of the truck. 'Looks like Fliss has a sweetheart,' said Carole. 'What's his name, Fliss?'

My head shot up, my cheeks burning. 'Don't be silly. I don't have a... a sweetheart.'

Rosie smiled. 'The way you're clutching that letter to your heart and the silly grin on your face tell a different story.'

I glanced down, yanked the paper away from my chest, folded it up and tucked it into my pocket. 'You're imagining things.' Happy little tingles rippled through me in spite of my denial.

Fortunately, Beaky arrived, forestalling any more teasing comments.

'Are we all ready?' she barked.

'Yes, ma'am,' I said. 'Everyone is on board. All kit is loaded and secure.'

'Then let's get going.'

It was a delight to be driving again, even with Beaky at my side, her nose buried in the map and occasionally coming up for air to growl contradictory instructions.

Kitty, Carole, Rosie and the other members of our troop all sat in the rear compartment on sideways wooden benches. Having never had to make allowances for multiple passengers travelling in the back of any vehicle I was driving before, I quickly learned that they object to being thrown around when you take corners too fast, or zip over humpback bridges without warning. Loud grumbles reached my ears. People started turning green and threatening to be sick. I slowed, apologised profusely and promised to be more careful. Before long, everyone had regained their sense of humour and settled down to chat, and it was impossible not to listen in.

'I wonder if there will be any handsome soldiers at this Renscombe place,' said Rosie.

'I hope so,' said Jane. 'No offence, ladies. I've never spent so long in the company of just women.'

'Me neither,' said Rosie. 'It'll be nice to see some fellas again.'

'There'll be soldiers, all right,' grunted Carole. 'But whether they'll be handsome is anyone's guess. Mind you, a uniform always improves a man's looks, even an ugly one.'

The last few weeks at Foxhalt had enabled the memory of that awful encounter with Jake to fade. The bruises had healed too. I found myself more inclined to think about men more favourably. Hearing Kitty, Carole and the others whisper and giggle about the fellas they fancied didn't make me shudder with horror. Instead, Daniel's face hovered in my mind. He had written, just as he'd promised. He'd spoken to me like an intelligent human being and treated me well. If I was honest with myself, I... well, I liked him. More than liked him. It would be nice to get to know him better. I decided I would send him a quick note back as soon as we were settled in Swanage. I'd tell him where I'd been posted and see what happened. He might write again. He might not. I would just have to wait and see.

We sailed along increasingly narrow and twisty lanes into the deepest Dorset countryside and, after several wrong turns, arrived in the village of Corfe, a collection of cottages built in the shadow of the picturesque ruins of a Norman castle. Having finally persuaded Beaky to ask for directions, we made it to Renscombe Down and a track that took us past a farm and on to a small collection of temporary buildings huddled at the base of two massive telecommunications towers set back from the clifftop. The path petered out into little more than a series of muddy tyre tracks and troughs that spoke of heavy vehicles struggling for purchase. I'm not sure what I had been expecting. It wasn't this.

I'd never driven under such tricky conditions and had to fight to stop the truck from sliding about on the slippery surface. 'Hold on,' I called back, conscious that my passengers were precious cargo and that it was my duty to keep them safe. My fingers gripped the steering wheel, my knuckles white, and my shoulders tensed as the truck repeatedly lurched off course.

The site was a mess. Apart from the boggy terrain, random, half-finished building foundations were dotted all over the place. It looked as if someone had originally had a grand plan, but they'd since lost the instructions and started throwing up slapdash structures left, right and centre, just for the heck of it, before giving up entirely and stomping off in a huff.

A group of men were hard at work on one of the closer structures. I steered in their direction. A grumpy-looking captain, with mud caked from his boots to his thighs watched our approach, his lip curling as if we were a pack of flea-ridden, mangy dogs. That we were unwelcome could not have been more evident.

'Who the hell are you?' he barked as I drew the truck to a halt alongside him. Several soldiers working on the building behind him paused to watch.

Beaky hopped down from the truck, gave the captain a crisp salute and passed over a thick envelope. 'Staff Sergeant Beaconsfield reporting for duty, sir. We're C company; here to help.'

'I asked for additional men,' he muttered, staring at Beaky in disbelief before tearing open the documents. 'Not a bunch of useless girls.'

Beaky took a deep breath, as if counting to ten slowly in her head. 'You requested assistance, sir,' she said, her tone unwavering. 'And that is what we are here to provide. My troop are very capable and will do whatever work is necessary.'

'Troop.' He snorted. 'It says here that you're responsible for housekeeping. Look around you, sweetheart. There are no houses for you to keep yet.' He stuffed our orders back into the envelope. 'You'll have to go back to wherever it is you came from.'

His dismissive attitude set prickles of outrage scampering across my shoulders. The intense glower on his face triggered unpleasant memories of Jake.

A red tide crept up Beaky's neck. Her mouth flapped open a few times but nothing came out. Something snapped deep inside me. While she and I might have our differences, she didn't deserve to be treated as if she was nothing and I wasn't going to sit idly by and watch it happen.

I scrambled from the truck to stand by her side.

Beaky threw me a questioning look.

I gave her a crisp salute. 'Staff Sergeant Beaconsfield, ma'am,' I said, making sure to use her full title. 'Shall I arrange to inform Commander Carter at Foxhalt, and our new Renscombe Commander, Senior Commander

Wilson, that we will need to be redeployed?' I placed a deliberate emphasis on each rank I mentioned. 'Or should it be Group Commander Williams or Senior Controller Adams at operational headquarters up in London?' I was making names and places up at this point; to hammer home the message to this patronising oaf that we weren't just a ragtag bunch of women who had rocked up by mistake. We had orders and a strong structure of command behind us.

'Hold on, Makepeace.' Beaky held up a hand. 'Captain,' she said, her tone conciliatory. 'We would much prefer to stay here, rather than move on to another site. Are you *sure* there isn't something we can do to assist?'

'Look around you, lady.' He scowled and stabbed a finger towards the wooden huts in the distance. 'This facility is about to triple in size. We'll have boffins coming out of our ears in a matter of weeks.'

'Boffins?' said Beaky.

'Scientists.' He spat the word out as if it tasted vile. 'Hundreds of them.'

'Goodness me,' she said. 'What a nuisance.'

The captain warmed to his theme. 'They'll bring truckloads of equipment and support staff with them. My men have to build accommodation for all the incoming personnel.' He raised his eyes to heaven as if praying for deliverance. 'So far, we've got foundations down for the canteen and two of the laboratories. The latrines are nearly done, apart from the doors, thanks to a mix-up with the delivery. The last thing I need is to waste time looking after you lot.'

Beaky cleared her throat. 'I understand, Captain. Be assured that my ATS troop do not need looking after. If there are no houses for us to keep yet, we are perfectly capable of helping to build them. As for the latrines, I suggest we sling a bit of old tarp over the doorway for modesty's sake and sing out loud to let others know when they're in use.'

He stared at her as if he didn't quite understand what language she was speaking. 'It's not just that, darling.' He waved at the jumble of part-built groundworks nearby. 'We've had apocalyptic rain. It's turned this place into a bog. I can't get building materials delivered close enough thanks to all the mud. Do you see that pile of bricks over there?'

We followed the direction of his hand to a mountain of bricks piled haphazardly near the entrance to the site.

'They aren't supposed to be there. Only the lorry delivering them got stuck up to its axles and had to abandon them there in order to get free. With that on top of everything else, we're never going to be ready. I don't have time to pussy-foot around delicate sensibilities.'

'I wouldn't expect you to, sir,' said Beaky, her usual no-nonsense attitude returning. 'We're fit and healthy, and very capable of moving bricks for you.'

He gave a puff of exasperation. 'You're not listening to me, lady. I need to mark outbuilding footprints, dig foundations, shift soil, lift beams, install drainage, erect buildings and everything in between.'

'None of that is a problem, sir,' Beaky shot back. 'My troop are fast learners. You only have to show us once what you need done, and we'll do it.'

The way she swept his repeated objections aside was splendid. My admiration for her grew with each word that left her mouth.

'In the meantime,' she continued, 'where do you want them?'

His forehead crinkled. 'What?'

'The bricks,' she said.

'Uh...' He scratched his head. 'Over there, by the new foundation trenches. But—'

'Can we use those?' She pointed to a stack of wooden planks.

'Yes, love, but—'

I couldn't take it any more. 'With respect, Captain,' I said, stepping forward and standing to attention. 'Please be aware that Staff Sergeant Beaconsfield is an officer in the Auxiliary Territorial Service. She does not answer to love, lady, sweetheart, darling or any other such term of endearment.'

He stared from me to her and back to me again, his mouth gaping but no sound coming out.

'That is enough, Makepeace,' said Beaky, her tone firm.

I turned to her and said, in a deliberately carrying whisper. 'Please, ma'am, it's not right for you to be addressed like that. The field marshal warned you, when you refused to accept an officer's commission, that people who don't know your family connections would treat you like this.'

She stared at me for several seconds, a crinkle appearing across her brow. I held my breath, convinced I had taken my ruse a step too far.

Then, she gave a brisk nod. 'Indeed,' she said, turned to the girls in the back of the truck and clapped her hands. 'Stir your stumps, troop. Dig your gloves out of your packs; we have a little pile of bricks to move.'

'Yes, ma'am,' they chorused, leaping to their feet.

The captain's bemused gaze bounced from me to Beaky and back again. I ignored him and hurried to follow orders. Using the wooden planks to build a temporary walkway over the boggy terrain, we formed a chain and passed the bricks along. The captain and his soldiers soon gave up watching and left us to it.

It was monotonous, thirsty work.

* * *

A couple of hours later, we stood to attention by the new, now very tidy, pile, exhausted and hungry but determined not to show it as the captain approached. He stopped in front of Beaky; tension crackled between them. With a short stab of his eyes in my direction, he sniffed, returned his gaze to Beaky. 'All done I see, Staff Sergeant Beaconsfield.' His use of her rank was pointed yet respectful, a marked difference to his previous disdainful attitude.

Beaky straightened and dusted off her hands. 'Yes, Captain. Now, with your permission, I'd like to take my troop into Swanage to settle into our billet. We'll be back tomorrow, suited, booted and ready to work.'

He gave a crisp professional nod. 'Very good, Staff Sergeant. Carry on.'

Turning to us, Beaky barked, 'Right, troop: about turn, quick march.'

We pivoted as one and paraded as best we could – given the slippery conditions – back to the truck and climbed aboard.

Beaky slid into the front passenger seat, shot me a quizzical look and said in a low voice, 'For the record, Makepeace, I've never even been in the same county as a field marshal, let alone the same conversation.'

'My mistake, ma'am,' I muttered with an unrepentant shrug. 'It worked though, didn't it?'

She let out a short puff of laughter and shook her head. 'You're incorrigible.' She pointed through the windshield. 'Drive on.'

I put the truck into gear and pulled away, a growing sense of triumph spreading a smile across my face. She hadn't told me off for interfering. Quite the opposite. And backing her up had felt good. I was determined to do it again should the need arise.

15

The next day, we arrived on site early, clad in overalls and thick jumpers, ready to muck in and do whatever was asked of us. The work wasn't difficult, merely exhausting and, thanks to a particularly wet winter, often cold and mucky. Keeping moving was the key to staying warm. I developed calluses on my hands and lean muscles all over from the intense physicality of the work yet, in spite of the many drawbacks, it was surprisingly satisfying to be involved in building something that mattered. The captain stopped scowling and even occasionally offered grudging thanks for our hard work. Ten days later, the extra manpower he had requested arrived. We continued to work alongside them until the canteen and the first four long wooden huts intended to house the new laboratories were complete.

* * *

A week later, the arrival of the incoming telecommunications research staff meant that we were pulled off construction duty to help assist the teams moving in. Beaky paired Kitty and I together and sent us to hut 4 with orders to do whatever was needed. A harassed-looking young man in a white coat, with floppy blonde hair and nervous darting eyes pounced on us the minute we approached. 'You can't be here. This is a confidential workspace.'

'We know that. We built it for you,' replied Kitty, with unaccustomed sass, pulling her security pass from her pocket and waving it under his nose.

I could understand her annoyance. We'd worked so hard on these buildings, it was impossible not to feel proprietorial about them.

The officious boffin blinked, evidently surprised that we weren't leaving.

'We have clearance for the whole site,' I assured him, producing my security pass too. 'We've been sent to help you move in.'

'Oh!' His expression cleared. 'In which case, there are three trucks on the way with equipment boxed into cartons. Everything is labelled with hut and room number. Be careful, though,' he urged. 'Some of the apparatus is fragile.'

Kitty's nostrils flared at his patronising manner.

I placed a warning hand on her arm. There was no point getting into a row. He'd only report us, and I was keen to see what research was going to take place.

'We'll treat everything like the finest bone china,' I promised.

Just then, the first of the promised trucks arrived. As soon as the tailgate was lowered, Kitty and I started unloading. The boffin watched us with grave intent for several minutes before, apparently satisfied with our conduct, he disappeared off with several boxes himself.

The rest of the day was spent unpacking. We mingled amongst the white-coated scientists opening cartons and removing their contents, complying with any direction issued. Empty rooms turned into functioning laboratories as shelves filled up and tables became operational workspaces littered with interesting pieces of equipment. Vast maps of the British Isles were attached to walls, with the location of each Chain Home Station identified and lines marking out the stretch of the English Channel that each monitored. Huge diagrams were pinned up of telecommunication towers. I read labels that said things like transponder and receiver and upper and lower gantry. The picture showed cables linking the two structures to a hut nearby and I realised that the arrangement was identical to that of the two metal towers right in the centre of the Renscombe site. I gazed from the diagram to the real thing, through the window, and wondered how each individual component worked. When I foolishly asked a question of a passing white coat, I immediately wished I hadn't, because he frowned and looked me up and down as if I'd said something genuinely offensive.

'You don't have to understand the science to unpack the boxes, woman,' he said, and stomped off, leaving me shaking with a combination of fury and embarrassment.

The whole morning was a curious mix of fascination and frustration. Desperate to examine all the strange pieces of apparatus to see how they worked, I didn't dare get too close. If I made a nuisance of myself and someone on the science team complained, Beaky would reassign me to another part of the site. I'd probably spend the rest of my days cleaning the latrines.

After lunch, whilst busy stacking textbooks onto a shelf in a room furnished with a series of long, high tables and tall stools, I watched from the corner of my eye as a junior scientist, who looked as if he should still be in the school-room, slotted a series of metal components together to build a small-scale model of the two towers outside. It was obvious to me that he had a couple of pieces near the base upside down, which meant that the upper sections wouldn't fit together.

'Sir,' I said, wondering how best to point out the source of the problem without causing offence.

'Don't bother me?' he growled, shooting me a look of thunder. 'Can't you see I'm busy. It can't be that difficult to stack books.'

Any desire to help him evaporated. 'Yes, sir. Sorry, sir.' I winced as he bent the last two struts in an effort to force them to connect. The urge to snatch them from him and sort the whole mess out was almost overwhelming. Why couldn't he see his mistake?

'Holloway?' A deep voice floated in through the open window. 'Where are you?'

The scientist's head jerked up. 'Here, sir.' He abandoned the model and dashed from the room.

I waited a few seconds, to see if he would return. When he didn't, I hurried over to dismantle the towers and rebuild them properly. Footsteps sounded in the corridor outside just as I pushed the last piece into place. I scurried back to the shelving unit and hauled a pile of books from a box mere seconds before Holloway stepped back into the room. In my peripheral vision I saw him frown at the model, run a hand over the top of his head and then glance over at me.

'Did you touch this?' he demanded.

I raised wide, innocent eyes. 'I'm sorry, sir. Are you talking to me?' Before he could reply, I held up a book. 'Should I arrange these according to colour to make the shelves look pretty?'

His eyes bugged in horror. 'This is a science lab, not your grandmother's parlour. Arrange them in alphabetical order, according to author's surname.'

'Yes, sir.' I turned back to the shelves and gave a mock-thoughtful sigh. 'The alphabet. That's a good idea. I'd better start all over again.' Tugging a few books from the shelf, I began shuffling them around muttering, 'A... B... um... C...'

Several beats of silence passed, before he turned and left the room.

With a sigh, I hauled the next armload of books from the box. On the top was a small, slim volume on basic radio detection finding. As a published scientific work, it wasn't in any way confidential. In principle, should such material be taken off site, it wouldn't count as a security breach. I don't know what made me do it. Perhaps it was curiosity, or maybe sheer defiance at being treated as if I was nothing but an airhead. I wedged it into the waistband of my skirt, underneath my blouse and then smoothed my jacket over the top.

* * *

That evening, back at our billet, as we drank cocoa in our landlady's doily-bedecked front room before bed, I thought of the book hidden under my pillow, and couldn't wait to start reading it. A small worm of guilt niggled deep down at my deception. However, I reasoned that if the scientists didn't want me bothering them with questions then I was doing them a favour.

I listened as Rosie regaled the others with an encounter she had had with another of the incoming research team that sounded almost identical to the one I had had with Holloway.

'Why are men so patronising?' she asked.

'They're not all like that,' I said, thinking of my train journey with Daniel. He had spoken to me like an equal.

'Ignore them,' said Carole. 'As long as they do their jobs, we'll win the war and all will be fine and dandy.'

I looked over at Kitty who was sat at a small table on the far side of the room. 'What are you doing, Kitty?'

She glanced up. 'I'm writing to a couple of the girls who were posted with Sergeant Matthews. Lilly and Diana asked to stay in touch and I do like exchanging letters.'

'That's nice,' I replied, remembering both girls vaguely from Foxhalt. 'I should write one, too,' I murmured.

'Is it to your mystery fella?' asked Carole. 'Haven't you replied to him yet? He'll think you're not interested.'

My cheeks burned. She was right. Even though we had been busy, it was no excuse. I should have written back by now. The problem was, I didn't quite know what to say.

'Leave her alone, Carole,' said Kitty. 'It's none of your beeswax who she does or doesn't stay in touch with.' She tugged a fresh piece of paper from the back of her notepad, put the lid back on her fountain pen and held them both out to me. 'Here, use these, if you like. I've just finished. I've a spare envelope you can have, too.'

'Thank you.' I shot her a grateful smile and crossed the room to settle into a chair on the opposite side of the table from her. With the blank page before me, the doubts about what I should say resurfaced. Before I could talk myself out of writing at all, I dived in and just said what I felt.

Dear Daniel,

Thank you for your letter. I am amazed it reached me, but I'm glad it did. Just in the nick of time too. We were just leaving. We have been posted to the telecommunications facility on the south coast of Dorset at Renscombe Down near Swanage. It's been hard work. The site is coming together now, though, and it's all very interesting. I am hoping to learn a lot.

We're staying here for the foreseeable future.

How are things with you? I hope you have found a direction that suits you in Southampton and that you are well. Should you—

I broke off, not sure how to phrase what I wanted to say without sounding forward. I'd not agreed to write to Daniel when he asked me before because of how scared I'd been by Jake's awful behaviour. I was better now. Allowing one awful man to stop me developing a potential friendship with another *nice* one was lunacy. I tapped the lid of the pen against my upper lip a few times before hurrying on.

Should you wish to stay in touch, I would be delighted to hear from you again.

Yours sincerely,
Fliss (Felicity Makepeace)

There. Now he knew my full name and my address. I tucked the letter into the envelope, determined to post it the next day. Hopefully, I hadn't left it too late. With luck, he hadn't forgotten me and would write back.

* * *

Over the next few weeks, the site continued to fill with new arrivals. I finished the textbook and snuck it back onto the bookshelf in hut 4. While fascinating, I found it had raised more questions than answers and, unable to resist the temptation, I borrowed another one. Similar to the first, it was small and easy to conceal. Much of what I read didn't make sense to begin with. However, with time, I found that things slowly started to slot into place.

As I mulled over my newfound knowledge, I assisted the others as they set up a series of offices ready for the incoming WAAF typing pool. Rosie, Jane and Kitty were particularly interested in this development and unboxed all the typewriters and other associated secretarial paraphernalia with squeals of excitement.

'Blooming heck,' said Carole, thumping one of the machines down onto a desk. 'They're heavier than they look.'

Kitty scooted into a chair and ran her fingers over the keys. 'Look at me. I'm a real secretary. Goodness.' She raised startled eyes. 'You have to press them quite hard to get them to move.'

Jane whipped the cover off another machine and prodded at a few letters too. 'Gosh, you're right.'

I grinned. 'You'll soon get used to it.'

'I wish I was in the typing pool,' sighed Jane.

'You should have joined the WAAF then, not the ATS,' said Carole.

'I think this one is broken,' said Rosie. 'Look, Fliss. Is it supposed to come apart like this?' She held up part of the carriage return mechanism.

I hurried over and examined it. 'No. It must have been knocked in transit. There are several tiny screws that have sheared off.'

'Watch out,' hissed Carole from the door. 'Beaky's on the loose.'

Kitty jumped to her feet and moved away from the machine she had been playing on just in time.

Beaky scanned the room, her brow furrowed. 'What's going on? Why aren't you working.'

'One of the machines is broken,' said Kitty, pointing towards Rosie and I.

Beaky stomped over, gave the damaged typewriter a cursory glance.

'I can probably fix it if I can source the right-sized screws,' I offered.

'There's no time,' Beaky said. 'The WAAF troop are arriving in three days. I've just had their sergeant on the telephone insisting that everything be ready for them. I'll request a replacement. There's a supply truck coming out tomorrow.'

'What shall I do with this one?' I said, sliding the cover back on it.

'I don't care what you do with it,' she said, waving a dismissive hand at the offending machine. 'Just get it out of my sight. Now, hurry up in here and get everything else straight. Carole, I need you with me. Come along.'

'Yes, ma'am,' said Carole, shooting us a wide-eyed look and following her from the room.

As soon as we were alone, Kitty said, 'It seems a shame to throw it out if it can be fixed.'

I wiggled my eyebrows at her and grinned. 'She didn't say to throw it out, though, did she?'

'That's true,' said Jane. 'She said to get it out of her sight.'

'Which is something else entirely,' agreed Rosie.

We exchanged glances, the air thick with suppressed excitement, all coming to the same conclusion in a single instant.

'Can you really fix it?' asked Kitty.

I lifted one shoulder. 'If I can get the right parts, yes, I should think so. There will be a hardware shop in Swanage somewhere. We just need to get it back to our billet.'

'And then when it's working, we can practise on it,' Rosie said, her voice breathless with excitement.

'Exactly,' I said. 'Mind you, it's not what Beaky meant. If she finds out, we might get into trouble.'

'It's not like she's in the same billet as us,' said Rosie. 'What she doesn't know won't hurt her.'

'True,' I said. 'If you can cover for me here, for a few minutes, I'll go and hide this in the cloakroom under my coat. We can sneak it onto the bus back to Swanage with us this evening.'

'Yes, go,' said Kitty, rubbing her hands together in glee.

I threw her a grin, scooped up the machine and left the room, glad to have the opportunity to help my friends.

16

Spring gave way to the promise of summer. Eventually, the influx of staff and equipment slowed and Renscombe Down became a thriving hub of scientific industry. Beaky took over a small office from which to supervise housekeeping rotas and our ATS troop settled into a range of new duties. In all that time, I received no reply from Daniel and was forced to assume that I had slipped from his mind entirely.

A dedicated team from the catering corps handled the bulk of the cooking for all personnel on site. Rosie, Kitty, Jane, Carole and I split our time between assisting them with meal prep, serving food in the mess hall before clearing and washing up, afterwards, and then systematically cleaning the whole of the research facility, restocking supplies and carrying out general maintenance. Then, in the evenings, the others took turns to practise their typing on the repaired machine, and I continued to read and absorb as much as I could about radio detection finding.

Kitty and I took to walking along the nearby clifftop path adjacent to the site during our breaks. We soon got to know the coastline well. Kitty enjoyed exploring the small, stone medieval chapel built just off the path at a place called St Aldhelm's Point and I fell in love with the view out over the English Channel from the edge of the bluff.

The onshore breeze was always brisk, laden with the scent of salt and seaweed. When the weather was good, sunshine glinted off the water in countless dancing sparkles. On cloudy days, the sea was a moving tapestry of greys, greens, blues and purples with dramatic white highlights when the waves crashed against the shore. It was hard to connect such natural beauty with the death and destruction that was happening in the world, and yet on the other side of the waves, the rest of Europe were fighting for their lives against the inexhaustible advance of Nazi troops.

Given the huge increase in air raids arriving in British airspace, it was easy to appreciate why the government were keen to develop aerial defences. The Nazi war machine continued to grind relentlessly towards us. We often saw squadrons of Spitfires in the distance over the Channel engaging in spats with enemy aircraft and watched with bated breath, willing our pilots to be victorious. The wheeling and diving of planes as they darted at each other was terrifying; the rat-tat-tat of gunfire carrying on the wind. The harsh rumble of Heinkel bomber formations heading inland became more frequent as time went on. We could do little but pray that they were intercepted and eliminated by the brave fighter pilots of the RAF before they could reach their targets. My thoughts were frequently with my family, hoping that Ma, Nana and the boys were still with Aunty Mo in the country and that Da was keeping safe. Bristol, with the port and all the industry, must surely be a target. Like everyone around me, I could only pray that those I loved were spared.

Commander Wilson, our ATS commanding officer, arrived to take charge. However, as she was splitting her time between Renscombe and two other local sites she was away a lot. This left Beaky running day-to-day operations. Apart from a little friction with Sergeant Thomas, the incoming WAAF sergeant supervising the WAAF typing pool, Beaky seemed content. The rumour that she came from a well-connected family had spread and the majority of people on site treated her with a degree of careful deference which had an unexpectedly calming effect on her. I made a point of backing her up on everything and our relationship improved dramatically.

It was with some surprise that I arrived at her office one afternoon to find her pacing the floor between desk and door, a look of panic on her face. Deep grooves gouged her forehead. Her eyes were unfocused, as if she couldn't really see me.

'Are you all right, ma'am?' I asked.

'Major Stapleton is coming tomorrow,' she whispered.

'Is she? Why?'

She thrust a piece of paper at me. 'To inspect us.'

I scanned the message. 'It says here that she's just coming to see how we've settled in and find out if we need anything.' Why was Beaky overreacting? 'I don't think it's something you need to worry about.'

Beaky shook her head. 'She's coming to check up on me. I know she is. And we're not ready. What if I lose my promotion?'

'You won't, ma'am.' I tried to infuse my words with as much calm encouragement as I could. 'You're really good at what you do.'

'But it's chaos around here. Have you seen the mess they're making in the new compound?'

With two out of four planned sections for the site completed, the building team had moved on to dig foundations for the third.

I kept my tone even, my manner soothing. 'Major Stapleton will understand. Remember, you aren't responsible for the parts of the site that aren't built yet.'

'I know, but what *is* here isn't good enough yet. And Commander Wilson isn't back for another week.'

'It will be fine,' I said. 'We'll make it fine. The others can manage in the canteen without me. Tell me what you need done. I'll stay until everything is sorted exactly the way you want it to be. Now. Where do you want me to start?'

I spent the rest of the afternoon making sure that the general cleaning duties in all buildings had been completed to a high standard, the toilet block gleamed, and all consumable office materials were topped up across the site. Meanwhile, Beaky ploughed through the paper records, determined that not a single aspect of the housekeeping administration could be said to be out of place.

The sun sank in the western sky, spilling stunning lakes of warm orange across the landscape. I scurried from the observation hut at the foot of the main tower across to the four long low buildings that housed the research laboratories, intent on refilling stationery supplies. The boffins always ploughed through reams of paper. It was usual practice to complete this task after all the scientists had left for the day, which suited me, because it gave me an opportunity to exchange my borrowed books.

However, time was an issue that day, so I slipped in and out of each room while they were still working, doing my best not to disturb anyone. It was interesting to see them actively engaged in projects that I usually only saw fragments

of at the end of the day in the form of scribbles on scrap paper, technical draw-
ings pinned to corkboards and piles of open reports littering desks. I'd often
passed the time, as I swept, mopped and polished my way around the site,
trying to figure out how all the experiments and data sets worked and how they
might link with the information I was learning from my reading.

A meeting was in progress in hut 4. Many white-coated men crowded into
one room, all listening intently to someone at the front who I couldn't see. As I
tiptoed across the back of the room, intent on sliding reams of paper into the
stationery drawers, a deep, gravelly voice spoke. 'As you know, gentlemen, we
are trying to increase our ability to detect incoming enemy aircraft. At present,
the Chain Home receivers are locked in position facing out to sea forming a
protective wall. Your challenge, today, is to find a way for receivers to move. We
need to be able to scan lower altitudes and we need to be considering
expanding the network to cover inland areas. Mobility is the key to scanning
the sky in all directions, even behind us. The question is, how?'

Voices from the crowd began suggesting a range of possibilities.

'How about adapting the new hydraulics systems in aircraft, sir?' said one
voice.

'Hydraulics? How exactly?' said another.

I crept silently away, but for the rest of the afternoon, I couldn't help
mulling over the problem. I might not understand the precise science behind
the transmitters and receivers, but I understood mechanics.

* * *

A couple of hours later, when the scientists had gone for the night, I returned to
hut 4 to clean. I had developed a particular affinity for this hut, and found the
work being completed inside it genuinely compelling. I was frequently late
finishing my rounds because I became engrossed in reading theories scrawled
on blackboards.

Today was no exception. I slipped back into the room where the meeting
about mobile receivers had been held, eager to see what solutions they had
come up with. Whatever it was would be ever so clever and way more sophisticated than the simple one I had formulated in my head. To my disappointment
the board had been wiped clean and there were no handy papers left lying
around to feed my curiosity. I sighed, my shoulders slumping even as my eye

darted to the chalk resting in the runnel at the base of the board and back up to the acres of clear space waiting to be filled. I checked over my shoulder. There was no one around. This was my chance to pretend to be part of something more than the cleaning team. What harm could it do?

Moving quickly, I picked up the chalk and, with firm lines, drew my simple method for moving gantries and receivers using a series of basic bicycle chains and cogwheels set at both vertical and horizontal alignments. No doubt there was a more scientific way of achieving the same thing via clever automation, but my muscle-powered rotation system allowed a full sweep of the sky, like an upturned bowl. Satisfied that I had represented my idea as well as I could, I dropped the chalk back into its rest, stood back and dusted off my hands.

It felt good, seeing my idea up there in black and white. I couldn't bear to wipe it off straight away and decided to leave it while I finished my chores. I could always pop back at the end of the evening to erase it before catching the bus back to Swanage.

Finishing up in hut 4, I headed for the typing pool where I polished desks with renewed vigour and took extra time to arrange freshly sharpened pencils on top of all the WAAF secretaries' notebooks.

17

The sun was gone by the time I had finished. Warm red and orange had dissolved into grey-blue shadows with silver highlights from the crescent moon above. I shivered in the cool night air and picked my way back across the grass towards hut 4 with care, wishing I could use a torch to see where I was putting my feet. The peace after all the hustle and bustle of the day was a relief. No doubt, back in Swanage, everyone would be huddled around the wireless listening to the latest dire war announcements.

I drank in the silence, aware that there was a skeleton staff on site, tucked away staring at screens in the observation tower. The guardhouse was occupied too. All else was still. For once, the sky was empty of all but heavenly bodies. No air-raid sirens keened and no engines roared. In this single precious moment in time, it seemed as if there wasn't a war on and all was right with the world.

A sudden noise came from hut 4, as if a window had swung in the barely there breeze and bashed against a wall. Strange. When I'd left it earlier, I had thought all windows and doors were shut, the blackout blinds secured. Perhaps I'd missed one. I pulled my keys from my pocket, remembering that I had to clean my drawing off that blackboard too. It was no trouble to check the windows again. I hurried across the grass to the entrance. Inside, I yanked the blackout curtain back across the door behind me and flicked on the corridor light.

What was that?

I froze. Was that a scuffle from one of the rooms at the end?

'Hello?' I called, my pulse racing at a million miles per hour.

Silence.

I crept along the corridor, the only sound the creak of hinges as I pushed each door open and scanned inside. 'Is anyone there?'

I paused and listened.

Nothing.

The hairs on the back of my neck stood to attention. There was definitely someone here – I was sure of it. My hands shook. If they were here legitimately then they'd speak out. If not, then... what did that mean? The sharp taste of bile filled my mouth. There were two rooms at the far end of the corridor, dark and empty. I crept into the first. A flurry of movement came from the other. A masked figure, dressed head to toe in black, dashed past me, a small rucksack bouncing against their back. Man or woman? I couldn't tell.

'Hey,' I yelled, making a grab for them. My fingers brushed fabric before closing on thin air. 'Come back.' My feet thundered down the passageway in pursuit. The distance between us closed as they wrestled with the blackout curtain before diving through the door. I snatched at a dangling strap of the rucksack and held on tight. They powered on, dragging me outside in their wake.

Dear heaven, they were strong. My body smacked against the ground, my skin scraping from my legs as I was dragged over obstacles. I gritted my teeth and ignored the pain, focusing instead on trying to make myself as heavy as possible.

They kept moving. I racked my brain trying to think what they might have been doing in the hut. Spying? Stealing secrets? Very probably. Fear vanished, replaced by red-hot anger. How dare they steal from my scientists? If I did nothing else in this war, I was damned if I'd let this person escape.

The fugitive twisted around, searching for whatever was impeding their progress. With an unintelligible curse they slapped at my arm and yanked on the bag.

I clung on like grim death, reaching to get a more secure hold with my other hand, grasping the neckline of the rucksack. It slipped from their shoulders. Gravel scattered like buckshot as they stumbled and I was pulled into a somersault of heads, arms and legs. We landed in a tangled heap. Grunts filled the air and the acrid smell of smoke and stale body odour caught in my throat. The intruder recovered before I did and leaned across, letting a fist fly. The blow hit my cheek, sending my wits begging even as my stubborn streak kicked in. I refused to release the bag, hauling it close to wrap both arms around it, twisting my body to fall between it and the thief. A second blow landed on the back of my head. Sparks jumped before my eyes.

A shout came from nearby. 'What's all that noise?'

And then another. 'Why is that blasted light on?' At last people were realising that something untoward was in progress.

Running footsteps crunched on stones.

The intruder cursed, turned and fled.

My vision went wavy around the edges. A pair of gentle hands grasped my shoulders and a low voice, one that I recognised but couldn't place, said, 'It's all right. You're safe now.'

'The bag,' I mumbled. 'I got the bag.' Then everything went black.

* * *

Sometime later, I was sat in the main guardhouse with a cold compress over my eye. A persistent heavy thudding in my head made it difficult to think and I struggled to answer the questions that the security commander fired at me about what happened. Eventually, he gave up and went to file a report with the base commander, and I watched the officer on duty rifle through the contents of the bag. Beaky set a cup of hot, sweet tea on the table in front of me.

'Who was that man?' I asked. 'The one who saved me?'

'Just one of the scientists,' said Beaky. 'Does it matter?'

'No, I just thought I recognised his voice.'

'Honestly, Makepeace, is that all you can think about?' Exasperation laced her words. 'This rumpus is the last thing I need.'

I bit back a sharp retort and reached for my tea. 'At least you can relax about Major Stapleton, now.'

'How do you figure that?'

I blew on my tea. 'She'll be more interested in all this drama than whether the windows are clean and everyone has enough soap and loo paper.'

'Let's hope so.' She leaned closer to prod at my bruised eye. 'I'll still have to write up incident reports for both Commander Carter *and* Commander Wilson.'

I winced as she poked a particularly sore spot.

'Don't be such a baby,' she tutted. 'If you will go tackling intruders in the dark, what do you expect? Anyway. You're lucky. I don't think your eye socket is broken. You'll have a bit of a shiner, that's all.'

The duty officer turned. 'There are a lot of confidential papers in here, ma'am, but as to how important they are, we'll have to wait until the boffins come back on site tomorrow.'

'Shall I take a look at them?' I said, desperate to see what was inside the bag.

'Don't be ridiculous, Makepeace,' scoffed Beaky. 'Leave it to the experts.'

I ducked my head, kicking myself for not thinking. Of course, no one would want my opinion.

The duty officer crossed to a black metal filing cabinet, pulled out the bottom drawer, saying, 'It's a shame the search party failed to catch whoever it was.' He dropped the bag and its contents inside, before closing and locking it. 'At least the information is safe. I suggest we follow this up in the morning, ma'am.'

'Thank you,' Beaky said and turned to me. 'Come along, Makepeace. There's a car waiting to take us to Swanage. We'll debrief properly tomorrow when you've had some rest.'

18

My right eye swelled shut overnight and random parts of my body ached with an intensity that made sleep almost impossible. The next morning, the bus journey from Swanage to Renscombe, with Kitty by my side throwing concerned glances my way every thirty seconds, was uncomfortable to say the least.

'Are you sure you didn't get a good look at them,' asked Carole, from the seat behind.

I glanced over my shoulder. 'They had some sort of balaclava on.'

'You must have seen something?' said Rosie twisting around from the seat in front of me.

I shook my head, and then wished I hadn't as my headache threatened to crank up a gear. 'Honestly, it all happened so quickly.'

'I wonder if it was an outsider, or someone from the site staff,' said Jane, who was sat next to Carole.

Rosie shuddered. 'It might be someone we see every day.'

'Someone we serve food to,' said Kitty. 'We could keep a lookout for anyone suspicious and put clues together at the end of each shift.'

I laughed. 'Like detectives, you mean?'

'Why not?' she said.

'Whoever they are, they're dangerous. Look at me.' I pointed to my face. 'They won't hesitate to hurt you, if they think you're on to them.'

Kitty snorted. 'I wasn't planning to confront them. I'm not daft.'

The more I thought about Kitty's suggestion the more it appealed. She was right. Everyone on site came through the canteen at some point or other during the day. 'I suppose it wouldn't hurt,' I said. 'As long as we're careful.'

'Are we looking for a man or a woman?' asked Jane.

'Difficult to say,' I said. 'They were an average height and had quite a slim build. Other than that, they could have been a strong, wiry woman, or an average but slender man.'

'Hmm,' said Rosie, her brows scrunched together in thought. 'That could describe a lot of people. We'll have to narrow it down a bit.'

'Given the state of your face,' said Carole, 'they'll have bruised knuckles, at the very least.'

'That's it,' exclaimed Kitty. 'That's our clue for today. We'll check everyone's hands as they pass us at the service area.'

I smiled at her. 'Fine. Only don't go challenging anyone. Just watch and report back.'

* * *

Half an hour later I was sat in an office with Major Stapleton and Beaky.

'Do you remember anything else at all?' asked Major Stapleton.

I was about to shake my head and then stopped. 'Whoever they are, they smoke. They had that claggy bitter smell about them that catches in your throat.' It wasn't much. So many people smoked.

'I see.' Major Stapleton leaned back in her chair and crossed her arms, fixing me with a look so intense she could have been looking right into my soul. 'It was brave of you to tackle them. Especially on your own. You could easily have let them get away with those papers and no one would have known. What made you take such a risk?'

'I don't know. I think… I just… well, whatever they were after was clearly important.' I shrugged. 'And I didn't want them to get away with it.'

'How did you know it was important?' she asked.

'Why else would they be breaking in?' I snapped. 'I'm not stupid, I—' A sharp gasp from Beaky reminded me who I was speaking to. I bit my lip. 'Forgive me, ma'am. I meant no disrespect.'

The major shook her head. 'That's fine. Go on.'

I took a deep breath, gathering my thoughts. 'The work I do around here isn't taxing, but that doesn't mean I don't know what's going on. In fact, I'd bet any money those papers were about the use of different metallic mixes in the construction of receiver dishes to improve reception capabilities.'

The major scanned down the report in her hands before looking up in surprise. 'What makes you say that?'

'Because the intruder came out of room 404, and *that's* what they are studying in there.'

'How on earth do you know that?'

I sighed. 'Major, the work I do every day is how I know.'

'Explain.'

'We ATS troops get treated like we're nothing. We're just the cleaners. Yet we go everywhere: the dining area, the latrines, the observation towers, the labs, the offices, the guard hut. Everywhere. To the world we are invisible. But we see things. We hear things. Not all of us do, I grant you. *I* do though. I can't help it.' I couldn't keep frustration from my voice. Being overlooked and dismissed was the story of my life and it was getting very boring.

The major's eyes narrowed. 'What sort of things?'

'I can't say.' I folded my arms, aware that I was being contrary, but I'd had enough.

Beaky exploded. 'For goodness' sake—'

'It could be confidential,' I said.

'Makep—'

'It's all right, Staff Sergeant. She's right. It could be.' The major leaned forward. 'I assure you, I have the highest clearance. Give me an example. Something relatively restricted but not earth-shattering.'

I uncrossed my arms. 'Fine. This morning, I overheard a discussion about the need for secure conversation between pilots and the observation tower controllers so that we can identify incoming planes as either friendly or hostile. That's the research the team in hut 2 are focusing on. They're making excellent progress, too. Communication like that should massively improve aerial interception response success rates. Apparently, the current technology we have could work, it just has to be smaller and they're working on a coded system.'

'I see. What else?'

'Enough to tell me that there are more weaknesses in the Chain Home system than we're led to believe in the news. If there is a full-on aerial assault as part of a Nazi invasion, we're toast. We might as well open the door and invite them in.'

'Don't be ridiculous,' said Beaky. 'You've overheard half a conversation and put two and two together to make seven, Makepeace.'

I ignored her.

The air between the major and I crackled with tension. Her gaze didn't waver. I could tell she knew I was right.

I shrugged. 'It's not just what I overhear. When I go into the labs to dust and sweep, I'm emptying wastepaper baskets. It's all there, scrunched up. It's on the blackboards, on documents left lying around. I'm not saying I go around reading everything – I don't have time for that. And I'm not saying I understand it all. I'm not a scientist. I'm just saying that...' I waved a hand '...I pick information up. It's the way my brain works.' I ground to a halt, cursing myself inside for rattling on.

The major studied me in silence for a few minutes before she said, 'Perhaps you can help to solve a mystery then.' She checked the report again. 'It says here that, as well as taking the exact documents that you predicted were taken, the intruder left something behind. It has the scientist in hut 4 baffled.'

I sat up, intrigued. 'What?'

'There's diagram on one of the blackboards.'

'Oh!' In all the excitement, I'd forgotten about my drawing. How mortifying. No one was supposed to see it.

'The scientists can't understand why it's there. It seems to be an attempt to answer the issue they were studying that afternoon. They say it's rudimentary but very effective. The question is,' continued the major, 'why would an enemy intruder take the trouble to do that, and how would they know what had been going on in that room earlier in the day?'

'Security thinks it means that the whole break-in was an inside job,' said Beaky. Her eyes narrowed. 'Why have you gone so red in the face, Makepeace?'

I had no choice but to admit what I'd done. 'It was me. The drawing. It's nothing to do with the break-in. I got carried away. I was going to clean it off before I went home, but then I hit my head and... well... I didn't. I'm sorry. It won't happen again.' I folded my hands in my lap and waited, the urge to squirm under the major's intense stare almost unbearable.

'Do you make a habit of interfering with the research?' the major asked.

'No, ma'am. That was the only time, and it won't happen again.'

'Damn right it won't,' said Beaky. 'Because I'm sending you back to Foxhalt immediately.'

My vision blurred as tears welled up at the thought of being sent away. 'Please, ma'am, don't—'

'No!' That single word from the major silenced both Beaky and I. 'That won't be necessary, Staff Sergeant Beaconsfield. We'll leave Private Makepeace in position for the time being.'

'But, ma'am, protocol states—'

Major Stapleton held up a hand. 'I can see that you run a very tight ship here, Staff Sergeant Beaconsfield, and I shall say so in my report. You are to be commended.'

'Thank you, ma'am.'

'I shall take it as a huge personal favour from you, if you will allow Private Makepeace to stay where she is. I'll inform security that the drawing is not related to the break-in and should not be included in their inquiries. Meanwhile *we* will keep her part in producing that drawing to ourselves. In my experience, scientists have delicate egos. There's no need to upset them with details. The less said about this whole thing, the better.'

Beaky's gaze bounced from the major to me and back again. 'If you insist, ma'am. Then, of course.'

'Thank you, Staff Sergeant.' The major gathered up her papers. 'I'll be on my way, now, secure in the knowledge that you have everything under control. And Private Makepeace...' she paused '...you've given me plenty to think about. I'll be in touch.' With that, she left the room.

Stunned, Beaky and I stared at each other, neither of us quite sure what to make of things. Eventually, she spoke, her voice thoughtful. 'I told you there was more to that woman than meets the eye, didn't I?'

'You did.'

'Be careful, Fliss.' Beaky's words were barely above a whisper. 'She's up to something.'

She'd never called me Fliss before.

Before I could reply, she snapped back into her usual brisk and efficient mode, and it was as if that quiet moment of reflection had never happened. 'You'd better get on, Makepeace. Try to behave yourself, and *don't*, whatever you do, draw on any more blackboards.'

'Yes, ma'am. I mean, no, ma'am.' I saluted and left the room.

What on earth did the major mean: *she'd be in touch*? I supposed I would find out. I pushed it from my mind as I hurried across the site towards the canteen, and focused instead on what the scientists had said about my diagram. *Rudimentary but effective.* I smiled, a wave of happiness waltzing through me. It worked. My little bicycle wheel and chain worked.

The minute I pushed open the door to the canteen, Kitty abandoned what she was doing and hurried over. 'Someone left you flowers,' she hissed.

'I beg your pardon?'

She gestured to a small bunch of wild flowers tucked into a tin mug sat on a shelf behind the serving area. 'One of the catering staff said a man came in with them and asked her to give them to you.'

'Who was it?'

Kitty shook her head. 'She doesn't know and wasn't able to describe him when I asked.'

'How strange.'

'Might they be from—' she glanced from side to side before continuing in an even lower tone '—you know who? To say sorry for hitting you?'

Remembering the force behind the intruder's punches, I shook my head. 'I sincerely doubt it. For them to come here openly, without a mask or anything, makes no sense.'

'Come along, you two,' barked the catering manager. 'This isn't the time for a mothers' meeting. There are people to feed.'

We hastened across the canteen and got to work. Further analysis of this unexpected development would have to wait until later. Even so, I couldn't help wondering what on earth the flowers might mean.

19

Over the next two weeks, my bruises settled and life carried on much as it had before. Keeping a lookout for clues in the canteen produced no useful results. There were so many people of average height with a slim build it was impossible to narrow it down, and only two of those had injuries to their hands, both of which on further investigation had plausible explanations. Meanwhile, I continued to puzzle over who might have sent me those flowers and why. One morning, I stood on the coastal path, listening to the sea wash in and out against the rocks below. A muted shout reached me. Kitty was picking her way along the tufted gravel path. I waved and went to join her.

The incident with the intruder had unsettled more than just me. The response from the security team had been immediate. Wire fencing went up around the whole site and regular patrols were introduced. Everyone was given extra training on confidentiality and security matters. We were ordered to gather all wastepaper at the end of the day and burn it in huge metal containers, making sure that every speck turned to ash. I found myself increasingly envious of those working in the laboratories; developing something that would help us win the war and perhaps save countless lives.

At breakfast the day before, I'd overheard a couple of scientists discussing a mechanised cogwheel system for moving the receivers. While it sounded more sophisticated than my drawing, it was definitely based on the same principles. Torn between delight that I had been right and exasperation that I couldn't chip in with a suggestion, I'd gritted my teeth and moved on. For a brief moment, I had been involved and now it was over. I felt as if something precious had been snatched away from me. I was left on the outside looking in, just as I had been at Makepeace Motors.

Mounting frustration made me appreciate how powerless Daniel must have felt at not being allowed to join the armed forces because of his arm. I wished, not for the first time, that the war hadn't separated us. If only I had written to him sooner, he might have replied.

'I've been looking for you all over,' said Kitty, arriving at my side with a merry laugh. 'I should have known you'd be staring out to sea. Sorry to drag you back to work, but we're nearly ready to serve lunch.'

'I was just coming.'

A pair of seagulls swooped over our heads, their sharp cries carrying on the breeze. Kitty fell into step beside me as we both walked back towards the canteen.

After several minutes of peace, she tucked an arm through mine. 'Just so you know, Carole has upset some of the WAAF girls.'

'Oh dear. Not again.'

The WAAF seemed friendly enough to me and they looked very smart in their blue uniforms. I ran a hand down my jacket and adjusted my belt. I rather liked the ATS uniform, even if we did have to cover it up with regulation aprons for all the messy jobs we were assigned.

Outside the canteen, the mouth-watering smell of rich vegetable stew wrapped around us, urging us inside. I gestured for Kitty go first. 'What did she say this time?'

'They were boasting that the WAAF was better than the ATS, so she put them in their place.'

'How bad was she?'

Kitty wrinkled her nose. 'Worse than usual.'

'Oh, for goodness' sake. We'd better try to smooth things over. We're all on the same side in this war. There's no point falling out with each other.'

'I know but—'

Whatever Kitty was about to say was drowned out by the raised voice of the canteen commander. 'You're late. Wash your hands and get ready.'

With clean hands and a fresh apron wrapped around my waist I set about dolloping portions of mashed potato onto each plate that was thrust out to me by the line of hungry personnel queueing for food. As soon as there was a lull, I grabbed a cloth and headed out from behind the serving platform to wipe down tables ready for the next sitting. I worked steadily from one side of the room to the other, keeping my head down, listening to the hum of multiple conversations. People were using hushed voices in light of a recent spate of confidentiality training, but they were still talking.

'If we change the angle and use aluminium to reduce the weight, it could work,' murmured one boffin.

'You're missing an important factor,' said another.

'It's the calculations that are off...'

'It needs to be small enough to fit inside the cockpit of the plane...'

'We need more speed...'

Snippets of intense discussions, taking place all around, fanned the flames of my discontent.

A sharp clatter of dishes came from a table in one corner of the room. A cry of pain pierced the air. I dropped my cloth and hurried over. A pretty blonde WAAF stared in horror from the edges of a broken glass to her hand. Blood spurted across the table from a deep gash in her palm.

My first-aid training kicked in. I grabbed her wrist and checked there were no signs of glass in the wound. Tugging free the clean tea towel I always carried tucked into the waistband of my apron, I wrapped it around her hand and applied pressure to slow the bleeding.

'It's all right,' I said, noting her jagged breathing and panicked whimpers. 'Try to stay calm. You're going to be fine.'

'I'm sorry, I think... I am going to... oh!' Healthy pink drained from her face as she turned a pasty grey.

I moved closer to stop her slumping off her chair onto the floor. A head injury wasn't going to help the situation. I looked at the girl sat next to her. Her eyes, wide with alarm, were fixed on a splatter of ruby red on the table. A forkful of mashed potatoes hovered midway to her mouth.

'Quick,' I said. 'Can you help steady her? We need to get her lying flat before she faints, but I daren't let go of this hand.'

The fork clattered to the table as she jumped into action, taking hold of her friend's shoulders. 'Come on, Lisa. Careful now.' With a little encouragement and a lot of support, Lisa lay down.

'Well done, Lisa,' I said. 'Now, I'll keep your arm raised because it will slow the bleeding.'

'I... I... My hand...' Lisa clutched at her friend's sleeve. 'Oh, Debbie, I...'

'I bet it hurts like billy-o,' said Debbie, her tone bracing. 'But we've got you. You'll be fine.'

'Yes,' I said, with a confidence I didn't feel. It was a deep cut. 'We'll get you sorted out. Concentrate on your breathing: deep, slow breaths in and then out. See? It's easy. You can do it.'

Glancing at a third WAAF, a well-upholstered brunette, who sat watching with her mouth hanging open, I nodded towards the serving area. 'Can you grab the first-aid kit, please? The green canvas bag hooked to the wall over by the trays.'

She leapt to her feet and dashed off, returning moments later, eyes full of concern. She laid the contents out on the table for me. I scanned the dressings, antiseptic cream and bandages, wondering if I should attempt to clean the wound. I eased my grip on the tea towel to see if the bleeding had slowed. The gush of crimson returned in an instant. I thrust a piece of sterile gauze over the cut and wrapped it up again, clamping down on the cut and cursing under my breath. 'I can't sort it out here. It's too deep. She needs a doctor and stitches.'

'What can I do?' said the brunette.

'Tell your supervisor we need transport to hospital.'

'Is my hand going to be all right?' asked Lisa, her voice barely more than a whisper as her friend hurried away.

'Yes. Absolutely.' I poured as much conviction as I could into my words. 'A few stitches and you'll be as right as rain. No, no, don't try to look – it'll make you feel queasy. Talk to Debbie instead.'

'Bonnie has gone to get Sergeant Thomas,' said Debbie from her other side. 'She'll get you to the docs and they'll patch you up in a jiffy. I expect you'll have to rest for a while, but you'll be fine.'

'The professor will be furious,' Lisa mumbled.

'You mustn't worry about him,' said Debbie. 'It was an accident.'

'Professor?' I asked.

Debbie grimaced. 'She types for him over in room 401. She's the only secretary he'll work with, grumpy sod.'

Room 401. Envy bloomed in spite of Lisa's injury. The WAAF got to work with the scientists, every day. What must that be like?

'He's a brilliant man,' said Lisa.

'That may be true,' said Debbie with a wry twist to her lips. 'But he says the rest of us are stupid.'

'Charming,' I said.

Debbie grinned. 'To be honest, we're all relieved that Lisa likes him, so *we* don't have to put up with him.'

'Well, one of you is going to have to until Lisa's hand heals,' I said, wishing with all my heart that it could be me. Grumpy professor or not, working in hut 4 was my idea of heaven.

'Huh! Not likely. We're short-staffed as it is, and the new secretaries aren't due to arrive for another two weeks.' She shook her head. 'To be honest, I don't know what we're going to do.'

'I can type.' The words were out before I could stop them.

'Can you?' said Debbie. 'What about shorthand and dictation?'

I nodded. 'I was a secretary before I joined up.'

'Well, don't let on or you could soon be working for the grumpiest man on the planet.'

Lisa gave me a wan smile. 'Don't listen to her. The professor is a sweetie underneath it all. He's only bad tempered when he forgets to eat. I bet he hasn't had any lunch today. Will you take him some for me?'

Just then, Sergeant Thomas arrived with a couple of beefy-looking men and a stretcher.

As Lisa was borne away, Kitty appeared at my side and started clearing the table. 'Well, that was dramatic. Are you all right, Fliss?'

'Yes, I'm fine,' I murmured, turning an idea over in my head. If I wanted things to change, then I was going to have to make them change. This might be my chance. 'Listen, Kitty. Can you cover for me? There's something I need to do.' Without waiting for an answer, I hurried to wash Lisa's blood from my hands. With a couple of sandwiches and half a dozen honey biscuits wrapped into a clean cloth, I dashed outside and across the grass to hut 4.

20

Conscious that I wasn't supposed to be inside the huts during the day, I slunk along the corridor, my head down, stepping back against the wall when anyone came by. Inside room 401, a tall, older man wearing a white coat over a dark suit, with greying hair slicked back from his forehead, stood near the far wall scratching mathematical formulae onto the blackboard. Shelving units to the left and right groaned under piles of documents. A wide table set under a window was similarly laden.

The man continued to write on the board, muttering to himself. My footsteps must have alerted him to my presence, because he paused. Without looking up, he growled, 'You took your time. Quick. Take this down.'

Startled, I glanced around at the otherwise empty room. He must think I was Lisa returning from lunch. Before I could explain, he began dictating in a loud, authoritative voice, whilst pacing up and down with his eyes fixed on the board. I hastened to Lisa's desk, grabbed her pad and pencil and started making notes.

Ten minutes later, he said, 'Now, type that up,' and resumed his scribbles on the board.

It had been a long time since I'd actually done any typing. Fortunately, it's like riding a bike – once learned, you don't forget. I sandwiched carbon paper in between two fresh sheets of paper – duplicates are always useful – and rolled them on to the main cylinder before snapping the paper lock into place. My fingers flew across the keys in a rhythmic click-clack. A nostalgic smile tugged at my lips; who would have thought that I would miss this quite as much as I had? I reached the end of the report and pulled it free of the machine, just as a shadow fell across my desk.

The professor loomed over me. Close up, his face was craggy and stern as if recently hewn from a granite cliffside. He glowered out from under bushy grey eyebrows. 'Who the hell are you?'

I scrambled to my feet, my heart thumping wildly in my chest, and stood to attention. 'Private Felicity Makepeace, sir.'

His eyes bounced from me to the typewriter to the report in my hands and back again. 'What are you doing here?'

'I came in, you said, "Take this down," so I did, sir.'

He paced away from the desk and back again, his eyes dropping to my apron. 'Where have you sprung from?'

'Housekeeping,' I said.

'You're the cleaner?' His nostrils flared as if something smelled bad. 'You shouldn't be typing my reports.'

'You asked me to, sir.'

'Don't be ridiculous,' he thundered. 'And where's...' he waved a hand '...whatshername? The quiet, blonde one.'

'If you mean, Lisa, she's been injured.' I ignored a flare of irritation. She'd been so quick to defend him and he didn't even know her name.

Disbelief and outrage chased each other across his face. 'That's not acceptable.'

'They've taken her to hospital. She'll be gone a while.'

'But...' His shoulders sagged. He gazed around the room as if he wasn't quite sure where he was. 'But I need her,' he whispered.

'I know. I'm sorry, sir.' I crossed my fingers behind my back, well aware that Beaky would flip her lid if she knew what I was doing, but I couldn't stop now. 'That's why she sent me.' I pulled the parcel of sandwiches and biscuits from my apron pocket and pushed it across the desk towards him. 'She said you would be hungry and asked if I would bring you these.' I placed the report down next to the food. 'And, yes, I am a cleaner, but I am also an excellent secretary. You'll find that I've typed your report both efficiently and accurately. Good day.'

Without waiting for a reply, I left the room, a strange energy coursing through my veins that made me feel more alive than ever before. I'd done it. For half an hour I'd worked in hut 4 with a real scientist and it had been amazing. No doubt the professor would complain. I didn't care. Triumphant defiance settled around my shoulders. Whatever the consequences, it had been worth every second.

* * *

Later that afternoon, Beaky arrived in the canteen just as the evening meal was being served and beckoned me over. I handed Kitty the spoon for the stew I was serving and stepped away from the tables.

'You'll be the death of me, Makepeace,' muttered Beaky. 'What on earth possessed you to go into the research huts during the day?'

'Lisa asked me to.'

'Who?'

'The WAAF who got injured. She was worried about the professor.'

Beaky fixed me with an intense stare. 'Well, I've just had your professor in my office shouting the odds and demanding to see you.'

'Oh!' Sadness crept over my shoulders, dragging them down. He really had complained. I took a deep breath and braced myself for a telling-off.

'He was very rude.' Beaky scowled. 'And if it weren't for the fact that Sergeant Thomas has been getting right up my nose, I would have sent him packing.'

Not following her logic and reluctant to ask for clarification, I waited to see if she would expand.

'She acts like the WAAF are better than the ATS. But your professor has refused all her girls. Apparently, only you will do and he wants you over there, now. Tell me you know what you're doing.'

'I do,' I said, not quite able to believe my luck.

'You'd better.' Grim warning laced Beaky's voice. 'Go on. It'll leave us short-staffed, but this is your chance to prove that my troop are not only as good as Sergeant Thomas' girls, they're better. Chop-chop. Take your apron off and get over to room 401.'

* * *

I ran over to hut 4, excitement lending me wings. Room 401 was packed with men wearing white coats over brown suits. They were all standing around in rapt attention, watching the professor draw on the board. He spoke in low, intense tones, periodically raising his voice and stabbing at the board with his chalk to emphasise a point. Half the men stared at the drawing in fascination; the others scribbled frantic notes on clipboards.

As I approached, he peered at me as if I were a stray rat that had accidentally wandered in. 'What are you doing here?' he boomed.

'You asked to see me,' I said.

He dragged a pair of small, round glasses from a pocket and examined me through them. 'Ah yes! You're the cleaner who can type.'

I ground my teeth. How dare he belittle me simply because I was assigned to housekeeping. *He* had asked *me* to come. I mentally sat on the urge to say something rude. I'd wanted things to change. This was my chance. What I said in this moment could mean the difference between me staying here or being sent back to my mops and buckets. Anxiety writhed in my belly like a nest of agitated snakes. I swallowed, forcing my voice to stay calm and professional. 'I have six years of technical office experience, sir. I worked in a mechanics firm before the war. For what it's worth I can also strip any internal combustion engine you name down to basic parts. I can reassemble it too. I can repair any vehicle from the point the wheels touch the road to the top of the roof. I can weld. I can panel-beat. I can drive. My grammar is excellent and my typing speed most efficient. But, yes, sir, as you say, I am the cleaner who can type.'

'Hmm, mechanics is all very well. What do you know about physics?'

I maintained eye contact. I couldn't admit to borrowing all those books without permission, and there was no other way to explain the knowledge I'd gained from them. I kept my tone respectful and firm as I answered, 'Very little. However, I have a good head on my shoulders, sir. If you need me to learn specific scientific terminology, spelling and usage, I can do that. Give me a list; I'll have it memorised by tomorrow.' I felt like adding *so there* and sticking out my tongue but refrained.

'She can also run like the wind and jump onto a moving train,' came a quiet voice from behind me.

I knew that voice.

My head whipped around and I searched the crowd for... there. Behind all the others. Daniel. Something inside me lifted at the sight of him, like a thousand birds taking off at once. What was *he* doing here? He twitched one eyebrow, his expression solemn. The air between us sizzled.

'Don't be ridiculous, Evans,' barked the professor, reclaiming my attention. 'This is no time for jokes.'

'This is the woman who chased off that intruder the other week,' said Daniel.

I knew I'd recognised that voice after the incident. It had been Daniel. I was sure of it. Why hadn't he stuck around? More to the point, why hadn't he come to see me afterwards? After all, he knew I was injured. Any decent friend would want to check I was all right. Perhaps I had misjudged him.

The professor's eyes nearly popped out of his head. 'Are you?'

'Yes, sir,' I said.

He scratched his chin. 'Well, well. That was brave of you.' He stomped over to a bookshelf crammed with documents and pulled out a huge textbook bound in leather with shiny letters stamped into the binding. He marched back and thrust it towards me. I took it, trying not to react to how heavy it was.

'Nothing in that is confidential,' he said. 'Take it away and learn the glossary of essential terms in the back. If you can manage that, then come to my office at nine o'clock sharp tomorrow and we'll get started.'

I wondered if he realised how pompous he sounded.

He turned back to the board. 'Now, gentlemen. Where were we?'

That I was dismissed was clear. I snuck one final glance at Daniel, but his attention was focused on the blackboard like all the others. He didn't seem remotely bothered that I was there and it rankled. It seemed that I had wasted my time, not only writing to him, but also hoping that he would write back.

* * *

Beaky pounced on me outside. 'How did it go?' she asked.

'Good. I think. He's given me some homework to do.'

'Excellent.' She dusted her hands together. 'You concentrate on that, and I'll request a replacement for you from Commander Carter.' She hurried off.

I cradled the book in one arm and flicked through some of the tissue-thin pages. The print was tiny and dense, and the glossary extensive. My stomach lurched. Oh my! What had I got myself into? I pushed that moment of doubt aside. This was what I wanted. A chance to contribute to something important in this war. If it meant I had to work my fingers to the bone, then that's what I would do.

21

That evening, back at our billet in Swanage, I retreated with my book to the attic where I shared a room with Kitty and Carole. The house was part of a large Victorian terrace and the attic was relatively spacious. The ceilings sloped but, as long as we were careful, the banging of heads could be avoided. There was room for three single bedsteads as well as trunks for us to store our kit, and a washstand with a jug and bowl for stand-up strip washes every morning. The only facility we had to queue for was the shared toilet on the floor below and the bathroom once a week on Sundays. Our landlady, Mrs Haines, was kind enough to allow us to use the kitchen to make cocoa, and the parlour to listen to the wireless.

I sighed as I repeated the spelling of one particularly long word over and over in my head, a small part of me longing to be with all the others downstairs. Some music would definitely cheer me up and might stop the confusing thoughts about Daniel that were playing tag inside my head.

How had he come to be at Renscombe? I didn't believe in coincidences. I'd written to him but he hadn't written back. Then all of a sudden, he was here, with no warning. It was unsettling. Why hadn't he come to say hello? I had thought, at the very least, we were friends.

A clatter of footsteps sounded on the stairs as if a whole herd of wild ponies had broken in and were busy cantering up to see me. Moments later the door burst open and Kitty dashed in with Carole hard on her heels.

'You'll never guess what's happened,' said Kitty, skidding to a halt on her knees beside my bed.

I raised an eyebrow. Why was she in such a tizz? 'I expect that they've finally announced that Mr Churchill is our new prime minister,' I said. It wasn't a wild stab in the dark. There had been rumblings for weeks ever since the public had lost confidence in Prime Minister Chamberlain.

Kitty shook her head. 'No. I mean yes, he *is* our new prime minister. But—'

'Germany has invaded France,' said Carole, her customary blunt delivery riding roughshod over Kitty's rambling.

'What?' My textbook fell to the floor with a bruising thump.

'It's true,' said Kitty, wringing her hands together, as if trying to wash them clean. 'But not just France, the Netherlands, Belgium and Luxembourg, too.'

Suddenly, there wasn't enough air. 'That's awful,' I whispered.

'We're next,' said Kitty, her voice barely above a whisper.

I swung my legs off the bed and crouched next to her, giving her shoulders an encouraging squeeze. 'France has one of the best armies in the world. Way better than Germany. It'll be fine. They'll stop them.'

'They might not,' said Carole. 'Luxembourg already surrendered.'

Kitty whimpered.

'Luxembourg isn't France.' I frowned at Carole and mimed for her to hush. I despaired of her sometimes. It was hard to dislike her, because she had a solid can-do attitude and wasn't afraid of hard work; nevertheless, she struggled to appreciate when others needed a little compassion. Could she not see that Kitty was terrified? Concern for my friend forced me to keep my own mounting anxiety in check, for fear that we would both spiral.

Carole blinked, genuinely confused. 'I'm just saying what happened. Kitty's right. If France falls, Hitler will be forcing his way over here next.'

'That's not going to happen,' I said, even though she was right. As unthinkable as it was, invading troops might arrive on our doorstep and force their way in.

'They could march in and take over,' whispered Kitty. 'Just like they did in Poland, last year.'

I gave her another squeeze. 'Prime Minister Churchill won't let that happen.' I got to my feet, my work forgotten. I needed to get outside in the fresh air. 'Grab your coat, Kitty. We're going for a walk.'

Kitty dashed a hand across her face and sniffed. 'Where?'

If I didn't get her away from Carole's doom and gloom, she'd never sleep. 'I want to show you something that might help put your mind at rest. Come on.'

'Rather you than me.' Carole shuddered and threw herself across her bed. 'It's late. It'll be dark soon.'

'It's only just gone eight,' I said. 'We have time.' Mrs Haines always locked the door at nine o'clock sharp.

Rosie and Jane were sitting on the stairs outside. They'd clearly been listening to our conversation. They both leapt to their feet.

Rosie crossed her arms over her chest as if hugging herself. 'Can we come?' The stiff set of her shoulders, and the way Jane was chewing her thumbnail, told me they were both scared too.

'Sure,' I said. 'The more the merrier. Remember to bring your papers in case we get stopped by a patrol.'

* * *

Outside, dusk crept over the town, reducing all colour to shades of grey. In the distance, a quarter moon rode high, ready to take charge of the sky once all daylight had faded. Walking through the empty streets of Swanage in the eerie silvery-grey half-light helped rid my legs of the jittery sensation that had flooded them the instant I had heard the news about France.

Kitty tucked a hand through the crook of my elbow. We paced in time with each other, brisk and rhythmic. I felt the tension in her grip gradually ease as the minutes passed.

'What was it you wanted to show me?' she asked.

'We're nearly there,' I replied.

Rosie called out from a few steps behind us. 'We're getting close to the beach, Fliss. We're not supposed to be here.'

Keen to see the sea, I'd come exploring shortly after we'd arrived in Swanage and been surprised to find the beach out of bounds. 'Don't worry,' I said. 'There's a side road along here, just before the blockade. If we take that one, we won't bother the guards. There's a good view of the beach from the top.'

'Is that what we're here to see?' said Kitty. 'The beach?'

'You and your obsession with the sea,' teased Jane as we reached the side road and turned off to the left.

I laughed. 'I'd never seen anything like it before I came here. We've got the

River Severn in Bristol, which is huge, but it's an estuary with smelly mud flats at low tide. It's nothing like a proper beach and the open ocean.' The sense of space and endlessness that came from seeing water all the way to the horizon was captivating. And now, it seemed all the more important. That water was an essential buffer between us and the rest of Europe, as vital as a firebreak carved through a forest to stop the spread of hungry flames.

We took the turning and walked up a rise until we reached the spot I had in mind. A series of semi-detached houses lined the left-hand side of the road, but on the right, there was merely a stone wall, which came up to about waist height. 'Here we are,' I said. I stopped and leaned against the wall, gesturing for my friends to look.

'Oh! Goodness,' said Kitty. 'You can see the whole of Swanage from here.'

'Not quite all.' I laughed.

The view was spectacular, even though it was one comprised of silver high-lights and deepening shadows. Swanage bay lay before us: a majestic curve of water hugged on both sides by protective cliffs.

'That's what I wanted you to see, Kitty,' I said, pointing at the beach. 'Look at all the defences they've built to stop an invasion.'

She stared down, nibbling her thumbnail.

'If France falls,' I continued, 'and, of course, I pray that it doesn't – but *if* it does, we have the whole of the English Channel between them and us. If the enemy try to cross it, we're going to fight them. Look at all the anti-invasion measures down there: concrete blocks, miles of razor wire, a wall of spiked metalwork, not to mention what's under the sand.'

Kitty's eyes flew to my face. 'You mean...?'

'Mines,' said Jane, her tone grave. 'That's why we're not allowed near the beach.'

'*And* in case we are spies,' added Rosie.

'Do you see up there?' I said, not wanting to dwell on the mines or the prospect of spies. I pointed to the headland on our right. 'That's Peveril Point. One of the security guards at Renscombe told me they're building a massive gun battery up there. Soon, they'll be able to shoot at enemy ships and planes all the way across this bay from up there. It'll cover the other side too. Durlston Bay and beyond.'

'I heard there are gun batteries going up all along the coast,' said Rosie.

'There are,' I said. 'As well as more radio telecommunications sites like ours, to combat aerial attacks too. And that's my point, Kitty. Prime Minister Churchill means business. We're going to fight. This is our country and no one is going to take it from us. Do you see that?'

She drew in a long shaky breath and nodded. 'I just wish there was something more I could do.'

'We're already doing our bit,' I said.

'I know, but I spent the best part of today peeling potatoes.' She spat the last word out as if it was sour. Such negativity was so unlike her. 'And then I had to go around all the science huts and empty wastepaper baskets.'

'I know what you mean,' agreed Rosie. 'It needs to be done, but it's boring. The WAAF are doing all the glamorous jobs, and we're either stuck in the kitchen, or doing battle with cobwebs and unblocking lavs.'

'No offence, Fliss,' said Jane with a sheepish shrug, 'even though you've taught us how to type and do shorthand and all that, it feels as if we're never going to actually get to do it. I'm beginning to think that we're wasting our time, bashing away on that old machine at Mrs Haines' in the evenings. The ribbon is so old now, half the letters don't show. It's soul destroying.'

I hadn't realised that they were feeling so frustrated. It wasn't just me chafing at the monotony of it all. Prepping veg for the cooks, serving meals, clearing tables, washing up, then prepping more veg for the cooks and then cleaning everywhere and everything. An ever-repeating cycle. 'I'm sorry,' I said, wishing I could wave a magic wand and fix everything for them.

'At least *you've* got a chance, Fliss,' said Kitty, a wistful edge to her words. 'If you knock that professor's socks off tomorrow, you'll be doing more, and who knows, maybe it'll be us next.'

I straightened up, as a thought came to me. 'If I'm inside the huts, maybe I'll hear of new opportunities for you. At the very least, I'll have legitimate access to a typewriter with a working ribbon. How about I save some work for you to type up for real. Something that's not confidential. You could take turns while we're supposed to be cleaning in the evenings after the scientists have all left.'

The other three pushed away from the wall. Their faces were in shadow, making it impossible to read their expressions.

I rushed on. 'I know it's not the same as having your own secretarial position, but it would give you some experience. Your shorthand is really good. And I've shown you everything I know about typing and filing. You just need to gain some confidence, and the only way to do that is to do some real pieces of work.

You're as good as any of the WAAF girls. And in the meantime, we wait for another opportunity to come up.'

'And then what?' asked Jane.

'We'll do whatever we have to, to get you a chance,' I said. 'I promise.'

Kitty threw her arms around me. 'Thank you, Fliss. That would be amazing.' She danced me around in a happy little circle 'This is going to work. I just know it is.'

'Hey,' shouted a deep voice from further along the road. 'What's going on over there?' Hurried footsteps beat against the pavement.

I freed myself from Kitty's embrace. 'Quick, this way,' I hissed and scampered across the road to an alleyway. We shrank back into the shadows, pressing ourselves against a wall out of sight. The last thing we needed was to be reported for causing a disturbance. Beaky would lose all patience with us.

The rhythmic sound got louder and two soldiers came into view, their upper bodies silhouetted against the sky behind the wall. I held my breath and prayed the others wouldn't make a sound either. The smallest cough or a sneeze would give us away. Then we'd be escorted back to our billet in disgrace. The soldiers scouted the area but didn't see the alleyway. After a few minutes, they ran on.

I waited until the sound of their boots hitting the pavement died away before creeping back towards the road to make sure they were definitely gone. 'Come on.' I beckoned the others forward. 'We really should be getting back.'

We walked briskly back to Mrs Haines, arriving just as she was about to lock the door, and hurried inside and up to our beds. It was good to see that smiles had replaced the worry on my friends' faces. The idea of doing something extra to help win the war meant so much to them. I only hoped that I could deliver on my promise.

22

The next morning, we arrived back on site early, ready to set up the mess hall for the first breakfast sitting. Instead of pitching in to help, I sat at a table in the corner and carried on studying. Kitty brought me a bowl of saltwater porridge and a cup of tea as soon as they were ready to serve. 'Good luck, today,' she whispered before bustling off as the first boffins trickled in and formed a queue at the serving table.

I concentrated on eating, reading and jotting down particularly difficult spellings on a scrap of paper and ignored frayed nerves that tumbled over each other in my belly. There was a lot riding on this. I couldn't bear the thought of letting everyone down.

Just as I was testing myself on a particularly difficult term, that strange magnetic pull crept up my spine and over the top of my head. I looked up, straight into the eyes of Daniel Evans as he walked towards my table.

I forced a polite smile to lips that felt like rubber.

He pushed the sides of his white coat back and shoved his hands deep into his pockets. 'How are you?'

I wanted to say: *What are you doing here? Why didn't you write back to me? And why on earth didn't you check up on me after that intruder knocked me for six?* None of which were acceptable responses. Polite pleasantries would have to suffice. 'I'm well, thank you. And you?'

'Yes, thank you.' He nodded. 'What do you know about radar?'

Radar wasn't one of the million terms I'd learned in the last twenty-four hours and it hadn't been mentioned in any of the books I'd read. If he was trying to make me feel dense, I was damned if I was going to let him. I tucked a non-existent strand of hair behind my ear. 'I've never heard of it. Why do you ask?'

'It's how the Americans refer to the research we're doing here. It's an acronym for radio detection and ranging. RADAR. The term is catching on in scientific circles to replace radio detection finding. The professor is horrified.'

'I can imagine!' I kept my tone cool. I was more interested in why he hadn't told me he was at Renscombe.

A deep line appeared between his eyebrows. He dragged the chair on the opposite side of the table out and sat down, plucking my pencil from my hand.

'Hey,' I said.

He waved an irritated hand. 'All hell will break loose here after last night's news. If France falls, our work becomes even more essential for national security. We'll need as many people on board as possible. That includes the secretaries. Especially if they are as bright as you are.' That comment threw me and delight bloomed in my middle. All my questions about why he was there scattered. Before I could round them back up, he charged on. 'If you understand the science in principle you'll find everything makes more sense. Do you want my help, or not?'

I gave a cautious nod.

'Good. Pass me that piece of paper.'

I slid the sheet towards him. He flipped it over to the unused side and started drawing. 'Radio detect... I mean, *radar*, uses radio waves to establish where something is. You need both a transmitter and a receiver.'

'Yes, I understand the basics,' I said. 'The transmitter sends the radio wave out. It travels to the object you're looking for and bounces back to the receiver, and the time it takes to do that tells you how far away the object is.'

He stared at me for a beat, before abandoning his drawing. 'Exactly. Using that data we can calculate not only where the object is, but also if it's moving, and if it *is* moving, how fast it's travelling and in what direction.'

'I know. The speed of the radio wave is the same as the speed of light, and the time it takes to travel back gives you the distance. Combining that with the angle of the echo from the receiver gives you your target's location,' I said.

He handed me back my pencil with a wry smile. 'You clearly understand more than I gave you credit for. Forgive me for underestimating you.'

I brushed his apology aside with a small shrug. 'What I want to know is what happens to that information afterwards? How does it get used?'

'Staff in the observation hut at the base of the tower send the data to Fighter Command.'

'And what do they do with it?'

'Feed it into the integrated air defence system.' He laughed and held up a hand. 'And please don't ask me about that. I just know the data is reported to them by telephone and they do the rest. Planes get sent up and they do their thing.' He gave a wistful sigh.

'Do you still wish you could go and fight?' I asked.

'Always.'

'I'm sorry,' I said. 'Can I assume that the department you went to in Southampton found another way for you to help the war effort and that's how you ended up here?'

He shrugged. 'Something like that.'

'Which of the projects are you working on?'

He started to answer and then stopped. 'What sort of security clearance do you have?'

'I signed the same confidentiality papers as all the other housekeeping staff, which is pretty extensive,' I said, tugging my pass from my pocket to show him. 'We have full access to all the offices and laboratories to clean. Plus, we burn your rubbish at the end of the day. You scientists are a messy bunch.'

He took it and turned it over, barely glancing at it before handing it back. 'You're right,' he said. 'Scientists are another breed entirely, obsessed with their work to the point that they don't register what's going on around them. A little thing like mess simply doesn't matter.' He smiled, a quick flash of brilliance that was gone almost as quickly as it arrived, leaving me with a strange urge to make him smile again.

'Do you include yourself in that description?' I asked.

Another brief, wry smile dashed across his face. If I'd not been watching, I would have missed it entirely. I was surprised to feel glad that I hadn't and reminded myself sternly that I wasn't sure that I liked him any more.

'I do. Although I'm not a proper scientist,' he said. 'I'm merely a school-teacher with an interest in physics. My colleagues are all researchers from top universities, and they don't hesitate to remind me of that whenever they get the chance.'

Whether I liked him or not, the idea of people putting him down annoyed me. 'That doesn't make them better than you.'

He leaned fractionally closer. 'It doesn't make them better than *you*, either.'

A warm glow spread through me at the intense look in his eyes. I scrambled for something to say to distract myself before I could do something ridiculous like blush. 'Your pompous windbag of a professor wouldn't agree.'

'No.' He laughed. 'He wouldn't. Mind you, pompous windbag or not, he is a brilliant man and on the brink of saving thousands of British lives. Given that, perhaps we can forgive him a little pompous wind-bagged-ness.'

'Pompous wind-bagged-ness.' A giggle escaped before I could stop it. 'Is that a technical term?'

'It is.' A slow grin lit him up from inside as if someone had turned the wick up in an oil lamp to maximum.

Mesmerised, I tore my gaze away, aware of a not unpleasant squirmy sensation in my stomach. 'It's a bit of a coincidence, don't you think? Us both ending up here.' There! I'd said it.

'They offered me the choice of several posts.' He drew a line on the table with one finger, refusing to meet my gaze. 'Renscombe was the only place I'd heard of before. You mentioned it in your letter. And...'

So, he *had* received my letter. And yet, he hadn't replied. I leaned a fraction closer. 'And?'

He shook his head. 'It's nothing, really, but I've followed the professor's work for a while in scientific journals. When I heard he was here, the opportunity to work with him was irresistible.'

'Oh.' I sat back, annoyed with myself for feeling disappointed. What had I expected him to say? That he'd missed me and desperately wanted to see me again? That he was keen to work on the professor's project made more sense. 'It was you, wasn't it?' I said. 'The night of the break-in. Afterwards, I mean. I heard your voice.'

'I was there, yes. I chased whoever it was away.' He dipped his head. 'I didn't catch them.'

'Why didn't you come and see me afterwards?'

He shrugged. 'I've been busy.'

A horrifying thought struck me. Perhaps he'd stayed away because I was part of the housekeeping team and he didn't want to be associated with me. He'd only revealed his presence here to me *after* the professor had demanded that I work for him. If that hadn't happened, would he have continued to avoid me? 'You've been here for a while, and yet you're only talking to me now. Did you not want to associate with me because I'm the cleaner?'

His eyebrows jerked up in surprise. 'Don't be silly. I arrived a day or so before the intruder struck. When I heard the commotion, I stepped in and gave chase. Unfortunately, I failed to catch him and by the time I got back, you'd left Renscombe for the night. The next day, I was sent off site, for a couple of weeks. There was no time to wait and see you, so I picked a bunch of flowers and left them at the canteen for you and—'

'The flowers,' I exclaimed. 'They were from you.'

'Yes.' He seemed taken aback at the vehemence of my reaction. 'Didn't you get my note?'

'No. I had no idea who had sent them. They were lovely. Thank you.'

Something passed between us that I didn't understand. A moment of connection that set my pulse racing. I dragged my eyes away and checked my watch. 'Heavens, I have to go. I need to get to Beaky... Staff Sergeant Beaconsfield's office before I go to the professor.'

'And I need some breakfast,' he said, getting to his feet. 'Good luck this morning.' He ambled over to the serving counter, nodding hello to a few scientists on his way.

I scooped up my things, chewing on the inside of my lip, deep in thought.

Carole came to collect my plate. 'Hark at you, hobnobbing with the boffins already.'

'Give over,' I said. 'We were only talking.'

'Give over, yourself. I wasn't the one staring into his eyes with my tongue hanging out.' She wiggled her eyebrows at me. 'Not that I blame you. He might not be a looker, but I wouldn't kick him out of bed in a hurry.'

'Carole!'

She laughed and sauntered off to clear the next table.

I dashed from the room, wishing I didn't feel so confused. I'd been wary before, after Jake's behaviour, and had wanted to avoid all men. Then things had changed and I'd been secretly hoping Daniel had come to Renscombe because of me. That smile of his made me go weak at the knees and... I shook my head. Enough! Daniel had come to Renscombe because of the professor *not* me. Then I remembered the flowers. No one had ever picked me flowers before. It was… nice.

I shook off the peculiar sense of longing that crept through me. I couldn't let the situation with Daniel distract me. There was work to do. I had to prove that I was good enough to become the professor's secretary so that I could help my friends. Opportunities like this didn't come around very often and I wasn't going to let this one pass me by.

23

I arrived outside the professor's room on the dot of nine and straightened my uniform before knocking. The door flew open, making me jump.

'You're late.' He gestured to Lisa's... no, *my* desk. 'Sit. We have a lot of ground to cover. Write this down and we'll see how you get on.'

My backside had barely touched the chair when he started talking. I wrenched open my notebook and started scribbling. He paced up and down the centre of the room, deep in thought. The words kept coming, allowing me no time for thought, or to worry about whether I was getting it right. I filled page after page with shorthand until my fingers began to cramp. Tears gathered behind my eyes as my notes got larger and sloppier in my haste to keep up.

Suddenly, footsteps echoed in the corridor outside and the door burst open, admitting one of the men from the group in here yesterday. Blonde and of medium height, his white coat hung off a slim, wiry frame. His breath was coming in huge gasps as if he had been running.

'What are you doing here, Havers?' barked the professor.

'Professor, excuse the interruption,' Havers said, between puffs. 'We need you in lab three. Jones has had a breakthrough.'

The professor stopped dictating mid-sentence and started for the door, calling back to me, 'Get that typed up, immediately. I want to see it when I get back.' Before I knew it, the door slammed shut and I was alone.

I flipped back through my pages of scrawl, my heart sinking. It would take ages to transcribe and I had no idea how long he was going to be. I could feel panic clawing its way up inside me. I hadn't expected it to be this hard.

The door opened, making me jump.

Daniel stuck his head in. 'How is it going?'

I shook my head, unable to think.

He glanced behind him as if checking he corridor was clear, then came right into the room and closed the door behind him. 'What's wrong?' The concern in his voice sounded genuine.

I shook my head. 'He... I...' I pushed my notebook towards him. 'He talks so fast. Look at it all. And then he disappeared saying he wants to see it all typed up when he gets back.'

'Can't you do it?'

'Of course I can do it,' I said. 'But it'll take ages. What if he comes back and it's not done?'

Daniel pulled a face. 'Then, it's not done. You can only work as fast as you can work.'

'That's easy for you to say,' I said, wishing I could have an ounce of his inner calm.

'Where did he go?' he asked.

'Someone came in saying that Jones had had a breakthrough. And he left.'

Daniel's eyes bugged. 'Jones? Are you sure?'

I nodded.

He spun on his heel and started for the door. 'I have to go. But, don't worry,' he called back. 'If Jones really has had a breakthrough, the prof will be hours. You'll have plenty of time.'

Alone once more, I rubbed at my palm to ease the cramping and pulled off the typewriter cover to reveal the black, shiny machine beneath. There had been no time to examine it the day before. An older model, it had seen better days. However, apart from needing a new ribbon, it was in reasonable condition. I tugged open the drawer, pulled out a spare ribbon, and set about installing it before I fed in some paper and started to type. My nerves settled and I fell into a steady, productive rhythm. After an hour, I took a short break to visit the necessary and came back via the mess hall, where I persuaded Kitty to pour me a mug of tea and wrap some honey biscuits up in brown paper. Back at my desk, I carried on typing. Occasionally, footsteps or voices in the corridor outside interrupted my flow, making me tense in case they heralded the professor's return. Whenever that happened, I repeated Daniel's words to myself. 'You can only work as fast as you can work.'

Eventually, I ran out of scribbles to transcribe. I pulled the last sheet of paper from the typewriter and placed it on the pile next to me and slipped the whole thing into an empty cardboard file I had found in the bottom drawer of the desk. Stretching, I got to my feet and walked over to the window to peer out.

The door crashed back against the wall, making me spin around in shock. The blonde scientist from earlier, Havers, called out, 'The professor wants you. Come. Bring your work.'

While his peremptory tone riled me, I dashed past the desk and grabbed the typed document as well as my pencil and a fresh notebook. At the last second, I scooped up the brown parcel of biscuits and tucked them in my pocket before following the man from the room. We ran across to the next building and along the corridor to the farthest room where the professor was once again at a blackboard, surrounded by acolytes.

He glanced up and held out an imperious hand as I approached. 'Let me see what you've done.'

I passed over the file and the pack of biscuits at the same time.

'What's this?' he demanded, staring at the wrapped parcel, great furrows marring his forehead.

'I thought you might be hungry.' I held my breath as he opened it.

'Hmm, good thinking.' He stuffed a whole biscuit in his mouth and chewed thoughtfully whilst scanning the papers.

He swallowed and pointed to a stool. 'Sit there. When I point at you, take down what I am saying. When I'm not pointing at you, don't. Understand?'

I nodded.

'Right, Jones.' He turned to a stocky, harassed-looking man near the board. 'Are you saying that...' He paused and pointed at me before continuing to speak.

I fumbled for my pencil and started taking shorthand, keeping a close eye on the professor's finger for my cues.

Over the course of the next two hours, the professor worked his way through all the biscuits and I filled another notebook.

24

That evening, the entire research team left at the usual time, leaving me alone in the building, engrossed in the notes I was transcribing. From what I could make out, Jones' breakthrough was a small but critical step forward in the development of a radar system that might work overland, rather than out over the ocean like the Chain Home early warning system did. Once I had finished, I filed the whole document ready for the professor to check in the morning and then spent the time glancing through the work I had kept back for my friends to do when they arrived.

The stillness of the building settled around me. I rubbed my hands to ease my cramped fingers and enjoyed the silence. A creak sounded behind me. My breath caught in my throat and I glanced over my shoulder to see the door ease open and a figure slip in. Havers crept towards the professor's desk and rummaged in the dustbin.

Something must have given my presence away, because he froze and then straightened, a crumpled piece of paper in his hands. 'I thought the room was empty,' he said.

'Evidently.' I kept my tone measured. 'What are you looking for?'

He coughed and swiped a hand over the top of his head. 'I... uh. The professor binned some of my research earlier. He said it was flawed. I think I know where I went wrong: it's the calculations and I thought I could... uh, correct them.'

There was a soft knock on the door. Kitty poked her head into the room.

Havers dropped the paper back into the bin. 'Forget it,' he said, dusting his hands together. 'I'll start again from scratch.' Before I could say anything, he barged through the door, almost sending Kitty flying.

'Don't mind me. I'm just standing here, minding my own business,' she called after him. 'Honestly, some people have no manners.'

Havers might simply be socially inept. Alternatively, he could be embarrassed that he'd been caught doing something nefarious. It was almost impossible to tell. Even so, he was of average height and of slight build, so I couldn't help but feel curious. I hurried over to the bin, trying to work out which piece of paper he had been interested in. It could have been any one of them, or all of them.

Kitty shuffled over. 'Is something wrong?'

'I don't know. Probably not.' There was something distinctly odd about Havers' behaviour. I'd have to keep an eye on him and I'd make sure the professor's bins were empty whenever I left the room unattended, from now on. No one was going to take anything on my watch.

Another knock sounded at the door. Rosie and Jane spilled in, bringing an assortment of brooms, dusters, mops and buckets.

'How did you get on today?' asked Jane.

'Good, I think,' I said. 'I haven't been given the boot, yet, anyway.'

'Here.' Rosie handed me a covered plate. 'I didn't see you at lunchtime. I thought you might be hungry. It's a ham fritter, some bread, and a slice of cheese.'

My stomach gave a grateful rumble, making us all laugh. I took a bite and gestured for Kitty to sit at my desk. 'Let's make the most of the time we have. Why don't you see if you can translate my shorthand for the next couple of pages and then you can swap with Rosie.'

Kitty ran a calculating eye over the page of my notebook and then set about loading a piece of paper into the typewriter. 'It looks simple enough.'

I gave her shoulder a reassuring squeeze. 'It is, I promise. Go on. I know you can do it.'

Kitty began to type, hesitantly at first, but within a few minutes her pace increased and a smile spread across her face as she settled into a steady, confident rhythm. Keys clacked and the intermittent ding and rattle of the returning cartridge filled the room.

'You clean in here, Fliss, so you're on hand if Kitty needs you,' said Rosie. 'Jane and I will give the next hut over a bit of spit and polish.'

Jane checked her watch. 'We'll come back at half past the hour and swap over. I can't wait for my turn.'

Their excited chatter as they disappeared through the doorway together was all the reward I needed, and I set about wiping down surfaces and then sweeping the floor with a spring in my step.

* * *

Twenty minutes later, the door swung open and Daniel reversed into the room, his arms full of papers. 'I heard you typing, Fliss. The prof asked if you could—' He looked up and spotted Kitty. 'Oh... you're not... uh.'

Kitty went bright red and glanced over at me.

'Daniel,' I said. 'How can I help?'

His eyes bounced from me to Kitty and back again. 'What's going on?'

The quizzical look on his face would have been comical if I weren't concerned that he might report us. There was little point making up an elaborate cover story. 'This is Kitty. She's practising her typing.'

'Hello, Kitty,' he said, giving her a smile, and then he looked at the broom in my hand. 'And you're cleaning?'

I shrugged. 'I've finished the professor's report. I thought I might as well make myself useful before the bus leaves for Swanage, and well... anyway.' I clamped my teeth down on the inside of my cheek, aware that I was starting to witter.

'Good for you. Don't let me stop you.' He placed a hand on top of the papers he had brought. 'I should have brought these over earlier. The prof asked if you could sort them out for him tomorrow morning? They need filing in date order.'

I put the broom down. 'I'll get onto it first thing. Thank you.' Silence hung between us. 'Was there anything else?'

He backed away. 'No. That's all. I... um, I'd better go. Goodnight.'

'Night,' I said.

'Happy typing, Kitty,' he called over his shoulder as he left.

'He's nice,' she whispered the minute the door closed.

'Hmm,' I said. 'Maybe.'

'Hark at you with your maybes.' She giggled. 'He couldn't take his eyes off you. I reckon he's smitten.'

'Don't be silly.' I frowned to cover the ridiculous skip of joy I felt inside. 'Come on. Let's keep working. Jane and Rosie will be here any minute.'

* * *

Over the next few weeks, we worked extra hard to keep up with cleaning all the rooms allocated to us in the time allowed, whilst also carrying out secret secretarial practice sessions. Every evening back at Swanage, we collapsed in a heap in the parlour, exhausted, and Carole – having made it clear that she thought we were all daft for risking Beaky's wrath – would bring us cocoa to drink. That was the time when we compared notes about unusual occurrences during the day. However, they were mere fragments, impressions here and there, nothing concrete that could be added together into anything that remotely resembled coherent evidence to track down the intruder.

'Hark at us lot, being all clandestine and watching everyone,' said Carole, one evening.

Kitty shrugged. 'It does no harm, to keep an eye out. Although, now I am watching, it's amazing how dubious people look in general, isn't it? That Havers fella always looks like he's doing something he shouldn't be.'

'You can't condemn someone because of the way they look,' said Jane. 'Mind you, I do find Holloway a bit shifty, and he's always throwing his weight around.'

I'd not forgotten the way he'd treated me the day I'd helped unpack equipment in hut 4. 'I don't like him. But that doesn't make him a traitor.'

'He's probably just insecure,' said Kitty. 'The more I think about it, the more I believe that the intruder was an outsider.'

'Clandestine,' murmured Rosie. 'I like that word.' She gave a soft laugh. 'If we called ourselves the Clandestine Auxiliary Territorial Service, that would make us the CATS.'

'Meow,' giggled Kitty. 'I love it.'

'Come on,' said Carole, rolling her eyes in disgust. She crossed the room to turn on the wireless. 'Let's listen to the evening broadcast.'

Unfortunately, the news wasn't good. Both France and the Netherlands were struggling against the invading Nazi forces. Hearing about the suffering of two of our neighbouring nations made it more important than ever that we did what we could to help the war effort, whether it was cleaning, typing or anything else thrown in our path. Whatever sacrifice it took to win the war had to be worth it, and no matter how tired or scared we became, we had to stay strong and keep going.

25

News reached me that poor Lisa's injury was far more serious than initially thought, which meant that she wasn't going to be able to return to Renscombe for a long time. I felt dreadfully sorry for her yet, at the same time, I was grateful for the chance to continue to work with the professor and his team. It wasn't just the work that appealed. Being in hut 4 afforded me snatched glimpses of Daniel. Being near him made me feel all light and bubbly inside, and I couldn't help wondering if Kitty was right. Might he like me, too?

The more I saw of him, the more I was convinced that he was totally different from Jake. He never once stood too close, or made me feel unsafe. He was kind and thoughtful, and whilst most of the time he was very serious, signs of a lively sense of humour occasionally surfaced, making me struggle not to laugh out loud.

Kitty, Jane and Rosie joined me every evening to alternate typing and cleaning. We got away with it for several weeks until, one evening, Beaky arrived to check up on us.

'What on earth is going on?' she demanded, startling me. I knocked the bucket at my feet and a tidal wave of soapy water slopped over both of our shoes.

I scrabbled for a couple of towels, handed her one and threw the other over the spreading puddle, ignoring the sensation of cold water as it trickled through my own brogues, my wet socks making every footstep squeak.

Beaky squelched over to a chair and sat to swipe at her feet. 'So, help me, Makepeace. I don't know what mischief you are up to, but if you—'

Kitty stood to attention beside my desk. 'She's taught me to type, ma'am. And I'm really good at it. Look.' She tore the sheet of paper she had been working on from the typewriter and held it out.

Beaky stalked over, snatched the page and examined it.

Drawn by the commotion, Jane and Rosie arrived at a run, both screeching to a halt when they saw who it was.

'Have you two learned to type, as well?' demanded Beaky.

'Yes, Staff Sergeant,' said Rosie, puffing out her chest. 'We are proficient in typing, shorthand, filing and answering the telephone, among other standard secretarial skills.'

'Our work hasn't suffered,' said Jane. 'We just want the chance to do more.'

I held my tongue. There was little else to add.

Beaky skewered me with a direct stare. 'Are they any good?'

I straightened, abandoning the puddle. 'Yes, ma'am. They are excellent secretaries. They just need an opportunity.'

She pursed her lips. 'It's very unorthodox.'

'Yes, ma'am,' I said. 'But these are strange times, and it seemed sensible to expand our skill set.'

'You should have come to me,' she said. 'If you want something like this, it should be dealt with through official channels.'

It hadn't occurred to me that she would support the endeavour. 'Yes, ma'am. Sorry, ma'am.'

'As it turns out,' she continued, 'I have recently heard a rumour that more typists are needed on site due to an increase in research workloads.'

An excited gasp escaped Kitty.

'No!' Beaky held up a hand. 'That does *not* mean that I'm pleased with the way you've gone about this. And I will definitely be informing Commander Carter, but...' She paused to make sure she had our full attention. 'I'll tell her that I wholeheartedly support your desire to better yourselves. While your approach is unconventional, your aim is in line with the spirit of our orders. We were told to do what needs to be done. And if this is what's needed, then so be it.'

I ducked my head to hide a grin. No doubt, Sergeant Thomas was supposed to be sourcing the new secretarial staff and Beaky relished the thought of getting a jump on her by producing typists of her own.

Beaky slapped the page in her hand. 'I suggest you all finish up here and get back to your billet. I'll see what Commander Carter thinks about getting you assigned to the secretarial pool.'

Jane, Kitty, Rosie and I stared at each other in turn, our eyes wide.

'Thank you, ma'am,' I said. My words were echoed by the others.

'Don't thank me yet,' she said. 'I'll have to request more girls from Foxhalt to replace these three in the housekeeping department. What with the planned expansion here and recent developments, I can't allow that work to slip. We'll just have to wait and see what happens.'

She marched out, leaving a trail of soggy footprints in her wake. Minutes later, we heard the outer door slam. Kitty giggled first, which set the rest of us off. It felt good to laugh. There had been so much tension over the last few weeks.

'Did you see the look on her face?' said Rosie.

'She's not a bad old stick,' I said. 'And she'll get plenty of credit for this, if we work out well. She might even get a promotion.'

'We'd better make sure we're good enough then,' said Kitty.

'You're good enough, don't worry. Come on. Let's clear up here and go catch the bus.'

* * *

Later that evening, we heard an official broadcast announcing the surrender of the Netherlands and describing the steady progress of enemy troops across northern France. Afterwards, with mounting horror, we listened as a BBC radio host explained how British Expeditionary forces and allied French troops had become trapped against the English Channel at Dunkirk.

Kitty slipped a hand into mine. 'Dear heaven, Fliss. Those poor men.'

I squeezed her hand, unable to find a single word of comfort to offer.

Cocoa forgotten, we listened in silence to the deep, reassuring tones of Prime Minister Churchill as he addressed the nation.

When the broadcast was over, Carole let out a low whistle. 'Three hundred and fifty thousand men. All evacuated on small boats. How on earth did they do it?'

'Thirty thousand killed, wounded or missing,' whispered Rosie.

'This war is horrible,' said Kitty. 'What will stop an invasion now?'

I squeezed her hand. 'You heard what the prime minister said. We won't surrender. If we have to fight anywhere and everywhere, you know, on beaches like he said and... and in fields and... well, we'll do it. That's how we'll stop them. You'll see.'

I could tell from the way that she wouldn't meet my eyes that she didn't believe me.

I didn't blame her. I wasn't sure I believed myself.

26

The intense atmosphere on site over the next few days made it clear that everyone had heard the news. Hushed diligence settled over the huts. Work was everyone's sole focus. I typed and filed reports at top speed, from the minute I arrived at my desk to the minute the scientists left. My fingers throbbed, my neck ached and I felt as if my brain was on fire. Regardless, it was good to be doing something of value, as if every report I completed was a brick in a defensive wall that would keep the enemy out.

Working alongside the professor a few days later, I glanced up at the clock, my stomach rumbling. It must be nearly time for lunch, surely? My gaze caught on a silent figure standing in the doorway. Major Stapleton raised one eyebrow and gave a small jerk of her head. I nodded to let her know I understood, then rattled off the last few sentences of the report I was writing, pulled the completed paper from the machine and locked it in my drawer before excusing myself to join her outside.

'Take a walk with me,' she said, striding off in the direction of the clifftop path, both hands clasped behind her back.

I fell into step.

'You have important work to do, so I won't beat about the bush,' she said. 'I happened to be at Foxhalt, yesterday, when Staff Sergeant Beaconsfield's report came in about you teaching your fellow privates to type.' She frowned at the ground. 'You intrigue me, Makepeace. It is rare for junior members of the ATS to act on their own initiative, and I've learned that, when it does happen, it's worth taking a closer look. Resourcefulness is something I'm keen to encourage.'

'It wasn't just me,' I said, not wanting to take credit for my friends' achievements. 'Kitty, Rosie and Jane were being resourceful too. They're hard workers, very quick to learn new skills and keen to do more for the war effort.'

'Noted,' she said. 'I will cast an eye over their records, seeing as you recommend them so highly, and see if we can put them to use somewhere.' We had reached the clifftop path when she spoke again. 'However, aside from you giving unofficial secretarial classes, I was particularly interested to discover that you have managed to get yourself assigned to hut 4 as clerical support.'

'It happened by chance,' I said.

She stared out to sea, taking in a deep breath of fresh air before exhaling and continuing in a light tone; the sort one uses to discuss trivialities. 'What you said the last time we spoke, about being invisible and yet *also* seeing and hearing things caught my attention.'

I waited, not sure where this conversation was going.

'Now that you *are* established in hut 4, might you be willing to add to your role there?' she said. 'Unofficially, I mean.'

'Add to it, in what way?' I shot her a narrow glance from the corner of my eyes. 'And unofficially how?'

'I recently had a little chat with Prime Minister Churchill.' Disbelief must have shown on my face because she paused. 'Is there something you wish to say?'

I shifted from foot to foot, searching for the right words. 'I appreciate that you are important, but how do you come to have little chats with the prime minister?'

She laughed. 'Connections. My family know his family. And, even though he is busy governing the country, he was kind enough to spare some time for me.'

With her refined accent and genteel ways, she was undoubtedly in a different social class to me, but I hadn't realised quite how posh she was until that moment.

'Would you like to know what we talked about?' she asked.

I lifted a shoulder. 'If you would like to tell me.'

'You.'

'Me?' She had to be teasing me. But, why?

'In a roundabout way, yes.' She turned to survey the communication towers and the rest of the higgledy-piggledy buildings behind us. 'The prime minister is interested in a number of projects being developed for national security. He is particularly interested in the research taking place here at Renscombe. And your professor's project is at the top of the list. He wants it to be properly protected.'

'Security has been tightened,' I said. 'There are plans to extend it further.'

'Which is good,' she replied. 'But I'm proposing something a little more unobtrusive.'

That sounded interesting.

'You said before that you pick things up, that you don't mean to, but it happens. How would you feel about quietly keeping an eye on things in hut 4, and if you see anything of concern, reporting it directly to me?'

I glanced down at my feet, rocking slightly from side to side. 'I... uh... I'm not sure that... um.' The memory of Havers rummaging in the professor's bin jumped to the forefront of my mind. I had managed to convince myself that he was merely a bit odd, with no malicious intent, but what if I was wrong?

'Are you asking me to snoop on the research team?'

'No.' An emphatic shake of the head accompanied her words. 'I am asking you to be an additional layer of protection for them. Off the record so to speak.'

'Why?'

She tipped her head on one side. 'You said yourself, it is possible to be present and yet not be seen. And as a woman, especially one of junior rank fulfilling a mundane role, it is easy to be overlooked.' There was a trace of bitterness in her tone that made me wonder if she had ever experienced being treated with that sort of disregard. 'I understand how frustrating that can be. Yet, it also gives one the opportunity to spot things that others discount. Yes?'

I nodded, wondering if this was the time to confess that my friends and I had already been keeping an eye on things from the canteen. I decided against it. After all we'd not discovered anything, and I didn't want to get them into trouble for overstepping the mark.

'My suggestion is that this is something we should be using to our advantage,' she continued.

'Does the prime minister agree?'

'Not as yet,' she said. 'However, he is willing to be persuaded.'

'You don't think he is humouring you?'

'He might be.' She shrugged. 'But if I can get solid proof that a woman undercover can offer valuable insight, then he might change his mind. As it stands, your professor's work and that of his colleagues is of huge interest to more than just the British government.'

'You mean Hitler.' This was starting to sound dangerous and I knew instinctively that my decision not to draw my friends into this was the right one. Taking a risk for myself was one thing, dragging them in with me was quite another.

'Yes. The secrets of radio direction finding technology are—'

'Radar,' I said.

'Pardon?'

'It's called radar, now.'

'You see?' A smile of satisfaction hovered around her mouth. 'You are already proving useful. As I was saying, the secrets of *radar* are most valuable. Control over them could make all the difference between winning and losing this war. I wouldn't put it past the enemy to have undercover operatives in the area with plans to steal what we know. Like that intruder.'

White-hot rage poured through me. If any of Hitler's henchmen came near my scientists or their work, they'd have *me* to deal with. I'd stopped the last intruder and I'd damn well keep stopping them, no matter how many they sent. 'What do you want me to do?'

'Nothing more than you're already doing. Simply pay attention. Ninety-five per cent of the time, you will be exactly what you are. A secretary.'

'And the rest?'

'Consider yourself to be an undercover agent answerable to the prime minister via me. Watch for anything that seems out of place, listen for things that don't sound right. You will know it, when it happens.'

'And then?'

'Get word to me.'

'How?'

'For now, send a confidential message via your section leader asking me to pay a visit. And I'll come.'

'For now?'

She laughed. 'This is a radio communication base. I am sure we can work out a more sophisticated way to message each other. Leave it with me.'

I blurted out a question. 'Are there others?'

She blinked as if startled by the question. 'What do you mean?'

'Other invisible women, working for you?'

'Ah! Well,' she said. 'A few. But mark my words, there will be more. If things continue to go against us in this war, who knows what we will have to do to survive?' She checked her watch. 'I need to get back. Have a think about what I said.'

She left me on the clifftop, my churning mind an echo of the water surging against the rocks below. I dry-washed my hands over and over realising that up until now I'd been playing at undercover observation; a bit of low-key detective fun, which had the added advantage of distracting Kitty, Jane, Rosie and Carole from the oppressive boredom of our repetitive routines. What Major Stapleton was suggesting was something else entirely. This was a high-stakes game of life and death, not only for me, but also for the many hundreds of thousands of people fighting to protect our country.

I'd wanted change. An opportunity to play an active role in the war. But this was huge. Amid my mounting excitement, there was a small voice urging caution. What if I'd bitten off more than I could chew?

27

Over the next few days, I struggled to herd my thoughts back into any semblance of order. I'd grown fond of the professor in spite of his idiosyncrasies. With the major's words echoing in my ears, I began to watch the other scientists more closely, only this time, I wasn't going to report back to Kitty and the others.

I noticed that Havers wasn't the only one who made attempts to access the professor's office when he wasn't there. Jones tried twice, as did Robbins, a nervous, redheaded fellow, who kept clearing his throat, and who darted away like a frightened rabbit whenever he saw me. Were these approaches sinister, or merely the result of enthusiasm to advance their research and defy the enemy?

When challenged, all gave valid reasons for their presence: looking for a missing file, checking to see if there was any new data, dropping off a report. The scientists were quirky in many ways, and some were total oddballs, yet all seemed dedicated to saving lives. As for Daniel... well. He was calm and, for the most part, annoyingly unreadable. He confused me but I liked him. More than liked. The thought of spying on any of them – him in particular – didn't sit well. Rather than completely commit to the major's request, for the time being, I decided that I would simply wait and see what happened.

The evening broadcasts continued. Newscasters described the march of Hitler's troops into Paris and then, horror of horrors, the fall of France.

Britain was on its own.

The enemy was knocking at the door.

If we weren't careful, we could soon go the same way as the rest of Europe. Protecting the project was now more important than ever.

The immediate response to the fall of France, as I could see it, was yet another flurry of activity on site. More scientists arrived and I was borrowed by several different teams and bounced between projects, helping out wherever I was needed. While I was never in one place long enough to grasp the finer details of the experiments in the other huts, other than the fact that they all were refining different aspects of radar technology for multiple defensive purposes, I could see from the faces of those involved when satisfactory progress was made. As the various research programs intensified, so did tension in the country as a whole. Emergency updates were reported on the wireless nightly. The threat of invasion grew.

Enemy U-boats mined the English Channel under cover of darkness, including the entrance to Poole Harbour, a few miles along the coast from us. Aerial bombings took out strategic targets, flying at night to confound our defences. The naval base at Portland was hit; Bournemouth, and Christchurch harbour, too. Countless disturbed nights. Sirens going off at all hours, forcing us outside to huddle in the air-raid shelter at the bottom of Mrs Haines' garden. Each morning the sky was painted with telltale plumes of black smoke rising into the air, grim flags heralding impending doom. Morale was wearing thin.

One evening, Carole looked up from the jigsaw she was working on. 'Did you hear about the ship that struck that mine today?'

I grimaced. 'Yes. I saw it sink from the clifftop. The keel cracked almost entirely in two.' Painful to watch, but impossible to turn away from. A crowd of site staff had stayed out in the sharp onshore winds sending prayers, watching as the doomed attempt to tow the ship ashore unfolded. 'It was awful. Thank heaven they saved the crew.'

Kitty lifted her chin. 'I've decided I'm going to concentrate on the good things that happen even if there are bad things too. Otherwise it's all bad and, if it's all bad, then what's the point?'

'I agree,' I said, relieved to see her so positive.

'Good,' she continued. 'Because I heard there's going to be a dance at the church hall down the road this Sunday, and whether you like it or not, we are *all* going.'

'That sounds like fun,' said Rosie. 'It will give us a chance to chat properly with staff away from the canteen.'

'Aye, aye,' said Carole, a teasing grin twitching her lips. 'Got your eye on someone, have you?'

'No! Not like that. Although there is that tall red-haired dreamboat from the observation room.' Rosie's gaze went all misty and distant.

'Which one?' said Kitty, plopping down onto the cushion next to Rosie, ready to gossip.

Rosie wrinkled her nose. 'None of your beeswax. All I'm saying is that we didn't get clues from watching people in the canteen. We might get a bit further if we can talk to them properly, that's all.'

I set my cocoa mug down on a small table near my chair. 'You mean clues about the intruder.'

'Exactly,' she said, throwing me a grateful smile. 'Other than asking: "Do you want mashed potato with that?" there's not much opportunity for meaningful discussion.'

'I'm not sure we should,' I said.

'Why ever not?' demanded Kitty.

'We could be getting into something more dangerous than we realise.'

'You've changed your tune,' said Carole.

'I know.' I shrugged. 'I just don't want any of you getting hurt.'

'I take it you've noticed there's a war on, Fliss?' teased Jane. 'There's danger everywhere.'

'Which is why we should be careful,' I said. 'If they realise what we're doing, they could get nasty.'

'I wasn't suggesting we pounce on them, tie them up and interrogate them,' grumbled Rosie.

Carole snorted. 'I'm planning to bat my eyelashes at everyone, and if I happen to hear or see anything suspicious, so be it.'

Kitty laughed. 'Flirting for your country.'

'Exactly,' said Rosie, a twinkle in her eye. She leapt to her feet, her finger pointing forwards in a mock parody of the classic Lord Kitchener poster from the last war. 'Your country needs you,' she said in a booming voice, 'to dance with as many men as possible.'

Jane stood to attention with a crisp salute. 'Yes, sir! Right away, sir.'

Kitty dissolved into a fit of giggles.

'Lighten up, Fliss,' said Carole. 'We're just having some fun.'

I chewed the inside of my cheek and watched my friends' playful antics. They had become so important to me over the last few months, taking me under their collective wing after I had arrived at Foxhalt alone and scared. I realised I would do anything for them.

'Fine,' I said. 'Promise me you'll be careful.'

28

Intruder aside, the idea of getting dressed up and going out for some fun was very appealing. However, having left Bristol in a tearing hurry, with few personal belongings, I had a huge problem. I had nothing to wear to a dance. Unlike me, my fellow ATS recruits had not followed instructions to pack light when joining up and soon, glad rags were pulled from trunks and hair, makeup and accessories were discussed in detail.

'I can't wait,' said Kitty, as she stood in Mrs Haines' kitchen in her dressing gown. The skirt of a pretty red and white polka dot dress was stretched over the ironing board. She squeezed out a damp cloth and laid it over the fabric before using another cloth to protect her hand as she lifted one of two black irons from the range. She spat delicately on the underside and listened for the satisfying sizzle that indicated the iron was hot enough to use before she ran it over the waiting fabric. A gentle hiss filled the air as wrinkles from months stored in a trunk were steamed away. 'It's ages since I wore civvies. It's going to be so much fun. And I've even got a pair of nylons that aren't laddered.'

'You'll look beautiful,' I said, glad to see my friend's natural bounce coming back.

'What are you wearing?' she asked, switching the now cool iron for the second, hotter one, waiting on the range.

I laughed. 'I only have the clothes I arrived at Foxhalt in or my uniform.

Both are far too hot for dancing.' I shrugged. 'I'm not much of a dancer anyway. I'll probably just watch.'

'You can't not dance.' Kitty's voice cracked with outrage.

'It's fine,' I said. 'I don't mind.'

'*I* mind.' The iron clanged back onto the range and she made for the door. 'Come.' Her commanding tone brooked no refusal. Up in our room, she flipped open her trunk and rummaged through it. 'I bought this at a jumble sale before I left home. It's lovely, but it's too long for me. I thought I'd have time to alter it in the evenings.' She laughed. 'As if there was ever going to be time for *that* to happen. Anyway, I bet it would fit you.' She shook out a silky blue dress and held it against me. 'Yes. It's perfect. You can have it, if you like.'

'It's beautiful.' I ran a hand over the fabric. It was nothing like anything I'd ever worn before: light and soft, with a sweetheart neckline to the fitted bodice and a skirt that flared. I knew it would be heaven to dance in. I gazed at it wistfully then shook my head. 'Thank you, but I can't.'

'Yes, you can.'

'I can't pay you for it.'

She made a rude noise. 'I don't want you to pay me. If it makes you feel better, take it in exchange for all the typing lessons.'

I hesitated.

'Go on,' she said. 'Please. I'm never going to wear it and it'll just go to waste.'

I gave her a quick hug. 'I'll borrow it. Just this once. That would be lovely, thank you.'

'Good. Let's go and iron it.' She clomped merrily back down the stairs, chattering nineteen to the dozen. 'Do you think the scientists will be going? Oh, my goodness, I just had a thought.' She shot me a look of horror. 'What if scientists can't dance? It'll be a disaster. We'll all be stood around staring at each other. And—'

'Kitty, relax. I imagine that some of them can dance, and if they can't, we'll teach them. And if that fails, we'll dance with each other.' Even as I said the words, Daniel sprang to mind. Would he be there? Might he ask me to dance? The thought of being held in his arms made me go all tingly inside. I gave a nervous laugh. 'Don't worry, we will have a good time, whatever happens.'

* * *

Jazz spilled from the open doorway of the hall, as we picked our way along the uneven flagstone path that ran around the side of the church.

It was six in the afternoon and the late June sun was still bright in the sky. With twilight not expected until at least nine o'clock, the thick blackout blinds at the hall windows were pulled back and the casements thrown wide allowing the heady mix of music and conversation from inside to reach out and draw us in.

Carole, Rosie and Jane hurried ahead, eager to secure dance partners.

'I'm already having fun.' Kitty giggled. I laughed too. Her effervescent excitement was irresistible. We stepped over the threshold, past the heavy velvet drapes standing to attention on either side of the door, ready to do their duty later and not to draw the ire of the air-raid warden. A wall of warmth and energy laced with aftershave, perfume and anticipation swallowed us whole. We shrugged off the light cardigans we'd worn for the walk, hung them on hooks near the door and turned to gaze around.

A big band melody rang out from a gramophone in the far corner and the dance floor was packed with couples jitterbugging. Groups of tables and chairs lined the walls. Refreshments were available through a hatch in the wall from the kitchen. I wondered what they were serving. Probably lemonade or maybe tea. Several of the scientists had planned to visit the pub before coming to the dance, because there wouldn't be any alcohol at the hall.

'Look,' said Kitty, pointing to Carole and Rosie being whisked around the dance floor by two laughing men in army uniform. She bounced on her toes in delight. 'There are so many people here, not just from Renscombe. Where do you think they've all come from?'

'There are troops stationed all around. I imagine everyone is ready for a little relaxation and those close enough to walk or cycle over have done exactly that.'

A dark-haired man in RAF blue dashed over to Kitty. 'Would you like to dance?'

Kitty shot me an uncertain glance.

I laughed and shooed her away. 'Go. I'll be fine.' She didn't need to be told twice and threw herself into the dancing. I watched like a fond parent on the sidelines, enjoying the energy in the air and it was impossible not to tap my toes to the rhythm. Clusters of people stood off to the side of the dance floor chatting. A movement on the far side of the room caught my eye.

Daniel, tall and handsome, stood with some of the scientists from Renscombe, a glass of lemonade in his hand. Things were so busy at work that I'd not had an opportunity to speak to him for ages and had to content myself with snatched glimpses across crowded rooms, each stolen moment triggering a strange fluttery sensation inside. If I didn't know better, I'd think there was a mysterious connection between us, drawing my eye to him whenever it could, my ear picking his voice out from all the others raised in discussion. I told myself not to be silly. We were nothing to each other, merely colleagues.

His eyes met mine and I felt a jolt to my heart that told me I wasn't being entirely honest with myself. There was something intangible connecting us, pulling me towards him. He raised a single eyebrow in my direction and nodded towards the dance floor.

Was he asking me to dance? I was about to move around the room towards him when a loud voice behind me said, 'As I live and breathe! Felicity Makepeace. What are you doing here?'

I whirled around and gasped. 'Carl Edwards. My goodness. I might ask you the same question. It must be, what... a year, since I last saw you?'

I vividly remembered him walking me home from Makepeace Motors that last evening and then... nothing. I'd not seen hide nor hair of him since. Yet here he was, fit and well and looking more like Errol Flynn than ever before.

He ran a hand down the front of his army uniform. 'I joined up as soon as war was declared and I haven't looked back.'

'Is that why you disappeared?' I said, the question out before I could censor myself. 'I... well, I wondered what happened to you.'

His smile faltered and he glanced behind me as if looking for someone. 'I thought you would still be in Bristol looking after your father and... I say.' He checked over his shoulder before leaning towards me and lowering his voice. '*He's* not here, is he?'

'Who?' I followed his gaze, confused.

'That man who works with your father.'

'You mean Jake?' Saying that name made me feel sick, even after all this time.

He nodded.

I squashed a sudden urge to find somewhere to hide, my eyes darting around the room. Unable to keep a wobble from my voice, I asked, 'What makes you think he might be here?'

'No reason,' said Carl. 'I just... well, he made it clear that I shouldn't... I mean that you were...' He flushed. 'His.' A tide of red crept up his face as he said the word.

'What?' Outrage in my voice carried over the music just as the song came to an end, drawing several interested glances. I ducked my head, turning away from the dancers and hissed. 'When? And... and how exactly did he make it clear?'

Chatter and dancing resumed as another song began.

Carl grimaced. 'He followed me one evening after I'd walked you home and then let rip with his fists. My own mother didn't recognise me, when he'd finished.'

A hand crept up to my mouth. 'Dear God. Carl. That's awful.' I didn't know what else to say. It certainly explained why he had stopped calling. 'I'm so sorry.'

Carl shrugged, a bitter twist to his lips. 'I recovered. He did me a favour really.'

I drew back as if he had slapped me. 'Well, thanks very much.'

He grabbed my wrist. 'I didn't mean it like that, Fliss.'

I stared at his hand, unable to not see Jake's hand there instead. My heart started pounding. I wrenched my arm away and stepped back. 'What *did* you mean, then?'

'Only that him beating me up made me want to learn how to fight properly. I went to stay with my cousins, Patrick and Niall in Ireland.'

At that moment, there was another lull in the music and a laughing Kitty returned to my side. 'That was so much fun, Fliss. You absolutely must dance. I insist.' She spotted Carl. 'Hello. Who is this?'

'He's an old friend,' I said. 'Carl, meet Kitty.'

Carl gave an exaggerated bow. Kitty giggled.

He reached an arm behind him to encourage a man who hovered slightly behind his left shoulder to step forward. 'And this is one of the cousins I was telling you about, Fliss. Meet Patrick. Patrick, meet Fliss and Kitty.'

While both men were the same height – an inch or two taller than me – and of identical slim but solid frames with the same dark hair, somehow the essence of the dashing Errol Flynn gene had skipped poor Patrick. To my eyes he was merely a faded copy of Carl, minus the movie-star-like polish. The tips of

Patrick's ears turned bright red and he gave a nervous smile, revealing a notice-able overbite.

The music restarted.

'Do you dance, Patrick?' asked Kitty.

He gave a half-shrug, half-nod.

'Good,' she said, tucking a hand through his arm. 'Come on, then.'

They disappeared into the throng on the dance floor. Carl wrinkled his nose and leaned in to shout above the noise. 'Don't mind him,' he said. 'He barely ever speaks. He's particularly shy around women. Anyway, *he's* the one who taught me bare-knuckle boxing. Him and his brother, Niall.'

My incredulous gaze shot to Kitty and Patrick doing the jive. Appearances were clearly deceptive.

'The exercise got me fit,' said Carl, patting his trim stomach. 'And then, when war was declared, Patrick and I joined up together. I think basic training was easier for us than it is for some, because we were already pretty tough.'

'Where are you posted?'

'A request came through for more security up at the telecommunications research site on the cliffs near here.'

'Renscombe?' I exclaimed. 'That's where we're based. I'm surprised I've not seen you before now.'

He grinned. 'I've only been here a few days. I took some leave just after the rest of my troop were deployed here so that I could go home to visit my family. Anyway, enough about all that.' He jerked his head towards the dance floor. 'Do you fancy a dance?'

'Well, I—' I suddenly remembered Daniel. I searched for him only he had gone. Covering a sense of loss, I nodded to Carl and was swept onto the dance floor and into a vigorous jive. Joining the mass of couples, laughing and twirling to the lively beat, lifted my spirits and it was a joy to surrender my worries for a while. Several dances later, I waved my hands to signal that I couldn't manage another step and retreated to the sidelines with a smile. Carl gave me a grin, a mock salute and headed off to find another partner.

Just as I was contemplating making my way around the edge of the room towards the hatch in search of a drink, Daniel arrived at my side.

'Friend of yours?' he asked, nodding towards Carl.

'He's the brother of a girl I went to school with.' As I said the words, an alarming thought occurred to me. 'Oh! Excuse me, Daniel. I'll be back in a minute.' I threw myself back into the heaving crowd in search of Carl again and soon spotted him spinning a pretty blonde in a pink dress. I wriggled past several other couples and tapped him on the shoulder.

'Sorry to interrupt,' I yelled above the music, casting his partner an apologetic smile as they both paused mid-step. 'I need to ask you something.'

Carl gave me a quizzical look. 'What's up?'

I stepped closer. 'If you write home, please don't mention that you've seen me.'

'Sorry.' He shook his head and pointed to his ear. 'I can't hear you.'

I tried again, but couldn't complete with saxophone and trumpets.

Carl put his mouth right next to my ear. 'I'll come and find you later. Walk you back to your billet. We can talk then.' With that he spun away with his partner.

I chewed the inside of my cheek. It was pointless chasing him. I'd just have to hope that we did catch up later. A vision of his sister or mother bumping into someone who knows my family and mentioning where I was brought with it a wave of nausea. It was a short stop to my father knowing and then... Dear heaven above! Jake.

I wrung my hands together with such force they hurt. I clenched them into fists, forcing them to be still. The music and dancing faded, replaced by my heartbeat thudding in my ears so loudly that I thought my head would explode. All I could think of was the fear I had felt as I ran along the station platform for that train. I edged off the dance floor, hoping to find somewhere quiet to tuck myself away. A tight band of panic wound itself around my chest, making it almost impossible to breathe and I stumbled towards the exit in search of air.

29

Fighting my way through the thick curtains that had been pulled across the doorway as twilight fell, I yanked at the door handle, stumbled out into the cool night and slumped onto a wooden bench set to one side of the path. I dropped my head into my hands. If I stayed very still, perhaps the world would stop spinning. Slow, deep breaths helped. The cool evening air soothed my agitated nerves.

'One too many glasses of punch before the party, perhaps?' said a familiar voice. The wood of the bench creaked and I sensed a weight settle beside me.

I glared at Daniel. 'I haven't touched a drop. Not even lemonade.'

'Then perhaps you *should* have a drink,' he said. 'Would you like me to fetch you something?'

A puff of exasperation escaped me. 'If there ever was a moment when I might turn to strong drink, it would be now. But, no thank you, I'll be fine. I just need a minute.'

He sat back, crossed his arms over his chest and stared up into the clear night sky. I copied him. The moon and a thousand stars gazed back. Several long seconds ticked by in which he remained silent.

'What are you thinking?' I asked.

He turned to me, eyebrows raised in surprise. 'Nothing. I'm merely giving you the minute you've asked for.'

Whatever I had been expecting him to say, it wasn't that. In my experience men always had an agenda, or an opinion on something that they wanted to explain to you. Merely sitting with one in silence was unusual and... unexpectedly restful. 'You don't have to stay,' I murmured.

'I know.' He returned his gaze to the stars, evidently not planning to go anywhere.

After another minute passed, I surprised myself by saying, 'I preferred it when no one from home knew where I was.'

He waited.

'I'm a runaway.' The words were out before I could wrestle them back down. I rolled my eyes at the absurdity of my statement. 'But then, you knew that, didn't you?'

'I suspected,' he said, as if it didn't matter.

'Carl, that man I was talking to, he's from home. It... it could cause problems.'

'Do you need me to have a word with him?'

'No!' The word exploded out with more force than I intended. 'I can speak to him. I'm perfectly capable, you know.'

'I know you are.' His tone was matter-of-fact. 'I was just trying to work out how I can help.'

'I'm sorry. That's kind of you, but there's no need. It's just...' Where did I start?

Silence stretched between us again, begging to be filled.

'When I left Bristol,' I said, 'I was running from someone. Someone dangerous.'

He turned serious eyes on me. 'Go on.'

'He...' I picked at a splinter of wood on the handle of the bench and muttered, 'It's not important.'

'It's important to me,' he said, his words dangerously soft. 'Because, whatever he did made you think you had no choice other than to jump onto a moving train. If I ever find out who he is and what he did, I promise I'll make him pay.'

The thought of Daniel defending me did odd things to my middle.

'There's no need,' I said.

'There's every need.'

'I'm safe here. Or, I thought I was, until Carl came.'

'So, it wasn't Carl who hurt you?'

'No. In fact, Jake beat him up for daring to spend time with me.'

Daniel shifted in his seat to lean closer, lethal intent clear behind his eyes. 'Jake who?'

I shook my head. 'It doesn't matter.'

'Tell me.'

I shook my head. Part of me would love to see Jake get some of his own medicine, but more violence wasn't going to help. Daniel finding and thumping him would only draw attention to my whereabouts.

'Carl got hurt far more than I did,' I said. 'That's why he learned to box. Perhaps that's what I should do?' I let out a long sigh.

'Learn to box?' He scrunched up his nose. 'Hmm. I'm not sure that's the answer.'

I stiffened. 'I can box if I want to.'

'Yes, you can. But there are better forms of self-defence you could choose.'

'Why, because I am a woman?'

'Not especially. It's more about your size than your gender.'

I frowned. 'Explain.'

'For the most part, boxing is a sport rather than an actual self-defence, unless you're talking about bare-knuckle fighting, of course. Whether you follow the Queensberry rules or not, that sort of approach to fighting relies on muscle, and sheer power; matching your adversary in terms of size and reach. If you are up against someone larger or stronger than you, you'll struggle. And with the best will in the world, most men will easily outmatch you.'

Try as I might, I couldn't fault his logic. 'What do you suggest then?'

'Something that allows you to take advantage of being faster and more agile than your opponent.'

'Can you show me?'

'Here? Now?'

I shrugged. 'Do you have something better to do?' I tipped my head back at the hall, from where the muted strains of music trickled out. 'Unless you fancy a waltz. I'm sure there are plenty of girls in there who'd love to dance with you.'

His lips twitched. 'I have no wish to dance.'

'Come on then.' I leapt to my feet. 'Show me how to defend myself.'

'Fine.' He rose in one fluid motion. 'Your best weapon is your voice. I'm not suggesting you do this now, for obvious reasons.' He jerked his head towards the party in full swing behind us. 'But you should scream. Shout. Raise merry hell. Basically, if someone grabs you, make as much commotion as you can. They will be relying on you being so scared that you'll be quiet and do what they want so they don't hurt you.'

That was exactly what I had done when Jake grabbed me. I had frozen. Why hadn't I yelled for help? We were alone in the workshop, but someone walking by outside might have heard and come to investigate. Instead, I had tried to reason with him. To smooth things over.

'I can scream. What else?'

'Kick and bite. Rake his face with your nails. Spit. Don't try to be ladylike about it. Cause such a hullabaloo. Make whoever is attacking you realise that you are more trouble than it's worth. Then, as soon as they release you, don't stick around. Run for the hills and don't look back.'

Could I ever do that? Not the running bit: the biting and spitting. Modesty, restraint and decorum had been drummed into me from birth, as it had all women. It went completely against the grain to do as Daniel suggested. But, with enough provocation, could I? I shuddered to think what such provocation might involve.

'It's not that easy,' I murmured. 'What if there's no one to hear you scream? What if he has grabbed you?' I reached forward to wrap my fingers around his wrist just as Jake had. 'Like this? And pushed you back against something so that you can't move?'

'Those are all good questions,' he said, his words quiet. Perhaps he could sense the tears hovering behind my eyes, threatening to ambush me along with the memories. He placed a gentle hand over mine, where my fingers barely reached around the width of his arm, and waited until I looked him in the eye. 'What did he do to you?'

'I... I... nothing. Well, he bruised my wrist. He frightened me, and made it clear that he enjoyed hurting me and was looking forward to doing it again.' I swallowed hard, realising anew just how unbearable my life with Jake would have been: constant fear, day in day out, for the rest of my life. Thank goodness I'd escaped.

'Was there no one you could turn to for help?'

I dropped my gaze. 'They didn't believe me.'

He cursed under his breath and before I realised what was happening he slid his arms around me and pulled me gently against his chest, resting his chin on the top of my head. 'No wonder you ran.'

The tears crept ever closer. I pushed them back, distracting myself with the interesting discovery that he smelled of spice and fresh, clean earth. Ripples of contented warmth ran from my head to my toes and back again. The urge to lean on him, to stay in his embrace forever was far too tempting. Dashing a hand across my eyes, I stepped back, my gaze locking with his before dropping to his lips. A fleeting thought of what it might feel like to be kissed by those lips danced through my mind. I took another step back, a scalding heat spreading up my neck. 'So,' I said. 'Um... can you show me what I could have done to break free?'

'If you like.' He shrugged. 'You say he grabbed your wrist and pushed you up against something. Did he have your other hand?'

'Not straight away.' I raised my fist. 'Should I have punched him or something?'

He covered my fist with one large, warm hand and pushed it back down gently. 'Your best bet at close quarters is your elbow, believe it or not. Here, let me show you. Pretend you're him and you've grabbed me.' He held out his arm.

I locked my small hand as far around his large wrist as I could, ignoring the tingling sensation that physical contact with him triggered.

'Now step closer,' he urged.

My mouth suddenly dry, I swallowed and edged forward, finding it hard to look at him, let alone breathe.

'Good,' he whispered. 'Now, remember, I'm you. I need to act quickly, use the element of surprise before you grab my other arm. Look.' He drew his fist up level with his armpit and swung his elbow towards my chin with a sharp upward jerk. 'It's called an elbow strike. It can be very effective, especially at close quarters. If you can step into it at the same time, all the better, as it will increase your power. Aim for whatever you can reach: chin, nose, throat, temple.' He demonstrated a blow towards each body part as he mentioned it, stopping just short of touching. 'Put everything you have behind it.'

He paused on the last mock blow, a strike to my temple, his eyes fixed on mine. A rapid pulse throbbed in his throat, matching the drumming of my heart. The world fell away. Time had no meaning. How long we stood like that, breathing the same air, I couldn't tell.

His eyes flicked to my mouth.

I licked my lips.

Just then, the door to the hall opened. A laughing couple tumbled out.

Daniel and I sprang apart, the abrupt distance between us bringing with it a palpable sense of loss. The couple dashed past, barely noticing us.

Alone again, I searched for something to say that would close the widening gap. 'Thank you. I'll remember to strike with my elbows in future.'

There was another creak of hinges from the hall door followed by a burst of laughter. Kitty battled her way through the blackout curtain and emerged, hand in hand with Patrick. It was only then that I registered the music had stopped; the dance was over and people were beginning to leave.

'There you are, Fliss,' she said. 'I wondered where you had got to. It's time to head back if we're to make it before Mrs Haines locks up.' She exchanged a sweet smile with her companion. 'Patrick is going to walk me. I'll see you there.'

I gave her a quick hug and whispered, 'Have a nice time.'

Another burst of sound from the hall produced Carole, Rosie and two RAF officers. Behind them was Carl. He came right up to us, nodded politely to Daniel before turning to me to say, 'I promised I'd walk you back to your billet, Fliss. Are you ready to go?'

Other than a brief twitch of one eyebrow Daniel's expression was unreadable. After what had just passed between us, it seemed wrong to disappear off with Carl. Nevertheless, I needed to make sure there was no chance that word would get back home about where I was. I hesitated, torn.

Daniel made the decision for me. He gave a short bow of his head and said, 'Goodnight,' before turning and walking away. He disappeared into the evening gloom.

Hiding a lake of inky-black disappointment behind a wide smile I turned to Carl. 'It would be lovely of you to walk me back. Thank you. Do you mind waiting a sec while I get my cardigan?'

'Of course. Take your time.' He pulled a packet of camels from his inside pocket. 'I'll wait here.'

30

I battled back into the hall against the flood of departing dancers, and once I had secured my cardigan and gas mask, I realised I needed to pay a quick trip to the lav. Slipping out of a small door at the rear of the building where the moonlight illuminated a short gravel path, I picked my way through the graveyard to the wooden outhouse. Conscious of the need to maintain blackout, I used the facility in almost complete darkness, my movements quick and minimal. Silence wrapped around me like a thick winter coat, as I mentally crossed my fingers that no large spiders lurked overhead in the rafters ready to drop on me. Just as I was about to leave, a whispered conversation began outside; hissed words carrying clearly through the paper-thin walls of the hut.

'Do you have the information?'

I froze. That harsh question sounded like it came from a man. The sharp scent of cigarette smoke seeped under the door.

'Not yet.' The second voice was softer. Whether it was a man or woman, I couldn't tell.

'Why is it taking so long?' The words carried a frown.

'It just is,' the second voice whined. 'I can't exactly tell them to hurry up, can I?'

Moving incredibly slowly, I inched my way towards the door. Perhaps if I peeped through a crack, I might be able to see who was talking.

'What was that?' demanded the first voice.

'What was what?' came the second voice.

I froze. It was better to stay still and listen rather than give myself away.

'Hmm! Probably a rat.' There was a definite lilt to the first speaker's accent that implied that their first language was not English. 'Find a way to speed things up. The Führer needs that data.'

'They are starting the first tests soon. I know that much.'

'Good.'

'The Führer can't seriously be thinking of invading using gliders.'

'It worked in Ében-Émael.'

My hands flew to my face to stop the gasp that almost escaped me, as crashing cymbals filled my ears. Recent news bulletins had been full of how the loss of Ében-Émael fortress in Belgium had allowed the Nazis into the low countries and paved the way for the invasion of France. I held my breath and prayed the conspirators outside hadn't heard me.

'That was one fortress,' the second voice mocked. 'Not a whole damn country.'

'The most heavily armed fortress in Europe. And we overran it in hours.'

'Yes, but gliders? They're so small, we'd need thousands.'

'The point is, they're made of wood. If the Chain Home system – which has been designed to pick up modern metal planes – can't register wood, then all the old wooden biplanes stored away in sheds since the last war can be recommissioned.'

The second speaker gave a low whistle. 'It's crazy, but it could actually work.'

'And if we can get enough troops over the Channel at night to neutralise strategic military defence targets, the Führer can walk in unchallenged.' The relish in those words triggered the sting of acid in my stomach.

The professor had recently received a communication from the British Air Ministry asking if the Chain Home system could pick up wooden gliders as well as metal planes. I remembered opening the envelope for him myself because it was marked urgent, and I'd handed it straight to him, so that it couldn't get mixed up and lost in all the paperwork on his desk. I also knew there were a series of glider tests planned. They were scheduled to start the next day. This wasn't just pie-in-the-sky. A glider invasion could actually happen. And these two monsters were keen to see it.

There was a rustle of something brushing against vegetation, then footsteps sounded on the path, moving away, before complete silence fell.

I waited several minutes until I could be sure they had really gone before I crept to the outhouse door and peered through the gap. My legs felt like rubber as I slipped back up the path to the hall. Major Stapleton was right – there really were spies at Renscombe. But who were they? Definitely someone with access to the research. The problem was there had been so many people at the dance from the site, it could be anyone. Most had left by the time I came through to find the loos, all drifting off in groups, heading for home. Only a few were left. I racked my brain; who had I seen? Two unknown airmen lurking in the hall by the gramophone, smoking and chatting whilst packing records away. A couple of ladies from the church clearing up in the kitchen. Other than that, I knew Carl was waiting out front for me, but it couldn't be him. Only... there was nothing stopping him from wandering around the back while he waited for me, so, what if it was him? Another thought struck me. Daniel had left on his own. Might he have doubled back?

I shook myself. It couldn't be Daniel... could it?

What if this clandestine meeting had all been prearranged and Daniel had just been killing time when he was showing me how to fight? What if, while I had been worrying about offending him by walking home with Carl, *he* had been trying to think of a way to get away from me so that he could meet whoever his contact was? He hadn't exactly objected, had just said goodbye and left. Only, neither of those voices had sounded like Daniel. But that was no comfort; people could change their voices. I should know; Jake had been good at it. Whenever he'd spoken to Da or Ma, he'd sounded perfectly civilised and reasonable, charming even. And then, when he and I were alone, it was a different story.

I clenched my fists in frustration and gave a low growl. This was too big to get my head around and I was too tired to think. First things first, I'd walk home with Carl and make sure he wasn't going to tell his sister he'd seen me. Not that *that* was as important as impending invasion, but it still needed to be done. Then, I'd think about what I'd heard and work out a plan.

I hurried out to the front of the hall, where Carl was stubbing out his cigarette.

'There you are,' he said. 'I was about to come looking for you.'

'Sorry, I took so long.' I glanced around. 'Did anyone come out this way a moment ago?'

'No. I think everyone else has gone. Why?'

'No reason.'

'Shall we go?' He offered me his arm. 'What was it you wanted to ask me, before?'

I shook off a lingering sense of unease from that furtive conversation and focused. 'I wanted to ask you if you could please not mention that you've seen me when you write home.'

He stopped walking, a deep frown creasing his brow. 'Why?'

'I'd prefer that my family not know where I am.'

'Why?'

I swallowed down a sharp lump that appeared in my throat. 'In case they tell Jake.'

'You think he might come after you?'

'I know he will,' I whispered.

His face fell. 'Oh Fliss,' he groaned. 'I'm so sorry. I already told Mam and Sarah that I thought you were here.'

'What?' Horror burned in my chest. 'When? How?'

'The day my troop arrived on site, I thought I saw you. I couldn't be certain. But then I went home on leave for a week and I... well, I happened to mention it. I...'

A swooshing sound filled my ears and I fought down rising nausea.

He grimaced. 'I'm so sorry, Fliss. I had no idea. I can write home and ask them not to say anything.'

I waved his offer away, struggling to find my voice. 'It's fine,' I croaked. 'I'm probably overreacting. After all, Ma, Nana and the boys are in the country with Aunty Mo.'

'Yes,' he said, relief ringing strong in his words. 'There's no reason to think that my mother would contact her. Why would she? I'll call home and say I was wrong. That it wasn't you, just someone who looked like you.' He placed a reassuring hand over mine. 'It will be fine, Fliss. Please don't worry.'

I wished I could believe him.

31

The next morning, on the bus up to Renscombe, I was still as confused as I had been after the dance. The girls chattered with enthusiasm, comparing notes on all the fellas they had flirted with. None of them had spotted anything suspicious which, in some ways, was reassuring. I didn't think I could cope with anything else nefarious having taken place at the dance. I forced a smile to my face and tried to join in with their light-hearted banter. My heart wasn't in it. There was no way I could share what I knew with them. It was too dangerous. This had to stay between Major Stapleton and me. My previous concerns about whether or not it was honourable to spy on my colleagues were nothing compared to key information like this falling into the wrong hands.

However, my immediate problem was communication. Major Stapleton had suggested I send a confidential report to her via my superior officer. That wasn't going to work. Beaky was my superior officer and there was no way she would agree to send a confidential report to the major on my behalf. Not without reading it first and asking awkward questions, which would totally blow my cover.

I stared out of the window at the passing hedgerows and concluded that the only thing I could do was keep an eye on the situation and hope I could find some other way to make contact. Having said that, if the radar failed the glider test, I would have to escalate things, because an imminent invasion using wooden aircraft might then be a genuine possibility.

* * *

Hut 4 was locked when I arrived. The first glider test had been scheduled to start shortly after dawn and would already be well underway. I took a brisk walk over to the clifftop, hoping that the exercise would calm my frazzled nerves. Maybe I would get to see the flight come in. I sent up a prayer that the scientists would get the results they needed. If the system could register wood, then the immediate problem of a German glider-borne invasion would be off the cards, which would give me more time to root out the spy.

At the edge of the bluff, sharp fingers of salt-stiffened breeze slipped through the fabric of my uniform, making me shiver in spite of the summer sunshine. Tugging my jacket closer, I stepped off the path, to a sheltered spot I knew, where thick gorse bushes formed a handy windbreak. To my surprise it was already occupied. Daniel sat in the long grass, with both knees up, his elbows resting on them to steady a pair of binoculars that were trained out across the water. My initial instinct was to walk away before he saw me. Quite apart from the fact that I'd wasted hours wondering if he could be the spy – in spite of the small voice deep inside me repeatedly saying he couldn't be – I felt awkward over the way we'd parted. I made myself stay; avoiding him wouldn't help me work out the identity of the traitor.

I sank down beside him, glad to be out of the wind. Memories of standing close to him outside the dance crowded in, stealing coherent thought.

'Morning,' I muttered.

He started, dragging his gaze briefly away from the sea. 'Hi.'

Did he feel as awkward as I did? I cast around for something to say. Anything at all. 'Are you looking for the glider?' Talk about asking the obvious.

'Yes. I'm to register the time that he becomes visible to the naked eye, so that we can compare that to any timed readings from the receiver.'

'That makes sense.'

His total focus on the view through his binoculars allowed me the chance to study him. He seemed his usual calm, contained self. He didn't look like someone desperate to find out the results of these tests so he could dash off and betray his country.

He'd removed his jacket and rolled up his shirt sleeves revealing muscular forearms with a light dusting of dark hair. His hands were beautiful: large but not brutish like Jake's. They were capable, his fingers slim and dextrous, the nails well trimmed and clean. A pale scar with puckered edges disappeared under the folded fabric at his left elbow. My heart squeezed at the difficulties he must have had to overcome as a child following his accident.

Seconds ticked by. Bumblebees danced among the ox-eye daisies; their gentle buzzing a soft contrast to sharp cries from gulls overhead. Sea thrift bobbed, a cheerful splash of bright pink in the long grass around us. The warm scent of wild flowers teased my nostrils, reminding me of summer picnics on carefree days gone by. It was almost possible to pretend that he and I were on a day out together and the war wasn't happening.

Eventually, I said, 'Whoever the glider pilot is, he must be very brave.'

'His name is Philip Wills,' murmured Daniel, not breaking his focus. 'And, yes he is. He's not supposed to go up if there have been any air-raid warnings.'

'We've had so many of those recently.'

'I know, and he's chosen to go up anyway.'

'Goodness!'

'They towed him up behind an Avro biplane this morning, released him twenty miles off the French coast and left him to make his own way back.'

'I see.'

'It's damn risky. And he'll probably have to do it several times so that we can get reliable readings of him approaching from different altitudes. But the key today is to see if the masts will register him at all.'

I realised I was nibbling at my thumbnail and pulled my hand from my mouth. 'Do you think he'll be all right up there on his own?' The stakes were already high yet, somehow, knowing the pilot's name made the whole venture seem even more dangerous.

Daniel gave a one-shouldered shrug, his profile grave. 'I honestly don't know. Quite apart from the fact that he has no engine and is therefore at the mercy of the air currents, if he runs into enemy planes he's completely defenceless.'

'And I'm assuming he can't have an escort of Spitfires up there because it will mess up the readings.'

'Exactly. The receiver will definitely detect Spitfires. Any pings from the glider could get lost. We need to know what a clear reading reflected off wood looks like, assuming we can get one.'

I shaded my eyes and pointed out to sea at a white speck hanging in the air. 'Is that him?'

Daniel checked to see where I was pointing. 'No, that's a seagull. But...' He examined the sky through the binoculars again. 'I do believe that dot to the right of it, *is* him.' He checked his watch and then looked back at the dot I couldn't see, yet. 'Yes. That's him. I'm sure of it.'

I shuffled a little closer and stared out along the same trajectory, straining my eyes until, at last, I could see what he was referring to. 'Oh, my!' A tiny fleck against the endless blue of the sky, which in time got steadily bigger.

Without breaking his focus on the glider's progress, Daniel gave a low laugh. 'I can hear you holding your breath, Fliss. Please breathe. I don't need you passing out on me.'

I dragged in a lungful of air. 'Sorry,' I muttered, shuffling away, suddenly conscious that I had edged towards him. 'I didn't mean to distract you.'

'It's fine, don't worry.' He threw me a quick smile. 'I'm praying for him to be all right too.'

I pressed a hand to my warm cheeks, relieved he had put my behaviour down to concern for the pilot rather than the disturbing fact that I found it difficult to think when he was so close.

He lowered his binoculars and climbed to his feet. I followed suit and we stood side by side on the clifftop and watched the graceful ballet of the glider swooping silently towards us.

'Is it just me,' I asked, after a few minutes, 'or does he seem a bit low?'

'He's very low.' Daniel tutted. 'If he doesn't catch a thermal and gain a bit of height, he'll crash into the cliff.'

The craft was now so close that I could make out the head and shoulders of the pilot inside. I wrung my hands together, willing him to find that upward current of air. He got closer and closer with no sign of any lift when to my horror the glider disappeared below the edge of the cliff.

'Oh, dear God! No!' I said, lurching forwards.

'Watch out!' Daniel's strong arms wrapped around me from behind and hauled me back against a solid wall of muscle. 'For goodness' sake,' he bit out. 'We don't need you in a broken heap down there too.'

Tears burned the backs of my eyes. 'I'm sorry. I just... Did he crash?' I turned my head away. 'Oh, I can't bear to look.'

'I don't know.' He released me, before creeping closer to the edge of the cliff to peer over. His foot slipped. 'Oh, my Lord!' He reeled back to safety, his complexion a pasty pale grey.

I grabbed his arm and tugged him several steps back towards the safety of the cliff path.

There was a whispering whoosh and a streak of white. The glider loomed into view, missing the cliff edge by inches. It continued to rise, passing over our heads – forcing us to duck – and soared on towards the tower.

'Oh, thank heavens. There he is.' I flung my arms around Daniel's neck, laughing in delight.

He lifted me off my feet and swung me around, letting out a whoop of joy. 'He did it. He actually did it. I honestly thought he'd bought it. He must have caught a thermal at the very last second. That's incredible!'

Relief flooded through me like someone had opened the sluice gate of a dam. Whether it was the joy at the glider's last-minute reprieve, or the fact that Daniel looked so jubilant, I don't know. The urge to kiss him was overwhelming. My gaze locked with his, and I was barely able to breathe. He set me back on my feet, took hold of my shoulders with both hands and lowered his head towards mine.

Any second now...

A shout came from behind.

I froze, remembering where we were, and volcanic heat raced across my cheeks.

Daniel stepped back, one hand rubbing the back of his neck. 'I should get to the observation room. Are you coming?'

* * *

The atmosphere inside the observation room at the base of the main receiving tower was one of muted jubilance. I waited just inside the door while Daniel conferred with a tall, stooped man in a white coat. They exchanged a hand-shake, a firm nod and a celebratory pat on the back, indicating the news was good. I scanned the room, noting faces, wondering who had also been at the dance. On my right, two WAAF officers in headsets sat with their backs to me, their attention focused on a series of display screens. A couple of RAF officers manned a bank of telephones on my left. In the middle, three scientists shifted markers on a large map of the coast laid out on a table. At least half a dozen other staff milled around. To my surprise, Kitty was among them, a pad and pencil in her hand. She gave me a little wave and hurried over.

'I was asked to come and take notes,' she said. 'It's so exciting. You should have heard everyone shout when they detected the glider.'

'I can imagine,' I said. 'It's good to know the results are positive.'

'Yes. Mind you, only the basic principle has been confirmed. Apparently, there are all sorts of other problems that need solving. They're planning a series of more detailed tests. I'm to type up a report for the Air Ministry. Who would ever have thought it? Me, writing to the Air Ministry.' She twirled her pencil in delight. 'And did you hear the news about Jane and Rosie?'

'No,' I said. 'What's happened?'

'They've been asked to give clerical support to a team from hut 2 heading over to the Chain Home site at Ventnor on the Isle of Wight.'

'Oh, my goodness.' I couldn't help wondering if Major Stapleton had something to do with their posting after I had mentioned their desire to do more to her.

'We did it,' said Kitty, giving my arm a gentle squeeze. 'We're all secretaries now, and it's thanks to you.'

I smiled, genuinely pleased for them. 'It's your hard work that has done this. It's wonderful news.'

One of the scientists called Kitty by name.

'Yes, sir,' she replied, glancing back at me. 'Sorry, Fliss. I'd better go. I'll see you later.'

I watched her dive back into the fray, thrilled to see her so happy, and ignored the niggle of worry burrowing away at the back of my mind. I could only hope that my interference on my friends' behalf hadn't placed them in danger.

Checking my watch, I realised it was time to head back to hut 4 to see what the professor needed.

32

Room 401 smelled of stale sweat and tension. I hurried to throw the window open and allow some fresh air in. The professor was scrawling on the blackboard in his room and muttering to himself again. He looked up as I approached.

'Durrington are stealing a march on me,' he said. He grabbed a sheet of paper off his desk and thrust it into my hands.

'Durrington, sir?'

'Do you think we're the only site developing ground-controlled interception?' he growled. 'Only Durrington are making theirs mobile. How?' He gave his head a vicious scratch. 'How in heaven's name are they making it mobile?'

I scanned the document as he paced away from me, the air around him thick with tension. It was a confidential letter from the Air Ministry, detailing a recent advance from another research facility at RAF Durrington in West Sussex.

'All that equipment,' he grumbled. 'Transponders, receivers, generators, observation units. It's impossible. There isn't a vehicle big enough to take it all. Unless they've managed to make it all really small, and I just don't see how?'

'It probably isn't all on one vehicle,' I said, re-reading the text. 'It doesn't imply the equipment is operational whilst on the move, merely that it will be able to be moved from one site to another in a relatively short period of time.'

'Does it?' He snatched the letter back.

'If that's the case, then it's possible to use as many vehicles as are needed and link them all up once they're parked.'

He stood stock-still. I could almost see the cogs turning in his brain. 'You're right.' He stopped and stared at the board. The unfocused look on his face and dark circles under his eyes made me wonder if he had been working all weekend, again. I'd seen this sort of obsessive behaviour before and it always concerned me.

'When did you last eat, sir?'

'Yes, yes. Good idea.' He scrubbed a section of the board clean before carving fresh white chalk lines on to it and annotating them with hurried half-formed numbers.

I ran over to the canteen to get him a tray of food, bringing back strong tea, a bowl of saltwater porridge and a plate of toast with Bovril. He pounced on the porridge, spooning in great mouthfuls whilst nodding meaningfully at his scribbles, before casting the empty crockery aside and taking up his chalk again. Short of insisting he go to bed – something I knew from experience he wouldn't react well to – there was little else I could do to support him. I settled at my desk to make a start on the mountain of notes awaiting transcription and kept a careful eye on him from across the room.

An hour later, Daniel arrived. My whole being lifted at the sight of him, like a hot air balloon taking flight, and then came crashing down again when he didn't acknowledge me. Instead, he made straight for the professor who was still scratching away at the board with chalk. I didn't know what I'd expected, but I didn't think he'd ignore me. Suddenly becoming invisible again was like a punch to the gut. The man had been about to kiss me on the clifftop in full view of the entire Renscombe site – how dare he act as if I didn't exist? Would it hurt to throw me a smile?

After several failed attempts to talk to the professor about the glider test results, Daniel finally turned to me. 'What's wrong with him?'

I squashed resentment down, concern for the professor more important than injured pride, and told him about the letter from the Air Ministry. 'I don't understand why he's so upset,' I whispered. 'Surely, the goal is to advance the technology and protect the country. It doesn't matter *who* has the breakthrough.'

'It might not matter to you, but it matters a hell of a lot to him,' said Daniel. 'This is his life's work.'

'I know that. Regardless, saving lives is more important. Why can't he collaborate with them and help advance everything together?'

'It would make sense at this stage. I agree.'

'Then, why doesn't he just telephone them?' I asked.

'Too risky. They can't discuss specific details in case the line is bugged. And a letter or reports will be too slow.'

'True, and I suppose a telegram would be too short to convey what he wants to say.'

'Exactly.'

'Then he'll have to go and see them,' I said. 'I know petrol is rationed, but there were several cars parked outside the main security hut when I arrived this morning. Can't he borrow one? Durrington is near Worthing, isn't it? That's just along the coast. It wouldn't take long. Three hours perhaps.'

'He doesn't drive. And I can't.' Daniel lifted his left arm. 'It's the gears.' I'd forgotten that his elbow injury restricted certain movements. He managed so well, most of the time. 'And everyone else here is needed to carry on with the project.'

'I can drive,' I said.

'That's it,' said the professor, snapping his fingers, making me jump. I hadn't realised he was listening. 'You.' He pointed a shaky hand at me. 'You can take me. Go and requisition a vehicle. I need to confer with Branson.'

I glanced at Daniel. 'Branson?'

'Doctor Branson. The next biggest brain in this field of research,' said Daniel. 'He is heading the project at RAF Durrington.'

'You can come too, Daniel,' said the professor. 'Get your equipment. We leave in an hour.'

I glanced from the professor to Daniel. The last thing I wanted was to spend hours in a car with a man who confused the hell out of me.

Daniel's expression was unreadable. He shrugged. 'We'd better do as he says.'

* * *

Requisitioning a vehicle wasn't easy. Patrick was on duty at the guard hut and he was no more talkative than he had been at the dance. When I explained what I needed, he stared at me as if I'd said I was planning to fly to the moon.

I sighed and pulled my papers from my uniform pocket to show him my driving licence. He scowled at the print in such a way that made me wonder if he could actually read. Just as I wanted to scream, a door opened behind him and Carl walked in.

'Carl,' I exclaimed. 'Can you please reassure Patrick, here, that I can drive? I need to take my professor to RAF Durrington.'

'Today?' Carl asked.

'Yes, right now,' I replied. 'Back this evening, with any luck.'

Carl grinned. 'Give her the Riley Nine, Pat. It's got a full tank. There's a spare jerry can in the boot as well.'

Patrick handed over a set of keys.

I jingled them, flashed Carl a smile of thanks and hurried outside.

With an enclosed body and shiny spoked wheels, the Riley Nine was a sporty saloon model with rear-wheel drive, a light body and sturdy chassis. It would be a delight to drive. I scanned the map in the glove compartment and estimated that even though I wasn't planning to push the top speed of sixty miles per hour, it shouldn't take more than two and a half hours to reach our destination.

* * *

Twenty minutes later, with Daniel and the professor loaded into the back along with a stack of important documents for them to work on as we travelled, and a satchel with a flask of tea, some sandwiches and honey biscuits to keep the professor's legendary temper under control, we set off.

It was a beautiful day. Gentle sunshine washed over resplendent hedgerows as we threaded our way north along narrow country lanes. Stunning as it was, none of that mattered. I was driving again and it felt amazing. The Riley Nine was in great condition, a smooth and responsive machine that gave me a heady sense of power. This was my way to fix the professor's problem.

Mindful that we had a fair distance to cover, over unpredictable and winding rural roads, I maintained a sensible speed. In the back, the professor lectured Daniel about the finer points of radar research, until finally the older man gave in to the warmth of the day and the rhythm of the car and fell asleep. I watched via the rear-view mirror as Daniel tenderly tucked a folded coat between the professor's head and the window he was leaning on and removed the papers clutched in his hands. To see him making sure the older man was comfortable, without waking him, tugged at my heart. Whatever else he might be, Daniel was a kind person. The next forty minutes passed in relatively companionable silence. He didn't speak, but I could excuse that because neither of us wanted to wake the professor. From time to time, I caught Daniel's eye in the mirror. Each time, my heart gave a little skip, which I ignored before dragging my focus back to the road.

Fifteen minutes from Durrington, I noticed two motorbikes behind us that were fractionally too close for comfort. I slowed into the next junction, giving them plenty of room to whizz past. Instead, they sat on my tail like two annoying gnats buzzing away waiting to pounce. If I sped up, they sped up. If I slowed, they slowed.

An uneasy feeling germinated in my middle and grew fast, like tendrils of ivy wrapping themselves around my vital organs and squeezing.

'Daniel,' I murmured, taking care not to turn my head. 'Don't look back. We seem to have picked up a tail.'

The professor snored.

Daniel stiffened. 'What can you see?'

'Two motorbikes. It's probably nothing to worry about, but they're a touch persistent.'

'I take it you've tried to shake them?'

'Yes. No joy. If I recall the map correctly, the road should open out a bit just up ahead. I'll keep an eye on them and see what they do.'

As expected, the road did open out. The bikes moved alongside the car to take up positions one on either side, level with the driver and front passenger doors. They made no attempt to fully overtake. That uneasy feeling morphed into something more concerning. The bikers' behaviour was downright sinister.

'It might be time to start worrying,' muttered Daniel.

'I agree. Brace yourselves, back there,' I warned. 'I'm going to speed up.'

'Sir,' said Daniel, shaking the professor's arm. 'You need to wake up, now, sir.'

The professor lurched forwards with a gasp. 'What?'

'You have to hold on,' he said.

Leaving Daniel to explain, I concentrated on the situation developing around us.

When I accelerated, the bikers accelerated. When I slowed down, they did the same. It was like an intense game of chicken.

I glanced at the one on my side. A black leather helmet, chinstrap and goggles covered the majority of his face. The only identifying features were lips pulled back into a wide, humourless smile revealing protruding front teeth, one of which was broken leaving half a stump. I tore my eyes back to the road to steady our course, but a glimpse of further movement from my unwelcome goofy companion forced me to look again. To my horror he withdrew a gun from inside his jacket and levelled it at the front car tyre.

'That is quite enough of that,' I said, jerking the steering wheel to edge the car into the path of his bike, not caring if I knocked him off. No one pulled a gun on me. Unfortunately, the road was straight and wide at that point, and while my manoeuvre made him ram the gun back into his jacket and reach to steady the handlebars to avoid a collision, it didn't stop him for long. I was nearing the car's top speed of sixty miles per hour. The engine was screaming and there was nothing else to do.

'Hold on,' I yelled, swerving the car across the carriageway onto a patch of gravel, forcing the armed biker to veer. I jerked the wheel back the other way, causing a spray of small stones to fly up from my tyres like buckshot. The armed biker wobbled and spun off the road into the bushes.

The second rider was closing in on my left. I spun the steering wheel over to the right, shifted into neutral and stamped on the footbrakes. The rear of the car swung around in a cloud of dirt, clipping the back wheel of the bike and sending him flying.

You can say two things about the Riley Nine. Firstly, it has an excellent braking system and secondly, if you get it right, you can turn on a sixpence. We ground to a halt facing in the opposite direction to the way we had been travelling. I threw the car into first and gunned the engine, sending up a prayer that it wouldn't stall on me because I was mistreating it. Bringing up the clutch, I forced an acceleration the poor vehicle wasn't designed to give and ratcheted through the gears one after another as we sped back down the road we'd just come along, checking the rear-view mirror repeatedly for signs of pursuit. If they weren't seriously hurt, they would give chase.

Careering around a hairpin bend, I spotted an open gateway. I threw the car through the gap and round behind the overgrown hedge, tucking the car tight into the dense unkempt foliage so that branches and leaves engulfed us. I yanked on the handbrake, tugged the key from the ignition and allowed the engine to die.

'Say still, and keep quiet.' I leapt from the car, ran back to the gate and rammed it shut, stuffed the length of chain hanging from it through the looped latch and forced the rusty padlock closed.

The sound of a bike being hammered at full capacity got louder, approaching the far side of the bend. I ducked out of sight just as the bike came into view. It slowed and I peered through the hedge at the rider. He came to a stop and glanced up the road, clearly thrown that he couldn't see a car ahead of him.

I pressed myself closer to the prickly hawthorn branches, the smell of engine fumes and worn rubber burning the inside of my nostrils.

He killed the engine, stepped off his machine, and gazed from side to side, before stepping over to the gateway to examine the field. It was the man with the broken tooth. I noticed that the front mudguard of his bike was now bent to almost ninety degrees from where it should be, damage caused when I'd forced him off the road. No wonder he looked cross. He pulled his gun out again.

All I could do was hold my breath and pray, my pulse thundering away in my ears. The car was out of sight, but he only had to climb the gate and walk a few paces into the field to see it.

He rattled the gate against the post. Using the barrel of his gun he lifted the chain and examined the padlock. A droning hum heralded the arrival of the second motorbike. The first man dropped the padlock and stalked over to his companion to exchange words. Seconds later, he remounted his bike and they both roared off down the road.

Shaking, I stumbled back to the car, breathing a sigh of relief. As I ducked in to speak to my passengers it was all I could do not to scream. The barrel of a gun was pointing straight at me.

Quiet, steady, Daniel had the professor pressed to the floor, and in his hands was a shiny black revolver.

'Have they gone?' asked Daniel, eyes narrowed, mouth grim. I nodded and he tucked the weapon away. 'You can get up, Professor. We're safe, for now.'

'For goodness' sake,' I said, pressing a hand to my chest to steady my breathing. 'Why is everyone playing with guns, today?'

I watched Daniel help the older man up and back onto his seat. White-faced and wide-eyed, the professor clutched his precious papers to his chest and mercifully stayed silent. I fished the flask from the front passenger side footwell.

'Here, sir,' I said, passing him a cup of tea and a biscuit. 'You've had a shock. Better get some sugar inside you.'

The poor man looked as if he didn't know who I was. I found myself wishing he would display a little of his pompous wind-bagged-ness just to reassure me that he was really all right. The silly phrase flitted through my head, making me smile. Then my face dropped. The Daniel who had made that quip wasn't the Daniel in the car. Neither was he the Daniel who had nearly kissed me on the clifftop at Renscombe. There was an implacable hardness to this Daniel, which made me wonder if I'd ever known him at all.

He climbed from the car, and paced over to the gate, tension radiating from every line of his body.

I followed and, from a cautious distance, asked, 'You carry a gun?'

'I do.' He swore under his breath. 'You shouldn't have got out of the car.'

'If I hadn't shut the gate, they'd have found us.'

'You should have let me do it.' He scowled.

I tutted. 'There wasn't time to ask you. I just did it.'

'You could have got hurt.'

Was that why he was so angry? The thought that he cared enough to want to keep me safe did strange things to my insides. I stepped closer, my voice softening. 'I'm fine. We're all fine.'

He slammed one fist into the palm of the other hand. 'This is my fault. I should have insisted on a security detail.'

'Who do you think they are?' I asked.

He shrugged. 'What's more important is how did they know we were here? This was an impulse trip. No one should know about it. Unless you told someone.'

'What are you suggesting?' I said, bristling at the implied criticism.

'Who filled that flask of tea for you?'

Part of me was outraged at the implication that I or one of my ATS team might be responsible, but he had a point. Someone at Renscombe must have set this up. It could easily be someone I worked with every day. Someone I trusted. The question was, who?

'What about you?' I asked. 'Who did *you* speak to when you were packing up the professor's stuff?'

'I don't remember telling anyone.' He rubbed his chin thoughtfully.

'Either they were watching the site,' I said, 'or one of our own people betrayed us.' My knees wobbled. 'I'm not sure which is worse.'

'We'll need a security detail before we attempt a return trip to Renscombe.'

'Come on,' I said. 'Let's get going in case they realise they've missed us and come back to search properly.'

'Are you all right to drive?'

'Of course I am.' I shot him a contemptuous look. He was not forgiven for mistrusting me. 'I'm not soft. It's a short drive on to Durrington from here. I suggest you and the professor sit back and hang on tight. I'll have us there in a jiffy.'

'There's one problem with that plan,' he said, pointing to the gate. 'Unless you have a key to that padlock, we're stuck.'

I gave a shout of laughter. 'I thought you scientists were supposed to be smart.'

'What do you mean?'

I pointed to the other end of the gate. 'It's a basic lift and drop mechanism.' The hinges were formed from two sections of reinforced metal tube that slipped over a couple of corresponding galvanised pins on the gatepost. 'If we remove the bolts, we can open it that side, drive out and then put it back on the hinges afterwards. Simple.'

He opened his mouth as if to say something and then stopped and laughed. 'Trust you to know that.'

I grinned and turned back to the car. 'I'll get the tool kit.'

33

Located a mile north of the coastal town of Worthing, RAF Durrington was an imposing site, surrounded by a high chain-link fence separating it from open countryside in all directions. The nearest buildings were a couple of derelict barns.

I'd been running on pure adrenaline ever since the bikers had started harassing us, and now the immediate danger was past, it was wearing off. I felt utterly drained. I was glad Daniel couldn't see my hands shaking as I changed gear. It was a relief to pull up at the guardhouse and put the handbrake on.

In a stark contrast to the relatively relaxed approach at Renscombe, security at Durrington was like a medieval fortress with the drawbridge up, the portcullis down and sentries poised with barrels of hot oil to pour down on unwanted visitors. Overkill or not, I found it comforting.

Our identity papers were scrutinised at length. The professor and I waited in the car as Daniel conferred with the security guards before we were escorted to a large building right in the centre of the compound. A sprawling brick-built construction, it was long, boxy and squat. A strange square tower section rose up an extra storey right in the middle. As I parked outside, I realised what was odd about it. There were no windows.

The guards must have telephoned ahead, because we were met on the steps by a man who could have been the professor's twin, right down to the tweed jacket and chalk-covered fingers. He grasped the professor's hand and pumped it up and down, saying, 'My dear chap. Why didn't you say you were coming? Come inside, come inside. Let's get you some tea.'

Daniel whispered to me, 'That's Doc Branson. Like I said, he's probably the next greatest mind in radio direction finding research in Britain, after the prof.'

We were ushered into a room that bore eerie similarities to the professor's own office – in that it was festooned with piles of papers and a scribble-filled blackboard. Refreshments were provided and the two top scientists fell into an involved discussion about the project, with no mention of our eventful journey.

Daniel leaned close and muttered, 'I'm going to find a telephone. To let Renscombe know what happened and see how they suggest we approach our return trip. Can you keep an eye here?'

'Are you sure that's wise? What if the line is tapped?'

His brow furrowed. 'That's a good point. It's a risk. I'll inform them of what happened today, because that's already happened and nothing can change it. Rather than get into specific details about our return trip, I'll ask them to establish a secure method of communication before we discuss the issue further.'

I watched him make his way to the door. There was no knowing how safe we were, either at Renscombe or here. Vigilance was essential. I should probably let Major Stapleton know what had happened too. This was exactly the sort of thing she'd be interested in. Before I could ponder how to contact her from Durrington, the professor demanded I take dictation.

An hour later, Daniel returned, just as the doc suggested a tour of the facility. He fell in step with me as we wandered through corridors lined with offices and laboratories, and then ambled outside to admire a small airstrip with ranks of temporary hangars on either side. Staff dormitories and washroom facilities were pointed out en route to the canteen for lunch where the smell of Lord Woolton pie made my mouth water. I soon got used to the lack of windows. From a practical point of view, if nothing else, it made managing blackout easier, and the whole building had to be more secure as a result.

Later, over lunch, while the professor and the doc continued to confer, a uniformed courier approached the table, escorted by one of the Durrington site security guards. The courier checked Daniel's identification papers, asked him to sign a form and then handed him an envelope before leaving.

Daniel checked over both shoulders before tearing open the envelope. He scanned the contents before folding it up and tucking it into his breast pocket.

'Today's events have rattled the higher-ups,' he said in a low voice. 'They're suggesting we remain here.'

'For how long?' I murmured.

'Indefinitely. Or at least for as long as this phase of the project lasts.'

Durrington was nice, but I didn't particularly want to stay. Everything I'd worked so hard for was back in Renscombe. Major Stapleton had asked me to keep watch over everyone in hut 4, not just the professor. I couldn't do that from here. I glanced along the table. The professor was leaning towards the doc over his empty dinner plate and stabbing at the table between them with a forefinger to emphasise whatever he was talking about. 'How do you think he'll take the news,' I asked.

Daniel gave a short puff of laughter. 'I don't think he'll be remotely bothered. Look at the two of them. They're happy as mud larks together.' The sight of the doc drawing imaginary lines on the table with his fingers too made me smile. What on earth must it be like inside those brilliant brains?

'There have been rumblings about possibly moving research sites for a while,' Daniel continued. 'I know there's been quite a bit of chatter about Renscombe and particularly this project in enemy radio transmissions.'

Would he know information like that if he were merely a scientist? I remembered the gun he was carrying in the car and my doubts about him resurfaced. Then, in a random leap of logic, it occurred to me that if we did move, it lessened the chance of Jake tracking me down. 'Is it possible to move the whole project?' I asked.

'I don't see why not,' he said. 'It makes sense to shift locations if there is a threat. They do it for munitions research all the time. The merest sniff that an armament development lab has been discovered and they up and disappear overnight before the Jerries can bomb the living daylights out of them.'

'Goodness. That must take some organising.'

'Not as much as you'd think. Jones, Havers and Robbins can pack everything up. The Renscombe security team will send an escort with them.'

'And what about billets?'

'There'll be space to accommodate us here. One of your troop can pack up your kit and arrange for it to be shipped here alongside all of the project equipment.'

My mind immediately flew to Kitty. She wouldn't mind doing that for me. Before I could reply, a no-nonsense woman in WAAF blue arrived at my side, self-importance rolling off her in waves. Daniel and I both rose to acknowledge her.

'I'm Sergeant Coombes,' she said, nodding to me. 'I've had orders to find you space in the WAAF dormitory. You should be comfortable enough.'

I exchanged a look with Daniel. That was quick work. We'd only just found out we were moving ourselves. Clearly the wheels of the War Office turned exceedingly fast when required. 'Thank you,' I said.

'And, as you're a secretary as well as a driver, I'll assign you to our typing pool, while you're here. We can always make use of an extra pair of hands. There's no point you sitting idle.' She delivered this suggestion as if she were doing me a huge favour.

The hairs on the back of my neck stood to attention. That was a step too far. If I was staying at Durrington, it would be on my terms. 'I'm sorry, Sergeant. I am permanently attached to the professor. He needs my assistance all day, every day.'

'Nonsense. You'll be no use to him during the day while they are building their contraption. And you won't want to get all dirty in the sheds with the machinery.'

'Forgive me, ma'am.' I didn't bother to sound contrite. 'Dirty machinery or not, I have to be available.'

She flared her nostrils and thrust her chest out like an offended gosling. 'In the absence of your senior officer, Private, you'll do as I say.'

'Makepeace,' barked the professor who had risen from the table with the doc and was heading for the door. 'Here.'

It sounded for all the world as if he were calling a dog to heel. I let it slide. It made the point to the sergeant that I wasn't hers to command far more effectively than I could. I shot her a helpless *do you see what I mean?* look and hurried after him.

The afternoon passed in the blink of an eye, with me desperately trying to keep up as the two greatest minds in radio detection finding sparked ideas off each other. That evening I fell into bed in the WAAF dormitory, in a pair of borrowed pyjamas, utterly exhausted.

34

Thirty-six hours later, Jones, Havers and Robbins arrived in two huge trucks, with other members of the Renscombe research team and all of our equipment. I was delighted to see Carl with them.

He grinned hello as he unloaded bags from one of the flatbeds. 'Can't get rid of me, can you, Fliss? I'm like a bad penny.'

'Are you here to stay?' I said.

'For now. We're here to get you all set up and act as bodyguards for your head boffin. Hey,' he called back over his shoulder. 'Patrick. Didn't you say Kitty gave you a letter for Fliss?'

Patrick emerged from the back of one of the trucks. He dug in his back pocket and handed over a crumpled envelope. With a non-committal nod, he picked up a large box and plodded off with it. I smoothed out the letter and slipped it into my inside pocket for later. It would be lovely to hear news from my friends.

Carl slapped a hand on the bumper of the vehicle. 'Your things are in the back here somewhere. They've even packed your typewriter. I'll take everything over to your quarters when we find it. Oh! and there's some officer here to see you.'

'Who?'

'I don't know. She arrived just after we did. Oh.' He pointed behind me. 'There she is.'

Major Stapleton stood on the main steps.

I hurried over. 'Ma'am. I was trying to work out how best to contact you.'

'Not to worry. Word usually finds me,' she said. 'Is there somewhere we can have a private chat?'

'Yes, of course.' I led her inside to an office that had been assigned to the professor.

Havers was crouched behind the professor's desk, rummaging in one of the drawers. He shot upright when he saw me and stood shifting from foot to foot, like a nervous child, whilst pushing his glasses back up his nose and refusing to meet my eyes.

Striving for a mild tone to hide my surprise, because Havers was notoriously jumpy, I asked, 'What are you doing?'

'Uh... I... uh.' He indicated at a box on the ground. 'The professor said to bring his files in.'

'I see,' I said. That wasn't an unreasonable explanation. The professor was outside supervising the unloading of sensitive paraphernalia into one of the hangars and could easily have sent Havers in with papers. 'Thank you. I'll sort them out from here.'

He nodded and dashed for the door as if a ferocious dog was snapping at his heels, leaving the major and I alone.

'I understand you had an eventful trip the other day,' said the major, sitting down. 'I've read a report, but I'd like to hear your version of what happened.'

I filled her in.

'Yes, that tallies with Daniel Evans' account. What do you make of him?'

The abrupt change of subject brought me up short. 'I don't think he's a scientist,' I blurted out. 'I mean, not like the others. I've been working with them for weeks now, and Daniel – while there's no doubt that he's very clever – he's not engaged in the work in the same way they are.' As the words tumbled out of my mouth, I realised they were true. He'd always been present in the labs, but usually a little to one side, as if waiting on the sidelines for something; watchful, analytical. And yet, at the same time, there was no doubt that he was completely supportive of the professor. Inspiration struck me like a tennis ball between the eyes. 'Could he be some sort of undercover bodyguard, ma'am?'

'It's possible,' she said. 'I'm not sighted on that particular young man's credentials. I'll get him checked out.' Her tone hardened. 'If he is what you're suggesting, then I have a pretty good idea who he's working for. Until I can be certain, we will have to hope that he's on the right side. I suggest you treat him with extreme caution for the time being.'

'You mean, treat him as if he were potentially an enemy agent? Surely not? He was protecting the professor.'

'Are you sure about that? Or was he part of the plot all along and ready to shoot you and force the professor to go with him once his accomplices turned up?'

'I...' I sagged in my chair. 'I don't know.' Every part of me wanted to scream out that Daniel wasn't like that. My gut told me he was on the right side. But things were getting too serious to rely on instinct and I had no proof. The Daniel I had interrupted in the car had a lethal streak a mile wide. I had seen it, clear as day. And no matter how nice he was to me, I'd be a fool to ignore it.

'Don't assume that there is only one enemy force at work here,' said the major. 'And don't assume your professor is any safer here at Durrington than he was at Renscombe. Nothing is ever what it seems in this war.'

I sat back, letting that last statement sink in.

'However...' she rested both elbows on the desk, and propped her chin on her hands '...you did well to outwit those bikers.'

'I just did what anyone would have done.'

'You give other people too much credit.' Her tone was dry. 'You're resilient and resourceful. Which is why I am keen to put what we discussed last time on a more formal footing. I want you to work with me to watch out for spies and protect British interests.' She placed a satchel on the table between us and pulled out some papers. 'However, before I go any further, I am going to need you to sign these.' She slid them across to me. 'What do you say?'

On His Majesty's Service was stamped across the top in large, important letters.

I scanned the first page before pushing it back to her unsigned. 'I have already completed confidentiality documents.'

'I know.' She nudged the papers towards me once again. 'These are... more stringent.'

'Stringent how?'

She tapped the top document. 'This is a copy of the Official Secrets Act. I need you to read it and then sign here.' She pointed to the last page of the second sheaf of papers. 'To confirm that you have seen the act and understand that you must comply with it. Because once you sign, you are obliged to stay silent on anything and everything to do with what I am about to tell you. On pain of death.'

On pain of death? My mouth was suddenly drier than any desert. It was all too much. I needed time to think, only there *was* no more time. I fought down a growing sense of panic and pulled the papers closer. '*If* I sign, who exactly would I be working for? You talk about hoping that Daniel is on the right side. How do I know that you're...?' There was no polite way to put it. 'How do I know that *you're* on the right side?'

A flicker of mild amusement ghosted across her face. 'Are you suggesting that I am in league with the Nazis?'

'It's not a daft question. This could all be a ruse to get information out of me on the very project you claim to be trying to protect.'

'It could,' she agreed. 'Particularly in these uncertain times with the worst enemy this country has ever faced knocking at the door. I assure you, I am working for the British government at the highest level.' She took a pen from her breast pocket and placed it on top of the papers before nudging them back towards me. 'Sign and I will tell you everything. If not, I leave, and this conversation never happened.'

Self-preservation warred with a deep-seated need to know more. My stomach churned. There was no escaping the fact that signing meant putting myself in the path of danger. Yet – what with first the intruder and now the car chase – danger seemed to be finding me anyway. People were putting their lives on the line for Britain every day. Why should I be any different? The chaotic events of the last six months had conspired to bring me here. Perhaps this was why. Did I trust the major? For some reason, I found that I did. The real question was: would I ever forgive myself if I walked away?

The answer was immediate and categorical. No.

I unscrewed the cap and signed my name in strong confident letters.

Private Felicity Makepeace.

I sat back in my chair. A surreal sense of detachment settled over me like the folds of a thick, warm blanket. Perhaps I was still in shock from all the recent drama.

Major Stapleton scooped the papers up from the desk between us and returned them to her satchel. 'Just to reiterate,' she said, screwing the cap back on her pen, 'everything I tell you from here on in is designated *Most Secret*.'

I nodded.

She steepled her fingers and took a deep breath. 'Recent developments in Europe are alarming. With northern France under Nazi occupation, larger enemy planes with bigger bombs can now reach British cities. Intelligence reports suggest that we are mere weeks away from a full-scale invasion.'

My chest suddenly felt too tight. 'The gliders,' I whispered, suddenly remembering what had happened at the dance.

'What about them?'

'I overheard two people at a dance in Swanage last week. I don't know who they were. I didn't see them. It was dark. One was definitely a man. His accent was foreign. The other, I couldn't say. But they mentioned an advance invasion via gliders to take out strategic military locations.'

She frowned. 'Why didn't you tell me?'

'I should have. I meant to. And then the first glider test took place, and the professor wanted to come here and... well, then it all got away from me. I'm sorry.'

'I'll report it as soon as I get back. Although, I understand the glider test results were positive.'

'Yes,' I said. 'Which, I suppose underlines how important the professor's ground-controlled intercept project is.'

'It's vital, because successful aerial attacks will be followed by naval advances and then boots on the ground. The government and the armed forces have already started planning for what might be needed if Britain were ever occupied like France.'

'How?' It made sense to plan for every possibility, even the unthinkable.

'There have been a number of different initiatives put into play, such as moving central government and key strategic forces into hidden locations, for example, and establishing secret methods for fighting back. They've recently set up what they are calling the Special Operations Executive.'

I nodded, not because I understood or had ever heard of it, but because it seemed expected. Still reeling from the major's casual suggestion that the country might end up overrun by Nazis, I thought of poor Kitty and the number of times I had reassured her that it wouldn't happen. Yet the government was already facing the fact that it could. And soon. Sharp needles of terror thrust into the deepest recesses of my soul.

The major continued, her tone matter-of-fact. 'I won't go into details for security reasons but, for the most part, they are involved with the training and distribution of specialised troops along with equipment and provisions to establish a number of most secret activities, mainly abroad. However, they also have a few schemes in mind here in Britain that involve sabotaging an occupying force in some rather ingenious ways.'

The thought of sabotage brought a tight smile to my lips.

'I can see that appeals to you,' she said. 'Well, in spite of the laudable bravery of all the men involved in these plans, I think they are missing a trick, and I've been trying to persuade the prime minister so. Not that I am making much progress.'

'What trick?'

'Women,' she said succinctly. 'As I've said to you previously, women are underappreciated and overlooked by everyone. Even other women. No one expects us to be capable of doing anything even slightly unusual, or brave, let alone extraordinary.'

I didn't disagree. 'It's the story of my life.'

'The right woman in the right place at the right time can make all the difference.' She raised both hands, palms up. 'Take what happened the other day for example. *Then*, the right woman was you. I would wager the minute those bikers realised there was a woman at the wheel of the professor's car, they assumed their attempted kidnap, or whatever it was, would be a runaway success. They didn't factor in what an excellent driver you are, or your ability to think on your feet. Or...' she paused '...your courage.'

It was hard not to blush at her words. 'It was nothing.'

'No, it wasn't. And I know there are other women out there, like you, who can be encouraged to use their unique skills to save this country. Women working in ordinary positions who could also operate effectively undercover. If we get enough talented women working together, we can make a real difference.'

I laughed. 'You sound like you're planning to build yourself an army.'

'Not for me.' She shook her head. 'For Great Britain? Yes. I am. An army of incredible women. I am trying to give us a part in this. The right to defend ourselves, not sit at home waiting for disaster to arrive.'

I couldn't fault her for that. 'Count me in. Whichever way all this plays out, I want an active part in it.'

'Good.' She picked up a small suitcase from the floor and laid it on the table between us. Slipping a key into a central locking mechanism, she released two clasps on either side. A satisfying double click resounded around the room. The lid lifted back to reveal a central metal board inside with black knobs, coiled copper tubing and a section of criss-crossed grille. 'This is a Type 3 Mark II transceiver, commonly referred to as a B2. It's fitted – as you can see – inside a nondescript piece of luggage for ease of concealment. There is space under the lid and above the main wireless unit to lay folded clothes to conceal the true contents. I suggest treating the whole thing as you would any other suitcase – store it under your bed perhaps. People tend not to notice the commonplace.' She pointed inside. 'That's your receiver, your transmitter and your power supply unit. Then in here...' she lifted up a flap to reveal a small compartment '...you have your headset and the tap key for sending Morse code. If you don't know Morse code, I'll leave you this booklet. I'm sure you can pick it up.' She pushed a small paper leaflet across the table towards me.

'Thank you,' I murmured, my eyes running over the wires and dials, trying to appear calm even though I was drinking in the cogs and dials. Direct communication would change everything.

'I've marked the frequency you should use on there,' she said. 'It's higher than that used by most chatter on the airwaves, so should be more secure. Nevertheless, keep messages short and coded. Is that clear?'

I nodded.

'There will be someone – not me, for obvious reasons – monitoring the frequency most of the time. If you have an urgent communication, it will get to me. However, other than emergencies, how about you make contact every Monday evening at six?' She glanced at me to check I agreed. 'Send a simple message, like "All's well and the weather is fine." Unless you have something more exciting to report, of course. Then, finish with your initials followed by the initials of your posting. Hence, you'd be FMD for Felicity Makepeace at Durrington. Wait ten minutes for any reply if it's coming and then power the unit down.' She demonstrated how to tune and operate the equipment. Then slotted everything back into place and closed the case with a double-clicked flourish. 'Excellent. Remember, not a word about what we have discussed to anyone. To all intents and purposes, you must continue to be exactly what you seem: a junior ATS officer delivering secretarial support in addition to driving the professor wherever he needs to go. Can you do that?'

'Yes.'

'Good.' She gave a brisk nod, getting to her feet. 'In which case, I will take my leave. I look forward to working with you. Good luck.'

I watched her go, feeling a strange fluttery dance going on inside my chest, a curious mixture of excitement and trepidation. I sat back in my chair. A crinkling sound from my pocket reminded me of Kitty's letter. I pulled it out and slipped a finger along the seal.

Dear Fliss,

How sad I am to know that you will not return to Renscombe for the fore-seeable future. It seems it is all change for the four of us. Rosie and Jane left for Ventnor yesterday. Carole and I think our digs feel quite empty all of a sudden, although Beaky says there will be two new girls joining us soon.

I've been moved into the observation room permanently. I love the work. It's so much more interesting than the canteen. And it wouldn't have been possible if it hadn't been for your help and encouragement. Thank you so much.

I've packed up all your things.

Sending you the best of luck. Do stay in touch. You know how much I love receiving letters.

Your friend always,

Kitty

x

PS: Beaky insisted I include your typewriter.

PPS: She also said to tell you to stay out of trouble.

The last made me smile. If only Beaky knew. I tucked the letter away, making a mental note to write back to Kitty later that evening. As long as I didn't include anything confidential, there was no reason we shouldn't stay in contact.

35

The next morning, the freshly transported Renscombe project was ready to get underway at Durrington. The professor gathered his team in his new office to brief them on the next stage of the collaboration.

'As you know, current overland reporting from the Observer Corps observation posts set up during the last war simply isn't enough,' he said. 'Aerial detection over British soil is patchy and unreliable, especially at night, or when the weather is poor. The Air Ministry is demanding that the ground-controlled intercept facilities we're developing, to deliver accurate inland cover to give our boys a fighting chance when they go up to defend us, be mobile.'

Robbins, a short scientist with a serious expression and floppy blonde hair, raised a tentative hand. 'When you say, mobile, sir, what exactly do you mean?'

'We've already been working on components for what they're referring to as the Air Ministry Experimental Station or AMES for short,' the professor said. 'What they're doing here at Durrington is taking that concept and mounting it on trucks.' The excitement in his voice was hard to miss. 'They've almost got a prototype ready.'

Havers gave a low whistle. 'What are they mounting it on?'

'Crossley tenders,' I said. You could hear a pin drop as all the scientists turned to stare at me with looks of stunned amazement, as if I had suddenly started can-canning around the room, complete with high kicks and flashes of my knickers, which in my sturdy A-line ATS uniform skirt would have been quite an achievement.

'Sorry,' I said, ducking my head to hide flaming cheeks. 'I didn't mean to interrupt.'

'Don't apologise. You know more about trucks than I do. Tell this lot,' the professor waved a hand towards the gathered scientists, 'why Crossleys are a good fit.'

Realising he was serious, I gathered my thoughts. 'Well, the three-ton Crossley tender is sturdy and adaptable. They can be modified to carry all sorts of military equipment. They have four-wheel drive so are excellent for a range of terrains. There's no reason why you couldn't mount a transmitter unit on one and the corresponding receiver on another. Aerial gantries and cantilevered platforms shouldn't be an issue either. Any half-decent mechanic can make elements of the array retractable so they can be secured for movement and then extended for operational use once in position. The tenders have a top speed of fifty-five miles per hour, which is reasonable. However, reliability is preferable to speed when moving sensitive equipment in convoy and the Crossley is more dependable than other similar vehicles. You can add trailers and mobile generators to follow as needed.'

Several beats of silence followed my words.

'Exactly right.' The professor rubbed his hands together. 'I'll be frank, my first response was that a transportable system wasn't possible. However, a convoy can be driven to any site and made operational within twenty-four hours of arrival. Doctor Branson and his team here at Durrington are in the middle of building such a system, and they are going to be using many of our components. If you'd all like to follow me, I suggest we go and take a look.'

He was through the door, off down the corridor and outside before the rest of the team realised his intention, leaving them scurrying to catch up.

Daniel fell into step beside me, bringing up the rear. We crossed the expanse of tarmac to the largest of the hangars on the far side. Constructed from steel poles and corrugated metal sheeting like many of the temporary buildings thrown up by the armed forces in recent months, this hangar was extra high with immense sliding doors, which opened to reveal several modified Crossley tenders parked inside. Although I had seen the set-up already, I'd not had a chance to really examine it. The urge to skip up and down like a child in a sweet shop charged through my veins as I ran my eyes over the machinery.

Breathing in the heady mix of motor oil and grease, I wanted to grab a wrench and dive in. Instead, I contented myself with walking behind the professor as he toured the length and breadth of the hangar, commenting on each vehicle in turn before returning to the first one where he began lecturing his team about issues relating to height and manoeuvrability.

A massive array of metal struts mounted on the flatbed of the truck supported a series of curved reflective dishes. Pulleys and chains led down from a gantry and were being fed into what looked exactly like spiked cogwheels from bicycles complete with pedals attached. It was so similar to the diagram I'd drawn on the blackboard all those weeks before – the night the intruder broke into hut 4 – that I gasped. Admittedly, it was a simple concept, and it was entirely possible that someone else had had the same idea. Regardless, it was a heady feeling to see the concept in reality.

A mechanic in blue overalls with MATT stamped across his shoulder blades in large friendly letters, was crouched on the truck bed adjusting something.

'Excuse me,' I said, in a low voice.

He raised an enquiring eyebrow. 'Yes, love?'

'This is the receiver, yes?'

He looked mildly surprised. 'Yes.'

'And turning those...' I pointed at the pedals and then up at the array above '...feeds these chains through that cog to adjust the orientation.' It wasn't a question. I knew what it did. I just wanted to revel in the moment.

'Yes. We should get complete coverage of the sky with it, too.' His voice was gruff but not unkind.

'And, once you have found a signal, I assume you will focus in on that specific sector,' I said. 'And then you can fine-tune for a number of eventualities.'

'Exactly.'

It worked just as I had imagined it would. 'Do you mind telling me what gave you the idea for this bit?' I pointed to the cogwheels. 'Did you not think of using something more sophisticated?'

He smiled. 'Your lot sent us a drawing of something similar, a while back. We've modified it, but not much. Our original plan was to develop hydraulics for it and we still might. In the meantime, this is cheaper and a lot faster to build and maintain. Given the time pressures we're under, it was an obvious choice.'

It *was* my design. I hugged my delight close to my chest, grinning from ear to ear.

Matt reached down to tighten a final bolt before jumping from the vehicle. He landed as light as a cat, right next to me. 'The only real issue has been getting the electrical feed down from up there, without it getting tangled up in the pulley system,' he said.

I hadn't thought about that.

'We've sorted it, though,' he said, patting a series of cables that led to the back of the truck bed.

'Where does that go?' I asked, aware that Daniel had crept up behind me and was listening intently.

Matt pulled a cloth from the pocket of his overalls to wipe his hands. 'Come on. I'll show you.' He moved towards the back of the truck. 'The plan is for it to feed into the operations room where the data will be displayed. We haven't quite sorted the hook-up yet. That's what we're working on at the moment. The data will identify the usual: bearing, position, height. Basically, what's needed to plot the position of any incoming aircraft. That will then be mapped and fed into the Dowding System at Fighter Control via telephone.'

'The Chain Home sites have a hardwired telephone system and dedicated lines. How are you going to achieve the same reliability with a mobile AMES unit?' asked Daniel.

'That's a point,' I said. 'There won't always be telephones installed nearby.'

'Agreed,' Matt conceded, wrinkling his nose. 'We plan to use a couple of Mark Two TMC field telephones to start with. They're not as dependable, of course, but we'll have spares as backup. We're looking to upgrade to something a bit more robust but, like everything, it's a work in progress.'

Daniel nodded, deep in thought. 'I suppose depending on where you set up, there might be an existing line you can tap into.'

'Potentially,' said Matt. 'That's the sort of variable that we will only know when we get on site.'

'And I suppose, Fighter Command will put the AMES data you send in with all the other information coming from other sources,' I said.

'Exactly,' said Matt. 'Data from Chain Home, the Observer Corps *and* the AMES units all added together will give pretty comprehensive coverage. With constant updates, all telephoned in as they happen, Fighter Command can build a precise moving picture of what is going on in the skies over Britain at any given moment.'

Daniel gave a low whistle of admiration that expressed my own sentiments exactly. 'Giving our pilots a huge advantage. Any defence force sent up will be able to zero in on a specific target deliberately, rather than stumble across them by accident at the end of a long patrol. It'll make a massive difference. If they can arrive fresh for a skirmish, with a full tank of fuel, detailed knowledge of what sized fleet they are facing, they'll be fast, efficient and deadly.' That last was said with intense relish. His delight at the advantage this system would give us as a country was both compelling and unmistakable. There was no way he was working for the enemy. I was sure of it.

Realising that I was staring at Daniel, my mouth hanging open, I snapped it closed and shuffled closer to Matt, dredging another question from the depths of my mind. 'And the operations trailer, how will that work?'

'We're fitting out that unit,' said Matt, indicating a four-wheeled trailer that resembled a large box-shaped caravan right at the back of the hangar. 'It's for a crew of three with space to house displays for the range and height finders, fighter control, and plotting. It's snug, but it does the job.' He shot us a quick smile, clearly keen to show it off. 'Come and see.'

The Renscombe research team spent the whole afternoon in the hangar as the Durrington team took us over their proposals for each vehicle in the convoy in minute detail and answered our many questions.

* * *

By the time evening came, I was exhausted but happy. To be a small part of such an important project was a huge privilege. After a tasty meal of hot pot in the canteen and a warm cup of cocoa, I slipped into my bunk, my head reeling with everything I had learned. Conscious that my radio set was hidden under my bed, I would be lying if I didn't admit to a few wobbles about what I had signed up for. Nevertheless, I comforted myself with the knowledge that the work being done here was vital for national security. I had to protect it, no matter the personal risk involved.

36

The next morning, we gathered outside the hangar to see those parts of the AMES unit currently on vehicles driven out onto the airstrip and placed in sequence, as they would be positioned when operational in the field. The scientists planned to confer on certain elements that required improvement. Mindful of the protective role Major Stapleton had charged me with, I stayed alert to those around me and observed the general interaction of the group. All appeared to be exactly as it should, two sets of scientists completely enthused with the details of the project they were working on and keen to move development forward to the next level.

Matt manoeuvred the receiver out of the hangar onto the tarmac and demonstrated how extra sections of the array would be reinstalled, once in position.

'You see these slots in this part here?' He pointed to the upper section. 'You slide an extra gantry on them, which gives you additional height.'

The wail of an air-raid siren interrupted him. While sirens had frequently sounded in Swanage, they'd rarely gone off at Renscombe. The remote location on the clifftop afforded a degree of protection. We often saw planes out over the water, and heading inland, but nothing so close that we needed to worry. In contrast, Durrington was close to three urban areas: Bognor Regis, Worthing and Brighton. It stood to reason that there would be more risk of aerial attack.

Icy prickles of panic scuttled down my spine and I prepared to follow everyone to a shelter, only no one moved.

'Relax,' said Matt, casting a casual glance up at the sky. 'They're a bit trigger-happy with the sirens around here. You wouldn't believe the number of false alarms we get. We usually wait until the last minute before taking cover. Nine times out of ten they're not after us, anyway. Enemy bombers have to pass over us to reach other targets. If we stopped work for every alert we'd never get anything done. Look.' He pointed off to the east, where a dozen or more planes were silhouetted against the morning sun. 'It's a dogfight rather than a bombing raid. Not much point taking shelter.'

The planes danced around each other as if playing tag. Two broke away from the main group and headed our way, one chasing the other. I squinted to make them out. A Messerschmitt with a Spitfire on its tail.

'Aren't you concerned that they might photograph the AMES units?' asked Daniel.

Matt gave a shout of laughter. 'The pilots are too busy to be getting cameras out. You're right, though, we should be careful not to have the array out in the open like this for too long.'

I couldn't take my eyes off the Messerschmitt dipping and diving, trying to shake the Spitfire loose. The sound of engines straining reached us on the breeze, becoming louder as they approached. The Messerschmitt pilot threw his plane into a barrel roll, which brought him almost directly overhead, before performing a sharp turn and heading back towards his fellow countrymen. As he retreated, the Spitfire closed in. There was sudden burst of rapid gunfire.

I took a step forward, shielding my eyes from the sun, as I watched with my heart in my mouth.

Smoke poured from one wing of the Messerschmitt, but the pilot held his course, eventually rejoining the other Messerschmitts and limping out to sea with them, the Spitfires hard on their heels.

'What if he had crashed here?' I asked, amazed that we were all standing around watching when an aerial fireball could have landed right on top of us.

Matt shrugged. 'The odds of that happening are small. I'd rather keep working.'

I exchanged a nervous look with Daniel, who merely wiggled his eyebrows in response.

'And if it's a bombing raid, rather than a dogfight, is there a bomb shelter over on this side of the site, or do we run for the basement under the dormitories they mentioned when we arrived?' Daniel asked.

Matt paused in tightening up a bolt on the array and waved his spanner across the site at the main building. 'There's only the one shelter. It's big enough for everyone. If you hear a night-time siren, grab your blankets and head down there. There are benches and an urn for tea. It's comfy enough.'

With the planes in retreat and no sign of them returning, we drifted back to work. I noticed a couple of men stood outside a small hangar on the far side of the observation tower. They were clad in dark-green overalls rather than the RAF blue that the AMES project team all wore. One was watching the sky; the other stared over the tarmac towards us. Tall and broad, with fair hair, he lingered when his companion went back inside. Something about his stance and the set of his shoulders tugged at my memory. The distance between us made it impossible to make out his features but an uneasy feeling slithered down my spine.

'Who's that, over there?' I asked.

Matt followed my gaze. 'There are other projects underway here, not just this one. That's an army hangar, over there. Hence the green overalls. He's probably one of their mechanics.'

At that moment, the professor called for me. I dismissed the stranger and hurried to see what he wanted.

We fell into a pattern of intense work interspersed with meals and short rest breaks as the two research crews collaborated from dawn until dusk. I filled notebook after notebook with cramped shorthand documenting anything the professor felt was important and typed it all up. Multiple daytime air-raid warnings went off, but nothing to cause too much concern.

* * *

A week later, in the middle of the night, the sirens went off. Then, a series of high whistles sounded, followed by loud crumps that were far too close for comfort. The whole building seemed to rock on its foundations. Groans, thumps and rustles rippled the length of the dormitory.

I sat bolt upright in my bunk, my mouth dry. The meaty drone of aeroplane engines growled overhead.

The girl in the next bed flicked on a torch and whispered, 'Grab your blanket and your dressing gown or coat, whichever is warmest, and follow me.'

I scrambled from the bed and shoved my feet into my slippers. My hands shook as I dragged my greatcoat on and bundled my blanket under one arm.

More whistling sounds pierced the air. I froze, waiting for the inevitable explosions. The ground shook beneath my feet. A smattering of small particles rained down and a low whimper escaped me before I could stop it. I reached to pull the radio from under the bed.

'Leave it,' she hissed. 'It's more important to save *you*, than your stuff.'

She was right, plus it would look really suspicious if I insisted on lugging a suitcase down to the basement. Abandoning it, I hurried after the other girls, out into the corridor. Sergeant Coombes stood at the bottom of the cellar steps directing women into the first room we came to and waving the men further along the passageway. I followed my dormitory companions without a word. Shuffling over to a bench against the far wall, I plonked myself down, my eyes darting back to those outside in the corridor, searching for the rest of my team.

The professor stumbled past the open doorway, his hair rumpled, a bemused look on his face. Daniel was two steps behind, his gaze locking with mine. He raised a hand in silent greeting. I smiled in return, my heart giving a little skip even as my cheeks warmed at the thought of him seeing my sleep-dishevelled appearance.

The lack of windows in the basement brought with it the advantage of no blackout requirements. Several oil lanterns had been lit and hung from hooks in the ceiling. The murmur of desultory conversations started as the girls tried to distract each other. Packs of cards, newspapers and books were brought out and cups of tea passed around. Someone handed me a part-finished crossword and the stub of a pencil and I did my best to relax, while my ears strained in anticipation of the awful whistle and crump of falling bombs overhead.

After a while, the girl sat next to me gave me a nudge. 'Do you know that man?'

I glanced up and followed her gaze to the doorway, in time to see a tall male figure turning away, his face hidden. I didn't see enough of him to answer her, but the unsettling sensation of being watched returned. Was it the same army mechanic from before? And if it was, who was he? 'I'm not sure,' I said. 'I don't think so. Why do you ask?'

She shrugged. 'No reason. He was just staring at you. I thought maybe... well, it was a bit strange. That's all. Forget I said anything.'

I flashed her a quick smile to hide my growing concern. It brought back memories of Jake and made my skin crawl. I brushed that thought aside. Jake couldn't get me here. Then, a more alarming notion presented itself. What if it was one of the bikers who had chased us? Might one of them have found a way onto site and be biding their time before striking?

When the all-clear sounded, I filed back to bed, checking over my shoulder several times. Things always seem so much worse in the dark. I spent the rest of the night huddled under the blankets, exhausted and terrified, wild ideas chasing each other around and around inside my head. What if the bikers weren't just after the professor? What if they wanted to kill me? After all, I'd outwitted them before. And I'd had a pretty clear view of one of them, despite his helmet and goggles. Those buck teeth with the single broken incisor were pretty recognisable. Telling myself not to be so dramatic and to be more vigilant in future, I finally fell into a fitful sleep.

37

Emerging from the main building the following morning, I sensed a distinct chill in the air. Geese circled overhead in an arrow formation, their mournful honking announcing their intention to head south for the coming winter. I paused to watch, one hand raised to shade my eyes from the glare of the sun, doing my best to shrug off the demons from the night before as well as a thumping headache from lack of sleep. Columns of thick black smoke rose from the rooftops of Worthing and a sharp acrid smell scraped at my lungs. I wrapped my arms around my torso and sent up a small prayer, hoping that no one had been hurt by the bombs, and hurried across to the hangar to join the research team.

'Ah! There you are,' said the professor. He held out a sheaf of crumpled papers. 'I made some notes last night. I need you to type them up. It's a method for improving the receptor array sweep angles. Make two copies please.'

I pinned a smile on my face, a tight band wrapping itself around my sore head at the thought of spending hours trying to decipher his cramped scrawl.

My typewriter was set up in the professor's office back in the main building, so I headed back across the tarmac, grabbed a cup of tea from the canteen and started work.

An hour later, engrossed in transcribing a particularly complicated paragraph, I didn't hear the door open.

'Felicity Makepeace.' A tall, broad, dark-green-overall-clad figure loomed at my side.

My whole body stiffened in immediate recognition. My stomach twisted into a knot. Dear heaven! It couldn't be. I shot to my feet, my chair clattering to the floor. 'Jake?'

'Yes. *Jake*,' he snarled and grabbed my shoulders, cruel fingers biting into my flesh. 'I bet you never expected to see me again.'

'I... I—' There were no words. No air. This made no sense. What was he doing here, dressed as a Durrington site mechanic? 'How did you find me?'

'Ha!' he spat. 'You gave that hag with the flowers your coat, but you forgot something didn't you?'

I sagged inside. Major Stapleton's letter.

He thrust his face closer. 'I followed you to that Foxhalt place. I wanted to see what you were up to. Marching around with all those other stupid girls.'

No wonder I'd felt as though I was being watched.

'I decided to go back and grab you the next week,' he hissed. 'Make you disappear forever.' He grunted. 'Only by the time I got there, you'd gone. You must have thought you were so clever.'

'No. I didn't. I just wanted you to leave me alone.'

'Shut up!' He gave me a sharp, neck-snapping shake, like a terrier with a rat. 'You made me look stupid.'

My head spun. 'I didn't... I—'

'All the old men down the boozer laugh at me, you know? They say girls would rather join the army than walk out with me.'

I lurched to one side, hoping to put some distance between us.

He mirrored my movement. A menacing smile spread across his face, shooting shards of ice-cold fear through me. 'I don't like it when you run.'

I threw my arms up between his, trying to break his hold, just like Daniel had shown me after the party. Jake's grip was too strong.

'Stop that!' He shook me again.

My teeth rattled. The only thing I could think to do was keep him talking. 'If you lost me after Foxhalt, how did you know I was here?'

'There was a rumour Carl Edwards had seen you. Then, his mam told your da he'd been deployed here to Durrington. I took a gamble that you were here too. And look.' He grinned, revealing sharp yellowing teeth. 'You are.'

I swallowed down the bitter taste of bile. 'This is a secure site. How did you get past the guards?'

He laughed, harsh and malevolent. 'That was a doddle. I waited in the bushes for a delivery and snuck under the truck chassis while they were checking paperwork. It's easy enough to hang on long enough to get on site. Then, I stole a set of overalls and a spanner and started tinkering with an engine. Everyone assumed I was a new mechanic. That I'd arrived with your lot, was superfluous to requirements and had been sent over to help another team out. Blending in was easy. Watching you was fun.' There was a ring of satisfaction to his words that told me how very pleased he was with himself.

'Why?'

'Because nobody makes a fool of me.' He leaned in close, his stale breath making me gag. 'You're going to pay. Bitch.' With a sweep of his arm he sent the typewriter clattering to the floor, and shoved me back over the desk, pinning me in place with one merciless paw as he tugged at my skirt with the other.

This couldn't be happening. Sour body odour made me gag. I could hear my breath coming in short, sharp gasps. Somewhere, someone was whimpering. It was several seconds before I realised that someone was me. As Jake's hand crept up my thigh, I remembered Daniel's words. *Make as much noise as you can.*

I dragged in as much air as I could and let out a piercing scream.

Daniel's voice was louder now. *Scratch, kick and bite.*

My hands curled into claws and I raked at his eyes, my nails tearing flesh. He jerked away, cursed and slapped my cheek so hard that for several heartbeats there were two of him. I blinked multiple times, desperate to clear my vision. He seized my wrists, trapping them together in one huge hand, his forearm pressing me down onto the tabletop while the other returned to drag at my skirt. The sound of ripping fabric filled the air.

I kicked out but Jake twisted his hips, making it impossible for me to connect with a target. In desperation, I wriggled and bucked, straining forwards, my teeth searching for part of him to sink themselves into, any part.

'Stop it.' His massive palm walloped the side of my face again, the force exploding through my head like a thunderclap.

My ears buzzed and the room spun. The will to fight leached from my limbs. I was not a physical match for his superior strength. I racked my brain for another tactic. Giving a small sigh, I closed my eyes and went floppy. He gave an evil chuckle and released my wrists to run both hands over my body: my chest, my waist and on down. Gritting my teeth to stop myself squirming away in revulsion, I dropped my hands to my sides and felt across the surface of the table in search of a weapon, anything I could use to gain an advantage.

My fingers curled around my pencil. Having checked which end was sharp with my thumb, I threw all the energy I had left into jerking upright. I swung my arm in an arc, stabbing at his neck with the pencil. The graphite point sank deep into the soft hollow above his collarbone.

Jake gave a howl of pain, backhanding me so hard that I flew several feet and landed in a heap on the stone tiles.

I was done. There was nothing left in me. All I could do was watch as he clutched his shoulder and advanced, his nostrils flared, his lips twisted in pure fury. I closed my eyes, braced for the inevitable.

It never came.

There was a bang, followed by thumps, grunts and the sound of scraping chair legs. I opened my eyes. Jake was sprawled on the floor.

Daniel stood over him, glaring down, fists clenched. 'Get up, I dare you,' he growled. 'Give me an excuse to rip your guts out.'

I dragged myself up into a sitting position and yanked what was left of my skirt back down. 'Leave him, Dan,' I mumbled, probing the split in my lip and running my tongue around my teeth to check they were all still there.

'Leave him?' He turned wild eyes on me. 'I'm not going to leave him. I'm going to *kill* him.'

'No.' I hauled myself to my feet, swaying slightly. 'He isn't worth hanging for.'

'What the...?' Carl stood in the doorway, surveying the room, with Patrick one step behind him. Carl's gaze landed on Jake. 'Jake Derwent!' he snarled. 'I've waited a long time to get my hands on you.' He stormed past Dan, and took hold of Jake by the throat, lifting him from the ground and shoving him back against the wall with a thump.

Daniel shot me a sardonic look. 'Why is he allowed to kill him, when I'm not?'

I sighed. 'Carl, don't—'

'Oh, don't worry, Fliss,' said Carl, his voice laced with lethal calm. 'I have no intention of killing him. This bastard and I have a lot of... well, let's call it *unfinished business*, shall we, Jake?'

I watched the colour drain from Jake's face as his eyes darted from Carl, to Daniel, to me and back to Carl again.

'Yes, Jake,' said Carl. 'Be afraid. You're coming with me. Official interrogation is going to be a long and painful process for you. Patrick,' he called over his shoulder. 'Give me a hand to escort our friend here into military custody.'

'You can't lock me up,' muttered Jake.

'Oh! I can do a lot more than that, buddy,' said Carl. 'You've broken into a high-security military base.' He gestured to Jake's army overalls. 'You're wearing an official uniform that doesn't belong to you. That makes you a spy.'

'I'm not a spy!' exclaimed Jake.

'Prove it,' said Carl, with a calculating smile. 'We have some very inventive interrogation techniques reserved for spies.'

Jake swallowed hard.

Patrick clamped a rough hand on Jake's shoulder.

Carl swept an inviting hand towards the door. 'Come along, Jake. You and I have hours of fun ahead of us and, depending on what you say, there might even be a firing squad at the end of it.'

'No,' gasped Jake, jerking away from Patrick, his voice laden with panic. 'Wait. Listen. I'm not a spy.'

Patrick shoved him face first against the wall and twisted both of his arms behind his back. Carl produced a length of rope from his pocket. Once Jake's hands were tied, he was led away, protesting with every step.

I lowered myself gingerly onto a chair, my battered body screaming in protest, and gazed around the wrecked office at the upturned furniture, the papers all over the floor, the wreckage of my typewriter. Daniel crouched next to me, wrapping his jacket around my shoulders. It was only then that I realised I was shivering so hard I didn't think I would ever stop.

'I'm sorry,' I said. 'I...'

'Never say you're sorry for this,' he hissed. 'This wasn't your fault.'

I sighed and closed my eyes, the pain in my head ramping up.

He got to his feet as the sound of someone approaching came from behind.

Sergeant Coombes, full of brisk bustle, leaned past him to examine my face. 'You've made a bit of a mess of yourself, haven't you, dear?' she said. 'Come along. Let's get you to sick bay and clean you up.' With gentle hands, she helped me to my feet and ushered me towards the door.

38

Trying to sleep that night proved impossible. The combination of thin mattress biscuits and my injuries was torture. Bruises throbbed, cuts ached and my brain tied itself in knots over the day's events. Major Stapleton repeatedly said nothing was what it seemed, but this development was beyond anything I could have anticipated. No wonder I had sensed someone watching me. Jake's attack wasn't part of some wider enemy plot threatening the project. It was an unexpected opportunity to take revenge on me for our personal history, rather than something more sinister. However, if Jake could get onto the base that easily, others could too. We were no safer here than at Renscombe.

The dark hours of the night dragged. Each time I flicked on my torch to check my watch, the hands didn't appear to have moved more than the smallest increment. My thoughts continued to tango around each other in tortuous circles. Tears crept out from under my closed lids, leaking into the hair at my temples, as my spirits sank lower than they'd ever been before. It had all been for nothing. I had tried so hard to escape Jake; had run away from my family and my home. I'd worked hard to fit in somewhere new, but Jake had found me anyway. Even though I had tried to learn how to defend myself, he had still been able to hurt me. If Daniel hadn't arrived when he did, Jake would have got what he wanted. I shuddered at the thought, realising that I was still the frightened young woman who had run along that platform so long ago. What made me think I could be different? That I could become someone who was strong, someone who deserved to be a part of something important? I had been fooling myself. It was time to wake up to reality.

I sat up in bed, sudden resolve coming over me. I had to tell Major Stapleton that she had the wrong girl. I couldn't do what she asked. I wasn't up to it. She needed someone braver, smarter and more capable than me.

It was 2 a.m. Major Stapleton had said someone would be monitoring the radio frequency at all times, but did that mean at night? Now that I had made my decision, I wanted to get it over with as soon as possible. I would message her now, and tell her we needed to talk, regardless of the fact that it was the middle of the night. Perhaps knowing that I had got the ball rolling to end this nonsense would help me to sleep. If there was no response, I could always send the message again, in the morning. I gingerly eased myself from my nest of blankets, stifling gasps of pain, and slid my feet into my slippers. Moving with utmost stealth, I pulled my suitcase from beneath the bed and limped along empty corridors to the professor's office. I paused just inside the door, running my eyes over the room. Everything disturbed during my fight with Jake had been tidied away. There was even a new typewriter on the desk in place of my broken one. It was as if nothing had happened. Only it had. With renewed determination, I placed the suitcase on the desk, opened the lid, connected the battery and slotted the headset into place. With one ear cocked for any disturbance outside the door, I rattled off the message.

```
It is time we met for tea. Urgent. FMD.
```

A few minutes later a response came through.

```
Message received.
```

I dismantled the components, tucked them away, and snapped the case shut before shuffling back to the dorm and stowing it back under my bed. A small inner voice asked if I was sure. I ignored it, even though my heart was breaking. It was the right thing to do. I'd go back to housekeeping in Renscombe, if Beaky would have me. The major would understand.

I couldn't face going back to bed. Tugging my coat on over my pyjamas, I tiptoed from the dormitory, along the corridor and out of a side door to stare up at the stars. Bright pinholes of light in an indigo sky winked back. I shuffled over to a bench set against the wall of the building, eased myself onto it and sat listening to the night. An owl hooted in the distance. All else was still. I took a deep breath of the fresh night air and my racing brain finally started to slow. Until...

What was that?

A faint scrape sounded off to my left.

Every ounce of me hurtled into high alert.

The owl hoot came again; this time, closer.

A dark shape moved, detaching itself from the building, running semi-crouched around the edge of the airstrip. Moving from shadow to shadow, it made its way towards the project hangar. Man or woman, I couldn't tell. They were hunched over, making it impossible to judge height or build. Loose clothing and a hood covering their head created an indistinct silhouette. Injuries forgotten, I was on my feet in an instant and took two strides before stopping and reminding myself I wasn't doing this any more. No more secret spy nonsense. I jigged from foot to foot for a few seconds and told myself to sit back down and ignore it. It wasn't my business.

The impulse to follow was too strong.

I cursed under my breath and trailed far enough behind the shadowy figure not to draw attention. Convinced that the hangar was their target, I was surprised when they continued past it, moving through the overgrown expanse beyond towards the chain-link fence. I paused at the corner of the hangar. The figure slipped from scrappy bush to scrappy bush. I was about to do the same when a hand clamped over my mouth and an arm as strong as an iron band slipped around my waist.

Jeepers! Not again! My hands curled into fists.

Before I could let them fly, a low voice said, 'You disappoint me, Fliss. I really didn't think you would betray your country.'

Daniel.

I twisted around, jerking my head free of his hand, I hissed, 'What in hell's name are you doing here?'

'I think that's my line,' he muttered.

'Shh! They'll hear you.'

A deep line appeared between his brows. 'Who?'

I stabbed a finger towards the person approaching the site boundary. '*Them*. You daft lummox! Who do you think?'

If the situation hadn't been so critical, the way his jaw dropped when he caught sight of the figure would have been laughable. 'Oh!' He released me. 'So, you're not the traitor.'

'No. I'm damn well not,' I huffed, dragging him down into a crouch beside me. 'Now for goodness' sake, let's find out who is.'

'Why is no one patrolling?' whispered Daniel. 'And what— Hey! Where are you going?'

I glared at him over my shoulder. If I thought *I* was bad at this cloak-and-dagger stuff, Daniel was worse. I put a finger to my lips and then stepped away from the hangar wall to slink across the patchy grass towards the fence, hunkering down behind a small bush.

A second shadow appeared beyond the fence and moved towards the first. They met, and the first shadow passed something through the chain links to the second.

I crept closer, and ducked down out of sight again, determined to get close enough to see or hear what was going on. The scrunch of a heavy footstep on loose stones behind me told me Daniel had followed. Unfortunately, it also drew the attention of the figures at the fence. They pulled apart, the one on the far side melting into the darkness. The one on our side started to run.

I gave chase, my battered and bruised body screaming in protest.

The hooded figure darted along the fence line, their trajectory curving away from us and around behind the furthest hangar. If they managed to get behind that and in through one of the doors, they'd be able to hide and with so much equipment stored inside, it would be difficult to find them. The thought galvanised an extra spurt of speed.

It wasn't enough. They were getting away.

Daniel dashed past, his long legs eating up the distance, closing in on our quarry. Just as they rounded the corner of the hangar he dived, tackling the shadow around the knees. Twin grunts rent the air as they both slammed into the dirt and a cloud of dust kicked up. I skidded to a halt by Dan's side as he wrestled his opponent into submission. He flipped the fugitive onto his back and yanked back his hood to allow the moonlight to illuminate his face.

We let out identical gasps and reeled back in shock.

The professor lay in the dirt, squinting up at us and gasping for breath.

39

A thorough search of the area around the site to see if the professor's contact could be apprehended failed. A few hours later, I stood in his office, all the piles of work waiting to be done unheeded, and watched the man I had come to respect so much fidget in his chair as we waited for a security detail to arrive to take him into custody.

Carl stood, with his arms crossed, blocking the door to the corridor, and glowered across the room like a lion preparing to tear his prey to pieces. Daniel paced the floor, fury radiating from every line of his body.

The professor tugged at the ropes tying his wrists to the arms of his chair. 'Are these really necessary?' he whined.

Daniel rounded on him. 'Yes, sir. They are. You're a traitor.'

'No!' The professor gave an adamant shake of his head. 'You've got it all wrong. I was merely conferring with a colleague for the good of the project.'

'If your actions were above board, you would have brought this so-called colleague onto site, through security.' Daniel's lip curled. 'I never thought you would betray your country.'

'I didn't.' The professor's shoulders slumped. 'You don't understand. It's not like that.'

It was hard to see him looking so defeated and hear the wobble in his voice. I'd grown used to his irascible ways in the months I'd been working with him. We'd developed a rapport.

I couldn't just do nothing. On impulse, I dragged a chair over to sit near him. 'What *is* it like?' I said, my voice soft. 'Tell me.'

He bowed his head and mumbled at his shoes. 'Three years before the war I met a German scientist at a convention in Munich. Dieter Braun. He is a mastermind. His theories on radio detection finding were nothing short of ingenious. We started writing to each other, exchanging ideas. The progress we made together was staggering.'

'Then the war started?' I asked.

'It all stopped.' He sighed, a long, sad sound, as if the weight of the world was squeezing all hope from his body. 'I miss him. Not just the intellectual exchange. I miss my friend.'

He suddenly seemed decades older. Only a monster would feel no sympathy at all for the grief radiating from every line of his withered frame. 'What happened?' I asked.

'Three months later, I received a message. A piece of paper passed to me in the street by someone who melted into the crowd before I could see who they were. It was from Dieter. Suggesting that we stay in touch.'

'How?' demanded Daniel.

The professor flinched at the unsympathetic tone and seemed to crumple in on himself even more.

I shot Daniel a look, warning him to back off. Couldn't he see that we'd get more information with honey than with poison? 'How?' I asked, keeping my tone soft and encouraging. 'How did you stay in touch, Professor?'

He raised confused eyes to mine. 'There's a hollow log on the cliff at Renscombe, near the chapel. I took a walk each morning. Sometimes there was a letter waiting for me. I'd leave one in return a few days later.'

Daniel cursed. 'And you didn't for one minute think that what you were doing was wrong?'

'He was *giving* me information,' implored the professor. 'Information that helped.'

'And you were betraying British secrets in return,' Daniel snapped back.

'I didn't give him anything critical.' A defensive edge crept into the professor's voice. 'Nothing that would actually help the Nazis.'

'How do you know that?' demanded Daniel. 'How do you know that something you told them didn't lead to a breakthrough on their side, or a successful bombing raid on British shores?'

The professor sat up straight, lifting his chin. 'War cannot be allowed to stand in the way of scientific progress. And anyway, I realised what I was doing was wrong. I tried to stop, but...'

'But?' I asked.

He shook his head. A single tear leaked out from under closed eyelids and trickled down his lined face to hang from his chin before plopping onto his lap. 'I... I don't think it was Dieter I was communicating with because there's no way he would blackmail me. He's a good man. A man of science.'

'Blackmail?' I asked.

He nodded. 'When I said I couldn't give them any more information, they said they'd hurt my wife.'

I'd not thought of him as someone with a family. To me he was just the professor. No wonder he'd been so grumpy and unapproachable, if all this had been going on.

'She wrote to me,' he continued. 'She said two strange men had turned up at the house and asked a lot of odd questions.'

'What did you do?' I said.

'I had no choice but to do what they asked,' he said. 'I tried sending them nonsense. Research with mistakes built in, but they soon realised. And she got another visit.'

'Did they hurt her?'

'No. But I couldn't take the risk that they *would* hurt her.'

'You should have reported all this,' said Daniel.

'I was in too deep,' the professor shot back. 'And *then* the intruder broke in at Renscombe.'

'They decided to take what they wanted,' said Daniel.

'It was a warning, too,' said the professor. 'Telling me they were deadly serious.'

'Do you know who it was?' I asked.

The professor shook his head. 'When those bikers chased us on the way here. I think they wanted to...' He swallowed. 'Well, either to scare me into sending more information or to kidnap me, or... I don't know.'

'What happened, yesterday?' I said. 'How was that rendezvous set up?'

He bowed his head again, shame rolling off him in waves. 'I received an anonymous note, tucked under my blanket in the dormitory – a few days after the rest of the team from Renscombe arrived here – telling me to meet a contact at the fence last night.'

Daniel gave a sharp intake of breath. 'Are you suggesting that someone travelled here *with* the project?'

The professor shrugged. 'I don't know. I only knew that it wasn't over. I gave them one more piece of work, and included a letter begging them to leave me, and my wife, alone.'

A sharp rap on the door alerted us to the security detail's arrival. A trim man in his middle years, wearing a colonel's uniform, walked in. Two armed soldiers followed.

Daniel stood to attention and saluted. 'Colonel Taylor.'

'At ease, Evans,' replied the colonel. He gestured for the soldiers to approach the professor. 'Take the prisoner into custody.'

'Please don't,' implored the professor, as the soldiers untied his wrists. 'I didn't mean to do it. I had no choice. I'm sorry. Please.'

'Be quiet,' said the colonel, his voice soft but commanding.

The professor subsided and was led from the room, a soldier on each side. Carl saluted the colonel and followed.

'Any luck apprehending his contact?' the colonel asked Daniel.

Daniel shook his head. 'Sadly, no.'

Brisk footsteps sounded in the corridor and Major Stapleton arrived in the doorway.

'What are you doing here, Stapleton?' demanded the colonel. Tension shimmered in the air between the two senior officers. Colonel Taylor's eyes darted to me, his eyebrows beetling together. 'Don't tell me you've got one of your little experiments going on here.'

'All right, sir,' the major replied. 'I won't.'

The colonel tutted. 'When are you going to give up on your preposterous idea for women to be undercover agents?'

Daniel threw a startled glance in my direction.

'Never,' said the major.

'Evans and...?' The colonel shot me an expectant look.

'Makepeace, sir,' I said.

He grunted. 'Evans and Makepeace, wait outside.'

Daniel saluted and gestured for me to leave the room ahead of him, and then closed the door behind us. He leaned one shoulder against the wall, crossed his arms and fixed me with an intense stare. 'What did he mean *little experiments*?'

I paid close attention to my feet. 'I've no idea.'

He lowered his voice to a whisper. 'Are you here undercover?'

'I don't know what you mean,' I whispered back, drawing a line on the floor with the toe of my boot.

He snorted in disbelief.

'Theoretically speaking, though,' I said, 'if I *were* an undercover agent, I'm much better at it than you are.'

'I beg your pardon?'

'You're not exactly subtle. I knew from the start that there was something dodgy about you, but you didn't suspect me.'

He turned to stand in front of me, square on. 'How do you figure that?'

'You admitted it. You said you didn't think I was a spy.'

'When did I say that?'

'Last night,' I said. 'Outside the hangar. You said – and I quote – "I really didn't think you would betray your country."'

His mouth snapped shut. 'I did say that, didn't I?'

I inched forwards, sensing victory, a smile on my face. It was fun teasing him. 'Whereas I *always* thought you could be a spy.' I tipped my head towards the office door. 'Your colonel arriving like this has rather blown your cover, hasn't he?'

He took a step closer. 'Only as much as your major has blown yours.'

We stood, mere inches apart, our gazes locked in identical narrow-eyed stares. My heart fluttered like the wings of a million tiny hummingbirds.

The door opened and we sprang apart. I rolled my eyes internally. Honestly! It was getting ridiculous. Why were we always being interrupted just as things were getting interesting? At this rate, he'd never kiss me.

Major Stapleton's eyes darted from Daniel to me. 'You two had better not be quarrelling.'

I gave her a crisp salute. 'I wouldn't dream of it, ma'am.'

She tipped her head. 'Walk with me, Makepeace?'

'Yes, ma'am.'

A voice came from behind her. 'Evans, get in here,' said the colonel.

40

The major and I strolled across the landing strip, thick coats pulled around us to combat the stiff September breeze.

'You've had a busy twenty-four hours,' she said.

I let out a long, heavy sigh as the reality of recent developments hit me. 'I never once suspected the professor, ma'am, and I should have.'

'Never mind. He's in custody, now.' She cast me a sideways glance. 'Although it looks like he put up quite a fight.'

I shook my head. 'Not a bit of it. He grumbled a lot, but didn't throw any punches. I think, in some ways, it will be a relief for him that it's all out in the open.'

'If the professor didn't hit you, where did you get that shiner?'

'Oh!' I'd forgotten that she didn't know. 'Jake Derwent tracked me down.' I explained that he was the man I had been running from when I left Bristol, and told her about the attack the day before.

'How bad are your injuries?' she asked.

'I'll live,' I said. 'I'll be honest. Jake was the reason I messaged you. I...' I took a deep breath. 'I was going to tell you that I can't do what you want.'

'You *were* going to tell me, or you *are* telling me.'

'I...' I glanced away, running my gaze over the busy site, aware of a renewed sense of purpose. Only hours before, I'd been on the point of giving up every-thing I'd worked for. Stepping away because of Jake. Now, I couldn't do it. If I let him and his bullying ways take everything I had achieved away from me, I might as well have stayed in Bristol all along. If the situation with the professor showed me anything, it was that I was good at what I do and I wanted to keep doing it. 'I *was* going to tell you.'

'Why?'

'I didn't think I was tough enough.'

'I didn't choose you because you're tough. I chose you because you're bright, resilient and adaptable. Something you made very clear the day we met.'

'How?'

'You waltzed into my office and fixed that damn telephone with no more than a paperclip and a bobby pin, like it was the easiest thing in the world.' She smiled. 'You don't have to be tough, you just have to be you. I'm glad you've decided to stay. There are going to be some significant changes in the light of the professor's treacherous behaviour. Added to that, in the last few weeks, intelligence reports have highlighted a growing enemy interest in both Renscombe and RAF Durrington. If that weren't enough, a recent bombing raid on Ventnor deliberately targeted the Chain Home site there.'

'Ventnor?' I gave a sharp intake of breath. 'Was anyone hurt?'

Her lips tightened. 'If you're thinking about your friends, I'm afraid I don't know. I believe the damage to the facility was significant. I'll know more when the full reports are in.'

I staggered back a step. *Oh Lord! Please no!* I could only pray that Rosie and Jane were safe. If they had come to any harm because I had drawn the major's attention to them, I would never forgive myself.

'The decision has been made for several of the research projects to be dispersed to safer locations,' she continued.

I fought against a fog of despair threatening to envelop me, and focused on what she had just said. 'Meaning what?'

'The AMES development unit here at Durrington is to be transferred to Christchurch to the Ministry of Supply's Air Defence Experimental Establishment. Which works in the project's favour, as the ADEE are all set up to manufacture radar components there anyway, so all to the good.'

Another radar research site? How many of them were there? She must have seen the question in my eyes, because she answered with a wry smile. 'The military don't ever put all their eggs together. It makes no sense to have just one facility. It's too obvious a target, and would leave us too vulnerable.'

'I see.'

'Daniel Evans will be in charge of the move. And by the way, my sources tell me that young man is trustworthy.' She tutted. 'Colonel Taylor might be one of the most annoying men on the planet, but his men are dependable.'

I watched her expression closely. There was more to the major's relationship with the colonel than met the eye, I was sure of it. The spiky intensity between them spoke of more than professional rivalry.

'Evans will deliver the project into the hands of Commander Bryant at Steamer Point. Commander Bryant will supervise the final stages of the build of your mobile ground-controlled interception unit and that will then be installed at a location nearby. The prime minister is keen to get it up and running as soon as possible.'

Given the battering the country was currently getting from enemy aircraft, it made sense.

'This new radar technology will be a beacon of hope,' she continued. 'A way to turn the tide on this awful Blitz. The radio callsign or codename for that operational site,' she continued, 'once its location has been identified, will be Starlight.'

'Starlight,' I murmured. I liked the sound of that.

'The callsign will be used in all ground-to-air transmissions between site and pilots once they are airborne. With luck Starlight will be the first of many and we'll give those wretched enemy bombers a real run for their money.'

She was right. Like everyone else in this war, there was nothing I could do to help my friends other than pray that they were safe. The project, however, was another matter. I dug my hands deep into my pockets, refusing to give in to the vast well of worry about Rosie and Jane that beckoned to me. 'And where do I go?'

'Colonel Taylor and I had a long discussion,' said the major. 'I've managed to persuade him that you should continue to work on the AMES project moving forwards. You're familiar with all the important components and training up a new secretary would be a waste of time. You will also act as a driver for whoever Commander Bryant tasks with surveying the area to find the right location for the operational unit.'

A tidal wave of relief washed over me. I wanted more than ever to see it through to the end. And, if I was honest with myself, part of me was keen to stay near Daniel.

'I expect you to continue to keep your eyes and ears peeled,' said the major.

'You still think the project is at risk?'

'I know it is,' she said. 'The professor might be in custody, but the enemy agents are still at large. Several rogue radio transmissions have been detected coming from here.'

'Transmissions before or *after* our arrival on site?' I asked.

'After.'

'The professor received that last note here, too. Which means that someone potentially travelled here with our team. The question is, who?'

'Exactly. I'll arrange a billet for you in Christchurch. You'll have plenty to keep you occupied. Officially and unofficially.' She pivoted and started back towards the main building.

'Wait.' The word exploded from me. I'm not sure who was more surprised: her or me.

She stopped and raised a single eyebrow.

I searched for words, leaning into them when they arrived. 'There's something I need. I want to know how to defend myself properly. I... after Jake... I want to be able to kill a man with my bare hands if I have to.' That statement fell into silence, the gulls overhead mute with shock. 'I'm not saying I'm going to do it. I just need to know that I can.'

She blinked as if I had presented her with a particularly puzzling maths problem.

The more I thought about it, the more I realised I was right. Was it the situation with Rosie and Jane that made me so adamant? I couldn't tell. I just knew that proper training was essential for anyone who became entangled in the major's scheme.

'It's only fair,' I said. 'If you are asking women to take risks, then you owe it to them to train them properly.'

'You make a good point. The special ops division have set up advanced training courses for the men they send undercover. I've asked for the same for my women.'

'And?'

'There's huge resistance to the concept. You saw Colonel Taylor's attitude. He's a pussy cat compared to some of them. Whether it's due to outdated chivalry or pure misogyny, the majority of the top brass cling to the belief that women should not be involved in any form of active combat.'

'Then they need to get over it,' I said. 'We're here and we're playing a part in this war whether they like it or not.'

'Indeed. I assure you, I will continue to push for proper training. In the meantime, get yourself embedded into this new phase of the project in Christchurch and I'll see what I can arrange in terms of private self-defence lessons for you.'

'Thank you.' The relief her words brought was immense. If the major continued to build her army, then those women would hopefully be better prepared for what lay ahead of them. And on a personal level, if Jake were ever released from custody, or I came up against one of those bikers or another enemy agent intent on killing me, with luck, I would stand a chance of beating the odds.

41

I travelled to Christchurch by train and walked down the high street. It was a typically beautiful English country town, yet the unmistakable signs of war were everywhere in the form of taped windows, queues outside shops and uniformed personnel milling around. For the most part the town appeared to have escaped the ravages of the ever-increasing number of bombing raids.

As I followed the directions I had been given to find my billet, I wondered how Daniel had managed the transport of the AMES GCI unit to the new site. He had not asked for my assistance, and I hadn't seen him since that conversation in the corridor outside the professor's office. For all I knew, he could be avoiding me. Perhaps the knowledge that I was an undercover operative, or maybe the tension between our senior officers, had changed his opinion of me. It saddened me to think so, but it was his loss. Any man who thought women didn't have the right to defend their country was never going to be the man for me. I wouldn't be put in a box by anyone.

I made my way to a converted outbuilding behind a pub, which my new landlady, Mrs Finch, also ran. She was a small, rounded, middle-aged woman with grey-streaked hair pulled back into a thick bun, who clucked like a mother hen around all the girls staying with her.

My roommate, Sally, was a cheerful WAAF who worked at the Steamer Point site. She showed me around and also found a bicycle for me to use to get to and from work every day. It was old and rusty, but after a few minor adjustments with a spanner and a quick squirt of oil I had the mechanism working relatively smoothly. As soon as I'd settled in, I dashed off a quick letter to Kitty.

> *Dear Kitty,*
>
> *I hope this letter finds you well.*
>
> *Unfortunately, I have received no news about Rosie or Jane. I am so sorry. We can only hope and pray that they are safe.*
>
> *Thank you so much for letting me know that you and the others will be moving from Renscombe soon. I appreciate that, for reasons of security, you cannot give me your new direction although it is good to know that you are not having to travel too far. Dorset is so beautiful. It is wonderful to know that Patrick will be reassigned with you and good to hear that he treats you well. How romantic.*
>
> *I have moved again too, and similarly am not allowed to say where or why.*
>
> *Thank you for giving me your parents' address in case the war keeps us apart for the duration. I hate the thought of losing touch with you. When I have any news that I can share, and/or when this is all over, I will send a letter to them and, hopefully, you will receive it.*
>
> *We will meet again, my friend.*
>
> *With love,*
>
> *Fliss*
>
> *PS: Please tell Beaky that I am doing my best to behave.*

Hot tears gathered unshed behind my eyes as I signed off. With luck it would reach her before she left Renscombe. It might be a long time before she and I had any contact with each other. I pulled on my coat and hurried to the post office to catch the last collection.

* * *

The next morning, I followed Sally and the rest of her WAAF troop as they cycled to the Air Defence Experimental Establishment. The weather was crisp and the gorgeous sunshine lifted my spirits.

'The ADEE caught a couple of stray bombs about a week ago,' said Sally, her legs pumping at the pedals, her cheeks red from the chill wind. 'There wasn't too much damage. No casualties. One was a dud. Most of the rubble from the other has been cleared away, now.'

'Goodness, that was lucky,' I called, wishing Ventnor had been as fortunate. 'Is it far from here?'

'No. It's only a couple of miles. It's right on the coast. At a place called Steamer Point. Apparently, some lord or other deliberately beached a steamer there in the early eighteen hundreds. Or so Mrs Finch was telling me. He used that as some sort of office for the workers who were repairing his castle.'

'Which castle is that?'

'Highcliffe. Well, it's called a castle, but it's more of a big, posh house than a castle, if you ask me. It's just up from the site, on the cliff, overlooking the Isle of Wight.'

'Stop wittering, Sally,' said one of the other girls. 'We're going to be late if we don't get a move on.'

The scent of salt and seaweed on the breeze would have told me we were near the coast, even without the cacophony from the seagulls whirling over-head. We stopped at a long, low hut set in a vast length of barbed-wire fencing. A vague collection of buildings huddled together in the distance beyond and past that I could see a splash of blue ocean against the sky.

Security was tighter than anything I had experienced before and I was forced to wait until all of the WAAF had passed through before my identity papers were examined.

The officious guard frowned and ran his finger down a list on his clipboard. 'I thought as much,' he said, a gleam of satisfaction in his eye. 'You're not on my list. Wait here – I'll make a call.' He disappeared into the hut and returned a few minutes later. 'Your project *is* here, but Commander Bryant says you're wanted over at the airfield this morning to drive someone.' My dismay must have shown, because his manner softened. 'You're all right. It's only another mile or so. Go back that way.' He pointed. 'Take a left, then a right at the end and then it's second left. You can't miss it.'

Twenty minutes later, I arrived at the airstrip, hot and flustered. It was little more than a grassed runway with a few wooden buildings. A sentry threw a bored look at my documents before waving me in the direction of a temporary hangar with a Morris Eight parked outside. 'There's a chap waiting over there for you. He seems a bit impatient.'

That must be whoever I was here to drive. I abandoned my bike against a hedge and hurried over, running greedy eyes over the vehicle, taking in the shiny black rounded bodywork, the chrome-plated radiator shell, honeycomb grille and bright red leather interior. I experienced a pang of sympathy for whoever had received the requisition order to surrender this beautiful family car to the war effort.

The scuff of shoes behind me made me turn.

Daniel.

I coughed to hide my instinctive delight at seeing him and reminded myself that things were different between us now.

'Why are you here?' he asked, his tone betraying genuine surprise.

'Commander Bryant assigned me to drive you today.'

'Well... You're late,' he said, his tone pointed.

I took a slow breath, fighting the urge to roll my eyes. He'd obviously got out of bed on the wrong side that morning. 'I apologise. I went to the wrong site. It won't happen again.'

A deep line appeared between his eyebrows. 'Why are you really here, Fliss?'

'I told you. I'm your driver.'

'Are you, though? Or, are you here keeping an eye on me for your Major Stapleton?'

So that was it. He thought I would spy on him. It was all I could do not to react. I couldn't let him see how much his words hurt.

'No more than you're keeping an eye on me for your Colonel Taylor,' I shot back.

'I've no idea what you're talking about.'

'Nor I you,' I countered. Two could play at that game.

'Let's get on, shall we?' His tone was clipped.

'Yes, let's. What's the plan for today?'

'Matt and the rest of the team are over at Steamer Point with Commander Bryant checking the convoy units arrived without any damage. They'll be making sure that all the connections still work and installing a new antenna designed from fresh research data that came in last week. As I understand it, several other new components need to be manufactured too. Hopefully, it won't be long before we can do a proper field trial. It's up to you and I to find where that field trial should take place.' He reached into the car for a map, which he opened out over the bonnet. 'The Avon Valley just north of here offers many of the characteristics we're looking for.'

I edged closer to see what he was pointing at, wishing that my pulse would stop going into orbit with every step that took me nearer to him. 'Characteristics like what?'

'Relatively open, flat land. Not too far from the coast. Preferably not close to a built-up area, no high buildings, dense woodland or rocky outcrops.'

'Nothing that would block the efficient transmission and receipt of the signal,' I murmured to myself as I examined a series of crosses marked on the map. One of those might be the Starlight site. A shiver of excitement skipped across my shoulders.

'Exactly,' said Daniel. 'There are several promising sites. We need to survey them all.'

'No problem.' I tugged on my driving gloves. 'You'll have to direct me.'

Daniel folded the map into a more easily manageable size. 'We'll go north to Ringwood and work our way south following the river. Then, once we've seen all of them, we can rank them in order of suitability.'

'And if we don't find anywhere?' I asked.

'Then we widen our search area,' said Daniel. 'We'll keep going until we find what we're looking for.'

'Fine,' I said, a hoppity-skip sensation starting in the pit of my stomach at the thought of sitting next to him all day, possibly all week, or maybe even longer. This could get really awkward. I checked over the vehicle as I always did before driving something new. I kicked the tyres and opened the boot to check the spare was in a decent condition. Who knew what state the roads were in? There was a full canister of extra fuel on board as well as a smaller one of oil. The keys were in the ignition. Satisfied, I slid into the driver's seat and started the engine. 'Are you coming?'

42

That first day was utter torture. Daniel was so close, mere inches away, and yet he might as well be on another planet. My hopes to clear the air were thwarted because he retreated into stiff formality. Colonel Taylor's disapproval of Major Stapleton's operatives – and therefore me – had been clear. Daniel must feel the same way. Why else would his behaviour towards me have changed so much? By the time I made it back to my billet that evening I was both exhausted *and* fizzing with frustration. The thought of sleep was impossible. After supper, I fired a brief radio communication off to the major at the usual time.

`The weather is fine and all is well. FMSP`

I waited the necessary ten minutes for a reply. Not expecting anything, I was about to unplug my headphones and switch off the machine, when a message started coming in. I jotted it down and frowned.

`Training, 8.30 p.m. Tonight. Courtyard.`

My spirits did a little high kick. If this was self-defence training, all to the good. After the day I'd had I was in the mood to thump someone. Courtyard must refer to the cobbled enclosure outside. The pub and the converted barn in which I was billeted formed two sides of a square, with a wooden shed on the third and a brick wall with a wide gateway onto the road on the fourth. The pub was closed Mondays to Wednesdays, or so Mrs Finch had told me, because the weekly beer ration was delivered on Thursday and generally ran out over the weekend. Thus, there would be no interruptions. Intrigued, I tugged on my coat at eight-twenty-five and slipped outside to stand in the dark and wait. All was quiet. A crescent moon sailed high overhead, throwing eerie silver-grey shadows over everything and the night sky was sprinkled with stars that shone all the brighter thanks to the enforced blackout. My breath generated little puffy clouds in the crisp winter air. I waited as the world settled for sleep.

Footsteps alerted me to an arrival. I stiffened.

A match flared. The tip of a cigarette glowed. I heard a deep breath drawn in. 'So, you're here,' came a light female voice.

'Mrs Finch?' She was the last person I expected.

'The one and only,' she replied, her husky voice descending into a chesty cough. 'Belinda tells me you want to learn to kill a man with your bare hands.'

I cleared my throat. 'Belinda?'

'Major Stapleton.'

I stepped forward. 'Yes, I do.'

'Come on, then. I owe her a favour.' She opened the back door to the pub, yanked back the blackout curtain that hung behind it and waved me inside. 'We'll use the tap room.' With the door closed behind her she flicked on the lights. The windows were covered with cardboard and thick blinds so there was no risk of drawing the ire of the warden.

I'd never set foot in a pub before. I gazed around me with interest at the solid oak bar. Rows of bottles and gleaming glasses stood to attention on the shelves behind. The air smelled of tobacco smoke and lavender polish. A poster on the wall encouraged customers to do their bit and donate whatever they could spare to the Spitfire Fund.

We pushed chairs and tables aside to create a clear space. Mrs Finch ran assessing eyes over me. I returned the favour, wondering what such a small, unassuming woman could possibly teach me.

She took a final puff of her cigarette before crushing the butt into an ashtray on the bar. 'I'm not going to ask why you want to do this. It's none of my business. Show me what you know already.'

I frowned, casting my mind back to that evening with Daniel in the church-yard after the dance, and ran her through what he had taught me.

She gave a grunt of appreciation. 'That's all good. How effective have you found it?'

I shrugged. 'Some of it worked. Some of it didn't. The thing is... I still felt helpless. Like I only survived last time because of pure luck.'

'That's often the way. When you are taught by a fella, no matter how well intentioned he is, the techniques aren't necessarily the most effective for a lighter, slighter female. You can't fight like a fella, because you're not a fella. You get my drift?'

I nodded.

'We women have to think differently. Be fast, sneaky and prepared to use deadly force. You won't get many chances to gain the upper hand. Make the most of them.'

I had to ask. 'How do you know all this?'

'You mean, how come an old woman knows how to fight.' A gurgle of laughter gave way to another coughing fit. 'Because I've been fighting all my life. Fighting dirty, too. It's the only way when you run a pub. Being good in a scrap comes with the job. Not that I go around killing my customers, you understand. It's not good for business. But knowing that I can gives me the confidence to deal with them when they get mardy, no matter how big they are.'

'I see.'

She rolled up her sleeves. 'Let's get down to it. Never go on the offensive, if you don't have to. Always try to defuse the situation. If that fails, you have to mean business. If you are carrying a concealed weapon, don't let them know you have it until you use it. What I mean by that is, say you have a knife—'

All of a sudden, there was a knife in her hand, a slim, narrow blade, approximately three inches long. I took a step back. Where had that came from?

'Don't threaten them with it,' she said. 'Get on and use it. If you wave it about trying to persuade them to back off—' she waved the knife in the air between us '—you're inviting them to take it from you. And they will. Then, not only will they be pissed off with you for drawing a weapon in the first place, they'll most likely use your own knife on you.' She paused to let that sink in. 'If you have a weapon, any weapon, then surprise is key.'

I nodded, thinking about Jake and the pencil. If he'd known that I'd had it, things would have played out very differently. I shuddered.

'Using a knife,' she continued. 'If you want to kill, strike here.' In a trice she was behind me, one arm wrapped around my neck, the tip of her knife touched my lower back. 'The kidneys are a good target. Mind you, if you want to stop a big fella in his tracks, then you want to go for the heart. Front or back, it makes no difference to how you strike. Fast and hard in an upward motion to get through the ribs midway down the chest on your opponent's left-hand side.' She dug a sharp pointy finger into my ribs both front and back to show me where.

Her matter-of-fact approach to stabbing someone was both shocking and awe-inspiring. I'd never experienced anything like it before. It was surreal, and yet alongside my discomfort, part of me was cheering with exultation. This was exactly what I needed to know.

'Get it right,' said Mrs Finch, 'and they'll drop like a stone. The jugular is another weak point.' She made a cutting motion with the same finger to the side of her neck.

'What if I want to stop them but not kill them?'

'Achilles tendon. That's here.' She gestured to the hard ridge at the back of my ankle. 'It joins the calf muscle to the heel bone. Cut across. One will do, both is better. Fast and hard. Then get out of range. Don't want them grabbing you on the way down.'

She handed me a wooden spoon. 'Pretend the handle of that is a knife and come at me.' We worked systematically through a whole host of moves and counter moves. When the clock behind the bar struck ten, she put up both hands as if in surrender. 'Time to turn in. Any final questions before you go?'

There was only one. 'Where do you hide your knife?'

She grinned and turned around. Reaching up to her head she slipped the blade into an ornate sheath hidden in the thick roll of hair at the back of her neck. Together the handle of the blade and the sheath made an innocuous-looking hair clasp. 'Now, off you go,' she said, putting out the light, and pulling the blackout curtain over the back door aside. 'We can practise again tomorrow, if you like.'

'Yes, please.' I thanked her and hurried across the courtyard feeling so much lighter than I had earlier on. Whether Daniel approved or not of my decisions, I was going to become the best undercover operative I could be. Anything I didn't know, I could learn.

43

It took two weeks to find the perfect site. Two weeks in which communication between Daniel and I reflected the autumn chill. Training with Mrs Finch in the evenings was the perfect foil, allowing me to work out my frustrations before bed. It made concentrating on work during the days easier, too. He and I were both very aware that time was passing and we needed to find a site to get the facility up and running. Intensely cold weather arrived with a vengeance. Frosts overnight were hard and driving conditions increasingly dicey. Maintaining a slow, steady speed was the only way to avoid ending up in one of the deep ditches that lined the country roads. This in turn slowed our progress, making tempers fray. Hail and sleet made taking readings unpleasant, no matter how many layers of clothing we wore.

By the time we reached the final site on the list – a field in the outskirts of a small village called Sopley – the last thing I wanted to do was walk the perimeter of yet another massive field and take yet more unedifying readings.

I tucked my scarf more securely around my neck against the biting wind, tugged my hat down, rammed gloved hands deep into the pockets of my greatcoat and stomped away from Daniel to tour the boundary, leaving him to take readings, check the map repeatedly and climb on to trees stumps to scan the horizon. Icy gusts bit through the material of my uniform skirt. Cold scratched at my lungs with each breath. By the time I was halfway round, I had lost all sensation in my toes and was feeling very sorry for myself. Even the sight of a patrol of magnificent Spitfires soaring overhead in perfect formation did little to lift my spirits. I returned to the car and grabbed the green Thermos flask I stowed there every day along with a pack of sandwiches, fruit and some biscuits. Using the bonnet as a table, I unscrewed the aluminium top from the flask, pulled out the stopper and poured myself a cup of tea, ramming the plug home again to preserve what heat remained inside. Leaning against the car, I allowed my gaze to roam over Daniel's tall, graceful form, his broad shoulders and easy stride.

Suddenly, he turned and hurried back towards the car. 'This is the one,' he said. 'It has everything we need.' He stopped short, 'Unless you found a problem with the boundary.'

I shook my head. 'Nothing of note, apart from the fact that we'll have to widen the gateway and reinforce the culvert for ease of access.'

He waved a dismissive hand. 'That won't be a problem. We'll have to lay a temporary surface too, and build a latrine, but that shouldn't take long. Other than those minor issues, I think we have a winner. I'll arrange to get Carl out here to check it over.'

'Carl? Why Carl?'

'Didn't he tell you?'

'I haven't heard from him since he left to escort the professor from Durrington,' I said. Why would he think I was in communication with Carl?

'He's been promoted. They want him to run security for the Starlight site.'

'Congratulations to both Carl *and* Starlight.' I raised a pretend toast to the absent Carl with my tea. 'What now? Do I drive you back to the airfield?' If our search was over, we had no reason to continue spending all day, every day together. I clamped my teeth down onto my lip and stared off into the distance. A lone goose circled the sky, calling out for companions who weren't there. Was it the lonely bird's plight that brought tears to my eyes, or the continued distance between Daniel and I?

'Not the airfield,' he said. 'We'll go to the main Steamer Point facility. I need a word with Matt about the convoy.'

I pulled the car keys from my pocket. 'Let's go then.'

* * *

Twenty minutes later, we arrived at Steamer Point. Daniel produced documents at the guard hut and we were waved through. The road led right down to the beach where I parked on a stretch of tarmac overlooking the sea. As I stepped from the car, I couldn't help admiring the view. My love of the sea hadn't changed. Clouds scudded across the sky above the ever-changing grey, blue and green of the water. The fresh tang of salt and seaweed hung in the air.

Something tickled my peripheral vision. Shading my eyes, I stared into the south-eastern sky. 'What in heaven's name is that?'

I felt, rather than saw, Daniel move to stand beside me. 'I don't know,' he said.

A large shadow loomed over the horizon. A low thrum grew louder. As it moved progressively closer, the shadow darkened and split into smaller shadows: pinpricks like a swarm of gnats over a stagnant ditch. Rooted to the spot, I watched each gnat grow until it was clearly identifiable as an enemy Heinkel bomber flying in formation, travelling with steady ruthless progress in a westerly direction parallel with the coast.

'Jeepers,' I muttered, nausea gripping my belly. 'There must be over a hundred of them.'

'Closer to two hundred,' said Daniel. 'Plus, their escort.'

He was right. Countless Messerschmitts danced around the edges of the main fleet.

'Where do you think they're heading?'

Deep grooves appeared either side of his mouth. 'At some point, they'll turn inland and find their target. Something strategic. A port, probably. Maybe Portland or Plymouth. Or something further north.' He turned, an inscrutable expression on his face.

'Bristol?' My voice no more than the ghost of a whisper. I took a shaky breath in. Were Ma, Nana and the boys still in the country with Aunty Mo, or had they returned? What about Da? I had thought about contacting them, now that Jake was no longer a problem. I hadn't yet, though. I didn't know what to say.

Daniel placed a hand on my arm, turning me away from the planes. 'You can't think like that. Those planes could be going anywhere. This is why we're doing the work we're doing. The formation is still over the water. Chain Home will have registered them.'

'They'll be overland soon enough, though. We don't have enough planes to take down that many enemy craft.'

'Chain Home will alert the Observer Corps. They'll track them as best they can. The RAF boys are incredibly skilled and enormously brave. Our duty is to keep doing our bit. We have to get the AMES unit up and running.'

'I know.' Hard as it was to ignore the urge to run around shouting out warnings, he was right. We had to concentrate on the areas where we could actually make a difference.

'Look,' he said. 'Why don't I drop all our data in to Matt. Then we can take a walk. There's a footpath that heads a little way up the cliff. I'm told it's a pleasant walk.'

I dredged up a wan smile. 'That would be nice.'

* * *

A few minutes later, he was back. We walked side by side along a dirt track that rose up and away from the research site into dense woodland. The climb was gentle but steady and shortly afterwards we arrived at a clearing on the edge of the cliff. The view across to the Isle of Wight was stunning.

'Are you feeling any better?' he asked.

I sighed. Our time working closely together was over. There would not be another chance to try and clear the air. 'If you really want to know, I'm sad.'

'Why?'

'Because you and I...' I shook my head, losing my nerve. 'It doesn't matter.'

He stepped closer, putting himself between the view and me, forcing me to look at him. 'You and I, what?'

'We stopped being friends,' I muttered. 'We were friends at Renscombe, and even at Durrington. Or, at least, I thought we were. Now we're not. I don't know why that changed.'

He reached a hand out as if he were going to take hold of my shoulder. Then he stopped, and instead clenched the hand into a fist and lowered it to his side. 'We weren't friends.'

My heart clanged to the ground faster than a dropped sledgehammer. 'I see. Yes, you're right. We were colleagues, nothing more. My mistake.' I drew what shreds of dignity I had left around me like a worn patchwork cloak and turned. 'When you're ready to leave, I'll be in the car.'

He grabbed my arm. 'Wait.'

I shook him off, swallowing down the huge lump that lodged in my throat.

'Fliss, please.'

Something in his voice made me turn back. 'What?' I said, steeling myself for more verbal damage.

'We weren't friends at Renscombe *or* Durrington,' he whispered. 'We were more than friends. Or at least, that's what I was hoping. I don't go around wanting to kiss my friends.'

'Kiss?'

He stepped closer, then closer still, until we were almost nose to nose. Wrapping his arms around me, he pulled me against his chest. Before I knew it, his lips were on mine and he was kissing me. Thoroughly.

My brain emptied as my knees melted. My arms slipped up around his shoulders of their own accord and my whole body sang with delicious, warm sensations.

Oh, my!

I never wanted it to stop.

Eventually, we broke apart. I laughed. 'If that's you and me not being friends, I hope that we're not friends for a very long time.'

He grinned. 'Me too.'

'So, why have you been so distant these last few weeks?'

'I was trying to give you some space. Time to recover from what happened with Jake and then the professor... I know you were fond of him. It can't have been easy for you to see him like that. Me wading in with my personal agenda seemed wrong. Especially as we *had* to work so closely together. I didn't want to put you in an awkward position.' He shrugged. 'The longer I waited, the harder it was to speak up.'

'I thought you didn't care.'

'I care all right. If anything, I care too much. It's been driving me mad, sitting right next to you, unable to touch you.'

I laid a hand on his chest. 'I thought you hated me. That you disapproved of... well.' I couldn't bring myself to mention being an undercover operative. Major Stapleton had said I could trust him, but I'd signed the Official Secrets Act and I wasn't going to break my word. He and I both knew what we were. There was no need to spell it out.

'I'll be honest, I don't know what to think about that. You're very good at appearing to be completely innocuous.'

'You mean, I'm better at it than you.'

He slid his arms around me again, pulling me close and kissing me again. I never wanted him to stop. The warm thrills returned, radiating out from my core to the tips of my fingers and toes.

Eventually, we both had to come up for air.

'Come on,' he said. 'We need to get back.'

We strolled down the path, hand in hand, and arrived back at the car just as an alarm sounded from inside the main hangar. Half a dozen armed soldiers ran around the side of the building.

'That's strange,' said Daniel. 'They're heading towards the project. I wonder what's going on.'

We followed them to a set of huge barn-like doors that had a smaller door set into them for ease of access. Matt was stood outside talking to a sergeant, his face the colour of ash. He looked up as we approached. 'It's the convoy,' he said. 'We left it unattended for half an hour. It was fine. The door was locked. When we got back, it was... damaged.'

* * *

I stared at the crumpled array: receptor dishes torn from their fixings, twisted metal props with sheared bolts sticking out. 'This isn't accidental,' I said. 'It's sabotage.'

Matt jumped down from the observation trailer. 'The screens are all smashed.'

Daniel emerged from the transmission truck. 'Several wires have been ripped from the connection unit. They'll all need replacing.'

Matt sighed and put his hands on his hips. 'This is going to set us back weeks. And we were so close.'

'Why would someone do something like this?' I groaned. 'Sorry. Silly question. Not why. How? How did they get in? It's almost impossible to get through security even *with* the right papers.'

'It has to be an inside job,' came a familiar voice from behind us.

'Carl!' I exclaimed. 'When did you get here?'

'Yesterday. And clearly not a moment too soon,' he said, gesturing to the damaged units. 'If this is what's going on.'

A rogue thought scooted through my head. If Carl was here, might he have had something to do with this? I told myself not to be silly. Carl was one of the good guys. I'd known him for years. 'How did they get in?'

He shrugged. 'I've just come from the team on the perimeter. There's been no breach and no sign of any broken locks or forced windows.'

'Do we know when it happened?' asked Daniel.

'It was fine at oh-sixteen-hundred,' said Matt.

'The patrol checked in here thirty minutes after that and all was well,' said Carl. 'Then, at oh-seventeen-hundred the damage was discovered.'

'Whoever it was knew how to cause maximum impact.' Daniel turned to Matt. 'What do you suggest we do?'

'There's nothing we can do, tonight,' said Matt. 'I'll inventory the damage and set up a schedule for repairs.'

'I'll station a guard in here permanently,' said Carl.

'How long is this going to set us back?' I asked. The importance of lifting the whole country's morale with the new radar was very much on my mind after the mass of enemy bombers we'd witnessed heading inland.

'I don't know,' said Matt. 'We'll have to see.'

* * *

The next few weeks were tough. We worked from morning to night, intent on getting the array repaired and operational as soon as possible. All the while, my mind went into free fall over who our saboteur could be. There were only two people that I knew for certain hadn't done it: Daniel and myself, because we had been together at the time. It had to be someone who had been connected with the project for a while. Someone who had been at Renscombe, Durrington and now Steamer Point. Try as we might, neither Daniel nor I could puzzle it out. It wasn't the professor, because he was in custody. It could be Jones, Havers or Robbins. They had all acted suspiciously, yet all three had seemed devastated at the damage and worked hard alongside us to repair it. There was a slim chance it was Matt, but that made no sense because he'd not been in Renscombe with us. Similarly, with Patrick, he had been at Renscombe and Durrington, yet he wasn't here at Steamer Point. Last I'd heard he was with

Kitty, wherever she was. The most likely candidate was Carl, only – much as I knew Daniel suspected him – even *he* wasn't a perfect fit. The only thing we could do was watch and wait.

Time crept inexorably by until, finally, the repaired units were driven the six miles from Steamer Point to the Sopley site to be installed. Progress was slow as the cumbersome units made their way north along narrow country roads, over the reinforced culvert and through the widened gateway into the chosen field. A degree of manoeuvring was required to slide each unit into optimal position, but at last the bases for the individual AMES component units were parked up and construction could begin on the transmitter and receivers. The team swung into action on the trailers – a well-oiled human machine raising cantilevered platforms and installing the retractable receiver array and a series of gantries supporting curved dishes. Cabling was run to link the units to the observation van, and two huge generators were installed.

The delay caused by the saboteur had given us time to install a temporary wooden hut at the site, which was large enough to host meetings and other essential gatherings. We had been informed that a VIP would be visiting to view the site in operation, along with members of the British Broadcasting Company press, and such a facility would prove useful for hospitality. In the far corner of the field, a row of small wooden sheds served as latrines.

As the last pieces of the unit were slotted into place, Daniel and I took a final walk around the site boundary, ostensibly to check the barbed wire fencing, although Carl was in charge of patrols and other security arrangements. Really, we were just taking a moment to see how far the project had come.

'Who would have thought it would actually happen,' I said.

'Yes. It's impressive, isn't it?'

'Are you nervous? About tomorrow, I mean?'

He shook his head. 'No. We've done our bit. It's over to the technicians now. There will be several fly-bys from RAF Christchurch. Fingers crossed the AMES unit will pick them up, and the VIP, whoever it is, will be suitably impressed and that will get reported in the papers.' He grinned. 'Why don't we go out this evening to celebrate? Just the two of us.'

I paused, locking eyes with him. 'Are you asking me on a date?' We'd been too busy to spend time together outside work. The rest of the world faded into nothing as I waited for his answer.

'I am.'

I smiled, feeling strangely shy yet at the same time bursting with happiness. 'In which case, that would be lovely.'

44

That evening, Daniel called for me at my billet and we walked into Christchurch to a pub near the Priory, a huge, medieval stone church in the centre of town. A fire roared in the hearth and a small group stood around a piano singing. Troops sat nearby relaxing over their pints. We found a small table in a quiet corner. After finishing a plate of bubble and squeak, followed by the most delicious bread pudding I had ever eaten, I sipped a gin and tonic and found myself unexpectedly tongue-tied.

Daniel raised his glass in salute. 'Here's to us. And also, to the first of many ground-to-air AMES systems.'

I clinked my glass against his. 'I've heard several of the team have been granted leave to go home to visit their families after tomorrow. Are you going?'

He shook his head and took a long swig of his beer. 'I'll go and see my parents soon, but not straight away. I'm hoping to get involved with building and siting another AMES unit, first.'

The mention of his parents made me realise how little I actually knew about him. 'Where are you from?'

'Originally, Sheffield. We moved to London when I was a teenager.'

'London! Goodness.' I touched his arm in concern. 'How are they coping with all the bombing? You must be worried sick about them.'

'I am.' He sighed, his brow creased. 'It's their home and they refuse to leave. I can understand that. They keep themselves busy. My dad is an air-raid warden and my mum and her best friend, Betty, spend the nights in the underground serving tea to anyone sheltering from the bombing. How about your family?'

I explained about Ma taking Nana and the boys to Aunty Mo's and Da staying behind to run the business. An unexpected pang of homesickness tickled at the periphery of my consciousness. I pushed it away and asked him about his childhood instead, and we compared stories about growing up in Sheffield and Bristol.

Eventually, he asked. 'How about you? Are you planning on going home?'

I shook my head, a well of sadness opening up inside me. There was no telling how much damage I had done by running away. 'I'm not sure going home is a good idea.'

'Why not? Jake is under arrest. Maybe it's time to mend some fences with your parents.'

I sighed. 'I love my family. But I'm not the same person I was this time last year. I'm not sure my parents will approve.'

'If they don't, it's their loss, and I'm more than happy to tell them so.'

The thought of taking him back to Bristol with me and introducing him to them as my... my what? My boyfriend? I dashed a flustered hand over my too warm face. 'I'll write to them and see what they say. In the meantime, I'm keen to see the project up and running, even though I'm not a proper scientist like the rest of you.'

'Don't give me that.' He grinned, his eyes sparking, little crinkly lines appearing at the corners. 'You know almost as much about the science behind it all as I do.' He leaned forward and kissed me. Slow and deep and oh so satisfying.

Whistles from the troops around us made us break apart with a laugh.

'Come on,' he said. 'I'd better walk you back before we're both locked out of our billets.'

We strolled arm in arm through the grounds of the Priory, along a pretty section of riverbank, our route a barely visible path of light grey stones winding alongside the inky water as it slipped quietly by. Owls called into the darkness. Night-time creatures rustled in the undergrowth with the occasional small splash as they plopped into the water. A warm sense of contentment settled over me as we approached Mrs Finch's pub and stopped outside.

I turned to him ready to thank him for a lovely evening.

'I want to ask you something, Fliss,' he said. His serious tone, at odds with the light-hearted camaraderie of our evening so far, made my stomach do a weird little flip of concern.

'Go on.'

He ran his palms down my upper arms and tugged me closer. 'Now that the Starlight site is up and running, or, it will be tomorrow, might you rethink your... well, might you rethink the situation between you and Major Stapleton?'

A sharp needle of pure ice punctured my bubble of happiness. 'I don't understand.'

'It's just...' He paused and sighed. 'I'm afraid she'll drag you in over your head.'

Was he suggesting that I didn't know my own mind? That I wasn't capable of making my own decisions? If so, I'd made a huge mistake. No matter how nice he seemed, if he thought he had the right to control me, he was no better than Jake. I clenched both fists, tamping down on the urge to shove him away from me. 'I'm still not following you.'

'I'm worried about you.'

Well intentioned or not, that comment triggered a tidal wave of rage. I stepped back and crossed my arms, every muscle in my body tense. 'Let me get this right,' I said, my voice deceptively calm. '*You're* worried, and you're asking *me* to stop doing something that is important to me to make *you* feel better?'

'No!' He frowned. 'Well, I mean... That's not exactly—'

'The situation, as you call it, between Major Stapleton and I, is the same situation that exists between you and Colonel Taylor.'

'And that's what bothers me.'

'Why?'

'Because it's dangerous.'

'It's no more dangerous for me than it is for you,' I ground out.

'That's different,' he said, swiping a jerky hand over the top of his head.

'Why? Because you're a man?'

'I... well, yes.' The word exploded from him.

I gaped, in disbelief. Did I not know him at all? 'I thought you were better than that.'

'Better than what? I'm trying to protect you.' He reached for me.

I knocked his arms away in disgust. 'I don't need protection.' I held both hands up palms out, preventing him from closing the gap. 'Hear this, Daniel

Evans, and hear it well. Don't *ever* tell me what to do.' My voice was tight with anger. 'If I wanted a man to control my life, I'd have stayed in Bristol.'

'That's not what I'm trying to do—' He sounded genuinely upset, which eased the intensity of my outrage.

'Isn't it? The world is changing, Daniel. You need to change with it or get left behind.' I fought to contain my anger before continuing in a more reasonable tone. 'You're trying to be chivalrous – I understand that. But don't try to wrap me in cotton wool and put me in a safe little box.' A beat of silence passed. 'Major Stapleton isn't dragging me into anything. I am doing what I am doing because *I* chose to, and I fully accept the risks.'

He stared at me in silence for several seconds as if lost for words.

'It's late,' I said, my heart heavy. 'Thank you for walking me back. I'll see you tomorrow.' Without waiting for him to reply, I pushed through the gate into Mrs Finch's courtyard and left him standing in the road. When I rounded the corner, I looked back over my shoulder. He was gone.

Tension as taut as an overstretched spring recoiled through me. I started to shake. Before I could gather my thoughts properly, the hairs on the back of my neck stood to attention, telling me I wasn't alone. Delighted at the opportunity to potentially punch someone, I demanded, 'Who's there?'

Major Stapleton stepped from the shadows. 'That was an interesting little chat you just had.'

'Don't start,' I said. 'I'm not in the mood.'

'Noted,' she said, her tone dry.

'What do you want, ma'am?'

'I thought you might like to know that your friends at Ventnor are well.'

'Thank heaven!' My words came out in a rush, relief bringing tears to my eyes as my throat thickened with emotion. *Rosie and Jane were safe*.

'The damage to the site was extensive, but there were minimal casualties.'

I frowned. Something didn't add up. 'You didn't really come all this way to tell me that, though, did you?'

'No.' She gestured towards the back door of the pub. 'Can you spare me a minute? We have a problem.'

I followed her into Mrs Finch's kitchen where the flickering light from an oil lamp threw a cosy glow over a wooden table and mismatched chairs. A black and white cat slept on a tattered rag rug in a puddle of warmth from the cast-iron range. The major poured two cups of tea from a pot sat on a cluttered dresser and passed one over the table towards me as we both sat down.

'I've received intelligence suggesting that there is going to be an attempt to disrupt tomorrow's launch,' she said.

'What sort of disruption?'

She stirred her tea with unnecessary force. 'An attack on the VIP.'

'Goodness. That's not ideal.' Intrigued, I sat forwards. 'Who is the VIP?' Rumours about the visit had spread like wildfire, yet no one had been able to confirm who was coming.

'The prime minister.'

'You're kidding.' I sat back with a whistle. 'But surely his security detail can deal with any threat.'

'They could, if they believed it to be true.' The expression on her face darkened. 'Unfortunately, they don't trust the source of the intelligence.'

'Why?'

'Because it's one of *my* sources, not one of theirs. Sadly, Colonel Taylor... well, let's just say, he has an agenda.'

I dry-washed my face with both hands, trying to erase the sense of exhaustion that landed on my shoulders as she spoke. 'You're saying that he's prepared to risk the security of the prime minster because he doesn't believe a woman.'

'Basically, yes. He says it's nothing but gossip. And he's convinced Winston that he's right.'

White-hot rage began to simmer inside me. 'So, the visit is going ahead.'

'It is. With no additional security. And with the eyes of the world's press in attendance.'

I leapt to my feet and paced the room, feeling like a hundred grenades about to explode. 'Typical bloody man. That's unbelievably insane,' I spat. 'It could be an assassination or a kidnap or anything. Imagine what that would do to the country's morale.'

'Agreed.'

I stopped pacing and rocked back on my heels. 'What do you want me to do?'

She steepled her fingers. 'The prime minister is scheduled to arrive at ten. I need you to be on site early. Mingle with whoever is there. Take a good look around. Be unobtrusive but observant.'

'What am I looking for?'

'Evidence that there is something untoward going on.'

'What sort of evidence?'

She shrugged. 'I don't know. I'm hoping you'll know it when you see it.'

'Then what?'

'Report to me. I'll stay as close to the PM as I can and keep him inside under cover as much as is humanly possible; either in the observational unit or the hospitality hut. Hopefully, if you can provide me with proof, I can persuade him to take appropriate measures to ensure whatever plot is afoot doesn't succeed.'

'I'll do my best, ma'am.'

'That's all I can ask.'

45

The next morning, I arrived in the Morris Eight and parked out of sight behind the latrines to leave room for official arrivals to park near the entrance, where a neat gravel path led towards the AMES observation units. Members of the press arrived in dribs and drabs until there was quite a throng waiting. Carl and his security team checked everyone's papers at the gate and escorted the reporters and photographers to stand to the far right of the hospitality hut, where they would be able to see everything without getting in the way. I took a quick tour of the site and checked the boundaries, finding nothing of note. Then, I took a large tray filled with mugs of tea from the hut across to the gathered journalists. I watched and listened as they stamped their feet and rubbed gloved hands together to help ward off the chill of the crisp winter morning. Spirits were high; they chatted about the upcoming VIP arrival but nothing about their interactions aroused my suspicions.

I slipped away, refreshed the tray of hot drinks and took it to the scientists, mechanics and administration staff operating each of the AMES project trucks. As before, all seemed in order, apart from the fact that I couldn't see Daniel anywhere, which struck me as odd. The way we had parted the night before weighed heavily on my mind. Had I been too forceful in my rejection of his concern? While I stood by the spirit of what I had said, I could have been more considerate of his feelings. The urge to protect women was deeply ingrained in society and it wasn't, in itself, wrong. It was not allowing us a choice and not respecting our decisions when they didn't align with a man's that was the problem. I could have explained that with more sensitivity. Maybe I could heal the rift between us if I could find him.

I wandered over to the receiver array, where Matt was making last-minute adjustments.

'Morning, Fliss,' he called.

'Morning,' I replied. 'How is everything?'

He wiped his hands on a rag and stuffed it into the pocket of the cleanest overalls I had ever seen him wear; no doubt a nod to the importance of the day. 'All good. We're ready for the fly-by.' He checked his watch. 'The VIP is arriving at ten, the fly-past is ten-thirty followed by refreshments in the hut at ten-forty-five and a press statement outside at eleven-thirty. We should be done and dusted by twelve, and then everyone who isn't part of the daily operational crew can disappear.'

A rumble of activity from the press pack alerted us to a procession of three shiny black Humber Pullmans, all sleek rounded lines and purring engines under prominent bonnets, pulling through the gate and onto the field. I threw Matt a smile goodbye and hurried over to join the reporters who surged towards the arrivals.

Prime Minister Churchill emerged from the central car. A hum of delight rose into the air from the crowd. That he and his party were here at Sopley underlined how important this event was, not only for the war effort, but also for the hearts and minds of the British people. There was a palpable sense that we were here to witness something important. I lingered at the back of the crowd, watching and waiting.

Commander Bryant, resplendent in full uniform, stepped forward to greet the prime minister. Colonel Taylor and Major Stapleton climbed from the rear vehicle. My breath caught in my throat when I saw that Daniel was with them. I felt as if the ground had been whisked from beneath my feet. My assumption that our roles in this operation were similar was clearly wrong. Whatever his position, he far outranked me if he was travelling *with the prime minister*. Two burly uniformed officers, and two of the drivers, flanked the whole party as they were conducted on a brief tour of the site. Camera bulbs flashed. Reporters scribbled notes.

The prime minister and his party moved from the transponder array to the receiver array and then on into the rest of the convoy.

Confusion gnawed at my belly as I watched Daniel stand at the bottom of the steps to the observation truck with the two majors whilst the prime minister and one of his bodyguards went inside. Major Stapleton stood with her back to Colonel Taylor, running her eyes over the site. As her gaze passed over me, she paused and nodded; a motion so clipped that it barely happened. I returned the greeting, noting the tension in her squared shoulders and rigid stance. Things might look fine, but it was clear that she thought otherwise.

I edged away from the press pack and wandered over to the prime minister's official cars, unable to resist having a closer look as I passed. They were stunning; perfect examples of high quality motor vehicles in pristine condition. One driver had remained with the cars. He greeted me before pulling a packet of cigarettes from his pocket. I wandered on, smiled at the guard on the gate and stepped out onto the road. It was deserted in both directions. I took a stroll to my right, examining the overgrown hedgerows, noting that the ditches were clogged and needed clearing. A flock of partridges took off from a nearby field, letting out noisy cackles as they flew overhead.

A break in the bushes revealed a rickety wooden stile into the next field. I checked my watch. It was nearly ten-thirty. The fly-by would be over us in a few minutes. The prime minister would be safe in the observation truck until that was over. There was no harm in taking a look in the adjacent field. In seconds I was over the stile and pushing my way through dried grass and brambles at the edge of an empty paddock.

About to retreat, something made me stop: a flattened patch of grass near the hedge and cigarette stubs littering the ground. Someone had been here. And they'd been here for a while. I crouched down and checked the paddock was empty before inching towards the flattened patch of grass. To my horror, it was possible to see through the hedge towards the AMES project – a clear unobstructed view. Major Stapleton's source was right.

I scanned the rest of the field. Other than an old tree trunk lying across the ground near the gate there was nothing to see. With no other leads, I skulked along the hedge line towards it, taking care not to step on twigs or dried vegetation that would snap or crunch underfoot. Another partridge took off, cackling with glee. All else was still. As I reached the tree trunk, I noticed the wheel of a motorbike tucked behind it. I froze, my ears on high alert. There was nothing to indicate that anyone else was there. Creeping closer, I could see that the front mudguard was bent out of line with the wheel, identical to the one I'd seen driven by the armed rider who'd attacked us en route to Durrington. A second bike was concealed behind the first. A cold sensation hardened in my midsection. Whoever they were and whatever they planned to do, they were *not* going to get away with it.

A low hum started in the distance, building into a formidable roar as a Spitfire thundered overhead, flying so low that every nut and bolt on the underbelly was visible. There would be three planes. All approaching from different directions at different heights, in a carefully choreographed dance to demonstrate the detection abilities of the array. Once it was over, the prime minister would leave the observation truck and move to the hospitality hut for a few individual interviews before he addressed the press pack as a whole outside. If whoever owned these hidden bikes was planning an assassination, the obvious target was the prime minister and the ideal time to cause the most disruption would be then – while he was speaking to journalists and photographers out in the open. There wasn't much time.

I thought about disabling the bikes. It would be easy to cut the brake cables, let the tyres down or throw dirt into the fuel tanks. The problem was that wouldn't necessarily stop whatever they had planned and Major Stapleton had told me to report back, not to act. Before doing anything irreversible, I needed to find her and ask how she wanted the situation handled.

46

I hurried back along the field, over the stile, along the road and into the AMES site. Rather than draw attention to myself by charging over to the observation truck in full view of the press, I slipped behind the prime minister's cars, thinking that I could hug the perimeter of the site until I was closer to my goal. Before I had taken more than a few steps I tripped. Throwing my hands out to break my fall, I landed on the cold ground and gasped in horror.

The prime minister's driver's lifeless eyes stared through me. Blood trickled from his head onto the ground only inches from my face.

Shock crackled through me like a lightning strike. Swallowing down a whimper of alarm, I pressed shaking fingers to his neck, searching for a pulse. Nothing. Dear heaven!

Snatching my hand back, I pulled my scarf from around my neck and gently placed it over his head and whispered, 'I am so sorry.' My gaze drifted past his body to the wheels of the car. Both front and rear tyres were slashed to ribbons. I lurched to my feet. Identical damage had been done to the other two prime ministerial cars. All the other vehicles that had borne scientists and staff to the site earlier in the day and were parked nearby had received similar treatment. Someone wanted to make sure that nobody could leave.

Whatever was going to happen would take place here at Sopley. I peered over the cars and surveyed the site. There was no sign of the VIP party. The press pack were loitering in a loose crowd. Nothing seemed to be happening. Aware that I had to get to the major without alerting the assassins that I was on to them, I moved as fast as I could, crossing the field to skirt the press pack in an awkward half-walk, half-run. There was no sign of anyone waiting outside the observation truck. Instead, two bodyguards were standing sentry at the steps to the hospitality hut. Forced to assume that this was where the prime minister was, I changed direction and headed over there.

Daniel fell into step at my side.

'Where did you come from?' I asked, not bothering to keep bitterness from colouring my words. 'I thought you'd be inside with all your important buddies.'

He ignored the question, instead asking in an unconcerned, conversational tone, 'What's wrong?'

I kept moving, my eyes straight ahead. He'd not been straight with me, so I didn't trust him. 'Nothing.' In my haste, I stumbled.

'Don't give me that,' he muttered, a hand clamping around my elbow to keep me on my feet. 'You're white as a sheet, Fliss,' he whispered. 'You're shaking. Something is wrong.'

I yanked my arm free and muttered, 'I have to speak with the major.'

We had reached the hut by then. The larger of the two bodyguards outside stepped forward, blocking my way.

'I need to see Major Stapleton,' I said. 'It's urgent.'

The guard frowned, ran his eyes over me as if searching for a weapon. 'You'll have to wait,' he said, making it clear he thought I was a timewaster.

Daniel cleared his throat. 'If Private Makepeace wants to talk to the major, then Private Makepeace gets to talk to the major. Do you understand?' I'd never heard him use such a commanding tone before. He slipped two fingers into his breast pocket and withdrew a card.

I couldn't see what was written on it. The guard's attitude changed in an instant. He opened the door to the hut, leaned in and said something to a soldier standing just inside. Seconds later, Major Stapleton emerged.

'Private Makepeace,' she said, her eyebrows rising as she took in Daniel's presence by my side. She indicated for us to move a few paces away from the bodyguards and Daniel and, as soon as we were out of earshot, murmured, 'Did you find what I need?'

'I did.' I leaned close to whisper. 'The PM's driver is dead and the tyres on his car have been slashed. I also found evidence that the site is, or has been, under surveillance by at least two unknown agents. I believe they are close by.'

'Wait here.' She slipped back into the hut. Moments later a reporter and two scientists emerged, deep in discussion. The major beckoned me in. I swallowed and climbed the steps, unable to believe that I was about to meet the prime minister of Great Britain.

It was warm inside the hut. A bowler hat and a long black coat hung on a hook, just inside the door. Colonel Taylor glared at me from across the room as I entered. At the far end of the space, two figures sat at a small table with cups of tea and an ashtray between them. Commander Bryant was one. The scent of expensive cigar smoke wrapped itself around me long before I dared raise my eyes to the other. There he was. Prime Minister Churchill. Looking just as he did in the news reels. Some might dismiss him as merely a balding, rotund man of a certain age, but there was an unmistakable presence to him. A sense of power and authority.

His gaze darted past me. 'Mr Evans,' he said, with a nod of greeting.

I glanced over my shoulder. Daniel had followed me in.

'Sir,' said Daniel.

The prime minister turned intense, intelligent eyes on me. 'And who do we have here?'

'This is Private Makepeace, sir,' said Major Stapleton.

Colonel Taylor tutted. 'This is hardly the time to try and advance your little project, Stapleton. We have—'

She raised her voice a fraction. 'Private Makepeace has important intelligence, Prime Minister, sir.'

I marvelled that she had the gall to speak over the colonel. He clearly didn't like it, but before he could object, the prime minister held up a hand. 'Stop squabbling, you two.' He clamped his teeth around his cigar, tucked a silver lighter into a small pocket in his waistcoat, and ran curious eyes over me. 'Makepeace. Hmm. I remember that name. Didn't you mention her to me before, Stapleton?'

'Yes, sir.'

He frowned. 'So, Makepeace, you're one of the major's infamous *women in plain sight*, are you?'

It took a second to find my voice. 'Yes sir. I am.'

He lifted a bushy eyebrow. 'You're not what I expected.'

I refused to react to the condescension in his tone. 'That's the point, sir. When I do my job right, people don't expect me. No one has noticed me so far today, and yet I have been here. In fact, I've been everywhere. Which is how I know, for certain, that you *are* in danger.'

'I am always in danger.' He waved his cigar in a lazy circle in the air. 'From what am I in danger from today, specifically?'

'Assassins. There are at least two enemy agents nearby, watching and waiting. *You* are the most likely target.'

'Assassins,' scoffed Colonel Taylor. 'Don't be ridiculous. We've got the whole site under surveillance.'

'If that is the case,' I said, unable to stop a thread of sarcasm from leaking into my words. 'I'm surprised you've not mentioned to Prime Minister Churchill that his driver is dead.'

'What?' the word exploded from the prime minister like gunshot. 'Taylor, you assured me that Stapleton's intelligence report was unfounded.'

'It is, sir,' Colonel Taylor insisted. 'This is all smoke and mirrors.'

'Smoke and mirrors that have slashed the tyres of all the prime ministerial cars,' I countered. A sharp intake of breath came from Daniel behind me. 'And two motorcycles, previously used in an attack on a senior member of personnel involved in this project are hidden in the next field with evidence of lengthy surveillance.'

Colonel Taylor turned a puce colour and made for the door.

'Stay where you are, Colonel,' barked the prime minister, stopping him in his tracks. 'It sounds as if Major Stapleton's operative *does* have some intelligence worth listening to. If you go storming off around the site to check it out, you'll blow any sort of advantage we have.'

'It's impossible. There are guards on the gate,' muttered Colonel Taylor. 'And regular patrols of the perimeter.'

'Patrols of the inside of the perimeter, yes,' I said. 'But the evidence is on the other side of the hedge. As for the guards on the gate, they only needed to be distracted by something like the fly-by for someone to slip past.'

'The question is...' boomed the prime minister. 'What do we do about it?'

'We have to get you out of here,' said Colonel Taylor. 'Your bodyguard can escort you out.'

'Out how?' said Major Stapleton. 'The prime ministerial cars are undriveable.'

Colonel Taylor rounded on her. 'We'll commandeer other cars. This is—'

'They're all damaged,' I said. 'I checked the other cars parked near the gate. Their tyres are slashed too. You could potentially cobble together enough spare tyres from all of them to repair one car, maybe two, but not without drawing attention to what you're doing.'

'We'll use the field telephone in the observation truck,' the colonel blustered. 'Commander Bryant can call for an armed response unit.'

Commander Bryant checked his watch. 'It'll take time to get here, but I'll see what I can do.' He got to his feet.

'No,' said the prime minister.

'But, sir,' said Colonel Taylor.

'No,' barked the prime minister, his gazed locked on me. 'I want to know what *she* thinks we should do.'

Colonel Taylor's eyes bounced from the prime minister to me and back again. 'Her?'

'Yes, her,' said the prime minister. 'I can tell that she's got an opinion. It's written all over her face.'

I swallowed, feeling like an insect being examined by a thousand microscopes. 'I... well, I think we should be looking at the bigger picture, sir.'

'Bigger picture?' scoffed Colonel Taylor. 'What's bigger than saving the prime minister from assassination?'

'Saving the country,' I said. 'With respect, Prime Minister, this project is more important than you.'

That was too much for Colonel Taylor. 'You jumped-up little... How dare you—'

'Be quiet, Taylor,' snapped the prime minister. 'I've always thought it best that the person in the room with the most knowledge about a situation should be the one who makes the decisions. For once, that person isn't me.' He gave a snort of laughter. 'And it certainly isn't *you*.' His eyes darted from Colonel Taylor to Daniel. 'What about you, Evans? What do you think?'

I daren't look around. The prime minister had put Daniel in an unenviable position. He was effectively being asked to choose between me and his superior officer.

Several seconds passed. I clenched my fists and waited, forcing my breathing to stay calm and steady.

Daniel cleared his throat. 'I think Private Makepeace has a point, sir.'

Heavy silence filled the room before the prime minister gave a shout of laughter. 'Ha! By Jove! You do, do you?'

'Yes, sir.' Daniel's voice was firm and unwavering.

'As it happens,' said the prime minister, 'I agree.'

Major Stapleton stepped forward. 'Sir, if—'

'No.' The prime minister held up an imperious hand. 'You've advocated for these undercover women of yours for months now. Let's see what this one has to say for herself.' His chair creaked as he turned to give me his full attention. 'Go on, Makepeace. What do you suggest we do?'

A thick expectant hush fell. I glanced from the prime minister to Major Stapleton and back again, stunned. This was the moment of truth: an opportunity to show that there was so much more to me than most people had ever imagined. I ignored my racing heart, herded my cartwheeling thoughts into a semblance of order and said, my tone intense and serious, 'These enemy agents have harried this project for months. They've followed us from Renscombe to Durrington to Steamer Point and now they're here, determined to cause trouble. We've no reason to think they will stop. I suggest we use what we have here, today, to draw them out and deal with them, permanently.'

'Makepeace,' said Major Stapleton, shock colouring the word. 'You are surely not suggesting we use the Prime Minister of Great Britain and the Commonwealth as bait?'

'I am, ma'am, yes.'

The room erupted as both Colonel Taylor and Commander Bryant objected. Underneath their protestations a low chuckle could be heard, a chuckle that morphed into a delighted whoop as the prime minister gave in to a full belly laugh. Everyone stopped what they were doing and watched in amazement.

I glanced at Major Stapleton who widened her eyes at me and shrugged.

The prime minister's chortles subsided. 'Go on, Makepeace, let's hear it. How do you propose to use me as a carrot to entice these miscreants out?'

I paused, as elements of a plan fell into place in my head. 'We're all going to have to play a part in this for it to work. We'll have to work together. Is everyone prepared to do that?'

'Of course,' said Major Stapleton.

'Yes,' said Commander Bryant.

All eyes fell on Colonel Taylor, and after a brief hesitation, he sighed. 'Yes.'

'Colonel Taylor.' I pointed to him. 'I need you to send a couple of your men to investigate the situation with the cars. Please choose those capable of acting. I want them to "discover" the prime minister's poor driver and raise a shout of alarm that will alert the whole site to a problem. Then, they must be seen hurrying straight back here to report to you.' Before the colonel could interject, I moved on.

'Commander Bryant, I want you to put the AMES staff on high alert. Colonel Taylor's men raising the alarm will trigger a commotion. Your team need to watch for any attempts to sabotage the units during any confusion that ensues. The project *must* be protected at all costs.'

Commander Bryant nodded. 'I can do that.'

'Major Stapleton,' I said. 'I need you to call in a few favours with the press pack outside. We're going to need some volunteers. Do you have any contacts out there who might co-operate? Anyone who is particularly fond of our prime minister?'

She nodded. 'I do.'

'Good.' Finally, I turned to the prime minister. 'There is one car on site that *might*, and I do mean might, still be driveable. I parked a Morris Eight over behind the latrines when I arrived this morning. I am hoping that the enemy agents haven't clocked it. It's light and highly manoeuvrable. My suggestion is that you leave the site in that vehicle with one bodyguard and *I'll* drive you.'

'That's preposterous,' roared Colonel Taylor.

I levelled a stare at him that brooked no argument. 'If everyone does exactly what I say, Colonel, there will be no risk to the prime minister whatsoever.'

'How?' he snarled.

'Makepeace is an excellent driver,' said Major Stapleton. 'She's outrun these fellows before, hasn't she, Evans?'

'She has,' agreed Daniel.

The prime minister got to his feet. 'If you were me, Evans, what would you do?'

I held my breath as Daniel cleared his throat. 'This situation is dicey, sir, but, for what it's worth, Private Makepeace is quite brilliant. I trust her with my life.'

A lump formed in my throat at his words. No one had ever paid me such a tribute. I swallowed hard, blinked rapidly to clear my vision, and tucked his words into my heart to examine later, when all this was over and, God willing, everyone was safe.

The prime minister clamped his lips around his cigar and mumbled, 'I rather think I trust her too.'

I glanced behind me at Daniel. 'I'm glad you say that, sir, because there is one more thing that I need you to do.'

47

The alarm when it was raised, was very noticeable. There was no way anyone on site wouldn't realise that something was going on. Minutes later two soldiers burst through the door into the hut.

'This had better work,' Colonel Taylor growled.

'It will,' I said, with more confidence than I felt. I stumbled from the hut, clutching my forage cap to my head and dashed clumsily in the direction of the latrines, my free arm flapping, partly to help keep my balance and also to make as much of a spectacle of myself as I could. The Morris was parked exactly as I had left it, the tyres intact. I sent up a prayer of thanks and slid behind the wheel. Making a point of gunning the engine, I drove back towards the hut.

The door flew open and two guards came out, brandishing pistols, followed immediately by the portly figure of the prime minister, in his trademark black woollen coat, a scarf wrapped around his lower face and neck and his bowler hat pulled down. The press pack immediately surged forwards, blocking the prime minister from wider view.

'Prime Minister, what is going on?' called one particularly tall reporter, brandishing a microphone.

'Yes, Prime Minister, sir,' called another tall chap shoving himself forward. 'Do you have any comment for our readers?'

'Over here, Prime Minister, sir,' called a burly photographer.

There were so many bodies surging around the prime minister that it was only possible to make out his bowler hat in between the caps of his two body-guards as they edged through the crowd towards my car.

I beeped my horn and the crowd shifted slightly, reporters and photogra-phers flowing around the car, allowing me to nudge my way forward. As soon as the prime minister was close enough, I felt the car lurch as he and one of the bodyguards climbed inside and slammed the door.

There was a cheer from the crowd, and reporters thumped the roof of the car, walking alongside it and screening the occupants from view, as I trundled towards the gate. 'Better hang on back there, Prime Minister,' I said. 'As soon as we're clear of your adoring press, I'm going to floor the accelerator.' I glanced in the rear-view mirror, glad to see that both passengers were hunched down away from the windows, meaning that an assassin would be unable to gain a clear shot.

I revved the engine again as we cleared the gate. The throng accompanying us stepped back with a final cheer. The wheels spun slightly, sending loose gravel flying before they found purchase on the tarmac road. The car leapt forward, and we sped away from the site.

No one spoke as the speedometer crept up from forty-five miles per hour to fifty. The maximum speed I could hope for with three people on board was fifty-seven, but I didn't push it. Instead, I kept my eyes on the road, periodically glancing into the rear-view mirror.

'Come on,' I muttered. 'Where are you?' This had to work. I prayed I hadn't miscalculated. 'Come *on*,' I urged, glancing back again. There! That was them. Moving in and out of sight just around the bend. It had to be.

Clad head to toe in dark leather, with goggles and helmets obscuring their faces, the bikers gained on me fast, and played a game of cat and mouse, harrying me from the rear quarters. Then, when we hit a long straight section of road, one zipped past on the passenger side. The other remained behind.

'Keep your heads down, back there,' I called out, spotting the rider in front pulling a gun. 'And brace yourselves.' I scrunched down myself, peering over the bonnet to weave from side to side on the carriageway, hoping to deny him a clear shot. The straight section gave way to a bend in the road, and then another one. The biker in front had to concentrate to stay balanced at the speed we were travelling. I scanned ahead, looking for a suitable gateway. There. That one would do.

'Any minute now,' I called. 'Hold on.' There was a shuffling in the back as my passengers readied themselves. We drew level with the open gateway. I swung the wheel at the last minute. The back end of the car skidded momentarily before we shot into the field and bumped wildly over the recently ploughed surface. I sent a quick apology to the owner, from whom the car had been requisitioned, for any damage I was causing to the suspension, and another to the absent farmer for ruining his crop.

The bike behind turned into the field too, and – making a better fist of crossing the uneven ground – it gained on us. The second bike followed. I swung the car to one side, deliberately causing a skid, before bringing it to a halt and hoping that the manoeuvre looked as if we could go no further. 'Now,' I said, scrambling from the car, one hand to my head as if dazed.

Prime Minister Churchill and his bodyguard climbed out. The former faced the car, keeping his back to the bikers. He gripped onto the roof with both hands as if to steady himself, the bodyguard moved to shield him, gun drawn.

The bikers drew alongside, leaping from their machines, brandishing weapons.

I staggered forwards, moving to block a clear shot of the prime minister. 'Wait,' I said. 'Please stop. Don't.'

'Get out of the way,' snarled the biker closest to me, flashing his overbite and that familiar broken tooth. *Broken Tooth, I knew it!* He shoved me hard and strode by, leaving me sprawled in the dirt. His companion in crime tramped in his wake as I scrambled to rise.

'Prime Minister,' said Broken Tooth. 'I suggest you surrender. There's no help coming.'

From a crouch behind both bikers, I watched as the prime minister tossed his bowler hat aside and slowly shrugged out of his coat, revealing a series of cushions strapped to his body. Daniel straightened up to his full height, and turned saying, 'There's no prime minister here.'

'What?' said Broken Tooth. He shot a look of consternation to his companion and spotted me creeping up behind him, ready to launch myself at him. Broken Tooth levelled his pistol and shouted, 'Watch out, Paddy!'

A shot rang out. I ducked my head as something whistled past far too close for comfort. Daniel and the bodyguard took advantage of the bikers' distraction to throw themselves forwards, rugby-tackling both to the ground. Daniel wrestled Broken Tooth's firearm from his grasp. The bodyguard wasn't so lucky and received a blow to the temple from Paddy's pistol. His eyes rolled up into his head and he slumped back. Paddy turned his gun on Daniel who was busy wrestling with Broken Tooth on the ground. I didn't hesitate. I launched myself into the air and landed on Paddy's shoulders, swung a leg either side of his waist to knock his weapon to the ground, and held on tight.

It was as if Mrs Finch were there with me, cheering me on. I wrapped one arm around his neck and locked it in place from the far side by looping my free arm around my wrist. He clawed at my arms, gasping for air, desperate to shake me loose. I clung tighter than any limpet. Seconds ticked by. His attempts to free himself weakened. I bit my lip, aware that the grip I had on his neck could kill if held too long. It wasn't my intention to kill him, but I knew I would if I had to. His struggles faded. Finally, he slumped forward. I released my grip immediately, allowing him to sink down onto the earth. I checked to see if he was still breathing, letting out a huge sigh of relief when his chest rose.

Seeing that Daniel had Broken Tooth subdued, I dashed across to the car to grab a couple of hanks of rope from the boot. I threw him one on my way back to tie Paddy's hands behind his back. The bodyguard groaned and rolled over, revealing a face the colour of porridge, and blood pouring from a cut on his head.

'Damn it,' he groaned. 'My head hurts like a herd of bulls just stampeded over it.'

'I'm not surprised,' I said. 'That was quite a whack he gave you.'

He struggled to sit up.

'Take it easy,' I said.

He shook his head, rolled onto his side and struggled to his feet. 'I'm fine.'

'If you say so,' I said, drawing his arm over my shoulder to steady him. 'Let's get you into the car. We'll head back to Steamer Point and get you checked over.' I poured him into the front passenger seat.

Daniel dragged first one unconscious biker over and then the other. 'Your plan worked like a charm.'

I grinned. 'Thank heaven.'

'How did you know the press would co-operate like that and willingly form a human shield?'

'I gambled on the fact that they're patriots. Most British citizens would do anything for Prime Minister Churchill. He's the only thing holding this country together.' I shrugged. 'Plus, I know that Major Stapleton has... contacts everywhere. She is going to make sure that nothing about today will ever appear in the news reports.'

'What? Nothing?'

I shook my head. 'It would be bad for morale. All that will be revealed is that the first Ground Controlled Interception unit was successfully tested. No mention of the prime minister's visit and nothing about an assassination attempt.'

'Wow.' His eyes bugged. 'She's scarier than I thought.'

'No,' I said. 'She's simply someone who knows how to get stuff done.'

'A bit like you.'

'If you say so,' I said, allowing the compliment to warm my insides. I kicked the foot of the biker closest to me. 'Who do you think they are?'

'Let's find out.' He yanked the helmet and goggles off Broken Tooth's head.

I gasped as recognition surged through me. 'Is that...? How in the world...? No, hang on.' I looked closer. 'It's not Kitty's Patrick, but it could be.'

'Yes, it could.' Daniel pulled the helmet and goggles from the other biker. *That* was Patrick.

'It's uncanny,' I said. 'They are so similar, overbite and everything *apart* from that one broken tooth.'

'Twins maybe,' said Daniel. 'Or merely brothers who happen to look very alike.'

Something lurked in the back of my brain. 'Carl mentioned staying with two cousins in Ireland when he introduced Patrick to me. What was the other one's name?' I snapped my fingers. 'Niall. That was it.'

'It would explain a lot,' said Daniel. 'Patrick would have access to information working on site. He could pass it to Niall who was lurking in the neighbouring area, who could send it on along a chain of informants.'

'Of all people,' I said, shaking my head. 'I never once suspected Patrick. Why would he betray his country? Oh hell.' Another thought struck me. 'How on earth am I going to tell Kitty?'

Daniel wrapped an arm around my shoulders and gave me a bracing squeeze. 'One thing at a time. First up, we need to get these two back to Steamer Point and throw them in the brig. Are you all right to drive?'

I nodded. 'I'm always all right to drive.'

He laughed. 'I think they must have broken the mould after they made you.'

'What do you mean by that?' I demanded.

'I mean, you're incredible.'

My face grew warm. 'Don't be silly.'

'It's true. Most people would be cowering wrecks hiding in a corner after something like this, but not you. You're steady as a rock. All *you're* bothered about is Kitty finding out she has a lousy boyfriend.'

I shrugged my shoulders, not used to compliments. 'I don't want her to be upset.'

'Exactly. Like I said, you're incredible, and utterly perfect.' He leaned in and pressed a firm kiss on my lips before stepping back. 'Come on. We had better get these two rats into the back of the car before they regain consciousness.'

48

The next day, inside a secure compound at Steamer Point, Daniel and I sat on hard, wooden chairs side by side in a cold, cramped interrogation room, and listened to Commander Bryant as he interrogated Patrick. A thin shaft of light from a window set high in the wall fell across the commander's tin of Lucky Strikes, a Zippo lighter and a glass ashtray set on the wide table between the two men. The air was hazy with smoke and tension.

The commander took a long drag on his cigarette and exhaled slowly before speaking. 'I'll ask you again. Why?'

Patrick, rigid with defiance, refused to respond.

The commander's chair creaked as he leaned forward. 'It will go easier on you, if you co-operate.' His voice was gravelly and his manner stern. There was no doubt in my mind that he meant what he said.

Patrick folded his arms. He didn't look anything like the Patrick I knew... or rather, the man I had thought I'd known. This wasn't Carl's cousin, a man so shy around women that he could barely breathe. No. This man radiated anger, rebellious insolence oozing from every pore.

An oppressive silence wrapped itself around us as long seconds ticked by.

'Fine,' said the commander, stubbing out his cigarette. 'You've had your chance. I'm not wasting any more time on you.' He nodded to a man dressed head to toe in black who lurked near the door. 'He's all yours.'

The man stalked forward, his movements lithe and menacing.

The commander rose to his feet, turning to Daniel and I. 'It's time we left them to it.'

Patrick's eyes darted to me. A brief flash of alarm in them was gone almost before I registered it. He looked away, his face settling into a blank mask.

Nausea flooded my stomach. I stood. I meant to follow Daniel, I really did, but somehow my feet took a step towards Patrick instead. 'Please, Patrick. Tell them what they need to know.'

Daniel put a hand on my arm. 'Leave it, Fliss.'

He was right, I knew that, but I had to try. 'What about Kitty, Patrick?'

Patrick's mouth tightened. 'What about Kitty?'

I gestured to the man in black. 'Do you want them to do this to her? Because they will. They'll think she was working with you.'

Patrick frowned and muttered, 'She had nothing to do with it.'

'Well, you had better convince them of that.' I leaned in until my face was mere inches from his and hissed. 'Or so help me, God, whatever they do to you, I'll do worse. Do you hear me?'

He turned away, a muscle twitching in his jaw.

Daniel tugged me away. 'Fliss, come on.'

I followed him from the room.

Outside, the commander fixed me with a level stare. 'I find it interesting that the only words he spoke in the last half an hour were to you, rather than me.'

I swallowed, lowering my eyes. 'I'm sorry, sir.'

'Don't be. If I get nothing more out of him, I'll be calling you back.'

'I'd be glad to help, sir,' I said.

'You're to report to Major Stapleton.' He waved a hand down the corridor. 'Third door on the left. Evans, You're with me.'

I shot a quick glance at Daniel. He gave me a reassuring smile that didn't quite reach his eyes, before he followed the commander.

Three doors down on the left, I knocked and waited.

'Come in.'

Inside, the major sat at a desk, a pile of paperwork before her. She pointed at a chair. 'Sit. Tell me how it's going in there. Has he spilled his guts yet?'

I sank down with a sigh. 'No, and I don't think he is going to.'

She steepled her hands, resting her elbows on the table. 'That's to be expected at this stage. He'll crack. They always do.'

'And what about the other one?'

She leaned back in her chair. 'Niall. He's not speaking either.'

I ran my eyes over the sparse office furnishings – regulation army-issue tables and chairs, bare walls – searching for the right words. 'I never for a single minute suspected Patrick. Yet, he was there the whole time. In front of me, large as life. Right from the break-in back at Renscombe. It must have been him, or possibly Niall, that I tackled in the corridor.'

'What makes you think that?'

'Neither of them is particularly big. Which fits with how I remember it. And it was a few days after the new security teams arrived. Carl was away on leave, but Patrick wasn't. I'm assuming Niall was lurking nearby.'

'Possibly,' she said. 'Do you think Carl was involved?'

I sighed. 'I really hope not. I've always thought he was one of the good guys.'

She frowned down at the papers on her desk. 'For what it's worth, I think you're right. As soon as he learned that Patrick and Niall were in custody, Carl presented himself for questioning. He has made no attempt to escape and is co-operating fully. We'll do our due diligence and investigate all his connections. If he's clean, we'll release him. The same goes for your friend, Kitty. Who, by the way, is already on her way here, under arrest.'

Nausea punched me in the gut. Poor Kitty. She'd been so in love. There's no way she was a traitor, not intentionally, but what if he tricked her? 'How is she?'

'Holding up pretty well and co-operating with everything.'

'May I see her?'

The major nodded. 'Of course. It'll be interesting to see how she interacts with you. It'll help us gauge if she's telling the truth.'

I blinked. I hadn't bargained on our friendship being used in that fashion. Although on reflection, if me having a chat with Kitty both supported her through this and speeded up the process for her, then who was I to refuse? And if she did admit to knowingly being involved then... It would break my heart if the Kitty I thought I knew turned out to be a figment of my imagination. I pushed the thought away. I trusted my friend. I had to hope for the best.

'Why do you think Patrick did it?'

She sighed. 'Both Patrick and Niall O'Hanlon are Irish nationals.'

'Why would that be an issue?'

'Ordinarily, it wouldn't be. With regard to the war, Ireland has remained neutral. Ostensibly, this is because they don't want to provoke Hitler by siding with Britain. Given the troubled history between Britain and Ireland, there is an argument that Irish neutrality is a way to assert their independence.'

'Which means what?'

'The Secret Service have raised concerns that – while the majority of Irish nationals are either genuinely neutral or actively anti-Nazi – there are a select few who side with Hitler because they consider Britain – mainly the English – to be an ancient oppressor. Patrick and Niall's father holds some intense anti-British views. It isn't a huge leap of the imagination to suppose that Patrick and Niall agree with him and believe in the old adage that my enemy's enemy is my friend.'

'Meaning that they would promote Nazi interests over British ones.'

'Exactly. Something that enemy intelligence would be quick to take advantage of.' Major Stapleton gave a grim nod. 'Hence, Patrick getting himself entrenched within a British Army unit alongside his cousin and using that position to help his brother steal important information and even attempting to kill Prime Minister Churchill when the opportunity presented itself.'

Sadness gnawed at my heart. 'I'm sure Carl doesn't think like that. And Kitty certainly doesn't. But why didn't I suspect Patrick? I should have. Looking back, the clues were there. It was Niall's blasted broken tooth that threw me. If it hadn't been for that, I might have recognised his resemblance to Patrick.'

'Hindsight is a wonderful thing,' said the major, 'but not something to judge yourself too harshly over. Without your insight, yesterday, their plot could have succeeded. We might have woken up today to a country in mourning for the loss of our prime minister – the only man, in my opinion, who stands a chance of bringing Britain through this war in one piece.'

'You've always said to me that nothing is ever what it seems.'

'And I'm right,' she said, not without a little satisfaction. 'You're not quite what you seem, either, you know. You've shown yourself to be significantly more determined than I anticipated. And, no doubt, you will be an even more valuable asset for future missions as a direct result of what you've learned from this one.'

I sat forward in my chair. 'Future missions?'

She got to her feet and started pacing the room, her hands clasped behind her back. 'I don't think you realise what you have helped to achieve here. As a direct result of what happened today, your contribution both behind the scenes and in the face of significant pressure, Prime Minister Churchill now appreciates that women have much more they can offer when it comes to the defence of this realm.'

'Meaning what, exactly?'

'He is willing to consider my idea for a secret army of women working undercover, on the watch for more spies like Patrick and Niall.'

'But?' I asked. 'You sound like there's a but coming.'

She shrugged. 'We mustn't run before we can walk. There are other senior commanders who still need to be brought around to the idea. However, with the prime minister on our side, in time, I am hopeful, it will happen. As soon as that happens, I will set up a proper training program. And when I do, I want you to come on board as an adviser.'

That was unexpected. 'What can I offer?'

'You can experience it from the recruits' point of view and tell us if we are meeting their needs.' She held up a hand. 'Self-defence is a must, of course, but there will be other things. How did you get on with Mrs Finch, by the way?'

'Mrs Finch was a revelation,' I said. 'I used what she taught me to subdue Patrick, yesterday.' I flexed my hands, the awful memory of what it felt like to hold a man in a death grip and wait for him to pass out was still very fresh in my mind. I shuddered. Thank heaven I hadn't killed him, although he might soon wish I had. The penalties for treason were dire.

'Excellent. I'll make a note. Perhaps we can persuade her to be one of our instructors.'

Our? She seemed to be talking to herself, yet also including me. Being involved in setting up such a unit held huge appeal. If other women were to follow my footsteps, I wanted them to be properly prepared.

Watching the major continue her pacing, a look of zeal in her eyes, a strange sense of contentment settled over me.

She suddenly seemed to remember where she was and returned to her desk. 'In the meantime, I want you to continue to work with the radar research facility.' She sat back down and started rummaging through her papers. 'Daniel Evans will brief you. I imagine you two have plenty to say to each other.' She shot me a quick smile. 'Just remember, while you might appear to be working for him...' She held up a hand as if to forestall my objection. 'It's a compromise I had to make in order to appease Colonel Taylor. You will really working for me, so make sure you take your radio. I'll be in touch. That will be all.'

A surge of delight had me on my feet in seconds. 'Thank you, ma'am.' I saluted and left the room in search of Daniel.

49

Outside the secure compound, the throaty roar of Spitfires passing overhead rolled over me, the intensity of the sound reverberating through my bones. I shielded my eyes against the glare of the midday winter sun and followed the graceful trajectory of the planes as they soared out over the sea. Hope surged in my heart. With such amazing aircraft, and the AMES unit to guide them, we would surely win in the end.

'Stunning, aren't they,' said Daniel, coming up behind me.

I whirled, excitement bubbling in my chest. 'They are.'

'How are you?' he asked, his expression serious. 'Any injuries from yesterday?'

I wriggled my shoulders. 'A few sore muscles and a couple of bruises, but... you know how it goes.'

He grinned. 'I do indeed. I never thought working in research would bring such excitement?'

'The major said something about us working together, but that you would brief me.'

'Ah, yes. The AMES unit has been so successful, we've been tasked with taking the research to the next level. Building more and making them more efficient.'

'Here, or Durrington, or back with the team from Renscombe, wherever they got moved to?' The idea of going back to Swanage appealed. It would be nice to catch up with Beaky and the others. And hopefully Kitty too.

He pulled a face. 'The Ministry of Defence have decided coastal locations are too vulnerable. The main radar research sites are being moved further inland.'

'Where to?'

'That is yet to be confirmed. Worcestershire, I believe. Probably Malvern. First, we're off to a place in Dorset called Leeson House to pick up the rest of the Renscombe team.'

How exciting! 'And what will my role be?'

'Officially, you'll be a junior researcher. It will involve a lot of clerical work, but your understanding of mechanics will prove useful to the project too. As for anything else.' He shrugged. 'That's between you and Major Stapleton.'

I nodded, suppressing a smile. He and I would continue to pretend we didn't know that the other was working undercover. There was no need to go into specifics. We knew each other and trusted each other and that was enough.

He rested both hands on my shoulders and gave a small tug to bring me close. 'You were utterly fearless yesterday.'

'Not fearless,' I said. 'I was shaking inside the whole time.'

'Then you were very brave.'

'So were you,' I murmured, distracted by the warm tingling sensation that spread from where he touched me.

'No. I was terrified that you were going to get hurt.'

'I was in no more danger than you. I know how to handle myself in a scrap now.'

His lips twitched. 'That much was very clear. I won't ask who taught you that death grip move.'

'You wouldn't believe me if I told you,' I said, the image of Mrs Finch flitting through my mind.

He rested his forehead on mine, staring deep into my eyes, and whispered, 'You can forget everything I said the other day about you needing to be careful. I was wrong. *I'm* the one who's going to have to watch out.'

'Don't worry,' I whispered. 'I'll keep you safe.' My gaze dropped to his lips. They were so close.

Then closer.

Oh my!

The electric connection between us was going to make working with Daniel in Malvern very interesting indeed.

50

MARCH 1942 HANNINGTON HALL. OUTSIDE MAJOR STAPLETON'S OFFICE

The baby grandfather clock along the hall rang the hour, a light ripple of chimes that snapped me from my reminiscence. I pulled the next report from the file on Sergeant Miller's desk and wondered how Connie was getting on in her interview with Major Stapleton. Part of me couldn't believe that this training facility was now a reality. Joining undercover as a cadet had allowed me to experience the special operations women's training program from the point of view of the women it was designed to help.

It had also allowed me to connect with some very special women. I'd never forget training alongside this first cohort, and living in hut six with Connie, Wren, Lexi, Jo and Louisa. They were strong, feisty, talented individuals who would make a difference in this war. It was a comfort to know that they were being offered comprehensive training that would give them every chance of survival, in spite of the danger that their missions would inevitably put them in. I planned to keep an eye on their progress, with a view to lending a helping hand if needed. I would never stop feeling responsible for those drawn into this life and I doubted the major would either.

The hinges of the ornate wooden door to Major Stapleton's office creaked as it opened and Connie appeared. White-faced and wide-eyed, she gave me a wobbly smile. 'It's time to say goodbye, Fliss.'

I swept her into a hug, giving her an extra-long squeeze of reassurance. 'Good luck, Connie. And don't forget what Wren and the others agreed,' I said, referring to the other four girls in our hut, who we'd spent the last three weeks training alongside. 'We'll all meet again in Trafalgar Square on the first of May. When this blasted war is over.'

'Yes. I'll see you there.' She picked up her kitbag, slipped the strap of her gas mask box over her shoulder, and headed down the corridor towards her first mission. I sent silent love and prayers after her, hoping that Wren was right, that we would all survive the war and see each other again.

Major Stapleton stood in the doorway, watching me watch my friend leave. 'She's stronger than she thinks, Fliss.'

'I know.'

'And she's perfect for the mission I've just assigned her to. In fact, she might be the only person who can pull it off.' She gestured for me to step into her office. 'Shall we?'

* * *

MORE FROM ALICE G. MAY

The next instalment in The Resistance Girls series by Alice G. May is available to order now here:

https://mybook.to/ResistanceGirls3BackAd

A NOTE FROM THE AUTHOR

Dear Reader,

Thank you for coming on this second Resistance Girls' journey with me. Fliss is a character who has surprised me at every turn. I have enjoyed getting to know her, and I hope you have too. While Fliss and Daniel are both fictitious, several elements of their story are based in truth.

The change in attitude towards the role of women throughout the years of the Second World War was significant. I have tried to reflect this in Churchill's, and other top brass like Colonel Taylor's, response to concept of female under-cover operatives in the Special Operations Executive. (The brave women who were recruited are referred to as Churchill's Secret Sweeties in some of the reports I have read. It is a term I am not comfortable with. Hence, I call them the Women's Secret Army).

The summer of 1940 was one filled with genuine concern that Britain faced an invasion from the German forces occupying France. Multiple initiatives were put in place to try and mitigate such a disaster. The SOE was responsible for many of these and Commander Beatrice Temple (the inspiration for my fictional character, Major Belinda Stapleton) played a key role in the way women were chosen, trained and deployed. While there are few formal records of what actually happened or who was involved, I have used what snippets of information I can find and imagined the rest.

Locations

The Renscombe Chain Home site is a genuine location. It developed from two towers, a few small huts and a handful of staff in early 1940, to a large radar research facility in only a matter of months. Approximately two hundred scientists arrived in May 1940 and the site continued to expand until there were over two thousand personnel working there. Whether an ATS troop were involved in this particular expansion program, your guess is as good as mine. However, many ATS teams were posted to do this type of foundational support work in order to free up men to go and fight.

RAF Durrington is also a real location. From what I have read it seems that during World War Two the main building really didn't have any windows. It has now been converted to a school, I am assuming that windows have been added.

The ADEE Steamer Point site continued to be used for Radar research and development long after the war was over.

The Sopley Starlight site and others like it played a critical part in strengthening the British response to the increasingly brutal waves of enemy aerial bombardment.

Radar

The Battle for Britain raged over the skies of England from mid 1940 onwards, and was followed by the Blitz. Britain came very close to losing the war in the face of persistent attacks. A significant factor that helped to turn the tide in Britain's favour was the development of radar and, among many other related projects, specifically ground-controlled interception (GCI) stations. Radar research and development was carried out by many scientists and took place at multiple sites, including Renscombe and RAF Durrington. Projects were moved to new locations when intelligence reports identified an enemy threat to their security.

The first operational GCI station, an AMES unit, was constructed at the Air Defence Experimental Establishment at Steamer Point, Christchurch, and installed in a field just outside the village of Sopley in December 1940. It is entirely possible that this technology was developed from a collaboration between multiple sites, which is why I had Fliss and Daniel's story hop from Renscombe to Durrington to Steamer Point to Sopley. Prime Minister

Churchill's presence on the day that the Sopley site became operational, is (as far as I know) a figment of my imagination. However, the prime minister was very interested in the project and it is highly likely that he did receive a tour of the Sopley GCI station at least once during the war. The site definitely received a VIP visit from King George on 7th May 1941. The Sopley GCI unit was mobile to start with, then became a more permanent fixture as the war progressed.

RAF Fighter Command

Data from sites like Sopley, was passed to RAF Fighter Command via telephone (and added to information from Chain Home and the Observer Corps) and fed into the Dowding System. This provided a comprehensive and real-time responsive air defence 'picture' of the skies over Britain. As I understand it, there was a huge map of the country on a vast table at Fighter Command. Multiple markers were placed on the map, denoting all the incoming information received via banks of telephones. Data included: which planes were spotted where, how many of them there were, what direction they were travelling in, what their heights and speeds were, et cetera. The telephones were staffed at all times, and the information on the map constantly updated. This enabled the efficient and effective deployment of British fighters.

The Gliders

The glider test flights I refer to really did happen. They were undertaken at Renscombe. One of the brave pilots involved was Philip Wills. I have read several accounts about these tests, and it seems that one of the flights did end with the glider almost crashing into the cliffs only to gain lift on a thermal right at the last minute. Whether there were two members of staff stood at the top of the cliff watching and urging the pilot on to safety – as my fictional characters Fliss and Daniel do – is unconfirmed; but I like to think there could have been.

And finally...

Speaking of Daniel, his wartime journey, including his backstory, is one that is particularly close to my heart. My grandfather was medically exempt from joining the armed forces due to a childhood fall from a tree resulting in a badly broken elbow, which didn't set properly. He had a limited range of motion in the joint thereafter. As a talented physicist, he was invited to work for the War Office as part of a top-secret research team. Every time his projects gained too much enemy interest, they packed up and disappeared, sometimes overnight, relocating to a new secret location where the work could carry on. It was lovely to be able to include a little family history in this particular book.

Please understand that *A New Recruit for the Resistance Girls* has been written for the purpose of entertainment, rather than education. Nevertheless, I have tried to keep to accurate historical facts where possible. Please forgive any mistakes, whether scientific, historical or geographical; they are entirely mine and unintentional.

Thank you again for joining me.

Until the next time, when we will find out what happens to Connie...

Love,

Alice

ACKNOWLEDGEMENTS

There were times when I was researching this book that I really didn't think I would manage to bring all the different elements of Fliss' story together. However, thanks to the unfailing support of my husband, Steve, who dragged me out on countless long walks for fresh air and a new perspective, and then supplied vast quantities of chocolate and endless patience, it is finally here. Phew!

The rest of my wonderful family have been instrumental in supporting me, too, whilst also teasing me about my obsession with all things related to World War Two.

In that vein, I would like to say thank you to Marcus White who kindly lent me a brilliant book (Dorset at War – Diary of WW2 by Rodney Legg) which, alongside my other research, proved hugely helpful due to its systematic layout of the timeline of events in Dorset as the war unfolded. With thanks also to Dave Lay for his unfailing support and willingness to chat about World War Two at the drop of a hat.

Gratitude and hugs to all my writer friends, especially Alex Stone and Sophie Beal, who have listened as I struggled with plot holes and confidence, and then dispensed practical advice and encouragement with a side of strong coffee. You are awesome.

And finally, thank you to my fantastic editor, Emily Ruston, and the awesome team at Boldwood Books for all the help and support, and for believing in the Resistance Girls series.

ABOUT THE AUTHOR

Alice G. May is an artist and the author of several fiction and non-fiction books. Born in Sheffield and brought up in South Wales, she went to Southampton University and then moved to the New Forest. She spent twenty years running a GP surgery, and now teaches art and creative writing as a casual tutor for the Hampshire Learning in Libraries program.

Sign up to Alice G. May's mailing list for news, competitions and updates on future books.

Visit Alice's website: www.alicegmay.com

Follow Alice on social media here:

instagram.com/alicegmay
x.com/AliceMay_Author
facebook.com/100013404690385
tiktok.com/@alicegmayartandbooks
bsky.app/profile/alicegmay.bsky.social

ALSO BY ALICE G. MAY

The Resistance Girls

A New Recruit for the Resistance Girls

Sixpence Stories

Introducing Sixpence Stories!

Discover page-turning
historical novels from your
favourite authors, meet new
friends and be transported
back in time.

Join our book club
Facebook group

https://bit.ly/SixpenceGroup

Sign up to our
newsletter

https://bit.ly/SixpenceNews

Boldwood

Boldwood Books is an award-winning fiction publishing company seeking out the best stories from around the world.

Find out more at www.boldwoodbooks.com

Join our reader community for brilliant books, competitions and offers!

Follow us
@BoldwoodBooks
@TheBoldBookClub

Sign up to our weekly deals newsletter

https://bit.ly/BoldwoodBNewsletter

www.ingramcontent.com/pod-product-compliance
Lightning Source LLC
Chambersburg PA
CBHW011759010726
47497CB00012B/3203

* 9 7 8 1 8 0 6 5 6 0 2 8 8 *